EDGE OF INSANITY

THE ALLIANCE BOOK 6

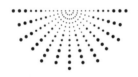

S.E. SMITH

CONTENTS

ACKNOWLEDGMENTS

I would like to thank my husband Steve for believing in me and being proud enough of me to give me the courage to follow my dream. I would also like to give a special thank you to my sister and best friend, Linda, who not only encouraged me to write, but who also read the manuscript. Also to my other friends who believe in me: Julie, Jackie, Christel, Sally, Jolanda, Lisa, Laurelle, Debbie, and Narelle. The girls that keep me going!

And a special thanks to Paul Heitsch, David Brenin, Samantha Cook, Suzanne Elise Freeman, and PJ Ochlan—the awesome voices behind my audiobooks!
—S.E. Smith

Montana Publishing
Science Fiction Romance
Edge of Insanity: The Alliance Book 6
Copyright © 2015 by Susan E. Smith
First E-Book Published April 2018
Cover Design by Melody Simmons

Summary: A human woman caught on an alien world will do anything to get back to Earth, even if it means freeing an alien warrior belonging to the species that caused the Earth to plunge into chaos.

ISBN: 978-1-944125-14-1 (Paperback)
ISBN: 978-1-944125-26-4 (eBook)

Published in the United States by Montana Publishing.

{1. Science Fiction Romance. – Fiction. 2. Science Fiction – Fiction. 3. Paranormal – Fiction. 4. Romance – Fiction.}

www.montanapublishinghouse.

SYNOPSIS

Sometimes the only way to survive is to let insanity take over...

Edge remembers little of his capture but all of what has happened since. Sold to the Waxians, he resists their efforts to gain information on the Trivator military and weapons systems. He can feel his mind splinter from their repeated tortures, but a soft voice in the darkness urges him to resist—and fight back.

Lina Daniels is used to fighting fire with fire. She isn't afraid of death, but she is terrified of being captured. As a resistance fighter on Earth, she knew the dangers. Those threats seem minuscule compared to those on the alien world where she now found herself.

Determined to return home, her plan is simple—free the Trivator warrior she discovered and force him to take her and the other women who are with her back to Earth. That plan turns out just as hazardous as being a fugitive on an alien world! The last thing Lina expects is for the Trivator to become intensely protective of her or his stubborn determination in believing she is his *Amate*!

The soft sound of Lina's voice is the only thing that prevents Edge's mind from completely shattering. With the Waxian and Drethulan forces on their tail, it will take more than a few daring moves to escape to freedom and safety. Can a tortured warrior and his rebellious rescuer escape the forces chasing them or will the threat of losing the last thing holding him together hurl Edge over the precipice and into insanity?

CHARACTER BIBLE

Lina Daniels: Human – sister of Tim Daniels.

Tim Daniels: Human – brother of Lina;
second in command for Destin Parks

Destin Parks: Human – Rebel Leader;
married to Jersula 'Sula' Ikera.

Jersula 'Sula' Ikera: Usoleum Ambassador to Earth

Gail Barber: Human: former Chicago police officer

Mirela Guinn: Human;
Hospitality and professional kickboxer

Mechelle Guinn: Human;
gaming programmer and actress

Bailey Reynolds: Human; Physician's Assistant

Andy Curlman: Human; Diesel Engine Mechanic

Edge: Trivator warrior; expertise in combat; weapons, piloting space-crafts, and combat medical training.

Thunder: Trivator warrior; expertise in tracking and moving behind enemy lines.

Vice: Trivator warrior; expertise in tracking and moving behind enemy lines.

Jag: Trivator Warship Commander; expertise in military maneuvers and combat situations.

Razor: Trivator Chancellor in charge of the Trivator military.

Hunter: Trivator diplomat

Jesse Sampson: Human; mate of Hunter

Kali Parks: Human; mate of Razor

Jordan Sampson: Human; mate of Dagger,
hacker extraordinaire

Dagger: Trivator warrior; expertise in combat weaponry; fighting

Prymorus Achler: Waxian; Prime Ruler

Katma Achler: Waxian; mate to Prymorus and former military commander of the Waxian forces.

Deppar Achler: Prymorus's half-brother, overlord of Oculus IX: Waxian Spaceport

Stitch: Trivator doctor

Dakar (Adron) Mul Kar: Kassisan Spy for the Kassisans and working with the Alliance.

CHAPTER ONE

Spaceport: Oculus IX—Deep in Waxian controlled territory.

The sound of cruel laughter pierced the periphery of Edge's consciousness. He wanted to fight the darkness, but it had become a welcome haven against the constant pain wracking his body. Despite his feelings of shame at his weakness, Edge knew he would court any brief respite from the agony ripping apart his mind and body. His head felt as if it might explode after the relentless inquisition he had just survived.

He wasn't sure 'survive' was the correct word. His mind was fragmented, his thoughts flashing at a nauseatingly rapid rate where one thought would start to form, only to be replaced with another in a dizzying kaleidoscope of colors that left him weak and disoriented. Whatever drugs his captors had pumped into him this time had come all too close to breaking the fragile control he had on his mind.

"Did you see the blood coming out of his nose this time? I swear I thought I could smell the bastard's brain frying," the guard gripping his left arm chuckled.

"We're just lucky Deppar had us double strap him or we'd all be dead," the guard on his right retorted.

"What are you talking about? I was expecting him to cry like a baby this time," the first guard replied with another laugh.

"I hope you know that you are going to be the first one he kills if he ever gets loose," the second guard muttered. "Open his cell door."

Edge heard another guard mumble something under his breath before the sound of metal scraping against stone screeched through the air. A groan mixed with the sound. It took a moment for Edge to realize the sound was coming from himself. Every sound was amplified in his head, causing sharp, excruciating pain to ricochet through his skull.

"He's drooling," the first guard chortled. "Next thing you know, he'll be pissing his pants. He can't even lift his head or keep the spit in his mouth. You really think he could fight me?"

"I heard Deppar is tired of dealing with him," the cell guard said as the first two guards dragged Edge through the doorway and dropped him to the cell floor. "Talk is that he has called in someone else to retrieve the information. I heard another Waxian wants all the knowledge the prisoner has about the Trivator forces and their technology. This Waxian is supposed to be working with the Drethulans. If he is, he's a crazy bastard. You couldn't pay me to have a Drethulan at *my* back. I doubt this Trivator will survive long once they get ahold of him."

"What could the Trivator know? He's been held captive for too long to have any current information of use. If you ask me, this other Waxian or the Drethulans should have gotten to him before he was sold to the mines," the first guard retorted before he spit on the floor near Edge's head. "Between working the mines and the drugs Deppar used on him, there isn't much left of the bastard's brain to interrogate. Deppar should just kill the big bastard now before he gets loose."

"Well, they didn't ask you," the second guard grumbled as he left the cell. "You're a grunt and grunts do what they are told. We keep our mouths shut if we want to get paid and live to spend it. Now, come on, I'm ready for some food." The cell door closed with a clang, and the sound of the cell guard locking it was loud in the small corridor. "That reminds me, Deppar said no food or drink for the prisoner. He wants him as weak as possible for the Waxian's visit," the second guard informed the cell guard.

"I haven't fed him anyway. They don't give us enough food, so I've been eating what they sent down. It all tastes like shit anyway," the cell guard muttered.

Edge rolled over in the narrow, dark cell as the guards continued to talk. A shiver ran through him as the toxic dregs of the drugs the Waxian had pumped into him seeped through his pores. He fought against the urge to throw up. The trembling in his body increased as the chill from the cold floor soaked into his sweat-dampened skin.

"Goddess, give me death," Edge whispered, hoping she would be merciful and grant him his wish.

"Like hell. You can't die now that I've found you, Trivator. I need you alive," a soft voice answered.

~

Lina Daniels peered through the narrow openings in the wall grill near the cell's filthy floor. Ever since she had overheard two men in the market talking about a Trivator, she had been searching for the alien warrior. It had taken her a day to discover where they were holding him. Then, almost another week to figure out a way in and out of the building. The last thing she wanted was to end up either in the cell with him or on the dinner table as the main course for the alien bastards holding him captive.

This tiny shithole of a cell had been the last on her checklist for the day. She had come up empty handed with her search of the other cells, and this one was empty too. She had been about to give up and had even started to scoot back down the drainage channel when she heard footsteps approaching and recognized one of the men's voices from the market.

Holding her breath, she waited to see what they would do. She was rewarded for her patience when the door opened. The man she'd been searching for was being dragged in by his arms by two guards. She watched with a combination of satisfaction and disgust as they dropped him to the floor.

The man was definitely a Trivator! She silently studied him while the guards talked. Personally, she didn't give a damn what his species or the Earth's government had said about the aliens responding to her planet's transmissions into space. As far as she was concerned, the Trivators and the Alliance had invaded Earth.

The resulting fallout had been devastating for humans. Her life and that of millions of others had gone to hell in a matter of hours. She'd spent the last decade since that unforgettable day fighting to free her fellow humans from the aliens and as well as from other humans.

It didn't help when memories of being sold by one of her own species filled her mouth with a bitter taste. She wanted to return to Earth so she could kill Colbert Allen. Who the hell cared that revenge was a bad idea? She'd had a lot of bad ideas in her lifetime and would deal with the consequences just as she always had—with a fight.

Lina ground her teeth to keep the curse from passing her lips. She wanted to tell the three guards to finish up with their sadistic enjoyment and get out. Now that she'd found what she'd been looking for, she had work to do.

It's about freakin' time, she savagely thought when the door finally closed behind the sadistic trio.

Returning her focus to the man in the cell, she watched as he rolled until he was facing the wall and unknowingly her. The grim satisfaction that coursed through her at the success of her mission was quickly replaced with a punch to the stomach as instant recognition hit her. Dark, painful memories threatened to choke her. Blood, pain, and despair flooded her as a vision of him standing over a lifeless body ripped her back to the past.

Deeply shaken, she closed her eyes for a moment and drew in a deep breath. There was no room for her personal feelings. Whether she liked it or not, she needed this man regardless of who he was or the painful memories that he awoke inside her.

Swallowing the bile that rose in her throat, she focused on her mission. This was not just about her. If it had been, she would have been tempted to help the Waxian with killing the Trivator.

At least, she reasoned, *I would be the more merciful killer. It might still come to that if he doesn't know how to fly a spaceship,* she thought.

"Goddess, give me death," he murmured.

Lina froze when she heard his barely audible mumble. A surprising rage swept through her unlike anything she had ever felt before—well, almost anything. She was reserving that little dose of overwhelming rage for Colbert Allen. Still, the words were like kerosene on an open flame to her. She totally ignored the fact that she had thought about killing him less than a second before.

"Like hell. You can't die now that I've found you, Trivator. I need you alive," Lina hissed out.

In the darkness, she could barely make out that his body had stiffened in surprise. Muttering a series of expletives under her breath, Lina felt along her side for the pocket of her pants. Slipping her hand inside, she pulled out a tiny red light and turned it on. Inserting it between the gaps of the grill, she got her first good look at the Trivator's face.

She drew in a deep, unsteady breath as the past and present collided again in her mind. There were two things which immediately caught and held her attention. First, he looked like shit. Second, she was surprised by the wave of compassion she felt when she saw the pain etched into his features.

"You were on Earth," she stated, unsure of what else to say.

"Yes," came his hoarse response.

"Can you fly one of those spaceships they've got here?" she demanded, forcing him to focus on her when his head started to roll back.

"Yes," he replied.

Lina's lips twisted and her fingers tightly gripped the light. She drew in another deep breath and wished she could just leave his ass here, but his admission sealed his fate as far as she was concerned. He knew where Earth was, and he could fly. She needed him alive.

"I'll be back. Don't you fucking die or get yourself killed before I do," she ordered.

Sliding backwards, Lina knew she didn't have much time. She was also going to need some help. As much as she hated endangering any of the other women who had escaped with her, she didn't have much choice in the matter. She couldn't haul this guy out on her own, and he didn't look like he was in any shape to walk, much less run.

She carefully retraced her steps, mentally adjusting her plans to get the warrior out of the building. As difficult a puzzle as the problem was, what worried her most was what to do after she got him out. There were too many variables once they were outside among the rest of the inhabitants on the Spaceport, and there were only so many places you could hide on a small rock in space.

CHAPTER TWO

"Are you sure, Lina? What happens if he turns on us?" Bailey asked, biting her bottom lip.

"Of course she is sure! Lina always knows what to do," Mirela retorted before she grimaced and added under her breath, "most of the time."

"Ha-ha," Andy replied, sitting back against the wall and stretching out her legs. "What's the plan, boss-lady?"

Five faces turned to Lina, their eyes watching her with anticipation. Gail and Mechelle, Mirela's twin sister, sat silently contemplating what she had told everyone. Gail was the oldest of them all while Mechelle was the youngest, even if it was just by five minutes.

"His injuries don't change the basics of the plan too much. We get him out, doctor him up as best we can, and make him take us home," Lina said.

"Well, that should be easy enough," Mirela replied with a roll of her eyes.

Gail snickered. "Be careful, Mirela. You might end up carrying this Trivator by his feet," she warned.

Mirela tossed her head. "It would take all of us to carry out one of those guys. I don't know about you, but I clearly remember them being big, muscular, and…."

"… Cute," Mechelle interjected, trying not to grin.

Mirela shot her twin a glare. "I never said I thought they were cute," she hissed.

Mechelle smirked. "No, you didn't. You whistled and said—"

"Okay," Lina cut her off. "Let's get back on topic and plan how we are going to get him out of his cell, past the guards, out of the building, and down into the access ducts without everyone on the Spaceport seeing us," Lina ordered in a slightly exasperated tone.

Andy leaned forward and rested her elbows on her knees. Lina could tell when the other women realized that this was probably their only chance of ever getting home. They had been lucky so far, but luck didn't last forever. Out of the eighteen women who had been abducted and spirited away from Earth by the alien ship, they were the only ones who had managed to escape.

"We're listening," Andy said in a quiet voice.

Lina looked around at the hopeful and determined faces. They had been through a lot together. Some of it good and some of it bad, but they had survived. Taking a deep breath, Lina motioned for everyone to gather around in a circle. Kneeling, she used the dirt on the ground as a drawing board.

"This is what we are going to do," she said in a determined voice. "I'm not sure he can walk, so I'll need one of you to go with me."

"I will," Andy volunteered immediately.

Lina nodded. "Mechelle, I want you to be ready at the entrance to the tunnels. We'll be coming in hot and heavy and will need to disappear fast. Mirela, I want you and Bailey to have a cart with a cover ready."

Mirela looked grim for a moment before she nodded. "There are a couple places where I can *borrow* one," she replied, using her fingers to place imaginary quotes around the word 'borrow'.

"Where do you want us to meet you?" Bailey asked, leaning forward and staring down at the roughly sketched map of the building.

"The building across from where they are holding the Trivator is empty. It has a chute that was left over from whatever they made there. The chute is located on the opposite side of the building. That's how I've been going in and out. I put a metal plank across from one roof to the other and crossed here. I guess they think because this is a Spaceport, no one would come in from the top. Anyway, there are no guards on this building because it is empty and none on the roof of the other one," Lina explained for the benefit of those who had not been in on the details of her scouting mission.

"What about cameras?" Gail asked.

Lina shook her head. "None that I could see. It is like they moved in and didn't bother with security except for hiring a bunch of moron guards. The main guy is a Waxian and is scary as shit. I've seen what he can do. It surprises me that anyone would be stupid enough to work for the man. I get the feeling the life expectancy of a guard isn't very long if you mess up," she explained with a look of distaste on her face.

"God, I hate the Waxians. They aren't as easy to kill as the Armatrux," Andy groaned.

"Yeah, I think we all do," Gail replied.

Lina nodded and continued. "The chute leads to an empty section on the top floor of the building. I've been crossing over and moving through the building using their ventilation and drainage accesses. Anyway, the chute comes out on this side alley. One end is a dead end, and the other leads to a larger alley that leads to the main market area. It is a dark and seedy section. Place the cart under the chute and stay in the shadows. Andy and I will get him out of the building, up to the top floor here, and shove his ass down the chute. He falls in the cart, we come down next, you cover him up, and move at a normal pace through the market while we take up positions on each side to cover you. We'll do it during rush hour when the market is chaos, which is in six hours," Lina instructed.

"What do you want me to do?" Gail asked.

Lina smiled and nodded to the blaster strapped to Gail's side. "You'll be undercover. I need you to cover our backs. Fall back and keep an eye out. If those Waxian bastards discover we've taken their golden egg, they are going to be pissed. You are the best shot out of all of us, especially from a distance. I'll need you to take them out if we are discovered," Lina said with a grim expression.

"I won't miss," Gail promised.

"I have one question," Mechelle said, frowning at her.

"What's that?" Lina asked.

Mechelle rubbed her chin. "If he can't walk, how are you going to get him across a metal plank nearly five stories up?" she asked.

Lina had hoped no one would notice that tiny detail. She glanced at Andy, who shrugged. Somehow they would get him across. Lina's eyes strayed to the bag in the corner.

"Bailey, what kind of drugs do you have that might help us?" Lina quietly asked.

~

Pain radiated through Edge's arms. His guards had left them shackled behind his back. The discomfort had finally pulled him from his restless doze. His head still ached, but it was back to the steady throb that he had been living with for months now.

His body was stiff from lying on the cold floor. Somewhere in his mind, he knew he should sit up, but he didn't have the strength. He kept his eyes closed. In the darkness, it didn't matter. He could see, but there was nothing to look at except the shadowy creatures that danced in his mind and along the walls.

Behind his back, he moved his fingers and tried to focus on counting. He could feel the claws of whatever beast they had poured into his blood this time tugging at him. Sweat beaded on his brow despite the cold.

The fire was heating up inside him, and he began to shake again. His reaction to the drugs was getting worse. He jerked his arms against the restraints in an effort to reduce the discomfort. As the fire grew to a fevered inferno, he twisted around and struggled up until he was on his knees.

Edge started shaking and his sweat poured out until a light film coated his entire body. His skin crawled with the imaginary insects. An agonized groan escaped him as the feeling of being eaten alive grew. The fireworks in his brain began to explode again, flashing colors at a sickening speed.

Gasping for air, he bent forward and rested his forehead against the cold floor. He squeezed his eyes closed to prevent the burning tears from escaping. He was dying. He could feel it, but he wasn't allowed to. The voice... The voice had told him he wasn't allowed to die. She needed him. She had found him, and she needed him.

Who had found him? another part of his brain demanded.

My Amate, the other part answered.

Edge knew his grasp on reality had finally snapped. There had been no voice answering his plea to the Goddess for death. It was a cruel hoax. The voice had been another trick to test his strength.

Straightening up, he parted his lips to shout his denial. He would never give the Waxians what they wanted. He was a Trivator warrior. Death before dishonor.

"Back up," a soft, feminine voice ordered.

The sound broke through the confusion, calming the chaos. A shudder ran through Edge and he opened his eyes. Along the far wall, he saw the insects that had been crawling over his body disappear.

"Goddess, I swear I will resist," he whispered. "I will die a warrior."

A barely audible sigh from behind made him frown. "Yeah, well, tell your Goddess to put your death on hold, sweetheart. There won't be any dying today if I have any say in the matter. Now, back your ass up to the wall behind you so I can see if I can get those damn wrist cuffs off you. It's going to be a bitch doing it from this angle," the voice demanded.

Edge tilted his head to the side. His frown deepened as his confusion grew. Shaking his head, he was rewarded with a wave of dizziness. Falling backwards, he grunted and stretched his legs out in front of him while he rested his head against the wall behind him.

"Why are you testing me like this?" he asked, closing his eyes again.

A soft snort answered him. "Welcome to our world, sweetheart.

Life is all about the tests - seeing who passes and who crashes and burns," the voice replied. "Can you walk?"

Edge was about to reply when he felt a movement against his skin. A shudder ran through him, and he started to shift to the side when he felt slender fingers wrap around his left wrist. Warmth poured through him. This wasn't the heat of a few minutes ago, but a soothing warmth that chased away the insects.

"Goddess?" Edge whispered in awe.

This time a chuckle answered him. "Darling, you can call me anything you want as long as I don't have to carry your ass out of here. That would make my life a lot easier. It might even give this harebrained plan a slim chance of success. As it is, we'll all probably be meeting up with this Goddess of yours for drinks by dinner time," the voice replied.

"I do not know if the Goddess drinks, or eats," Edge replied, feeling several tugs on his wrists.

"Yeah, well, I'll have to make sure I bring a few cases of beer along then," the voice muttered before uttering a long string of curses that had Edge opening his eyes again in surprise.

"You have very colorful language," he stated.

Another soft chuckle echoed behind him. "So I've been told," she replied.

The sudden release of pressure on his arms took him by surprise. He slowly pulled his arms around, wincing at his protesting muscles. Bending his elbows, he rotated his arms until the feeling began to come back. Flexing his fingers, he suddenly twisted until he was lying on the floor, facing the wall.

A tiny red light shone from the hole where the grill had been. His top lip curled and he snarled. If the Waxian thought giving him hope would break him, he would show the man he had made a serious mistake.

"Well, you're still fast, but that doesn't answer my earlier question," the voice hissed.

Edge tried to get a look at the face in the depths of the hole, but the red light was shining in his eyes. A low growl shook his frame. He wanted to reach into the hole and drag out whoever was within by their neck.

"What question is that?" Edge demanded, curling his fingers into a fist.

The red light wavered for a brief second, and Edge could make out the delicate lines of a very feminine face. The woman stared back at him, as if she, too, was assessing his features. Her dark brown eyes locked with his in a silent battle.

"Can you walk?" she asked.

"Yes," he said, hoping it was true.

A small grin curved her lips. "Good, though if you can run, it will be even better. Expect company in ten minutes," she replied, turning off the light.

Edge heard a soft scraping sound on the other side of the wall. Unsure if he had imagined what had just happened, he shot his hand out and he stuck it through the opening. He reached as far as he could and felt around the other side.

Then he pulled his hand back, and slowly pushed up until he was in a sitting position again. His gaze ran over his arms while he used his fingers to trace the raw circles around his wrist where the restraints had been. Reaching down, he picked up the metal cuffs in his left hand. His grip tightened around them.

Can you walk? Can you walk? Can you walk?

Her words kept repeating over and over in his head. Unsure, he braced his free hand against the wall and pushed up off the floor. His legs trembled, and he fell against the smooth wall of his cell. Gritting his teeth, he forced his legs to straighten until he was standing.

CHAPTER THREE

A wave of dizziness washed over Edge, threatening to send him back to the floor. Once again, sweat coated his skin, and he could feel the legs of insects crawling across his body. Nausea churned in his stomach.

He kept his head up and focused on the other side of the narrow cell. It was three steps. He could make three steps. His lips parted and he licked them.

Step, he commanded his body. *Move your leg.*

His body refused to follow his mental command. The sweat began to form rivulets trickling down from his temple and between his shoulders. The metal from the wrist cuffs cut into the palm of his clenched left fist.

Step, he commanded again.

This time, his leg moved with a jerky, uncoordinated movement. He kept one hand braced against the wall. Swallowing, he sent the command again. His steps were jerky and unsure, as if he were an infant learning to walk. He made it two steps before he started to tilt. He quickly stretched out his arms and braced his hands on the wall across from him.

His jaw ached from clamping his teeth together. He desperately wanted to pull his hands away from the wall. The insects were coming back out of the metal. A small part of his brain knew that they weren't really there, but his eyes saw them, and his skin felt their touch. The sweat was pouring off his body now as he began to shake.

Expect company...

Someone was coming. The thought sent another wave of panic and rage through him. Had the woman been real? Was she part of the Waxian's plan to get information from him?

"Walk," he desperately mumbled. "I have to be able to walk. She doesn't want to carry my ass out of here."

Turning, he continued to force his body to listen to him even as the number of insects doubled and then doubled again. Soon, he felt like he was wading through a sea of them. They were crawling up his legs. Their numbers continued to increase until they were up to his knees. His breathing became more erratic. He could feel his heart pounding until he was sure it would explode.

He turned his head when he heard a muffled sound outside the door, followed by a thump. Shaking, he continued to grip the metal handcuff in his hand as he fell back against the wall away from the door. Blinking his eyes to clear them, he gritted his teeth and waited.

The rattle of metal on metal and the turn of a key reverberated through his brain. Even the sound of his own breathing brought him a large amount of discomfort.

Edge braced himself for what was about to enter. He refused to fall without a fight. Nothing would stop him this time—not the insects, not the explosions going off in his mind, not the trembling and weakness of his body, not even the sudden presence of his imaginary Goddess giving him false hope. The time had come to end this nightmare once and for all.

The door slowly opened, and a shaft of light from the corridor cast a shadow on the figure pushing against it. Edge waited, sweat rolling down his trembling body, gripping his only weapon so tightly that he could feel the warmth of his blood sliding down from his cut palm to his wrist.

"Bloody hell! Can they make these damn doors any heavier?" a woman's voice muttered.

"Just hurry, Lina. I know you said they don't have any cameras, but I'd sure feel a lot better if we were already out of here," another feminine voice replied.

"Almost... there," Lina grunted.

Edge watched in disbelief as the door opened enough that the shadow could step inside. His pupils tried to contract because of the light. He pushed off the wall, his arm rising toward the person silhouetted in the doorway.

"Watch out!" the woman behind his goddess warned.

"Son-of-a-bitch! Don't make me have to knock out your ass," his goddess threatened, stepping forward and wrapping her hand around his uplifted wrist. "Drop it or I will."

Edge's breath caught in his throat. He swallowed several times before he could speak. His gaze remained locked in disbelief on the defiant face looking up at him.

"You... You are real," he finally said in a hoarse voice.

The woman grinned at him with a wry expression on her face. "It's good to see you standing. Now, let's see if we can get out of here alive," she replied, standing to the side. "Andy, take the lead."

Edge watched as the other woman nodded and started to turn away. He took a step toward the door. His vision blurred and he shook his head to clear it. In the distance, he could hear a voice utter a low string of very colorful curses. Warm hands wrapped around his waist to steady him.

He caught snippets of words. It took a moment for his brain to translate them.

"Hold him," one voice said.

"Shit! This isn't going to be good," another responded.

"We'll have to drag him," the first said.

Edge shook his head again. "No, I... can walk," he muttered.

The arms around him tightened. The voice of his goddess sounded harsh but determined. Her refusal to allow him to give up was like a living thing in his mind.

"Prove it, warrior. Move your feet. We've got to get out of here now or we're all going to die," she stated. "Walk."

"I can walk," Edge muttered, lifting his foot and stepping forward.

"Andy, you lead. Shoot anything that gets in our way," his goddess ordered before she turned her attention back to him. "Move your damn feet faster, soldier."

"You are a very... bossy Goddess... with colorful language," he informed her, his voice breaking as he tried to focus on not falling.

The other woman ahead of them snorted. The periphery of Edge's vision grew dark and he blinked to clear it. The arm around his waist squeezed his side. His arm was draped over her shoulder.

"I'm too heavy," he said, unable to do anything about it.

His goddess made a very unladylike noise. "No kidding. What did they do to you?" she asked.

Edge felt their pace slow, and the woman ahead of them murmured it was clear. Turning the corner, he braced his free hand on the wall to keep himself upright and steady. His hand slid across the smooth surface.

"Next left," his goddess said.

"Drugs. My brain... skin... hurt," he finally admitted.

"Damn!" the woman in front muttered.

Edge gripped the frame of the door when it opened. This room was darker than the corridor. He breathed a sigh of relief. The light hurt his eyes. The woman tugged him forward into the room.

"There's a service lift in the back of the room, thank God. I forgot how big you aliens are," his goddess groaned.

The other woman hurried forward and pressed the control button. The doors parted to show a lift. Edge stumbled forward into the small box. He closed his eyes and leaned against the lift wall. When the lift suddenly moved, he breathed deeply through his nose, trying to keep his stomach from expelling the churning acid inside.

"How in the hell are we going to get him across to the other building?" the other woman asked.

His goddess had guided him to the corner and was pressed up against him in an effort to keep him upright. He wanted to answer, but the effort to keep the nausea under control kept his mouth firmly closed.

"He'll make it," his goddess replied. "He has to."

"He doesn't look so good, Lina," the woman remarked as the lift began to slow.

His goddess didn't answer. Edge cracked his eyelids open when the lift drew to a stop. The woman with them stood to the side with a laser pistol leveled at the door. His goddess had stepped in front of him. She was standing protectively with her back pressed against his chest and her hands gripping another gun. The doors silently slid open to another dark room.

The woman by the door peered through the opening before she cautiously stepped out of the lift. A second later, she motioned for them to follow her. Edge automatically lifted his arm when his goddess turned and wrapped her arm around his waist again. Leaning heavily on her shoulder, he stumbled forward.

They were halfway across the room before he spoke. His throat was dry from dehydration and his voice rough from lack of use. Still, he could feel the danger surrounding them and knew he was a liability. His mind and body were shutting down.

"You... need to... leave me," he croaked in a raspy voice.

"Shut up," his goddess hissed in response.

A frown creased Edge's brow. Anger began to build inside him. No one told him to shut up.

Licking his lips, he tried again. "I said... you need... to leave me... here. It is.... It is too dangerous... for you," he insisted.

The woman glanced up at him with a scowl. "And I said shut the fuck up," she replied, scanning the empty room.

Edge could feel the muscle in his jaw twitch at her response. A low growl of disapproval rumbled in his chest. Goddess or not, she needed to understand that he would not risk her life for his own.

Focusing inward, he commanded his body to listen to him. He felt the woman's body stiffen in surprise when he straightened and tried to pull away from her. Her arm tightened around his waist while her fingers curled into the vest he was wearing.

"I will not endanger you," he growled.

Her fingers curled against his side. "Don't go getting all huffy and noble on me now. You can do that after we save your ass. Trust me, Trivator, we aren't doing this for any other reason than that we need you, otherwise I would have left your ass to the Waxians," she snapped.

"Roof is clear," the other woman said.

Edge was surprised when he felt his body being turned and shoved up against the wall. The woman pressed her free hand against his chest. Somewhere in the back of his mind, he noted that she was surprisingly strong for someone so small. Her eyes flashed with a warning that made him want to smile. That astonishing fact registered in his tortured brain. He wanted to smile!

"I need you to keep your shit together for this next phase. We have to get across to the other building. We doubled the planks, but it is still too narrow for Andy or me to support you. You have a choice. You can either walk or we can try to carry you. If you screw up, it is a fifty-foot drop to the ground. It is only a matter of time before they discover you're gone. Can you do this or not?" his goddess bit out in a soft, cold voice.

Edge gazed down at the face staring up at him. In the dim light, he saw her features better than he could before. Shoulder-length, dark-brown hair framed a face with a long nose, full lips, and fierce dark-brown eyes. Her black shirt and jacket highlighted the creamy column of her neck and the slight curve of her breasts, while her form-fitting black pants and boots showed an undeniably feminine figure.

"Why are you doing this?" he quietly asked.

The woman's expression hardened. She slowly dropped her hand and stepped away from him. Lifting her chin, she stared at him with a look of challenge in her eyes.

"We need you. You are bigger than I remembered and there is no way Andy and I can carry your ass out of here. So, here's the deal, if you want to get out of this dump, you need to prove it. It's your call," she stated in a voice laced with steel before she turned toward the door.

Edge watched the woman walk through the door. He took two steps and paused to grip the doorframe to steady himself. His gaze remained focused on her as he pushed away from the door and began to follow his Goddess.

He ignored his body's demand that he stop and give up. Instead, he focused on the woman's back as she walked away from him. He needed to stay with her. She was important. He needed... to help her... to protect her.

Once again, the instinctive knowledge of who she was flashed through the haze threatening to overtake his mind. The one thing a warrior craved above all. She belonged to him, his *Amate*. Adrenaline surged through him when the distance between them increased and he picked up speed to close the gap.

CHAPTER FOUR

$\mathcal{A}$s much as she wanted to, Lina resisted the urge to look back over her shoulder to see if the Trivator was following her. She could sense that his body was shutting down. As much as she would love to feel sympathetic toward him, such a feeling now wouldn't do anything but get them captured or killed.

Too many times in the past, she had noticed the same situation among those fighting back home. Hell, she'd even felt it herself on more than one occasion. Sometimes there had been an overwhelming urge to just give up and let whatever was going to happen occur.

Lina shook her head at Andy when her friend turned to look back at her with a worried expression. If there was one thing she had learned when fighting these bastards back on Earth, it was that they didn't give up—ever. Her hope was that somewhere deep inside the man behind her, there was a steel spine and a cast iron will to survive.

Andy slowed as she reached the low wall running around the roof of the building. The buildings on this section of the Spaceport butted up against the floor of the section above it. Stacked like the game with the wooden blocks, all it would take was to move the wrong one to make it collapse and bring the entire Spaceport crashing down.

Lina paused when she heard the echo of shouts from below.

Glancing over the side, she saw several men running down the alley toward the entrance to the building, frantically issuing orders for the guards to spread out. Their attention was momentarily captured by the Waxian angrily striding down the alley five stories below. Fortunately, neither the Waxian nor his guards had looked up yet.

"Life is about to get very exciting," she said, nodding to Andy.

Andy grimaced and looked over the ledge. "Tell me about it," she said, turning to look back at the open door. "We need to bar the door. You get our ticket out of here across to the other building, I'll try to delay them as best I can."

Lina started to shake her head, but realized Andy was right. The Trivator seemed to have bonded with her and was more likely to follow her lead than Andy's. Turning, she faced the warrior whose eyes were glued on her.

"Follow me," she instructed as she shoved her gun into the waistband of her pants and reached out her hands.

She breathed a sigh of relief when he automatically gripped her hands. Pulling him forward, she stepped up onto the planks they had laid across the yawning gap between the buildings.

Lina slowly walked backwards. "Focus on my face," she ordered.

Behind him, she could see Andy disappear through the doorway again. Her gaze moved back to the Trivator holding her hands in a surprisingly gentle grip. He stepped up onto the plank.

Her stomach twisted when she felt the uncontrollable trembling in his hands. Sweat glistened on his brow, and his face was very pale under his naturally dark complexion. She could see the wild expression in his eyes and knew he was fighting to maintain the fragile hold he had on his control.

"How long have they been drugging you?" she asked, moving backwards, taking one step at a time.

"I don't... remember. It... it feels like forever," he admitted.

Lina squeezed his hands when she saw him start to look down. "Focus on my face," she sharply ordered before softening her tone. "How long have you been here?"

A shudder ran through him. "Too long.... I... Everything is a blur. My head.... It feels like...," he started to say before his voice faded.

He shook his head. Lina could immediately tell that was a huge mistake when he groaned and started to sway. Fear swept through her. If he fell, he'd take them both down.

"Close your eyes," she ordered.

He started to shake his head again, but stopped. "I can't...," he started to say.

Lina stopped and pulled him closer to her. She tightly squeezed his hands. Her gaze remained locked on him.

"What's your name?" she asked in a soft voice.

He blinked. "Edge. I am called Edge," he replied.

"Edge, I need you to trust me. Please, we are almost there. Close your eyes," Lina insisted.

She watched indecision and confusion flash through his dazed eyes. Behind them, she saw Andy thrust a metal bar in the door panel before running across the roof. Andy paused, her concerned gaze locking on Edge. Lina jerked her head for Andy to come forward.

"We've got to move, Lina. What I did won't hold them for long, and they are bound to work their way up here," Andy warned, coming up behind Edge.

Lina felt Edge stiffen and start to turn. She gripped his hands and pulled him closer to her again. He was very close to losing it.

"Edge, honey, I need you to close your eyes and trust Andy and me. We've got this. We won't let anything happen to you. I promise," Lina said.

"You should leave me, little goddess," he murmured, closing his eyes.

Lina saw Andy's eyes widen and her mouth silently repeat the words 'little goddess' with a raised eyebrow. Rolling her eyes, Lina shook her head at her friend. They were in a critical situation. Now was not the time to go into the political correctness of words.

"Andy is going to hold you steady while I guide you across," Lina continued.

Andy made a face at her and quickly shoved her gun into the

waistband of her pants. Lina nodded grimly, and they began working their way across the plank to the other roof. It seemed to take forever before Lina felt the drop off to the roof.

Stepping down, she quietly instructed Edge to step down after her. Once they were all down, Andy took his one side and she took the other. Edge was done.

"The planks...," Andy said, looking over her shoulder.

Lina shook her head, grunting under Edge's weight. "Doesn't matter now. We won't be coming back here. Get him to the chute. He needs medical attention," she huffed.

Andy nodded, looking at Edge's pale features. "Do you think Bailey will be able to help him?" she asked, staggering under Edge's collapsing weight.

"I sure as hell hope so or we are going to be living in the sewers for a very long time," Lina replied.

Lina slid around behind Edge and supported his upper body, while Andy grabbed his legs and lifted them onto the lip of the chute. Slowly crab-walking forward, Lina pushed Edge's now unconscious body as far as she could into the chute without losing her grip on him. She would have to slide down with him. There was no way she was going to risk him breaking his neck now that they had made it this far.

"Follow me as fast as you can. It won't take them long to figure out what we did once they reach the roof," Lina ordered, climbing into the chute and wrapping her arms around Edge.

"See you at the bottom, Lina," Andy said, pushing on Lina's back to give her momentum.

Lina locked her hands together around Edge's broad chest. She could feel the bones of his ribs through the leather vest. Resting her chin on his shoulder, she used their weight and her legs to help guide them down the chute and as a way to slow them down when they reached the bottom. Less than a minute later, Mirela and Bailey were helping her lay him down and cover him up in the cart. Andy handed her a cloak. All hell was about to break loose and they were all anxious to get out of there before it did.

CHAPTER FIVE

"Clear," Andy murmured, stepping around the corner onto the crowded street.

Lina nodded to Bailey and Mirela and they pushed the cart out into the gathering of pedestrians. They each wore the elaborate headgear of the traders who frequented the Spaceport and masks depicting an alien visitor's face. Mechelle had created different costumes for each of them so they could move around the station with ease.

Lina merged into the crowd with several people between her and the cart.

Their small group had become experts at blending in over the past two years. They worked as a team, each scanning the crowded lane. Shouts sounded behind them and the crowd slowed as most people tried to glimpse what was causing the commotion behind them.

Lina gripped the pistol in her hand as she peered through her mask.

"Move out of the way," a harsh voice ordered.

A patron who was standing behind Andy was shoved aside by one of the Waxian's guards. Andy turned and stepped to the side to avoid a collision as the men swarmed the market.

Mirela and Bailey continued to push the cart at a steady pace several yards ahead of them. Lina bit back a curse when she saw the Waxian striding down the lane. People parted like the Red Sea, quickly moving to the side. Anyone who didn't move fast enough was tossed aside or shot.

"Search every cart! Find him," the Waxian ordered.

"Yes, sir," one of the guards replied as he lifted his hand and signaled the others in the hunting group.

Lina's eyes moved to Andy. Her friend had already slipped into the shadows and was working her way through the crowd and down a narrow alley.

Turning to glance down the lane, Lina's mouth tightened when she saw that Bailey and Mirela were ordered to stop. Both women stopped and bowed their heads. Lina pushed her way through the crowd toward them.

Fear washed through her when the Waxian paused by their cart. His penetrating look ran over Mirela and Bailey before he turned his attention to their cart, and he reached out to pull off the cover on the top.

As he yanked off the cover, Lina lifted her gun. Two guards moved, effectively cutting off her view of the cart and the Waxian. Frustrated, she pushed between several patrons so she could get a clear shot. Her eyes widened when the Waxian turned back in fury.

"Find him!" the Waxian yelled.

The guards pushed past her while the Waxian turned and retraced his steps. He had only gone a few feet before he stopped and slowly swiveled in her direction. Lina hurriedly stepped into the shadowed recess of a doorway and froze. After a few seconds, the Waxian pivoted on his heel and disappeared into the crowd.

Releasing the breath she'd been holding, Lina turned back toward Bailey and Mirela who were again proceeding down the lane. *Where in the hell had they hidden Edge? He should have been in the cart!*

Lina quickened her step until she was even with the two women. They turned down the next lane and Gail fell into step next to her. Near the end of the lane, Mirela and Bailey abandoned the cart they'd been pushing and grabbed the handles of another cart waiting in front of a cloth vendor. Andy nodded and fell in behind them.

The small group continued, sometimes close together and other times spread apart. Two dozen turns and three levels down from where they had started, they slowed as they neared a series of grates barring access to the internal workings of the Spaceport.

The third grate from the end swiftly opened. Mirela and Bailey pushed the cart inside. Lina, Andy, and Gail turned to make sure no one had followed them, then nodded to Mechelle, and swept past her. A moment later, the grate sealed behind them.

Only after the second door had closed behind them and the lift descended deeper into the belly of the Spaceport did Lina look over at Mirela and Bailey. She couldn't see their faces behind the masks, but she could feel their excitement. The lift slowed and opened into a dark tunnel.

Andy and Gail took the lead, Mirela, Bailey, and the cart were in the middle, and Lina was in the rear. In the year and a half that they had been in hiding on this Spaceport, they had never encountered anyone down this far. Still, there was always a chance it could happen. The engineers or whoever had designed and built the Spaceport had used the remains of a small moon that had been locked in orbit around the Waxian home planet. Lina and the others had discovered this section which had been built with surplus supplies after the Spaceport's main construction was completed.

They all paused as Mechelle punched in the code to a large abandoned storage bay they now called home. The small door set in the larger bay door clicked and slid to the side. Gail entered first, making sure the area was clear before motioning to Andy and Mechelle.

Mechelle stepped inside while Andy stood by the door and motioned for Mirela and Bailey to push the cart through. Once they entered, Lina followed with Andy, double-checking the corridor before stepping inside and resealing the door. Only when they were safely inside their makeshift home did they relax.

Lina slipped off the hood of her cloak and removed her mask. She took a deep breath before walking over and folding down the tarp covering Edge. He was pale, sweat covered his face, and his body was violently shaking.

"Bailey," she said, looking up at the other woman.

Bailey handed her cloak and mask to Mechelle and stepped up close to the cart. She bent over Edge, and shone a small light into his eyes, observing his dilated pupils. She looked back at Lina.

"Did he give you any indication of what they did to him?" Bailey asked.

Lina pursed her lips. "He said drugs. I imagine it was more. Can you help him?" she bit out.

Bailey frowned and raised one shoulder. "Without knowing which drug, how it affects them, and what can counteract it, the only thing we can do is hope he can make it through detox without severe withdrawals. If he has internal injuries, that is going to be even worse. I've only got a rudimentary understanding of the alien medicine we stole," she explained.

Lina nodded her head in understanding. She reached out and gently touched Edge's forehead. He was burning up. He softly groaned at her touch.

"Let's make him as comfortable as possible. Bailey, I'd like you to examine him as best as you can," Lina instructed.

"Of course," Bailey said, motioning for Mirela to grab the other handle. "Let's get him over to one of the beds."

"He can have mine. I'll make another one," Lina said.

"Why don't we just leave him in the cart?" Mirela suggested. "This way, if he dies, all we'll have to do is wheel him up to the top level and leave him."

Lina scowled at the other woman. "He's not going to die!" she snapped, motioning for them to take him to the section she had created for herself. "Bailey, I'll help you."

It took all of them to lift Edge out of the cart and onto Lina's bed. Fortunately, they were able to use the blanket he was lying on as a stretcher. Once he was on the bed, Bailey motioned for everyone but Lina to leave. Lina pulled the curtain closed, giving them privacy.

"What do you need me to do?" she asked Bailey.

Bailey looked up from where she was taking Edge's vital signs. Lina patiently waited until Bailey was done. Bailey used the side of a crate to write down some numbers.

"Get some water, lukewarm is best. We need to get his fever down. I can't tell exactly what his temperature is, but I know it is higher than is safe. If it stays high for too long, there's a chance of brain or organ damage. I'll check him over for any visible physical injuries," Bailey replied.

"I'll be right back," Lina murmured and turned around. She pulled aside the curtain, then paused to look at Bailey. "Do you think he'll make it?"

Bailey looked up, and her expression softened into a look of compassion. Lina shifted uncomfortably. There was a lot riding on this Trivator's health. They all knew it. Just because she was remembering how he had looked at her, and how his voice had become an intimate growl when he called her goddess, didn't mean she wanted him to get better more than the rest of them did.

"Let me assess him first and I'll feel more comfortable answering that question. We know that he's been through a lot. Still, he's a Trivator. We know just how tough they can be," Bailey answered.

Lina's smile was bittersweet. "Yeah, we do. I'll be back in a few minutes," she said and stepped through the opening.

Taking a deep breath once again, Lina pushed down memories of the man from more than a decade before and focused on the task at hand. Walking across the storage bay to the bathroom, she grabbed a bucket along the way. She stepped inside, placed the bucket in the sink, and turned on the faucet.

Her attention was drawn to a soft knock on the door behind her. Looking over her shoulder, she saw Andy leaning against the doorframe. She turned back around and stared down at the water filling the bucket.

"That was pretty clever, switching the carts like that," Lina commented.

Andy straightened behind her and walked over to lean against the wall so that they were facing each other. Lina kept her head down and continued to watch the water pouring into the bucket. She finally looked up when Andy didn't immediately respond.

"Yeah, it was. Gail must have seen the guards and realized what was about to happen before we did. She warned Mirela and Bailey. They commandeered another cart while Gail pushed the one with the Trivator in it. Bailey told me, and I met up with Gail and took over the cart while she fell back to give you guys coverage if you needed it," Andy explained.

Lina nodded. "That was really a smart move," she said again, reaching over the bucket to turn off the water.

"Lina, you know that the Waxian isn't going to stop until he's torn up every inch of this station," Andy warned, reaching out to touch her arm.

Picking up the bucket of water, Lina nodded. "I know," she replied before pushing past Andy and exiting the room.

Lina was all too aware of the can of worms they had just opened. Her hope was that they would be gone before the Waxian found their hiding place. One thing in their favor was that the clientele of the Spaceport appeared to hate the idea of surveillance cameras. There were some on the upper levels from what she had seen, but none in the lower, seedier sections. The few that had been installed down there were usually gone within an hour.

Still, Lina wasn't positive whether they had been seen or not. All this anxiety was making her nauseous. If the bucket weren't so heavy, she would have carried it with one hand so she could rub her aching stomach. She really hoped she wasn't getting an ulcer.

CHAPTER SIX

"Hey, how's he doing? Do you need fresh water?" Mechelle asked, peering through a small opening in the curtain.

Lina glanced up from where she was running the damp cloth over Edge's bare flesh. For the past three hours, she had been tenderly running the tepid water over his hot skin. Goosebumps covered his body now.

"No, I think I'll give his body a chance to rest before I do any more. I could use some soup for him, though," she replied.

Mechelle nodded. "I have a pot warming. I'll bring some for you both," she said.

"Thanks, Mechelle," Lina replied, carefully folding the wet cloth and hanging it on the side of the bucket.

"Hey, Mechelle," Bailey said.

Lina listened as Bailey and Mechelle talked quietly outside the curtain. She pulled the thin blanket over Edge's body. He jerked, groaning softly, and she smoothed her hand over his brow. She hated that they were forced to tie his wrists to the metal frame of her bed. It felt a lot like kicking a wounded or sick animal when they were too defenseless to do anything about it. Still, they'd had no choice when he began to violently thrash as Bailey was examining him.

"It's okay, sweetheart. No one is going to hurt you here. I promise," Lina softly vowed, falling into the soothing tones she used to use back home when she helped doc in the infirmary.

Bailey had been the first to notice that the big guy appeared to calm down whenever she spoke to or touched him. Bailey figured it was because he associated her touch and the sound of her voice with freedom. Whatever worked was good enough for her. She'd touch and coo to the guy all the way back to Earth if she had to.

Her fingers traced the outline of his face. She remembered him. Her brother, Tim, used to freak out about her ability to remember a face, but her memory of his face was for a different reason – a personal one forged by tragedy. She always thought faces told so much about a person. The lines on their faces, their mouths, and their eyes told a story about their life and who they were deep inside.

This guy had been one of the Trivators who patrolled the city near the river. She'd seen him five times before she and the other women had been taken. The last time she'd seen him would forever be burned into her memory.

Tears burned her eyes as she remembered the night that she had tried so hard to forget. Why did the Trivator have to be him? She'd thought she had finally closed and locked the door on that part of her life, the night when the last of her innocence, her belief in love, hope, and happiness, had been stripped away in a hail of gun and laser fire. The night a huge alien warrior stood over the man she loved, unaware of the devastation he, the other warriors, and the humans they had been fighting with, had left behind.

Unable to cope with the sudden rush of emotions, Lina slammed the door shut on her memory of that night. Now was not the time to reopen old wounds. Once they were free and back on Earth, she could let the memories come and deal with them, but not right now. The dark emotions connected with that time in her life still carried enough weight to pull her down into a dark abyss she wasn't sure she could crawl back out of again.

Drawing in a deep breath, she instead focused on trying to under-stand the story etched into Edge's face. She slid her fingers down to his mouth and ran her thumb along his bottom lip. She hissed when his lips suddenly parted and the tip of her thumb brushed against the sharp edges of his teeth.

His lips closed around her thumb. They both released a soft moan when he gently sucked on it. Lina was surprised at the physical response she felt with the intimate gesture. She quickly pulled her thumb free when she heard Bailey say she needed to see Edge.

"Lina, I found something that might help him if we can get him to drink it," Bailey said, pulling the curtain back and stepping in.

Lina looked up at Bailey. "What is it?" she asked, unconsciously laying a protective hand on Edge's chest.

Bailey smiled and held up a container. "Super water! Do you remember the supplemental packs the Trivators handed out in an effort to get into our good graces back on Earth?" she asked, gently shaking the dark gray bottle in her hand.

Lina's eyes widened and she grinned. "Yeah. It was like a super dose of energy drinks, only better," she replied, reaching for the bottle when Bailey held it out to her.

Bailey pulled one of the empty boxes closer to the bed and sat down. She nodded at the container Lina was now holding. A smile pulled at the corner of her lips.

"A few days ago, Andy and I were out looking for new stuff. I remembered spying a vendor unloading cases of this stuff. I saw them on display today in the market. Mirela recognized them as well. We sort of helped ourselves to a few bottles when the Waxian and his guards made an appearance," Bailey admitted. "I wanted to make sure it was what I thought it was before I gave it to your friend there."

Lina ignored the friend comment. "So, you drank some? Did it give you that familiar oomph?" she asked.

Bailey laughed and shook her head. "No, I didn't try it. I left that wonderful test to Mirela. She's got a good buzz going," she shared.

Lina looked down at Edge. She had been alarmed when she felt his ribs nearly poking through his skin. Twisting around, she sat so that she was next to his head.

"Help me prop him up. I don't want him to choke on the liquid," Lina instructed.

Bailey had already stood up and moved to the other side of the bed. Together, they gently raised Edge until he was at an angle where he would be less likely to choke. Lina scooted behind him. Bailey unscrewed the top for her. Holding the metal container to his lips and whispering in his ear, Lina quietly coaxed him to take a sip.

"Come on, sweetheart. Drink a little of this. We need you up and kicking ass as soon as possible," she whispered.

A few drops dampened his cracked lips, and she saw his Adam's apple move. Careful to not spill the liquid, she tipped it a little more. A soft moan escaped him, and his arms jerked as he tried to lift them.

Lina saw his eyelashes twitch before his eyelids slowly rose. He moved his head to the side, away from the lip of the container. Every time Lina tried to place it against his lips, he would turn away his head.

"Listen, Edge. You've got to drink some of this. You're dehydrated. That isn't a good thing, in case you didn't know it. This is some of your Trivator super water," Lina murmured against his ear.

"Re... lease... me," he ordered.

Lina looked up at Bailey. She could see the expression of uncertainty on the other woman's face. Neither one of them was sure how safe it would be to grant him his request.

"Yeah, well, let's not, until I know you aren't going to beat the shit out of us. I'm already sporting a few bruises from just cleaning you up a bit," Lina joked, stroking his arm with her free hand.

His head moved again, and she could tell he was trying to look at her. Her arms tightened around him when he started to slide to one side. Bailey reached out and took the container from her so she could use both hands to steady him.

"I...." He stopped and licked his lips. A frown creased his brow as he tried again. "I... hurt you?"

Lina couldn't stop the chuckle that slipped out. Her breath brushed against his forehead, and she pressed a kiss against his temple. She could feel Bailey's surprise at her intimate response. Lina shot the other woman a warning glance.

"You couldn't hurt a fly at the moment, big guy. How about giving me a little trust? I want you to drink this super water so you can fight off whatever it is they pumped into you. You work with me and we'll talk about untying your wrists," she promised.

His eyes darkened. "No," he said before clamping his lips together.

Lina pursed her lips in irritation when Bailey snickered. Hard-headed, stupid, irritating... the list of words ran through her head. With a muttered oath, she reached down and released the cord holding his right wrist.

"Lina, are you sure...?" Bailey started to protest.

Lina gave a sharp nod of her head. "Untie him please, and leave us alone," she said.

Bailey reluctantly untied the rope holding Edge's left wrist. She held out the container with the water. Edge's eyes remained glued on the other woman's uncertain expression and her every movement—and not in a good way.

"If you need us, we'll be here in less than a second," Bailey said, returning Edge's hard glare with one of her own.

Nodding her head again, Lina waited until Bailey stepped out of the small enclosure. Lina sighed and leaned back against the pillow that Mechelle had made for her. Edge shifted and she felt him relax a little once he was confident that Bailey wasn't coming back.

"Give me... the... water," he ordered.

Lina's lips twisted in an effort to contain a smart-ass reply. She held out the container. His hands shook as he lifted them. She could feel and see his growing frustration at his own weakness.

"Hold on," she muttered.

Pushing against him, she tilted him forward and slid out from behind him. Still supporting him with one hand, she grabbed a spare blanket from inside the crate she used as a nightstand. Between the blanket and her pillow, they gave him enough support to lean back without being at an uncomfortable angle.

She twisted around until she could sit on the bed, and she took the container from him. Removing the lid, she picked up his left hand and wrapped it around the metal bottle. His skin felt cool to her touch now.

"Okay, now try," she instructed.

She didn't look away. He lifted his shaking hand. Lina didn't help him, even though she could hear the liquid sloshing inside the bottle. It was obvious that he wanted to do this on his own. He raised his other hand and grasped the container with both hands so he could steady it before lifting it to his lips.

Lina followed his shaky movements. He took a tentative sip and paused. A few seconds later, he took another one, this time drinking nearly a quarter of the contents. On his third helping, Lina couldn't stand it anymore and lifted her hand to cover his.

"Easy, big guy. Something tells me it has been a while since you've had anything in your stomach besides the lethal cocktails the Waxian was feeding you. The last thing you want to do is get sick," she cautioned.

He took another defiant gulp before he lowered the nearly empty container. Lina carefully took it out of his hands. His color already looked better than it had when they'd found him. She wasn't sure how much of the stuff Mirela and Bailey had pilfered, but she might need to send them for more if it helped get him back on his feet this quickly.

"Who are you, and where am I?" he demanded, glancing around the enclosed area before returning his attention to her face.

Lina raised an eyebrow and lifted the container. "I told you before, but in case you missed it, my name is Lina Daniels. I'm a human. I'm guessing this stuff works pretty damn fast. You're already becoming the arrogant ass that most of your kind are," she observed.

He frowned at her. "I don't remember the females of your kind using such colorful language. Where am I?" he questioned again in a more demanding voice.

Lina didn't miss the way his gaze returned to the container. She held it out to him. Her eyes widened when he wrapped his hand around her wrist instead and jerked her off balance with a strength that surprised her.

Fury at being tricked flashed through her. She raised her hand and pressed it against his chest to brace herself. They were practically nose to nose.

"Don't piss me off, Trivator. We may need your help, but I'm not above killing your ass if you pose a threat to my friends or me," she hissed.

For a few seconds, they stared at each other. She couldn't help but notice that his eyes were an unusual color of brown with golden flecks in them. His pupils were still slightly larger than normal for a Trivator. Lina curled her fingers against his bare skin.

"Lina, I have the...," Mechelle said behind her. "Oh! I... Do you need help?"

Lina felt a shudder run through Edge before he slowly released her wrist. She leaned back until she was sitting on the bed again, and flashed a look of warning at Edge before she turned her head to look at Mechelle. Rising to her feet, she stepped up to Mechelle and held out her hands for the tray. Lina nodded to Mechelle when her friend asked if everything was alright again.

"Everything's fine. I was checking Edge's pupils," Lina replied.

Mechelle raised an eyebrow. Lina resisted the urge to roll her eyes at the skeptical look on the other woman's face. Mechelle looked at Edge who was watching them with an intense expression.

"Bailey said to make sure he ate this slowly. His system may have some issues if it's been a while since he's eaten," Mechelle murmured.

"Thanks, Mechelle," Lina replied, turning to place the tray on the crate.

"Right...pupils," Mechelle muttered under her breath as she was leaving.

CHAPTER SEVEN

*E*dge carefully observed the exchange between the two women. He knew that they were human. What he didn't understand was how they could be here. Leaning his head back, he fought against the desire to close his eyes again as a wave of fatigue hit him.

Grasping the container with the nutrient-rich water, he raised it to his lips. His hands shook so badly he was forced to grasp it with both of them. Frustration and rage burned through him. He had never in his life felt so weak.

He followed the woman with his eyes as she placed the tray on the crate next to the bed. Two bowls sat on the thin sheet of metal. Spirals of steam rose from each bowl. The fragrant scent of the soup made his stomach clench with hunger. It had been weeks since he had eaten anything.

"You might want me to help you with this," she said, picking up one of the bowls.

Edge ground his teeth together when he saw her glance at his shaking hands. He lowered the container of water back to the bed. His mind felt disconnected and fuzzy. He was trying to piece everything together, but the effort caused his head to pound.

"Where am I?" he asked again, this time in a softer voice.

Lina gave him a rueful smile. "You're basically in the sewers," she said, lifting the spoon to his lips. "You eat, I'll talk."

Edge grunted his agreement. This woman – Lina – was very bossy, he decided, opening his lips and accepting the warm soup. The liquid hit his taste buds and he moaned in bliss.

Lina chuckled. "I swear Gail is the best cook in the universe. She can take the most unappetizing stuff and create a dish that will make your mouth water." Her expression sobered as she continued. "There are six of us all together. You've met Bailey. She was the one who helped doctor you up a bit. Mechelle is the one who brought us the soup. Her twin sister, Mirela, is here as well. Then, there is Gail, Andy, and myself," she explained.

Edge frowned. "How...?" he asked between mouthfuls.

Lina's mouth tightened, and she looked down at the bowl in her hand for a second before spooning up more soup and lifting it to his lips. There was anger in her dark brown eyes. He was fascinated by how they could express so many emotions in them.

"A son-of-a-bitch named Colbert Allen sold us to a blue prick named Badrick. He was the Usoleum who the Alliance council assigned to Chicago. Badrick was supposed to be working to end the battle between Destin and Colbert. Instead, Colbert and he had come up with a partnership to sell human women to a bunch of other aliens. Those in our shipment were divided up. A group of aliens known as the Armatrux took us," she bitterly explained.

Edge lifted his hand and touched her arm when she placed the spoon in the soup. Between the water and the soup, he was feeling stronger. What she was telling him was unbelievable. The Armatrux would never let such precious cargo escape them.

"You expect me to believe you... that a group of... human women were able to escape... the Armatrux?" he demanded, his voice filled with suspicion.

Her mouth tightened again. His weakened condition appeared to be hindering his ability to hide his emotions and thoughts. She turned on the bed and placed his bowl of soup on the tray. Edge caught his breath when she twisted back around with surprising speed. Her hand wrapped in his long hair, pulling his head back while the front edge of the pointed spoon pressed uncomfortably against the soft skin where the main artery in his neck was located.

Her grip on his hair tightened when he dropped the water container. It hit the floor with a loud metallic clunk. She was straddling him. Rising up on her knees, she forced his head back a little further.

Edge wrapped his hands around her waist. Out of the corner of his eye, he saw the curtain that had given them the illusion of privacy being jerked open. Five additional women suddenly surrounded the bed. Each held a weapon trained on him.

Edge's grip on Lina tightened. His gaze remained locked with hers.

"I can take him out," Gail said, drawing a bead to the side of his temple.

Lina's eyes held a satisfied challenge and he understood her message: even if he was able to hurt her, he'd be dead in seconds. A wry smile curved his lips, and he forced his fingers to relax.

"Just give the word, boss lady," Andy said.

The tension grew as the silence lengthened. Lina slowly removed the spoon from his neck and slid down across his lap. Another feeling of discomfort swept through him. This feeling had nothing to do with the fact that he was weak and everything to do with the woman rising from the bed.

He watched as she skillfully twirled the spoon between her fingers before placing it in the bowl of soup. The other women were a little more reluctant to lower their weapons. He moved his gaze to each one before returning to Lina.

"Tell me… what happened," he asked in a soft voice.

Lina nodded. She raised her hand and spread her fingers. As quickly as they had appeared, the women retreated. The oldest woman shot him a warning look before she closed the curtain.

"We've lived, worked, and fought together for years," Lina said, sitting on the crate near the bed.

She picked up the second bowl of soup and drank it before placing the empty bowl on the tray. She wiped her mouth with the back of her hand. Then she picked up his bowl, and was surprised to see that the bowl was almost empty.

Edge started to shake his head, but stopped as a wave of dizziness threatened to send him sliding sideways. Whether he wanted the soup or not, his body needed it. He curled his fingers when they began to tremble.

"I had forgotten how fierce the women on your world could be," he said, grateful when she held the rim of the bowl to his lips instead of the spoon. He drank deeply, then leaned back against the pillow and closed his eyes as the warm liquid hit his stomach. "How long have you been here?"

"Almost two years," Lina replied, "give or take a few weeks."

Edge opened his eyes in surprise and met her gaze. She gave him a wry smile and indicated that he should finish his soup. He drank the remainder.

"Two years," he repeated in disbelief.

Lina nodded and placed the empty bowl on the tray. "From what we could surmise, the Armatrux were planning on selling us. Unfortunately for them, they met up with some other aliens who were even bigger and badder than they were – Jawtaws. During the fight, the electrical system went haywire for a bit. The cells the Armatrux were holding us in opened and we escaped. It wasn't too hard for us to find a place to hide. Spaceships are pretty damn big. The Jawtaws must not have realized that we were a missing part of the cargo and, from what we could see, the bastards didn't leave any survivors to tell them about us. With a skeleton crew, it wasn't difficult for us to remain out of sight. Two and a half months later, they docked on this Spaceport. Mechelle is brilliant when it comes to costumes and makeup that allows us to blend in. The Jawtaws were selling off things left, right, and center from the ship. We dressed up, pretended to be shopping merchants, and walked off the ship. My brother once told me that you could get away with anything as long as you acted as if you belonged there. We slowly worked our way down, learning more about the

Spaceport. Seven months ago, we found this place and here we are," she said.

Edge blinked as he absorbed what she was telling him. The dangers were almost too many to comprehend. The possibility of their surviving this long without being caught was impossible to calculate. A shiver ran through his body followed quickly by another one.

"Lina," he suddenly hissed, his head fell back and his jaw fiercely tightened.

"Bailey!" Lina yelled, reaching out and gripping Edge's hands when his body began to jerk uncontrollably.

From the recesses of his mind, Edge heard the sound of the curtain opening. A burning pain was beginning to overtake him. His stomach twisted and churned. He felt the touch of cold metal against his neck. He jerked in surprise when the injector hissed before darkness surrounded him, mercifully pulling him down into its inky embrace.

CHAPTER EIGHT

*E*dge came awake to the soft sound of singing. He didn't recognize the song, but he'd heard it several times through the haze of pain. The words and melody calmed the raging torment tearing him apart.

He kept his eyes closed, listening. He could hear the soft murmur of women's voices in the background, but it was the sound next to him that held him spellbound, the barely audible singing of his goddess. Her voice mixed with the sound of water as it was poured into a container.

A moment later, he felt a warm cloth slide across his brow and down along his cheek. The process was familiar, as if it had happened numerous times over the past few days. The cloth continued to move down his body.

He focused on each gentle stroke. A delicate hand lifted his arm and the damp cloth was moved over his skin from shoulder to fingers. He couldn't remember the last time he'd ever felt anything so sensual. He recognized the gentle touch of the woman caring for him as she replaced his arm on the bed. Once again, he heard the sound of water and knew that she was refreshing the cloth.

Flashes of memory came back to him in slow, uneven waves: dark brown eyes that challenged him, language that seemed too harsh to be coming from someone so feminine – and then he was falling as a never ending fire ripped through him.

The hand and the cloth returned, moving with slow, methodical precision over his other arm and chest. He continued trying to connect the pieces of his memories.

The face of the woman appeared again. Her eyes flashed with a fire that burned as brightly as the one searing through him. Whenever the insects came, she had soothed them away from his flesh and mind, preventing them from eating him alive. Her voice calmed the chaotic thoughts inside his head and made the pounding go away.

He moved his hand with lightning speed when he felt the sheet over his waist begin to slide downward. He forced his fingers to loosen slightly when he felt the fragile bones underneath them. Opening his eyes, he met a pair of intense, amused brown ones.

"I was wondering how far you'd let me get before you'd open your eyes," she chuckled.

"You knew I was awake?" he asked, looking up at her with a rather droll inquiring expression.

She glanced down his body before turning back to peek at him with a wry grin. He followed the path of her eyes. His own eyes widened when he saw the tented sheet around his crotch. A rueful smile curved his mouth. He dropped his head back against the pillow.

"Yes, I guess that would explain how you knew," he admitted before he grew silent for a moment. "How long have I been... like this?" he asked.

She leaned over and dropped the cloth in the bucket of water on the crate next to the bed. His eyes followed her when she lifted a hand and tenderly brushed his hair back from his face.

"Good, no fever. You've been in and out of it for over a week," she admitted. "This is the first time since right after we brought you here that you have actually been lucid enough to understand what is going on."

"The fire...," he said, running his hand over his flat stomach.

Lina nodded. "That and you kept saying something about insects.

That was when your withdrawal symptoms were the worst," she commented, fingering his hair.

He remembered the fire and the insects—and her touch and voice, nothing else. He noticed that his hand still shook. He clenched his fingers into a fist. His gaze snapped to hers when she reached up and covered his hand.

"Why? Why did you risk your life to help me?" he demanded.

"We want to go home and you are our only hope," she replied. She released his hand and stood up. "I have some things I need to get done. Bailey will come to sit with you."

He was surprised by the sudden change in her. It was as if a wall had suddenly gone up between them. He could almost taste her desire to escape.

"Lin... Lina...." He paused, hoping he had correctly remembered her name.

She paused at the curtain and turned back to look at him. "Yes?" she asked.

"Thank... you," he said.

Her lips twisted into a wry smile. "Don't thank me yet, big guy. You aren't out of the woods and neither are we. Until I know we can trust you, you'll be under guard. Just don't try anything stupid or...." She stopped and looked at him in silence before she shook her head. "Just don't try anything stupid. I'll let Bailey know you've made it back to the land of the living."

Edge watched Lina disappear through the wall of curtains. He flexed his fingers back and forth as he tried to control their trembling. Glancing up at the ceiling, he prayed to the Goddess that the worst of his withdrawal from the drugs was over. He needed to get his strength back as soon as possible. If there was one thing he had learned during his captivity, it was that the Waxian would never give up. Whether the women were aware of it or not, they had started the countdown that would only lead to death and destruction if they didn't find a way to escape, soon.

∾

Four days later, Edge watched as Lina quietly chatted with the woman named Gail. He had finally learned all of their names. What normally would have taken a few minutes had taken him two days to achieve.

There were times during those first few days when he felt like pulling his hair out. At other times, he had felt like doing something much worse just to end the agony and find peace. During the first few days, he swore he could feel thousands of small legs climbing over his body. At other times, an unexpected fire would flare up inside his stomach. The fire was hot enough to drive him to his knees.

Then, there was the nausea that kept him over the waste unit throughout the day and halfway through the night. The few moments when he would try to rest, dizzying swirls of uncontrollable thoughts would start. By the end of each episode, he was left weak, shaky, and sure that he was either going crazy or dying.

Yet, during each occurrence, Lina had been there. Talking to him, washing his face, and softly singing the lullaby she had told him helped her when she felt lost or unwell. She never looked down on him as if he were weak or… unworthy.

"Hey, how are you feeling?" she asked, walking over to where he was sitting.

"Stronger," he replied, coming back to the present.

She chuckled at the stubborn tone in his voice. "That's good. Andy and I are going to go topside for a bit. We need to see if we can pilfer some more of that miracle water for you. Gail, Bailey, and the others will be here," she said.

"No," he immediately responded.

She blinked at him in surprise. "I beg your pardon?" she replied, frowning at him.

Rising from his seat, he clenched his fists against the panic winding its way through him. The thought of her going to the top, where the Waxian could find her, sent a chill through his body.

"I forbid it," he said.

"You…. Listen up. I don't take orders from you. If you are going to get your strength back, you need more of that water. We also need to see what is going on up there. The only way to do both is for us to go up top," she explained.

A muscle ticked in his cheek. Behind Lina, the other women were watching them with a mixture of amusement and fascination. He returned his attention to Lina.

"Let someone else go," he finally said.

She looked at him with a confused expression. "And why would I do that?" she demanded.

A part of his mind warned him that he was treading on dangerous ground. What kind of warrior offered up a defenseless female to go into a hostile territory? His gaze moved to the locked door that opened to the outer corridor.

"I will go," he suddenly said.

"Oh, hell no," Andy commented behind her.

Edge heard the other women murmuring the same sentiment. His jaw tightened. He drew up to his full height and glared back at them.

"I am a warrior…," he began.

"Exactly, big guy. Not just any warrior, but a Trivator warrior who has escaped from the Waxian and who happens to be hiding under the prick's arrogant, pathetic nose," Lina retorted.

Gail shook her head at him. "Talk about a bull in a china shop. We might as well put a target in the center of his forehead if he goes up there," she remarked.

"He can't go. We need him to…," Mechelle started to say before she bit her lip and looked at her sister.

"I say we get Bailey to knock out his ass again," Mirela replied, straightening and fingering the gun at her side. "Or, I can shoot him in the leg."

Lina twisted and scowled at Mirela. "We are not shooting him," she snapped in exasperation before she turned back to glare at him. "But Bailey knocking out your ass if you try to leave sounds like a good plan."

"I'm ready," Bailey replied, pulling the injector out of the medical case and twirling it around on her finger.

"Listen, Edge, you're only just now getting back on your feet. You need time to regain your strength," Lina said.

Anger flared inside him. He would not live his life hiding in the sewers or behind a group of women, and he would definitely not allow the women to put their lives in jeopardy again because of him.

"I will not allow you to endanger yourselves for me," he quietly replied.

Andy and Mirela both snorted. "Oh, please," Mirela said. "Lina could take you down and you'd never even know what hit you."

"Do you honestly believe that any of you could stop me?" he asked with an incredulous expression.

Andy grinned. "We just need Lina," she quipped.

"You gals are not helping the situation," Lina growled, turning to glare at the women behind her.

An idea formed in Edge's mind. Perhaps if his head were clearer, he might have been faster or thought it through better, but tossing her over his shoulder and perhaps stealing a kiss was an appealing plan.

He bent and wrapped his hands around her waist. The second her feet left the ground, she struck out. The first blow was to his groin. Stars danced in front of his eyes, and the air he had drawn into his lungs exploded outward in a loud hiss.

Edge's legs began to tremble as the pain in his crotch registered in his mind. He might have stayed on his feet if the second blow to the tip of his nose hadn't occurred. His hands loosened enough for Lina to slip out of his grasp. She practically rolled over his shoulder onto his back, her arms around his neck and her feet around his waist.

The thought that this would have been much more pleasant if she had been in front of him flashed through his mind before he fell forward. He shot out his hands to keep from hitting the floor with his face.

If he thought she was done, he was sadly mistaken. Lina used the weight of her body, his pain, and a move he had never seen before to flip him. Lying on his back, Edge blinked to try to clear the moisture from his eyes. He wasn't sure which hurt worse, his aching groin or his tender nose. Her hand tangled in his hair and she pulled his head back far enough to press the blade of her sharp knife to his throat.

"I remember you... doing this... before," he replied in a hoarse voice. "Thankfully without... the other pain."

Lina's eyes glittered with an emotion he didn't understand. For a second, she looked as if she wanted to cry. Her throat worked up and down and her hands trembled. She was taking short, deep breaths.

"Sometimes you drive me crazy," she whispered, gazing down at him for a second before she pulled away the knife and pressed her lips against his.

Edge lay stunned when she released him and climbed off his aching body. He rolled sideways and onto his knees. He moved his hand to his aching groin and watched as Lina sheathed the knife at her side and grabbed a pack near the door.

"Don't let him leave," she ordered, stepping out of the door when Andy opened it.

Edge bowed his head and breathed deeply. Lifting a hand to his nose, he was surprised that there was no blood. He looked up and rose to his feet when Bailey walked toward him with a chemical ice pack.

"Not sure if you need this more on your nose or your...." She waved at his crotch with a sympathetic smile.

"Where did she learn to fight like that?" he asked, taking the pack from her.

"The same place we all did—on the streets," Mirela replied, walking toward the kitchen. "Anyone hungry?"

Edge nodded, though he continued to stare at the door. Gail had taken up a position in front of the entrance, and she stared back at him in warning.

"Edge... You have a choice. Mystery package number one or mystery package number two," Mirela called out.

"God, I just hope they don't have the dehydrated worms in them this time," Mechelle groaned.

CHAPTER NINE

$\mathcal{T}$he days seemed to be passing by faster than before. No one had been topside since Andy and she had last gone. If anything, the chaos on the upper levels had increased. After talking with the other women, they decided to hold off as long as possible in the hope that the Waxian would give up, and reduce the chance of someone seeing them slip into the service grate.

With a soft sigh, Lina rolled onto her side. She was trying to ignore the man lying on the bed, but it was impossible. Edge wasn't the kind of guy a girl could ignore. Hell, he had been practically glued to her side since they had rescued him. All she knew was that he was driving her crazy.

I never should have kissed him, she thought, remembering his face and the pain in his eyes.

She hadn't planned to kiss him. She wanted to make the excuse that she had done it as a reaction to adrenaline, or because she felt sorry for hurting him when she knew he wasn't at his best, or a hundred other excuses. Anything except the truth. She wanted him. There was something about him that made her physically attracted to him. Emotionally, well, emotionally she wasn't ready to admit that there was something about him that was making her respond in a way she hadn't to anyone in a long, long time. It was those feelings that were the most difficult to deal with. How could she want someone that she should hate? The problem was that caring for him all these weeks had shown her a different side to him. She was finding it harder and harder to see him only as an alien, and not as a caring, compassionate man.

Protect your heart, Lina, she thought. *You know what happens when you fall in love. It doesn't end well. Remember, he's the alien who broke your heart once already. Don't give him the chance to do it again.*

A small amount of relief swept through her at her mental conclusion. She and Edge literally came from two different worlds with too much history between them. They would return to their respective planets if they survived the plan that she and the other women had been working on for over a year. Hell, if she wanted to throw in a few more obstacles, none of her fears would matter in the end. They were all probably going to die in this hellhole.

That last thought actually gave her a measure of comfort in a weird way. It was a *What happens in Vegas stays in Vegas* type of attitude, only it would be on a Waxian shithole.

Lina's gaze moved to Edge again. She could tell he was getting better. He was definitely stronger than he had been the day before. Curling her hands under her cheek, she listened to his breathing. He'd made it through the last four nights without being sick, and today she had noticed that his hands were shaking a little less. It had been heartbreaking watching him fight the effects of the drugs the Waxian had pumped into him.

She had seen her fair share of people addicted to heroin and crack on Earth. For the first year after the Trivators arrived, there had been a surge in drug use. When the supply lines ran out, people had turned to making their own. The death tolls had risen so quickly that Destin Parks had issued a mandate that anyone caught making, distributing, or using drugs would be banished from the city and barred from entering it again.

Unfortunately, Colbert Allen had seen the drug crisis as an opportunity to control those under him. Colbert had taken to distributing the drugs as a form of payment for loyalty. She would never understand how two men who had been close friends at one time could be so vastly different in their morals.

The sound of a soft moan pulled Lina back to the present. She rose up on her elbow to peek over the edge of the bed. Edge's eyes were closed, and his breathing had changed from a calm, even rhythm to a more agitated one. Nightmares—she knew all too well about them.

Pushing the blanket to the side, she silently rose to her feet and sat on the side of the bed. She laid her hand on his forehead. It was cool. His fever hadn't returned.

A soft hiss slipped from her lips when his strong fingers suddenly wrapped around her wrist, and she found herself lying on her back with Edge's large body pinning her to the bed. His eyes were dazed, as if he was still locked in the nightmare. Afraid to startle him in case he turned violent, she reached up with her free hand and tenderly cupped his cheek.

"Edge," she whispered. "It's okay. It's just your little goddess checking on you, big guy. I promise I'm not here to kick your ass again."

She'd found that touching him and using a teasing tone in her voice appeared to calm him more quickly than anything else. He'd suffered from night terrors every night, sometimes multiple times. Bailey had told her that it wasn't uncommon after trauma.

"Lina?" Edge murmured, his voice rough and slightly hesitant.

She continued to stroke him. Her hand moved down his cheek, along his throat to his shoulder and back. She tugged her other hand free so she could play with the strands of his hair that hung down to form a curtain around her.

"Yeah, it's me, big guy," she replied in a hushed voice. "You were having a bad dream again."

"You feel real. I dreamed…," he started to say before he buried his face against her neck and pressed his lips against her soft skin.

A shiver ran through her. She lowered her hands to push him away, but somehow her hands seemed to have a mind of their own.

Her fingers fluttered across his bare chest. A wave of pleasure and yearning hit her hard.

Closing her eyes, she turned her head to the side, trying to push the emotion away. Her thoughts from minutes earlier teased her mind, whispering to her. What would it hurt for just one night to take what she wanted without worrying about the future? Who knew what tomorrow might bring? At least she would have this memory—this night to hold onto in the dark days ahead.

Every time she had touched him had been another step leading up to tonight. She had soothed him when the demons threatened to drag him down to the depths of hell. Tonight, he could erase the demons that threatened to choke her. For one night, she would allow herself to feel again.

Lina had already tried denying her attraction to him, and had ended up kissing him. She couldn't help but see Edge as a man and not an alien. This was not the man she'd thought she knew from years ago, but one who she had grown to respect – and desire.

"Edge." A soft whimper escaped her when he ran his teeth along her neck.

"My *fi'ta*. My little goddess. You are my *Amate*, Lina," he murmured.

The fire burning inside her ignited. The touch of his lips against her skin and his warm breath feathering across her flesh severed the thin thread of her resistance. Tonight, for one night, she wanted to be with him. It had been so long since she had felt the warm touch of a man. Tomorrow would come soon enough with its uncertainties.

"Only for tonight," she murmured, gazing up at the ceiling with shimmering eyes. "I can only give you tonight."

She felt him stiffen at her quietly spoken words. He slowly lifted his head and gazed down at her. Lina could see the confusion in his eyes. She knew he was about to argue with her—possibly even reject her because of what she'd said. She slid her hands up and cupped his cheeks. Then she met him halfway, capturing his lips with hers.

She deepened the kiss, refusing to break their connection. She moved her hands from his cheeks and down his arms to the waistband of his loose-fitting trousers. Slipping her fingers inside the band, she pushed his pants lower on his hips. Her intention was clear, she wanted them off.

Edge broke their kiss and stared down at her for a brief moment before he rose up. Standing by the bed, he pushed his trousers down and stepped out of them. Lina followed him, gripping the hem of her shirt and pulling it over her head before removing her own pants.

Her eyes roamed over his body. She traced his ribs with her fingers. He was still too thin. The past couple of weeks had helped some, but he still wasn't eating as much as he should.

She looked up when he wrapped his hand around her wrist and brought it to his mouth. Her lips parted when she felt his tongue across the inside of her wrist. His gaze clashed with hers in a silent challenge. Lifting her chin, she slid her hand down to his hip before stepping closer and wrapping her hand around his cock. He drew in a shuddering breath at her touch.

"Tonight," she whispered again, not breaking their connection.

He wrapped his arm around her and pulled her tightly against his body. She lowered her eyelids to conceal the sadness in her eyes when she saw the possessiveness of his smile. She knew that their time together would fade all too quickly into a distant memory. Lifting her head, she met his lips halfway.

But, first, I have to build the memory to hold onto, she thought as her lips parted.

～

Edge saw the haunted expression on Lina's face. The desire to chase the shadows away struck him hard. She had given so much of herself to him over the past weeks. Her tender touch had awoken an instinctive protectiveness he'd never realized that he possessed.

As a warrior, he was trained to protect those who were weaker, but this was different. Lina was not weak. She was fierce, proud, strong, compassionate, and so much more.

He knew there was something more deeply rooted in her insistence that they only have tonight, but she was not ready to share it with him. He would be patient. In time, she would grow to trust him.

For now, Edge would eagerly take tonight with Lina and do everything in his power to entice her to want more. She was giving herself to him, and he would use any means possible to keep her. He bent down and captured her lips.

He found this intimate act much more rewarding than the Trivator way of running his nose along the pulse points of a female to leave his scent so other males would know that she was spoken for.

He ran his tongue along her smooth, even teeth. He liked them. He was rewarded when Lina touched her tongue to his. Their breaths mingled and heated as their need for each other grew.

He slid his right hand along her back while his left tangled in her hair. She caressed his skin, moving up his chest to his shoulders before winding her arms around his neck. He could feel her breasts pressed firmly against his chest. His cock brushed against her stomach, the head so sensitive that a shudder ran through him at the sensation.

Lina must have felt his body tremble because she broke their kiss to look up at him with a searching gaze. He raised an eyebrow and glanced down between them. Her eyes followed his, and a look of comprehension dawned quickly when she saw his cock. With laughter in her eyes, she bit her lip.

He relished seeing that delight in her eyes. The shadows were gone, if only for this moment. She stepped back and grabbed his hand. He slowly followed her when she sank down onto her thick pallet on the floor.

He was surprised when she knelt and then straddled him. The position was incredibly arousing because of the way his cock rubbed against the soft hair between her legs and also allowed him access to her beautiful breasts and sexy mouth.

They faced each other. A muscle in his jaw twitched when she began moving her hips. He automatically raised his hands to cup her breasts. She tilted her head and leaned forward to kiss him again.

His body was on fire for her. She was teasing him, rubbing her clit against the head of his cock while tantalizing his lips with her tongue. The tip of his cock was slick from their combined desires, making each stroke a painful pleasure.

"Lina," he whispered when she broke their kiss to run a series of tiny kisses along his jaw. "My *Amate*...."

"Shush," she whispered against his ear. "No talking, just feel what is happening between us."

He tightened his fingers on her nipples, causing a moan to slip from her lips. She bent her head and bit down on his shoulder. He tilted his head back at the feel of her teeth on his skin. He slid his arms around her when she rose up and, with agonizing precision, slowly impaled herself on his thick shaft.

"Sweet Goddess," he hissed, feeling her channel wrap tightly around his cock.

"Damn, but you feel good," she murmured against his neck.

'Feel good' was an understatement. He caressed her back, moving down to her hips as she rode him. He leaned back against the bed when she pressed on his shoulders. He'd never been with a woman in this position before. The feel of her riding him, the view of her face flushed with desire, and the freedom to explore and watch her was intensely arousing.

While he rocked his hips, he slid his hands along her sides to her breasts. She rose up and down on his shaft, and he cupped her breasts again and pinched her rosy nipples until they both stood out like hard pebbles. The areolas around her nipples darkened.

Her body stiffened and her lips parted in a silent cry. Determined to extend her orgasm, he continued to rock his hips. A shudder went through her, and her body melted against his.

Wrapping his arms around her again, he rolled until he was on top of her. Her legs spread farther apart, opening her to his possession. He buried his face against the curve of her neck as he drove into her with increasing need. The tingling at the base of his spine warned him that he was about to come.

He swept his tongue along the sweat dampened skin of her neck. He opened his mouth, gently biting the creamy flesh. Another moan, muffled by his grip on her neck escaped him as he stiffened. He buried his cock as far as he could go inside her.

His release was powerful—his body jerking and his cock pulsing along her sensitive core. She raised her legs and wrapped them around his waist, digging her heels into his buttocks to push him deeper until he swore he could feel the tip of his cock against her womb.

He knew she was locked in another release. Her tight depths spasmed around his cock, milking every drop of semen from him. Her arms held him against her. It took him a moment to realize that he had bitten her hard enough to draw blood. Running his tongue over the mark, he knew it would be the first of many if he had his way. Tonight would not be their only night.

They lay locked together. Neither of them spoke. Instead, they caressed each other, using their touch to communicate. Once he had relaxed enough to withdraw from her, he rolled to the side and reached down for the blanket they had kicked off. He could hear Lina's soft, even breaths and knew that she had fallen into a relaxed sleep.

She rolled onto her side with her back to him when he covered them with the blanket. Smoothing her hair back, he pressed his warm body against hers and wrapped his arm possessively around her waist. Brushing a kiss to her shoulder, he slowly relaxed and fell into a deep, contented, and dreamless sleep.

CHAPTER TEN

"What have you found?" Deppar asked, staring out the window over the crowded lanes of the Spaceport.

He could feel the guard's wary gaze on his back. The man had a right to feel nervous. Deppar had already eliminated two of this guard's predecessors. He impatiently waited for the man's response. He moved his hand down to his sidearm.

"We are still searching. We know that he must still be on the Spaceport," the guard said.

Deppar turned to stare at the man. The muscle in his jaw twitched. His pale, almost sickly white complexion flushed with an unnatural red hue as his blood heated.

"How do you know he is still on the Spaceport? It has been three weeks since he escaped. He had assistance. I have no answers. I want that escaped Trivator found!" Deppar snapped.

"Ye.. yes, sir. I have men thoroughly searching every transport and container before they depart. No one leaves without being searched," the man swore.

"You've posted a reward?" Deppar asked.

The guard nodded. "Yes, ten thousand credits for any information," he replied.

Deppar gritted his teeth. Ten thousand credits and yet no one had come forward. The Trivator had been too weak to escape on his own. If there had been other Trivator warriors on the Spaceport, the entire forces on the Waxian home world would have been on high alert. What confounded him was that very few people knew he'd had the Trivator captive. He'd been very careful and guarded about his communications.

The alert of a message coming through broke the silence. Frustrated, he turned on his heel and stepped around to his desk. A grimace of distaste crossed his features before he looked up at the guard who was still standing at attention.

"What are you waiting for? I don't care if you have to tear apart this Spaceport! Find him!" Deppar ordered with a wave of his hand.

"Yes, sir," the guard said, backing toward the door and, with an expression of relief, disappeared through it when it opened behind him.

Deppar sat down in the chair and reached for the screen. He tapped in a code and cleared his expression before pressing the command key. The glowering face on the screen facing him didn't look any more pleased than he felt.

"Prymorus," Deppar greeted.

"You've found him?" Prymorus demanded in lieu of a greeting.

Deppar shook his head. "Not yet. I suspect since his body hasn't turned up yet, that he is still alive," he replied.

Prymorus's expression hardened. "You suspect? How did you lose the Trivator in the first place when he couldn't even walk?" he demanded in a cold voice.

Deppar curled his fingers into a fist. "He had help. We later discovered how they were able to get him out of the building. I believe he is still on the Spaceport. I have guards searching every section. No transports are allowed to leave without a thorough search. We will find him and those who have helped him," Deppar promised.

Prymorus was silent for a moment. Behind him, Deppar could see a group of Drethulans entering and exiting the bridge of the spaceship. He was honestly surprised that Prymorus was still alive after their disastrous assault against the planet which had most recently joined the Alliance. Deppar had half-expected the Drethulans to have killed his half-brother for that failure.

"I will be arriving in four days. Find him, Deppar," Prymorus ordered.

"I will, brother," Deppar stated before ending the communications.

He rose from his seat, and walked back to the window. From the upper level of the Spaceport, he had quite a view. He had four days to find the Trivator. If he didn't, Deppar's tenuous blood connection with his half-brother would do little to keep Prymorus from spilling his blood.

"Where are you? Who would dare to help you when we are in the center of the Waxian stronghold?" Deppar wondered aloud.

In his mind, he ran through the different alien species on the Spaceport. There were few who would not only be bold enough to try but would have the slimmest chance of successfully pulling off such a daring mission. The only species he knew of were the Trivators, the Kassisans, and perhaps the Elpidiosians. The Jawtaw, Raftian, and Armatrux knew better than to challenge a Waxian force, especially considering their current alliances with the Drethulans. The Usoleums were too arrogant and would never soil their own hands with such a dangerous endeavor.

"Computer, search for the following alien species on the Spaceport," Deppar commanded, calling out the list he'd compiled in his head.

"Affirmative," the computer responded and then replied. "There are currently zero matches for your criteria aboard the Spaceport."

Irritation flared inside Deppar. Turning around, he walked behind his desk and sat down. Drumming his fingers on the desk, he broadened his search. If he had to sort through every single being currently inhabiting the Spaceport, he would. There had to be an answer, and when he found it, he would crush them all.

~

"Two hundred fifty-two, two hundred fifty-three, two hundred fifty...," Mechelle counted.

"Enough! You are driving me crazy," Mirela groaned, looking up from the computer screen she was studying.

"Shut up, Mirela. I have a new shirt riding on this," Andy said, popping a snack into her mouth.

"Earlier you said it was a pair of pants," Mirela said in exasperation.

Andy stuck out her tongue at Mirela. "I lost... again. Edge is working on his abs now," she retorted.

Edge was having a hard enough time staying focused on what he was doing. The women's constant teasing was highly entertaining and completely unexpected, but it was his memories of the night before that were distracting him.

Lina had been gone from their bed when he woke. All morning, she had avoided looking directly at him. The wall she was trying to erect between them was almost tangible. Frustrated, he'd spent the morning focusing on rebuilding his strength. Unfortunately, his mind and body were more in tune with Lina than on what he was doing. He finally gave up when he heard Lina's muffled laugh and lowered himself to the floor.

Breathing heavily, he turned his head to follow Lina as she exited the area they shared. He sat up when he saw the way she was dressed. Once again, she avoided his eyes. He raised an eyebrow at her and Mechelle released a long sigh.

"Oh man! Lina! You should have waited two more seconds before you came out," Mechelle groaned.

Andy stood up and pumped her triumphant fist in the air. "Yes!! I won," she crowed.

Mechelle turned and glared at Andy. "That shouldn't count. He was only four away for me to win again. He would have made it too, if Lina hadn't distracted him," she complained.

This time it was Andy's turn to snort. "Are you kidding me? He hasn't been able to take his eyes off of her all morning. If I didn't know any better, I'd think someone has the hots for Lina," she teased with a knowing glance.

Lina looked over at Mechelle and shook her head. "Don't blame this on me. I can't help it if lover boy here has a case of puppyitis for me," she retorted in a seemingly light, playful tone, but one that fell a bit flat. She turned her attention to tightening the strap over her laser pistol. "Gail, do you have the bags?"

He frowned and rolled to his feet. "Where are you going?" Edge growled.

"Uh-oh," Bailey said, stepping out of their makeshift kitchen.

He didn't bother to hide his displeasure. The idea of her leaving the safety of their hideaway made him feel the darkness closing in around him. The fear that she might not return nearly suffocated him.

Lina raised an eyebrow at him. Flexing his fingers, he tried to calm the rising desire to throw her over his shoulder and haul her to their private quarters. He'd already tried that, and it hadn't gone well, but he was stronger now, better able to think and maneuver. If it was a fight she wanted, then he would give it to her, he decided. He would fight even his *Amate* to keep her safe.

"Don't even think about it, Edge," Lina softly warned with a confused, almost desperate look in her eyes.

He tilted his head at her. She'd been trying to avoid physical contact with him all morning. He raised his eyebrow at her in return.

"I bet a pair of pants that Lina wins," Andy crowed, watching the standoff with a grin.

Mechelle scowled. "I'm not betting on this one. He's stronger than he was the last time," she said.

"Oh, yeah. I could look at that tight ass with no pants on," Andy murmured.

His lips twitched when Lina shot her friend a heated glare. Taking advantage of her distraction, he darted forward and wrapped an arm around her waist. This time, he kept her back to his front. Lina's outraged gasp was drowned by the other women's laughter. He continued walking until he swept them through the parted curtains.

"Damn! Sex in the afternoon. I can't remember the last time I did that," Gail commented, drawing snide responses from the others.

"We are NOT having sex!" Lina snapped in irritation, pushing her hands against his.

"Yet," Edge replied, gently lowering her onto the bed. He covered her body with his, caging her beneath him. "Where are you going?" he quietly asked.

Her eyebrows rose, and she pursed her lips together. He didn't miss her slightly shaky breath or the tremble in her bottom lip. Her eyes were filled with emotion. Unable to resist, he lowered his head and gently pressed his lips to hers.

She resisted at first, keeping her lips firmly pressed together. He teased her lips, the way she had done to him last night. He felt a shudder run through her body before her lips parted, and she ran her tongue along his top lip. Sliding his arm under her head, he pressed a series of small, light kisses to her lips.

She released a long sigh. "You are such a tease and totally not fighting fair," she muttered, sliding her hands up his arms to his shoulders. "If you are going to kiss me, you might as well do it right."

He chuckled at her defiantly spoken words. Goddess, but he loved having her under him. If not fighting fair was how he could keep her at his side, then he would learn every way he could in order to be successful at unfair-fighting practices. He placed a line of kisses along her jaw before he pressed a lingering one to the side of her neck. Tonight, he would mark her there.

"Are you okay?" she murmured.

A wry smile curved Edge's lips. "No," he replied near her ear, suggestively pressing his hips downward. "Will you make me feel better?"

A soft groan escaped her. "I swear you've been hanging around with Andy and Mirela too much," she said, pushing against his chest. "Move, before I make you hurt there in a different way."

He chuckled. Instead of moving off of her, he lifted his head and rubbed his nose along her cheek. Pleasure swept through him at his species' particular way of intimately showing affection to an *Amate*.

"I don't want you to go topside without me," he stated, looking down at her.

Lina turned her head away from his intense gaze. He took advantage of her exposed neck, bending and lightly nipping at the soft flesh. He was rewarded when her hips jerked. A soft hiss slipped from her lips when she felt his increased desire. She turned her head and he could see on her face that she wanted him as much as he wanted her. Both of them grimaced when they heard the women on the other side of the thin curtain.

"Lina, daylight is burning," Mirela called out.

"Knock it off, Mirela. If the roles were reversed, you and I both know that you'd be burning more than a little daylight. We wouldn't see you for a week," her sister retorted.

"Oh yeah, I could live with a week of continuous sex," Bailey replied with a loud, dreamy sigh, drawing more laughter.

Lina groaned and shook her head. "They won't stop now. I have to go. I... we won't be gone long. Promise me that you won't do anything stupid. If you try, I've given... I've given Andy and Bailey permission to knock out your ass," she murmured.

"It is better than Mirela shooting me in the leg," he grudgingly conceded, running his nose along her cheek again.

"What in the hell are you doing to me?" she groaned, her hands going back and forth between pushing him away and pulling him closer.

"I am marking you. If I were on your planet, I would be courting you. It is something I learned while I was there. I met a nurse there named Chelsea. She was very interesting. Her husband, Thomas, was also very enlightening," he replied, pressing his lips over her pulsing vein. "I want to mark you here to show the world that you are mine."

"You want to.... Oh, hell, no! Move!" Lina ordered with exasperation, pushing harder this time.

He rolled to the side, confused by her sudden panicked tone and vehement protest. She rolled in the opposite direction, half-falling from the bed before she straightened. He sat up and watched her run a nervous hand over her disheveled dark brown hair before she adjusted her shirt. Rising to his feet, he frowned when she took a few steps back.

"What is wrong?" Edge quietly asked.

He took a step toward her only to pause when she held up her hand and took another step away from him. Her throat moved nervously up and down along with her hands. Finally, she released a barely audible curse and looked up at him.

"Listen, I know that you think you are attracted to me in some... sort of, you know, way, but it isn't real. I mean, you may think it is real, but it really isn't—real, I mean. I think they probably have some fancy name for it in the medical or science world. I was never very good at either one so I couldn't tell you what it might be. I just know that it is something that makes a person feel like there is something real when there really isn't, and I really don't think we should go there. If you know what I mean," she finished in a voice that faded on the last word.

Confused, he returned her gaze. "I fear I did not understand any of what you just said. Can you repeat it? Are you trying to say that what happened between us last night was not real?" he asked in frustration. "It felt very real to me."

She growled before turning on her heel and sweeping aside the curtain. "Gail, let's go."

He remained where he was for a split second before he followed her. He was still trying to decipher what she had been trying to tell him. It took another second for her most recent words to register. She was still determined to go topside.

Following her, he brushed the curtain aside. A frustrated snarl escaped him when he saw Andy, Mirela, and Bailey all standing between him and the exit. Mechelle shot him a sympathetic glance from where she was operating the door.

"I do not want her to go! It is too dangerous," Edge snarled, glaring at the other women.

Mirela chuckled. "And you aren't? Honey, you've got a lot to learn about Earth women if you think acting like a Neanderthal caveman will get you anywhere," she retorted.

"I am not this caveman. I am a Trivator warrior," he snapped.

"Yeah, well, if you ask me, there isn't much difference between the two of you," Mirela replied.

"You… Earth women are very frustrating," Edge growled.

"You might as well get used to it," Bailey replied with a shake of her head. "You've got six of us to keep you in line."

Edge watched as Andy walked over and sat down on the chair by the door. She laid her laser pistol across her lap. His fingers clenched into two tight fists. He was stronger, but not strong enough to take on all of the women.

He grudgingly admitted they were smart. Instead of huddling together, they each took different points in the room where they could monitor his movements, yet still have a clear shot with their weapons. Even Mechelle, the quietest one of the group, stayed far enough away from him that it would be difficult for him to use one of them as a hostage—not that he would do that. It would be beneath the honor of a Trivator warrior.

But, that doesn't mean I can't think about trying it, he thought, his eyes narrowing on Andy.

"She'll be back soon, Trivator. Don't you worry about Lina. She knows how to survive on the streets, even alien ones," Andy said, waving her hand at him. "If you need to burn some energy, I could always use a new vest. Mechelle, you game?"

"I think he should rest and build his energy," Bailey interjected. "How about lunch instead?"

He reluctantly nodded, his gaze still focused on the door. He forced his fingers to relax. Turning toward the kitchen area, he looked down at his hands. They were trembling again.

CHAPTER ELEVEN

*T*rivator home world of Rathon:

"What have you found?" Jesse asked, peeking over her sister's shoulder.

Jordan glanced up and scowled before she returned her attention to the screen in front of her. Her fingers flew over the keyboard. Eight different screens displayed various data. One had a star map, another screen was filled with rows of data that constantly changed, as if thousands of conversations were running all at once.

"I'm not sure yet. I need to follow this thread," Jordan replied. "Are the kids being good?"

"They are napping. So is Scout. I think they wore Grandpa out today," Jesse replied, pulling up a chair to sit next to her sister. "So, you've worked like a maniac the last couple of months. What are you working on, and do Hunter and Razor know about it?"

Jordan nodded. "Yes, they know. In fact, they asked me to research all this data. They have recently received additional information from Destin and Sula," she explained.

"Is this about the missing women?" Jesse asked, her eyes moving over the screens. "I swear, I don't know how you do this, Jordan. All the data flashing across the screens makes my head and eyes hurt. I don't understand any of it."

Jordan chuckled. "I know. Dagger says the same thing. It is like listening to music, only I see it," she confessed. "Each part is a piece of a puzzle and when it all comes together, I finally get to see the whole picture. I love the challenge and seeing the symmetry of lines creating data which tells a story."

Jesse shook her head. "You are such a nerd," she teased.

"I know," Jordan admitted. "I'll be out in a little bit. I need to finish compiling this latest lot of data."

"Okay. I'll fix you something to eat. You've been in here all morning. You probably didn't even eat breakfast this morning either," Jesse chided.

"Don't tell Dagger," Jordan murmured.

"Don't tell me what?" a deep voice demanded.

Jesse turned and grimaced. "Uh-oh! Busted. I'll be in the kitchen," she muttered.

Jordan bit her lip and managed to enter two more commands before she felt her chair being turned. Her large eyes looked straight into those of the man kneeling in front of her. Her gaze softened when she saw the worry in his eyes.

"I'm fine," she said.

She tilted her head to rest her cheek against the warm palm that cupped it. Dagger leaned forward and pressed a tender kiss to her lips. She loved the way his thumb gently caressed her cheek.

"When Hunter and Razor asked me if I would object to you helping them, I said no," he began.

Jordan's lips twisted into a wry smile. "Only because you knew I'd do it anyway," she softly retorted.

Dagger sighed. "Yes, you would have done it anyway. I worry about you," he said.

Jordan's heart melted at the expression in his eyes. Her hands rose to cup his face and she leaned in and kissed him. His lips parted when she traced them with her tongue. Deepening the kiss, she poured her love for him into every touch, every breath before she reluctantly ended the caress.

"I love you, Dagger. You and our daughter, Helena, are my life," Jordan murmured, brushing another kiss against his lips.

"You are an amazing woman and I love you very much. I want you to take care of yourself more," Dagger said, his voice growing deeper with the depth of his emotion.

Jordan glanced over her shoulder at the screens. "I'm so close, Dagger. I can feel it," she said, turning back to look at him with a pleading expression. "I can't give up on them."

Dagger drew in a deep breath and stood up, pulling her with him. Jordan wrapped her arms around his waist and held onto him as if she would never let him go. After a moment, he rubbed his chin against her soft brown hair.

"Ten minutes, then take a break to eat. I will take care of Helena when she wakes up. Find them, so we can have you back," he murmured.

Tears burned the back of Jordan's eyes. "You will always have me, Dagger," she promised.

"Ten minutes, then food," Dagger insisted, releasing her.

Jordan grimaced. "And the bathroom," she laughed.

Jordan watched Dagger step out of the electronics room, which was set up at Hunter and Jesse's house specifically for her. Razor had suggested installing the computer system at their own home, but Jordan had declined. She knew herself well enough to know that she needed to be away from easy access to such an elaborate setup if she was to maintain her sanity.

Sinking back down into her seat, she scanned the data coming in. Her heart sped up when the filters she had programmed into the software she had designed suddenly began to go crazy. Her fingers flew over the keyboard again, pulling the information from one screen to another and combining them.

"*Prymorus.*" Jordan's fingers touched on a program to identify the man's voice.

Voice recognition at ninety-nine percent: Deppar Achler, Waxian mercenary.

"You've found him?" Prymorus's voice demanded.

"Not yet. I suspect since his body hasn't turned up yet, that he is still alive."

"You suspect? How did you lose the Trivator in the first place when he couldn't even walk?"

"He had help. We discovered how they were able to get him out of the building. He is still on the Spaceport. I have guards searching every section. No transports are allowed to leave without a thorough search. We will find him and those who helped him."

"I will be arriving in four days. Find him, Deppar."

"I will, brother."

"Spaceport…. Where are you? Where are you?" Jordan muttered, her fingers trying to find the location of the signal.

The dot on the top center screen moved across the star charts, until it slowed and stopped. Jordan's hand shook slightly as memories flooded her mind from another time when she had done this, the time she had finally found Dagger. She turned her focus toward the screen in front of her. A detailed image of the Spaceport the two men had been talking about appeared on the screen. Tears burned her eyes when she saw the location.

"Jordan, time's up," Dagger said behind her. "Jesse has lunch…."

Jordan heard Dagger's voice fade as he caught a glimpse of the screen. She slowly turned. His face was pale but composed.

"You found something," Dagger said.

Jordan pursed her lips together and nodded. Drawing in a deep breath, she stepped closer to Dagger. She needed to feel his warmth again.

"Yes. I can't be completely sure it is Edge, but… but, I'm ninety-nine percent sure," she whispered, laying her cheek against his broad chest.

"That is the Waxian home planet," Dagger said.

Jordan tilted her head back and nodded again. "I know. The Spaceport was built around its moon," she replied.

Dagger tore his gaze from the screen to look down at her with a frown. "Are you sure he is there?" he asked.

Jordan looked over her shoulder at the screens. "I heard Prymorus asking his half-brother about a Trivator who had been captured. Dagger...." Jordan turned and looked back up at her mate. "They are looking for him. He has escaped. Deppar Achler said the Trivator had help."

"Help," Dagger replied, startled. He looked back at the screen. "Who could have helped him that far into Waxian territory?"

"I don't know. Maybe Razor or Hunter may know," Jordan replied.

"I'll contact them while you eat," he said, staring at the screens.

Jordan laughed. "Bathroom first. I've really got to go," she admitted with a grimace.

~

"Bathroom, then food. I'm sure Hunter and Razor will want to talk to you," Dagger murmured, stepping to the side so Jordan could pass him.

His attention remained locked on the screens even as he pressed the activation button on the communicator clipped to his ear. He stepped closer to the screens, staring down at the Spaceport. It was in one of the most hostile star systems known to the Alliance.

"This is Hunter."

"Hunter, Jordan found something. Razor and you may want to see this," Dagger said.

"I'll contact Razor, and we'll be there in half an hour," Hunter replied.

"I'll let Jordan know," Dagger said, ending the call.

A shudder ran through his body and he sat down in the chair. Memories of his time in captivity flashbacked through his mind. Sweat beaded on his brow and he clenched his fists as he fought the flashbacks. The knowledge that Edge had probably suffered the same conditions as he or worse hit him hard. He should have stayed with him. He shouldn't have left him defenseless.

"Dagger," Jordan's voice pulled him back from the precipice that he still found himself teetering on at times. "Dagger, come sit with me."

Dagger took a deep breath before he stood up. Stepping away from the monitors, he reached for Jordan's hand. She wrapped her arm around his waist and leaned against him.

"He escaped. He isn't alone like you were," she quietly said.

Dagger's arm tightened around her. "I was never alone, Jordan. You were always there with me," he murmured.

CHAPTER TWELVE

"**You**'ve got a shadow on your tail, Lina. Seven o'clock," Gail murmured into the headset.

"Turning left at the parts cart," Lina replied.

Lina wanted to growl in frustration. This trip had been fraught with one hazardous situation after another. They had scavenged no food, no supplies, absolutely nothing! Lina had all but given up when a group of Waxian guards had swept into the market. Gail and she had been forced to split up at one point and hadn't yet been able to safely reconnect.

She was thankful Gail had found her again. Turning just past the cart containing junk parts salvaged from space, she headed down a long alley that cut over to the next street. She was almost to the end when two guards stepped into the alley and cut her off.

Turning on her heel, she started to retrace her steps when another guard blocked her way. Lina took a step back and stopped. She was trapped. Her only hope now was that they would just bypass her.

Lowering her head, she picked at the light blue fabric covering her pants. The material looked like a skirt but had slits in it that separated in case she needed to run or climb. She slid her hand down to her side as the sound of their footsteps drew closer.

She wrapped her fingers around the butt of the laser pistol strapped to her thigh. Through the eye holes cut in the textured mask, she could see a pair of worn black boots. She lifted one gloved hand to pull the hood of her cloak lower. Coarse threads of white hung down over her left breast. Maybe she should have chosen one of the hairy men as her costume today instead of that of a Driserian woman.

"You are pretty quick," the guard who had been following her stated.

Lina kept her head down. Seeing as she could only understand what they were saying, but not respond in their language, she decided pretending to be mute might be her best option at the moment. She swallowed when she saw another pair of boots stop in front of her.

This isn't going to be good, she thought.

"We've been ordered to search every person on this Spaceport. Any that resist will find themselves imprisoned—or worse," the guard in front of her stated.

Lina wanted to roll her eyes when the other two guards laughed. Really? Like she hadn't heard that before back on Earth. Some males were pigs no matter where they lived in the universe.

"Let's get a look at what we are about to have fun with," the guard on her right said, reaching out to grab her arm.

Left with little choice, Lina pulled her gun and fired it at the man on her left while kicking her right foot out and connecting with the crotch of the man standing in front of her. She then turned into the male who had grabbed her arm.

This one was a little more with it. He dropped his hand down and wrapped it around her left wrist, preventing her from bringing around the laser pistol.

Lina stepped into the man and kneed him in the crotch. His fingers nearly crushed her wrists when he tightened them in reaction to his pain. Despite her own pain, she tilted her head back and then slammed her forehead against his nose. His loud groan filled the alley. He released her wrists and fell backwards.

A searing fire hit her side, and Lina twisted and jerked back several feet. Her back struck the wall behind her. Lifting her pistol, she fired a round into the center of the shooter's chest.

She was just about to do the same to the man she had kicked when he slammed into her. Pain exploded through her. He pulled her arm back and smashed it against the wall. The pistol fell from her hand.

She choked as the man held his beefy forearm against her throat. Her right hand slammed into his side with as much force as she could muster, but he barely reacted. Her fingers trembled as dark spots began to blur her vision.

"What are you? You aren't a Driserian," the man snarled.

He released her right arm, reached up, and ripped off her wig and mask. Shock registered on his face.

"I'm... your... worst... fucking... nightmare," Lina gasped, pulling his pistol free from its holster at his side and shooting him.

She leaned against the wall, gasping for air. The male she had kneed was scrambling to his feet. As if in slow motion, she saw him raise his pistol and point it at her. Lina fought to raise hers first. She didn't have to bother. A large black hole appeared between the man's eyes before he fell backwards, his pistol sliding across the alley.

"Shit! I tried to get to you sooner, but there were a couple of merchants in my way," Gail said, running up to her. "Are you okay?"

Lina leaned her head back against the wall and felt her side. She grimaced when she felt warm wetness spreading on her clothes. Blinking at Gail, she gave the other woman a wry smile.

"I've had better days," she admitted in a terse voice. "I need you to help me put the mask and wig back on."

Gail turned and looked down at where Lina was holding her side. Bright red blood stained her hand. She tried to grin when Gail released a long string of unfamiliar expletives.

"That's a good one. I'll have to... try to remember it," Lina joked before she gritted teeth. "Damn, but this hurts as bad as a bullet."

"Just... Shut up," Gail ordered, ripping a strip of material from her own outfit and folding it. "You do know that Edge is going to go ballistic when he sees you covered in blood, don't you?"

Lina chuckled before she winced in pain. She held herself still while Gail tried to stem the flow of blood. Once the other woman had done what she could in the short amount of time they had, they decided to hide as much of Lina's face as they could. Gail shoved the mask and wig into her pocket.

Lina leaned heavily on Gail when the other woman wrapped her arm around her. Once they reached the end of the alley, Gail murmured to take it slow and easy. Lina couldn't help the strained chuckle that slipped out.

"We're just two old ladies out for a Sunday stroll in the park," she whimpered.

"Shut up, Lina, or I swear I'll leave your ass here," Gail ordered under her breath.

∾

By the time they made it back to the entrance of their underground hideout, Lina was ready for Gail to leave her on the side of the lane. Given how weak she felt, she knew she had lost a lot of blood. Her biggest fear was that she might have left a blood trail behind. The last thing she wanted to do was create a neon sign saying 'here we are'.

"Are you sure there is no blood?" Lina asked for the hundredth time.

Gail glanced behind her. "I'm positive. I can go back and make sure if you want," she replied.

Lina shook her head. "No, I think... we've taken enough chances today," she whispered.

She released a sigh when Gail opened the door to the grate. Gail helped her inside before closing it. They made sure no one else was around before Gail opened the second door. Peering inside, Gail wrapped an arm around Lina's waist.

"Not much farther, Lina," Gail said.

Lina wanted to laugh, but at the moment, she didn't think she had the strength. The ride down in the lift seemed to take forever. She was a bit worried when she realized that she couldn't lift her head.

"I've ruined Mechelle's outfit," Lina observed, staring down at the long red streak on her right side. It was easier to look down than to try to lift her head. "I wonder if she can wash it out."

"God, I hate it when you get hurt," Gail muttered as the lift slowed to a stop.

Lina tilted her head to the side. "I'm a nice wounded patient," she declared in a faint voice.

Gail grimly nodded. "That's what scares the hell out of me," the older woman admitted.

"Gail," Lina whispered as her eyelids began to droop and shivers of shock took hold of her body.

"What is it, boss lady?" Gail questioned, wrapping her arm around Lina's waist.

Lina tried to think of what she had been going to say. The words and thoughts were all jumbled in her head. She wondered if this was how Edge had felt the day they rescued him. If it was, then it was a miracle that he had managed to make it as far as he had.

"I'm cold," Lina whispered, her head rolling back and her eyes closing.

CHAPTER THIRTEEN

*E*dge turned when he heard the banging on the outer side of the door. Andy jerked out of her seat, sliding the chair to the side and aiming her gun at the door. Bailey and Mirela came around to each side. Mechelle stood next to Edge.

Another impatient knock echoed through the room, this time in a distinct pattern. Mechelle hurried forward and threw back the locks. Andy was shouldering her weapon while Bailey ran to be next to Mechelle. Mirela disappeared into the bathroom.

"She's hurt bad," Gail said the moment the door opened.

"Shit," Andy said.

Bailey was already trying to assess what had happened. Edge surged forward. He reached between the women and picked up Lina's limp form in his arms. Turning, he strode quickly across the room to their quarters. He gently bent over and laid her on the bed.

"Let me see," Bailey said, sliding in next to him.

Mirela appeared and handed Bailey a knife. Bailey lifted the material and tried to cut it away. Frustrated with the amount of time it was taking, he reached down and grabbed the ends, ripping apart the bloodstained material.

"Thanks," Bailey muttered, carefully lifting the makeshift bandage that Gail had pressed against the wound.

"What do you need?" Mirela asked, placing a medium-sized container filled with medical supplies on the crate next to the bed.

Bailey choked back a bitter laugh. "A sterilized operating room back on Earth and a team of doctors," she replied.

"You can fix her up, can't you, Bailey?" Mechelle asked.

Edge watched as Bailey dropped the bloodied bandage into a bucket that Andy had silently brought in and placed next to her. He saw her look of indecision as she looked at the supplies. It dawned on him that Bailey wasn't sure what to do.

"Give me the blue box," he ordered. "Bailey, the green container has an antiseptic cleanser in it. Clean the wound."

Bailey looked up at him with a startled expression before she reached for the green container that Mirela was holding out to her. Edge took the blue box and opened it up. Inside was an emergency field kit. He inserted one of the vials containing a numbing agent into an injector, placed the business end of the injector near the wound on Lina's side, and depressed the button.

"Bailey and I will take care of Lina," he said.

Gail motioned for the others to step out, and paused in the doorway after they had left. Her gaze moved from Lina's pale face to Edge's. Edge looked up from what he was doing.

"Don't let her die," Gail said.

Edge nodded. "We need to stop the bleeding," he instructed, kneeling down and focusing on the deep wound.

"Tell me what you want me to do," Bailey responded.

Deppar walked down the lane. He was surrounded by five of his guards. Crowds of merchants and visitors warily eyed the group as they passed by.

"You said they were found an hour ago?" Deppar asked.

The guard walking next to him nodded. "Yes, sir," the guard replied.

The small unit of men turned into the alley. Deppar slowed when he saw the three dead men. Standing to the side was his new Captain of the guard.

"What have you discovered?" Deppar demanded.

The guard glanced down at the men. "Witnesses state that one of the men was following a Driserian female," he said.

Deppar walked around the bodies, scanning the ground. He paused. Kneeling, he picked up several bluish-white colored strands and rolled them between his fingers. He stood up and held out the strands to the guard.

"Analyze this," he ordered, rotating to study the dead men.

Stepping closer to the man lying in the middle of the alley, he noticed a clip attached to the man's vest. Scanning the area, he turned to look at the guard.

"He was wearing a vidpod. Spread out and find it," Deppar directed.

The guard turned and waved his hand. "You heard him. Find it," the guard repeated to the other men.

Deppar searched along the wall, two men checked under the bodies, and the rest spread out. The vidpod would be small and difficult to find in the ill lit alley. On the third pass, one of the guards called out. Turning, Deppar held out his hand when the guard hurried over.

"I need a reader," he snapped.

The guard turned to the men. They all shook their heads. Deppar's attention returned to the dead man.

"Check the body," he ordered in irritation at the blank looks on the guard's faces.

The guard bent over and searched the man's pockets. Deppar impatiently waited. Several minutes later, the man held up a vidpod reader that he had pulled from the man's leg pocket.

Slipping the tiny camera into the device, he skimmed through the videos. The guard had a penchant for taping his encounters with women. From the flashes of video he saw, the three dead men had worked together to target their victims. He slowed the video when he reached the guard's first sighting of the Driserian.

The men had followed the Driserian for several blocks. There was something about the way the woman moved that didn't feel right. Driserians tended to be hesitant and walked with a different gait due to the joint structure of their legs. Their knees were reversed, bending backwards instead of to the front.

This female had walked with a steady, smooth stride that spoke of confidence and... determination. She was searching for something. Deppar noted the vendors where she had paused, touching certain items. He saw her head turn. Frustration burned inside him because the hood of her cloak hid most of her face.

He caught the movement of her hands, as if she were speaking to someone before she turned and moved down the line of carts. At one point, she disappeared. The vidpod captured a 360 degree view as the guard turned trying to locate the woman.

Deppar sped up the video until he caught a glimpse of the blue gown the woman was wearing. He glanced at the time. It had taken the guards almost thirty minutes to find her again. She was coming down the alley where he was now. Behind her was one of the other guards.

Once again, frustration burned through Deppar. This reader model did not have audio capability. He watched as the scene unfolded. The laughter on the men's faces, the woman's bowed head, the discharge as she shot the guard to her left. The guard with the vidpod fell to the ground, so the front of the woman and the ground were all that was visible. The woman moved again. This time, Deppar was able to see clearly that her legs were not jointed like a Driserian's.

She was quick, he noted. The vidpod angled upward as the guard rose. He could see red against the blue of her outer covering. She was bleeding.

The vidpod aimed straight now and for the first time, Deppar was able to get a view of the woman's face. At first glance, she looked like she was a Driserian, except for her dark brown eyes. His hand tightened on the device when the guard's arm blocked the view of the camera. A second later, the vidpod jerked as the guard stumbled backwards.

He froze the image on the face of a species he had never seen before. Frowning, he enlarged the image. The woman's skin was darker than his. Rich, dark-brown hair matched the color of her eyes. Her lips were pressed together as if she were in pain. This confirmed that it had been her blood that he had seen on her outer clothing. He let the video continue playing. Her head turned, but he never caught sight of who she was looking at because at that point the vidpod had fallen off the guard's vest and rolled until it was facing the back wall.

His hand closed around the recording device. He breathed deeply. A strange species like this, especially a female, would have been brought to his attention. Who had she been looking at? Could it have been the Trivator?

He looked over at the guard with a clean shot between the eyes. A shot like that wasn't impossible to make, but it was not one most species would have picked first. Was it possible that this female had something to do with the Trivator's escape? If so, how had she managed to get him out of his cell, through the building, across the planks that had bridged the gap across the alley, and spirit him away without being caught? It was impossible to believe—yet....

"Follow the blood trail," he quietly ordered.

"Sir?" the guard asked, unsure if he had heard Deppar correctly.

Deppar turned and shot the man a heated glare. "I said follow the blood trail. The woman was injured and bleeding. Follow the blood trail and you will find her. When you do, inform me at once. I want her and whoever is with her brought to me alive," he demanded.

"Yes, sir," the guard replied.

Deppar swiveled on his heel and retraced his steps down the alley. He wanted to return to his office and further analyze the vidpod. He wanted to know who the female was and who was with her.

CHAPTER FOURTEEN

*P*ain, that was the first thing that Lina expected when she woke. Well, in all honesty, she was surprised that she was still alive and capable of waking up. After that pleasant surprise, she moved on to expecting the pain. A frown creased her brow. An analysis of her body resulted in her noticing a pleasant numbness.

"I'm paralyzed," she whispered in horror.

That had to be the reason she didn't feel any discomfort. She blinked, trying to clear the fog from her brain. Focusing, she imagined her fingers moving.

The feeling of horror changed to puzzlement when she realized she could feel the cloth covering of her bed. She also realized that she could feel the material against her bare skin, including her legs.

"Okay, maybe semi-paralyzed," she murmured, concentrating on wiggling her toes. "Or, not."

"You are awake," a voice grunted, sitting up beside her bed.

Lina turned her head to the side and blinked. Edge was sitting on her makeshift pallet on the floor. She gave him a critical look.

"You look like shit. Are you feeling okay?" she asked in a voice that felt surprisingly weak. "What happened? How long have I been out?"

Edge's expression darkened. Lina wondered if she should close her eyes and pretend that she had fallen back asleep. From the fire burning in Edge's eyes, she had a feeling she was about to receive an ass-chewing.

"I'll tell you what happened," he growled. "You almost died! You have been unconscious for two days! I told you not to leave, but you refused to listen to me. You are the most hard-headed, irritating...."

Lina grinned when his voice faded, and she could see him trying to think of other names to call her. She relaxed against the pillow and raised an eyebrow. It was nice not to be in pain.

"How about lovable, smart, witty, cute, kick-ass, and a good kisser?" she suggested.

Edge glared at her with a frown. "No, those are not what I was thinking at all," he replied before his expression changed, "but, I do agree with the last one."

Lina chuckled, then moaned. Her hand slid up to her side. Okay, it did hurt when she laughed.

Mark off laughing from the list for a few days, she thought, closing her eyes.

"I cannot give you more medication for the pain yet. There is not much left," he said, rising from the floor and sitting on the edge of the bed.

Lina hissed when he pulled away the covers enough that he could gently grasp her hand in his. She fumbled to cover herself. Without the covers, half of her right side, including her breast, was exposed.

He surprised her again when he lifted her hand to his lips and pressed her fingers against his mouth. His eyes darkened with emotion. Lina felt that familiar flutter in her stomach whenever they touched. Hell, whenever she thought of him.

This isn't good. Not good at all, she thought.

"Water," she whispered.

Edge nodded. "It is a good thing that Bailey and Mirela kept several containers in reserve," he commented as he reached over and picked up a container of water on the table beside the bed.

Lina winced when she tried to sit up. A shiver ran through her.

She clutched the bedsheet to her chest when he slid his arm underneath her back and helped her sit up to drink some water.

"Thank you," she muttered.

She raised her hand to hold the container, but he kept one hand on it and the other wrapped around her shoulders. The cool liquid felt good going down her dry throat. She drank nearly a third of the container before the effort became too much and she needed to lie back down again.

Edge tenderly lowered her back to the bed. He brushed a hand along her cheek. His fingers warm against her cool flesh.

"Edge...," she started to say with an uneasy tremble in her voice.

He slid his hand down and laid his thumb against her slightly parted lips. His eyes flashed with a warning and a determined look came into his eyes. Lina was too tired to fight—at the moment, but she had to let him know that there could never be anything between them. Well, at least nothing serious.

"You are mine, Lina. Mine to care for, mine to protect. You are my *Amate*," he stated with a mutinous glare.

Lina shook her head. Her eyes closed despite her desire to stay awake. It was as if her body knew that she needed the rest even if her mind fought it.

"I can't be yours, big guy," she whispered.

She couldn't be his—ever. It was hard to belong to someone when you didn't have a heart. She had given hers away years ago to someone else.

～

Edge tenderly tucked Lina's arm back under the covers and bowed his head. He looked at his hands. They were trembling. The chaotic thoughts and trembling were slowly diminishing, but he still had issues with them. Both issues became noticeably worse when he wasn't near Lina.

The sound of the curtain moving drew his attention. He turned and saw Gail silently standing in the opening. She looked tired.

"How is she? I thought I heard her voice," she asked.

Edge felt an unfamiliar smile lift the corner of his mouth. "Hard-headed, stubborn... but also cute and lovable. The last two were her words, not mine. I used a few others," he admitted.

Gail chuckled and looked relieved. "I'll let the others know that she is going to be okay," she said.

Edge saw her turn, then pause and look back at him. Gail had kept her distance from him since the beginning. She had always looked at him with an expression of suspicion. He couldn't blame her. He remembered what had happened to her world after the Trivators were sent there.

"I won't hurt you or any of the other women," he said.

Gail glanced at Lina's peaceful face before looking back at him. "It isn't us that I'm worried about you hurting. Lina can be tough as nails, but under that tough exterior is a warm and loving heart. She would give her life for those she loves. She's come pretty damn close to doing that more times than I can count in just the few years I've known her. I see the way you look at her. Don't confuse being grateful that she saved your ass for something deeper. In the end, you are still one of the aliens who changed our world forever and someone we can't trust," she said.

Edge rose to his feet. Gail didn't move. She straightened and stared back at him.

"Lina is mine. I have claimed her as my *Amate*. It is my responsibility to protect and care for her. This is not about gratitude," he replied.

Gail shook her head. "You can't just claim her, Edge. Lina isn't a pet. You say you won't hurt any of us, and part of me believes that you mean it. I don't think you would intentionally hurt any of us, especially Lina, but...." She shook her head and was silent a moment before she spoke again. "Just a word of caution, Trivator. You might want to protect your own heart," she quietly said before she stepped out of the room.

He stood there as the curtain swung closed behind her. Returning to his position on the bed, he picked up Lina's hand and studied her pale, slender fingers. Lifting them to his mouth, he pressed them against his warm lips.

"You are mine, little goddess," he murmured, rubbing her hand against his cheek. "You keep the insanity away, giving me peace, and warming my soul. We will find a way out of here, and I will keep you safe."

CHAPTER FIFTEEN

culus IX

"Prymorus," Deppar said grimly. "You arrived early."

Prymorus' mouth tightened at the expression of consternation that crossed the younger male's face before Deppar hid it. He didn't need to ask if Deppar had been successful in finding the Trivator—his expression told him that he hadn't been. Pushing past Deppar, Prymorus entered his half-brother's office.

"I suspected you would need assistance," Prymorus stated, walking over to the wall of windows. "What have you discovered?"

Behind him, he could hear Deppar walk over to the bar. The sounds of Deppar removing the stopper from a liquor bottle and pouring the liquid into two glasses echoed through the otherwise silent room. In the reflection from the window, he observed Deppar's nervous movements.

"He was helped," Deppar said, walking over and holding out the glass of liquor.

Prymorus took the glass. His mouth tightened in irritation. He wanted information he did not already know.

"What have you done so far?" he asked.

Prymorus watched as Deppar gazed out the window and down at the levels below them. If it wasn't for the fact that Deppar was useful at times, he would have already eliminated him long ago. Deppar's only value to him had been the way he oversaw the Spaceport. Now he wasn't even beneficial for that.

"There is a woman who I believe helped him," Deppar admitted.

Prymorus turned and stared at Deppar with a look of disbelief. "A woman? You are telling me that a single female infiltrated your stronghold, overpowered your guard, broke through a locked door, and carried out a Trivator warrior—all on her own? Who is this incredible female warrior?"

A flash of anger crossed Deppar's face at the sarcastic tone, and he walked over to his desk. Moving to stand behind Deppar, Prymorus watched him enter a series of commands into his computer. A moment later, the image of a woman's face appeared.

"I don't know her species yet. She was dressed as a Driserian, but as you can see, she isn't one. She wasn't alone. She, and whoever was with her, killed three of my guards in an alley near the Trader's Market eight levels below," he explained.

"Human," Prymorus replied with a curl of his lip. "The woman is a human. How did she get here?"

Prymorus watched the play of emotions cross Deppar's face as he studied the woman's features for a moment.

"There is no record of her or anyone else like her arriving on the Spaceport. I've searched all the arrival documents for the past year. No one has ever seen her before. I've ordered reward notices posted for her capture on all levels. Interviews conducted with all the vendors in the Trader's Market came up with the same response. No one recognized her," Deppar replied in frustration. "It is like she suddenly appeared, then vanished. Even before this incident, I've had every departing spacecraft thoroughly searched, so there is no way she could have coming and going without notice. I do know she was wounded in the attack. My guards are tracking the faint residue of her blood. The process has been hampered by the activity in the area."

Prymorus could almost feel his half-brother's frustration. It matched his own. He rubbed the tender flesh of his gun wound. Gripping his drink, he returned to the window to look down at the activity on the Spaceport.

"The Drethulans on the warship will assist in the search for her and the Trivator," Prymorus informed Deppar.

"The Drethulans…. Can they be trusted? We supply them with weapons which they could easily use against us," Deppar replied with distaste. "My men will find both the woman and the Trivator. I don't want the Drethulans on my Spaceport."

Prymorus's chuckle was soft and mocking. Deppar thought he was in charge, when truly he had lost his command position on the Spaceport the moment Prymorus had stepped onto it. With the Drethulans behind him, not even the Prime Ruler was a match for Prymorus and his power.

"This is no longer your Spaceport, Deppar. I will oversee the search for the human and the Trivator henceforth," Prymorus stated.

"The Prime Ruler will…," Deppar snarled, rising from his office chair.

Prymorus waved his hand in dismissal. "Our uncle is old and weak, Deppar. Be careful how you challenge me, half-brother. The star systems are about to change." He turned to study Deppar's outraged expression. "The Alliance will fall."

Deppar gave him a skeptical look. "Just as it happened on that primitive planet? There was only a small regiment of Trivator warriors there. What about Dises V? You are the one who will fall, *half*-brother. You and your overweening ambitions will drag all of us down with you. If the Alliance doesn't retaliate against us, then the Drethulans will. If I had my choice, I would choose the Alliance," Deppar snarled.

Rage swept through Prymorus. Throwing his glass against the wall, he pulled the pistol at his waist and aimed it at his incompetent relation. Deppar's sneer changed to wariness.

"Do not test me, Deppar," Prymorus warned in a soft but dangerous voice. "The Trivator you allowed to escape could provide us with valuable and much needed information in the coming conflict."

Deppar shook his head. "He would die before he would talk. Not even the drugs I gave him would loosen his tongue," he argued.

Prymorus's eyes narrowed. "I won't need drugs to make him talk. I only need the human who helped him escape," he replied, lowering his weapon and looking thoughtful.

"Why would that matter?" Deppar asked, confused.

CHAPTER SIXTEEN

athon:

Razor studied the information that Jordan had discovered. Once again, he appreciated that she was on the Alliance's side. Her skills rivaled the best programmers in the coalition, but it was her tenacity and intuition to search through data others would dismiss that gave her an edge most lacked.

"I know you have men searching for Prymorus. I had a program running in the background searching for anything concerning him. I never would have connected him with Edge's disappearance. I shouldn't have been surprised though, considering what happened to Dagger," Jordan said.

Razor's gaze focused on the Spaceport in orbit around the Waxian home world. It would be suicidal to send a team to extract Edge. At the moment, they could still only guess which Trivator the Waxians claimed to be holding. If by some miracle, a team was able to infiltrate the Spaceport, they would have to locate him and then retreat through hostile territory.

"It might not be Edge. He has been missing for over two years. From the content of the transmissions, the Trivator warrior they are talking about hasn't been in Waxian custody for very long," Hunter observed.

"Edge is the only one who keeps coming up on my filters as a probability. What I would like to know is why would they want a Trivator warrior in the first place. I checked through all the information I could find and neither Deppar nor Prymorus have had dealings in the fight rings the way Kelman did with Dagger," Jordan said with a perplexed expression.

Dagger frowned. "Kelman was greedy for credits. Prymorus is greedy for power. The Waxians have always dealt with the Drethulans on a business level. This is something else. The attack on Earth is evidence of that," he said.

Hunter shot Razor a wary glance. "If you know anything you aren't sharing, now would be a good time to divulge it. I know the Alliance Council has been convening almost daily behind closed doors in secret sessions since we returned from Dises V," he reflected.

Razor's jaw tightened. Yes, the council had been meeting. The increase in Drethulan forces and the attack on Earth had initially drawn the wrath of many of the council members, but since then they had quickly dismissed the hostile action as a rogue attempt at colonizing a new world and not as a threat to the Alliance.

Even the situation on Dises V was brushed off as a mutual trade agreement between the Waxians and the members of the ruling government on Dises V. There was nothing in the agreement that mentioned the Drethulans and there was no hard evidence that anything inappropriate was being done. It didn't matter that Taylor had testified before the council after her experiences there.

For the safety of the rebel bases hidden on Dises V and the rebels still fighting for control, some information was being withheld. Razor, Hunter, and Ajaska Ja Kel Coradon, the new Kassisan ambassador to the Alliance, thought it best to keep the sensitive information to themselves. It was all too obvious that there were some on the council who did not have the best interests of the

Alliance at heart. Razor and Ajaska would work on uncovering what was going on inside the council. Hunter's assistance outside the circle of those looking over Razor and Ajaska's shoulders was invaluable.

"We must get Edge out. I was instructed by the council to clear any mission orders through them first. They are concerned that any troop movements toward the Waxian or Drethulan borders might be interpreted as military aggression," Razor dryly replied.

The corner of Hunter's lips lifted into a smirk. "It is fortunate that I do not have the same constraints. Thunder and Vice are the two with the best chance of getting in and out under the Waxians' noses and crazy enough to volunteer for the mission. I won't order them to go. This will have to be a strictly voluntary mission," he warned.

"But... how will they get close enough to the Spaceport without being seen?" Jordan asked with a frown. "A freighter would be too slow. A fighter would be too obvious. You'd need something that was fast, yet not obvious."

"Or something invisible," Dagger said with a growing grin.

"Ajaska...," Hunter murmured under his breath.

Jordan looked thoughtful before she nodded. "The cloaking device he uses on his spaceship would work," she agreed, surprising the three men.

Razor frowned. "How did you know about the cloaking device?" he demanded, looking at Dagger with a raised eyebrow.

"I didn't tell her," Dagger swore, raising his hands in the air.

Jordan smiled and wrapped her arm around Dagger's waist. Razor watched as the delicate-looking young woman tilted her head. Her eyes brimmed with mischief.

"Did you forget that Taylor was on board?" she reminded them. "She thought it might be useful information to have so I could develop a program that can track a concealed ship—as a security measure," she quickly added.

Razor chuckled and shook his head. "I didn't think she had been aware of the ship's capabilities," he admitted.

"Taylor notices everything. It was important if we wanted to survive. Even then, there were no guarantees and we still came close to dying many, many times," Jordan said.

Razor didn't miss the haunted expression in Jordan's eyes or the way Dagger's arm tightened around her slender body. His thoughts turned to his own mate. Memories of the dangers Kali had lived through – barely – swept through his mind.

"I will contact Ajaska. Hunter...," Razor said, looking at his brother.

Hunter nodded. "I'll contact Thunder and Vice and let you know by this evening," he replied.

"Jordan, continue monitoring any other communications dealing with Prymorus. I want to know what that bastard is up to," Razor requested.

Jordan nodded. Razor bit back a chuckle when he heard Dagger mutter that she had already done enough. Razor agreed, but Jordan's unique expertise was needed, and he would use any resource he could to save one of his men.

"We meet again tonight," Razor announced.

Hunter chuckled. "I'll tell Charma to expect extra company for dinner," he said.

"Make sure Kali and Ami come. Taylor will be so bummed out to miss this. She and Saber are still on vacation," Jordan added with a sigh.

"I will. Ami loves playing with Lyon, Leila, and Helena. She likes that there are more girls than boys," he chuckled.

"Not for long," Jordan said without thinking.

Dagger stiffened beside her. His surprised eyes locked on her face. Jordan's face flushed a charming rosy color and she bit her lip, looking up at Dagger with an excited expression.

"Excuse us," Dagger muttered, turning Jordan toward the door.

With an expression of amusement, Razor watched the two disappear through the doorway. He heard Hunter's chuckle. Returning his attention to the screens, he took a deep breath.

"My gut tells me there is more to what is happening than the council is willing to see or acknowledge," Razor murmured.

Hunter turned to look at the screens as well. "The cryptic messages from the red crystal ship, the attacks on Earth, Ajaska's insistence that Destin be protected, and now this. Why would he want Edge, if he is their captive, that is? Who helped him escape, and where are they all now?" Hunter mused.

"I don't know, but I intend to find out," Razor said, suddenly turning. "Contact Thunder and Vice, see if they are willing to volunteer for this mission and if so, when they can return to Rathon. In the meantime, I will speak with Ajaska."

Hunter nodded. "I know they are already on their way back to Rathon. I spoke to Vice earlier this morning. He said they had located all but six of the missing women on an Armatrux slave ship bound for one of their mining operations. They rescued the women they found and decided it was best to return to Rathon for the time being since it was closer than Earth. Several of the women were ill," he replied.

Razor's lips tightened. He would issue a formal complaint to the Armatrux council. They will also need additional sanctions and patrols to ensure that they remain in compliance with the Alliance accord that they had recently signed. Trafficking of humanoid species was against Alliance law.

"I'll see you later tonight," Razor murmured.

Striding through the house, he briefly glanced through the window out into the garden. Dagger was sitting on the swing under the tree, holding Jordan. Razor paused when he saw the pleased smile on Dagger's face.

His focus moved to Jesse and his parents when they stepped out of the playroom onto the veranda with Lyon, Leila, and Helena. The children squealed with delight when their grandfather playfully growled at them and began chasing them all.

His thoughts moved to his own mate, Kali, and their young daughter, Ami. A sudden need to see them and hold them swept through him. Refocusing on his mission, he decided he could contact Ajaska from the secure line at his home just as well. This way, he could take care of his obligations to his people and the desire of his heart.

~

Later that night, the small group sat in Jordan's office. They had enjoyed a boisterous dinner with the family before quietly excusing themselves. Razor waited for Dagger to close the door before he looked over at Hunter.

"Ajaska is sending a cloaking device. Due to the delicate nature of the Kassisans' new membership in the Alliance, we both agreed that it was better to keep any link between the Kassisans and what we are doing now limited to our core group. Until the council concludes that the Waxians are working with the Drethulans on a larger scale than they are currently admitting, our hands are tied. As Chancellor, I am assuming responsibility for this mission in accordance with our treaty with Earth to provide protection," Razor said.

"Thunder and Vice have agreed to go," Hunter said with a nod.

"They'll need support to handle a ship large enough to travel that far, yet small enough to get in and out with a crew," Dagger added.

Hunter nodded. "Jag will command the *Nebula One*, a new Class V warship that is smaller and sleeker, yet can handle greater distances. He has been working with Thunder, Vice, and a small but trusted crew to hunt down the missing Earth women," he explained.

"Now all we need to find is the location of our missing warrior. It's going to be nearly impossible for Thunder and Vice to get on the Spaceport without getting caught. If we could pinpoint the warrior's location, it would help tremendously," Razor said, turning his gaze to Jordan.

"I'll have it by the time they get close enough to need it," Jordan said, a look of determination on her face.

"I know you will, Jordan. If anyone can do it, you can," Razor chuckled.

"Just ask my brother Trig," Dagger muttered under his breath. He grunted when Jordan elbowed him. "What? It's true."

Jordan leaned to the side and brushed a kiss across his lips. "You were worth every second of driving your brother crazy," she said.

"When will the cloaking device arrive, Razor?" Hunter asked.

"Tomorrow night," Razor replied. "I already have the schematics for Jag's engineer. He can begin preparations for the installation and make the necessary modifications. They will finish it all here once the Kassisan transport arrives. I want them to head back out as soon as the warship is ready."

"Jordan, go over everything you've discovered so far. I want to be able to debrief Jag, Thunder, and Vice as soon as possible," Razor instructed.

Jordan nodded and turned to the screens. "This is what I've found out so far….," she began.

CHAPTER SEVENTEEN

*W*axian Spaceport - Oculus IX:

"What are you doing up?" Edge growled.

Lina teetered for a moment before she fell back against the pillow with a groan of frustration. She needed to use the bathroom and she was ready to do it without Bailey's help and a bedpan. Struggling to sit up again, she gritted her teeth to keep the moan of pain from slipping out. Sweat beaded on her brow and black dots danced before her eyes. She blinked.

No, black chest hair, not dots, she silently groaned in frustration.

"I need to use the bathroom," she bit out.

"Bailey…," he started to say, stopping when she shook her head.

"No! I am not using a damn bedpan again. Now, either help me up or get the hell out of my way," she snapped, gripping the front of his vest.

Edge grunted, but he didn't argue with her. She had woken up in a bad mood. While she might be a good wounded patient, she was a bitch of a patient when she was healing. A hiss escaped her when she was gently lifted. She raised her arm and wrapped it around his neck.

She allowed her head the luxury of resting against his shoulder. If she were to be honest, she was exhausted from her attempts to get up. If it hadn't been for her protesting bladder, she would have said to hell with it.

Her lips twisted when all of the other women turned to look at them. It was obvious from the amused expressions on their faces that they had heard the conversation. Lina decided that curtains made lousy walls.

"I could have helped you, Lina," Bailey said.

Lina grimaced. "I know. You've done enough and I need to get on my feet," she said as Edge carried her to the bathroom.

She breathed a sigh of relief when he placed her feet on the floor. She sighed again, this time with aggravation, when Edge started to close the door—with him still inside the room. Holding a hand to her side, she raised an eyebrow and looked pointedly at him.

"You're on the wrong side of the door," she stated.

He had the nerve to shake his head at her. "No. You should have someone in here with you," he replied.

Lina ignored the pain in both her side and her bladder. She lifted her hand and gripped the edge of the door frame. There was no way in hell she was going to give in.

"Out! Now!" she ordered, pointing to the door.

She ignored the way his jaw tightened. He was going to try to argue with her. She wasn't in the mood to negotiate. The pain in her bladder was beginning to overshadow the one in her side.

"You are a frustrating woman," Edge replied with a scowl.

"Yeah, well, just keep remembering that," she retorted with a wiggle of her fingers. "If I need you, I'll holler."

He opened his mouth to respond before snapping it shut and stepping out of the room. A rueful smile lifted her lips when he closed the door while muttering under his breath. Drawing in a deep breath, she stared at the door for a moment. She could hear the teasing comments the women were giving Edge.

"That man is going to drive me crazy," she whispered with an amused shake of her head.

～

An hour later, Lina sat on a crate and rested her head against the wall as she watched Mechelle and Bailey quiz Edge about life on Rathon, the Trivator home world. She hoped Edge didn't realize that they were also asking pertinent questions to help them understand if the risk they had taken was the right one. Deep down, Lina's gut told her it was right despite the complexity of the situation between them.

"So, you know how to fly spaceships?" Mechelle asked. "Like all kinds of spaceships or just Trivator ones?"

Edge frowned. "I can fly anything that has been made. The dynamics of most ships are the same," he replied.

"What is life like on Rathon? I mean, do all the women have to bow down to the men or do they have some say in what goes on?" Bailey asked.

Lina's lips twitched at Edge's startled expression. "If you ask my father, he would say my mother has more say than most. Why should a woman feel she must bow to a man? She is what balances him. Without her, he only has half a soul." Lina sucked in a breath when Edge turned his glittering gaze to her. "Finding our *Amate* is a gift from the Goddess. It is her way of showing a warrior that he is worthy," he said.

She flushed when Mechelle looked at her with wide eyes while Bailey fanned herself. Mirela's soft 'What the fuck?' rang in her ear. Lina bowed her head and tried to pretend she didn't understand what Edge was publicly telling her. She wasn't up to dealing with the emotions he was causing inside her.

"Somebody definitely has the hots for you. I think it is more than a one-night stand kind, too," Mirela murmured.

Lina scowled and shot Mirela a warning look. "He'll get over it. It's survivor's emotions. Once he's out of here and back on his world, he'll find some poor Trivator girl and shower her with his affection," she retorted.

"Mm, yeah. That would be easier to believe if no one had heard the hushed moans and groans coming from your area a few nights ago. If you were trying to keep things a secret, Lina, you need more than a curtain," Mirela dryly replied.

"It didn't mean anything, Mirela," Lina quietly retorted.

She ignored Mirela's skeptical look. Her eyes turned toward Edge. He was explaining to Bailey what the different medicines in the box were and how to use them.

Even though she had only been up for an hour, she was already exhausted, but she resisted the urge to go lie down again. She knew it was because she was worried about Andy and Gail. The two women had gone topside while she was in the bathroom.

"Changing the subject, when are you going to tell him about the you-know-what?" Mirela asked.

Lina knew what Mirela was asking. They had agreed they wouldn't mention anything about how they planned to escape until they felt the time was right. Part of that timing included not only getting Edge recovered and detoxed from the drugs, but also knowing that they could trust him.

"He still has the shakes. They aren't as bad as they were, but he still has them," she softly replied. "At night, when he thinks I'm sleeping, I can hear him still fighting against the effects. Whatever the Waxian did to him—whatever happened to him before—it continues to affect him."

Mirela leaned her head against the wall next to Lina and released a long sigh. Lina watched the other woman draw up one leg onto the edge of the crate and wrap her arm around it. She could tell from Mirela's hard expression that the woman was remembering the things they had lived through.

"We all have our ghosts at night, Lina. I was in the same cell as you and heard your nightmares just as you've heard mine. I say he is ready and so do the others. If we are going to get out of here, we need to do it sooner rather than later. He's the only one out of the lot of us who knows how to pilot one of those damn alien spacecrafts. The longer we stay, the greater the odds are that we'll be discovered. We've already outlasted the statistics for that probability," Mirela replied in a slightly bitter tone.

Lina watched Edge nod as Bailey repeated what he'd told her as she replaced the items. Mirela was right. The longer they stayed, the more likely it was that something else could happen to one of them.

"I'll talk to him tonight. Do we have the rest of the supplies loaded?" Lina asked.

Mirela nodded. "Yeah. Mechelle and I did a run yesterday, and Andy and Gail did the last one before they went topside," she said.

"We don't even know if it will work. Maybe that is why the ship was left behind," Lina muttered.

Mirela slid her leg down and sat up. "It has to. I don't want to fucking die in this shithole," she replied, standing up. "I'm going to get a drink. Do you want anything?"

"No, thanks, I'm good," Lina replied.

Lina watched as Mirela walked over to the others. She chatted for a moment before disappearing into the kitchen. Looking down at her hands, she realized that she was playing with the hem of her shirt. A part of her had been dreading this moment ever since she first heard the guards talking about having a Trivator in their custody.

She wanted to get off this rock as much as the rest of them, but she was also worried that their one hope would turn out to be a dud. What if the spaceship they had found during their explorations turned out to be a piece of junk? When they first discovered it, they had been so excited. It was the hope that kept them going day after endless day.

Now, it was time to see if that hope was a pipe dream or a reality. She looked up at Edge, and watched him quietly walk across the room toward her. There was something in the big guy that melted the ice around her heart, and it scared the shit out of her. She had promised herself it would be just one night, but she quickly realized that one night would never be enough.

They had been together pretty much 24/7 since she'd found him. You got to know someone when you spent that much time together in close proximity, and it hurt so much to lose them. Tears burned her eyes for a moment before she blinked them away. She had given up on tears and love a long, long time ago, she reminded herself.

"You should be resting," Edge said, stopping in front of her.

She tilted her head back and glanced up at him. "I am," she retorted with a wry smile. "That was nice of you to show Bailey how everything works."

She smiled when he pressed his lips together at her avoidance. Turning, he sat down on the crate that Mirela had abandoned just a moment before. He leaned against the wall and folded his arms across his chest.

"We are trained in advanced field medicine," he replied. "Why did Mechelle and Bailey want to know what types of spaceships I can pilot and what my home world is like?"

Lina briefly closed her eyes. She turned her head and gave him a rueful smile. He was looking at her with a raised eyebrow. He had known exactly what the two women had been doing.

"We have a spaceship," she softly admitted.

He sat up and twisted until he was facing her. The humorous expression in his eyes had quickly faded into an intense look, and he stared at her with a sense of purpose that shook her. She took a deep breath and stiffly straightened.

"Where is it?" he demanded.

"Before you get too excited, we don't even know if the damn thing will work," she cautioned.

His jaw tightened, and he studied her face. Lina tried to keep her expression neutral.

"That is why you risked your life to release me—so that I would fly this spaceship. Was that the only reason?" he asked, searching her face.

"Yes," Lina replied, staring back at him.

His eyes narrowed and she saw a flash of anger in them before he concealed it. She didn't flinch when he lifted his hand and ran his fingers along her jaw. Her heart pounded in her chest when he rubbed his thumb along her bottom lip.

"And now? Am I just a pilot to you?" he asked softly with a smoldering look.

Lina hesitated, but knew what she had to say. "Nothing has changed, Trivator," she whispered regretfully.

"You are not a very good liar, Lina Daniels," he murmured.

Her lips softened when he bent his head. His hand moved along her jaw and his fingers spread along the back of her neck to keep her from turning away from him. Her eyelashes fluttered closed when he captured her lips in a tender kiss.

She could have handled keeping her heart protected if he had just kissed her with heated passion. It was his gentle touch and the tender way his lips moved against hers that melted her resistance. This huge alien warrior confused her. Every time she thought she was beginning to figure him out, he did something totally unexpected.

Her lips parted under his gentle probing. His tongue swept along the smooth surface of her teeth while his other hand came up to cup her heated cheek. He gave her a series of kisses, some deep, while others were light and teasing. The combination was enough to draw a soft moan from her.

"Edge," she whispered, her hand sliding up the front of his vest.

The sound of something dropping on the floor drew Lina back to the fact that they were not alone. She tilted her head and gazed over his shoulder. Mechelle, Mirela, and Bailey were standing there with their mouths open, staring at the two of them. Mirela had dropped the spoon she was using to stir her tea.

"We need our own space," he muttered.

Lina started to reply when she heard the soft sound of knocking on the other side of the door. Mechelle quickly turned and hurried to it. The rhythmic knock came again. Mechelle unlocked the door and pulled it open. She had barely opened it far enough for a person to enter when Andy pushed by her followed closely by Gail. They both wore grim expressions as their eyes swept the room before locking with hers.

"We've got to go now. The Waxians have some kind of creatures that are tearing apart the lower sections. They are heading this way," Andy informed them.

CHAPTER EIGHTEEN

*N*o matter how many times they had prepared for this moment, it still caused a rush of adrenaline, but despite the stress and danger, they worked in a cool, confident, and organized manner. Bailey collected the medical supplies, while the others packed up the few remaining weapons as well as their personal items.

"Here you go," Mirela said, tossing a laser rifle to Gail.

Mirela turned toward Edge with another one in her hand. "This is for you," she said, holding it out.

Edge looked at the rifle before taking it and slinging it over his shoulder. Lina saw that he had grabbed the bag she kept packed and ready to go. Biting her lip, she stiffly walked over to the pistols lying on the crate. She picked up two of them before glancing around.

"Let's go," she said, refocusing on the small group. "Andy, how long do you anticipate it will take them to reach this section?"

Andy slung her backpack over her shoulder and gripped her rifle. "Gail shorted out the lift down here. I set off the charges on the doors to the stairs on the various levels. Each door all the way down is sealed. They'll have to break through each one," she said.

"Those things, whatever in the hell they were, looked like they wouldn't have much trouble doing that," Gail replied with a shudder.

"What did they look like?" Edge asked.

"They looked like most aliens until they shape-shifted. They had these tentacle things, six eyes, and a circular mouth with rows of teeth. They scared the shit out of both of us," Andy said.

"And they smelled like roadkill after a week in the Georgia sun," Gail added.

Lina saw Edge stiffen as the two women described the creatures. "They are called Drethulans. They evolved in a desert climate, living and breeding underground. That is their natural form, and in that form they are the deadliest. If they are here, it means they are working with the Waxians," Edge grimly replied. "We need to leave now."

Lina stood back from the group. Her teeth worried her bottom lip as she thought of what they could do to delay those searching the access tunnel. Her eyes lit on the cases of explosives they had found shortly after they discovered this section of the Spaceport. She suspected the explosives were left over from the Spaceport construction. If they could use them, it was possible to get to the spaceship which was another two miles away through winding tunnels. The only way to give them a chance was to seal off this section of the tunnel.

She turned and looked at the others with a determined expression. "I can delay them. I'll give you as long as I can before I set off the explosives," Lina said.

"What the hell are you talking about?" Gail demanded, turning to glare at Lina.

Andy shook her head. "Don't start talking bullshit, Lina. We all go or we all stay," she said.

Lina shook her head. "I'm about ready to collapse right now. There is no way I can make it two miles. There are enough explosives here to collapse this section of the underground. I can detonate them and give you all enough time to take off," she explained with a wan smile.

"There's no guarantee the spaceship will even power up, much less fly," Mechelle pointed out.

"All the more reason to give you additional time," Lina replied, sinking down on a crate. She lifted a shaking hand. The pistol shook from the effort. "Go. That's an order."

"Fuck that," Mirela replied, folding her arms across her chest. "I've decided I don't like your orders anymore, boss lady."

"Lina's right. You need to go," Edge instructed.

"What?!" a chorus of startled voices sounded through the room.

"I said go. We will catch up with you," he repeated.

Gail gave Edge a skeptical look. "What are you going to do?" she demanded.

"Lina is correct. We need to stop the Waxians and Drethulans. I will wire the explosives to go off, then pick up Lina and run," he replied. "I am very fast when I know there is going to be an explosion."

Soft, relieved chuckles trickled through the air. "I'll bet on that," Mirela replied. She turned toward Edge. "Don't make me lose, Trivator. I hate losing."

Lina caught the silent message that passed between Edge and Mirela. Gritting her teeth, she decided arguing would just waste more precious time. She slowly rose to her feet, and walked over to the crates of explosives. She pushed off one of the lids.

"Andy, you go with Mirela, Mechelle, and Bailey," Gail said. "I'll stay here and help Edge and Lina."

The grin on Andy's face faded and she nodded. "Let's go," she said, pulling the door open and checking the outer corridor. In the distance, they could hear banging.

"Whatever you do, hurry," Andy instructed before she and the other women disappeared in the opposite direction of the lift.

"What do you want me to do?" Gail asked.

"I'll stack the cases of explosives around the main support beams and near the entrances. Once they detonate, there will be no turning back," Edge explained, picking up two of the cases.

Gail nodded. "I worked for the Explosive Ordnance Disposal Unit in the Army for six years and on the bomb squad with the police force for another eight years. I can set up some remote detonators," she said.

"I'll help," Lina replied.

They worked as a team. Edge carried the crates of explosives and set them up while Lina and Gail worked on the timers and detonators for each one. Gail figured they would only need a handful. Once the first explosions began, it would create a chain reaction.

"That's it," Gail said twenty minutes later. She lifted a hand and wiped her brow. "I guess my time in the EOD unit and the Trivator invasion came in handy after all."

"They are getting closer," Lina replied, listening to the sounds of explosions.

Edge came in and nodded to Gail. Lina raised her arm when he bent over to sweep her up into his arms. Gail held out one of the remotes. Lina took it and held it against her chest.

The timers were set to go off in fifteen minutes. Just in case they didn't have that much time, Gail had added a remote that would be good for about five hundred yards. That didn't give them much of a head start when they would have several tons of moon rock and metal construction materials coming down all at once.

The echo of something heavy hitting metal rang out along the corridor. Gail was ahead of them by several yards. Lina clung to Edge, trying not to cry out from the pain in her side.

"What was...?" she tried to ask.

"A Drethulan. One of them must have dropped down the lift shaft. It will tear through the metal of the lift, then open the doors. When I tell you, press the detonator," Edge ordered through gritted teeth.

"You need to...," she hissed.

"Don't argue, Lina. The Drethulans aren't easy to kill and they won't hesitate to kill the other women," Edge warned.

Lina started to nod before horror struck her. Coming straight at them from out of the darkness were twin beams of light moving at a rapid speed. Gail slid to a stop and dropped down onto one knee. She slid her backpack off and raised her rifle to her shoulder.

"Don't shoot!" a voice yelled out as the lights veered to the side when the vehicle turned at a sharp angle.

"Mirela?" Gail exclaimed, rising back to her feet and grabbing the backpack. "Where in the hell did you get that thing?"

"She can tell us later. We are about to have company," Lina urgently said, looking over Edge's shoulder.

The screeching sound of metal as it was ripped apart made Lina grimace. Her eyes widened when she saw the tip of what looked like a tentacle protruding between the doors of the lift. Edge climbed into the back of the cargo vehicle and placed her onto the seat. Gail slid into the front passenger seat.

"Mirela, get us out of here," Edge instructed.

"No shit," Mirela muttered, seeing the Drethulan's limb.

Edge and Gail both raised their rifles and aimed at the pale, wiggling mass even as Mirela was turning the vehicle around in a tight circle. They fired at the same time, and the visible part of the tentacle exploded. A loud howl of fury resounded from the lift.

"The doors are buckling," Lina warned.

"Blow the charges," Edge ordered.

"Not yet," Lina and Gail replied at the same time.

Lina silently counted as Mirela increased the speed of the cargo transport. The doors of the lift began to contort before they were ripped open. One of the most bizarre creatures Lina had ever seen squeezed through the opening. Blood from the stump of the severed tentacle left grotesque smears on the doors and wall.

"Now," Gail said.

Together, the two women pressed their detonators. A brilliant flash of white temporarily blinded Lina before they turned a corner and out of sight of the lift doors. Edge wrapped his arm around her, holding her protectively against his body as Mirela swung close enough to the wall that their vehicle scraped against it.

"Brace for the concussion," Edge warned, turning so that he covered as much of her as he could.

Lina felt the heat a moment before the shockwave hit them. Mirela struggled to keep the vehicle from smashing into the walls. A rolling ball of flames rushed at them before the backdraft grabbed it. The shaft of the lift opened up, pulling the flames back to the top like a chimney that had suddenly been cleared. A second later, the entire tunnel trembled before the section behind them also began to collapse.

"Well, that was fun—not," Mirela stated, regaining control of the vehicle and pressing the accelerator.

"Where are the others?" Lina asked, leaning heavily against Edge.

Mirela glanced over her shoulder before refocusing on the dark tunnel. "They were heading for the spaceship. We should meet up with them before too long," she said.

"I hope to God that spaceship still works," Gail muttered.

"Me, too," Lina murmured, her hand moving down to her side.

She felt Edge move his hand over hers. He tightened his arm around her when he felt the same warm dampness that she did. She was bleeding again.

"How bad is it?" he quietly asked.

Lina closed her eyes. "Bailey can patch me up while you get us out of here," she replied.

As her adrenaline subsided, so did her remaining strength. She was still weak from her earlier blood loss and her side hurt like hell. She would close her eyes for just a little while and recharge herself a bit. They were still in a lot of danger, perhaps more so than before now that the Waxians and those other creatures knew they were down here. Lina could only hope that they had killed a bunch of the bastards.

"There are the others," Gail said.

Lina tried to open her eyes, but it felt like someone had placed lead weights on her eyelids. Instead, she listened as Mechelle, Bailey, and Andy climbed onto the back. A ghost of a smile crossed her lips when she heard them excitedly talking about the 'big bang'.

Nothing like a nice explosion to lift the spirits, she thought.

CHAPTER NINETEEN

*T*he only lights in the dark tunnel came from the cargo vehicle. Beyond the headlights, scattered crates, left over from the construction of the Spaceport or forgotten by thieves, littered the side of the tunnel.

The stale smell of moon dust and the poignant smell of Lina's blood teased his senses. She was relaxed against him, but every few seconds her body would tremble.

He tenderly rubbed her hip. He'd seen and heard stories of the bravery of the human women during his tour on Earth. His mind replayed the time when, Sword, Thunder, and he had been sitting in the dining hall at the Earth compound. There had been a young human female, Taylor Sampson, in the dining hall. Young, nimble, and very vocal, Taylor had been amazing to watch as she tried to evade Saber who had been trying to catch her.

Memories he had thought forgotten flooded his mind. The young human had covered Saber in food particles before jumping up on a row of metal shelves. He had never seen anything like that before. The three huge Trivator warriors had been amused at first until the shelf had started to tilt. It was a few moments later, when she was safely on the ground, that Taylor had told Saber in a tortured voice how she had lost her father. Edge would never forget the regret he'd felt while listening to her pain.

Tilting his head to the side, he rested his cheek against Lina's soft hair. His remorse for the devastation of Earth was a feeling that would never truly leave him. The people of Lina's world had not been prepared for first contact. They had risen up in force, both against the Trivator forces and against each other. It had shocked Edge – and the council – that the humans were not only willing to die to be free of the Alliance, they were willing to destroy their entire planet in order to achieve that goal.

It was the Trivators' function within the Alliance to guide new worlds through a peaceful transition into the federation of planets. Instead, the humans had fought with a stunning savagery and tenacity, despite repeated reassurances from the Trivators themselves and their own governments that the Trivators were not there to capture or harm them.

Seeing the heartbreak on the young human's face and hearing how their presence had affected Taylor and her sisters had stayed with him. Now he had another tangible demonstration of what Earth had become, in Lina. Still, a part of him could not regret their actions because if they had never gone to Earth, he would never have met her.

"I will get you to safety, my little goddess," he murmured, rubbing his cheek against her hair.

Ten minutes later, the tunnel opened into a large delivery hangar. Lights automatically came on as they entered the area. He blinked as his eyes adjusted to the muted glow.

Edge took a swift breath when he saw the spaceship in the center of the hangar. He didn't recognize the ship immediately. At first, he thought it was a Waxian fast dispatch supply ship. The outer hull had been modified to resemble one of the older model ships, but there was something different about it. Edge knew that some of the supply ships were upgraded with a faster engine system and new weaponry, but even without upgrades, the ships were still considered the most agile in the Waxian fleet.

As they drew closer, he could see the retracted mounted turrets on the sides. It looked like this one had been used for pirating. He turned his gaze to the numerous empty crates.

"We found this not long after we made our way down into the bowels of the Spaceport," Lina murmured in a faint voice. "We monitored the area for weeks before we finally decided it was abandoned. The ship was covered in dust and there was no evidence that anyone had disturbed it or even been here in years."

Edge loosened his hold on her when she stiffly pushed against him to straighten. He immediately looked down at her wound. She was still holding her side, and he could see the dampness of fresh blood between her fingers and on her shirt.

"This hangar would have been used during the initial construction of the Spaceport. Once it was no longer needed, it would have been sealed. A Waxian mercenary probably discovered it. I noticed as we came into the hangar that the blast doors were open. It was probably used to import and export items on which the Waxians wanted to avoid paying a hefty tariff. They were probably caught or killed topside and the ship was forgotten," Edge deduced.

"Why do you think that?" Mechelle asked, leaning forward.

Edge nodded at the ship. "If it is a Waxian supply ship, it has been modified. Regardless, I can fly it," he said.

Mirela swung the vehicle closer so they could unload. Everyone froze for a moment when they heard a distant explosion and the ground trembled beneath them. Alarms sounded, and red lights began to flash in the hangar.

"What's going on?" she asked, looking up at Edge.

Edge slid out of the vehicle and motioned for everyone else to hurry. Behind them, the blast door began to close. He truly hoped that the Waxian ship was in functional condition—at least the environmental system. They were going to be needing it soon.

"There has been an atmospheric breach to the Spaceport," he replied. "Mirela, move the vehicle. Lina, *fi'ta*, slide your arm around my neck. I need to get you inside. Bailey, she will need your help as soon as we are out of here. Gail, Mirela, Andy, and Mechelle, I will instruct you on how to use the weapons. It is time to leave," Edge stated, picking up Lina and cradling her with the utmost gentleness.

"Got it," Mirela stated, waiting as the others grabbed their bags and weapons.

"I think you have someone challenging your bossiness factor, boss lady," Andy teased.

"You're just now figuring that out," Mechelle retorted.

The easy way the women worked together reminded Edge of how it had been with the Trivator warriors he'd served with. There was an easy camaraderie between them even while they remained focused on the seriousness of the mission.

He waited until Gail opened the back platform. The flashing red lights were beginning to switch to a solid red glow. Once the last one stopped flashing, the upper containment doors would open. It was a safety measure to ensure that any spacecraft could leave quickly in an emergency.

Striding up the platform, he carried Lina through to the storage bay. The other women quickly followed him. He heard Mirela slap her hand over the control to the platform. Running lights lit the walkway, illuminating their passage.

He stepped through the door from the storage bay into the main corridor. The ship had three levels. The top level housed the bridge, captain's quarters, some storage and equipment closets, and access to the upper weapon turret. The middle level housed the living areas for a crew of ten or less and the medical bay. The lowest section housed the storage bay, engine room, and also had access to the undercarriage and the weapons turrets on the sides and rear of the ship.

Edge braced his shoulder against the wall when the Spaceport rocked again, even more violently than before. Outside the spaceship, he could hear the alarm sounding as the upper doors prepared to open.

"Bailey, follow me. The rest of you move to those benches along each side of the door and strap in," he ordered.

"I guess I don't have to tell you where the medical bay is," Bailey replied, hurrying after him.

Edge glanced over his shoulder and shook his head before refocusing on where he was going. The other woman's attention was fixed on Lina's pale face. He hoped to the Goddess that the mercenary pirate who had operated this ship had upgraded the medical bay with a surgical cylinder table.

Turning at the end of the hallway, he paused at the entrance to the medical bay. When he didn't see a cylinder table, he motioned Bailey toward the touchscreen panel on the wall as he walked across the room.

"There's no power to the ship," she protested.

"It will come on when you touch the panel. The medical bay has a power source separate from that of the rest of the ship in case of an emergency. Once the landing bay loses pressure, the ship's main power system will automatically come online," he explained.

Almost as if the spaceship were listening to him, lights began to flicker and the ship began to hum. Bailey's eyes widened as she looked around. She reached out and touched the panel on the wall. The cylinder table he'd been looking for slid out of the wall and opened.

He gently laid Lina down. Her eyes fluttered open and she gave him a tired, strained smile. He stroked her cheek.

"Now, it is my turn, *fi'ta*, to rescue you," he murmured.

Edge leaned over and brushed his lips tenderly across Lina's before he stepped back and closed the cylinder. Straps automatically wrapped around Lina. Several thin lights ran down along her body, pausing on the wound in her side before moving down to her feet and back again. He splayed his hand over the glass. Lina's eyes locked with his as a light mist filled the cylinder.

"What is it doing?" Bailey quietly asked.

Edge watched Lina's eyelids flutter for a moment before they rested like the twin crescent moons of his world. The anesthesia was working. He reluctantly stepped back and turned.

"It is a surgical cylinder. They are installed in most spaceships this size due to the limited number of crew members. They are a necessity if there are no healers available or if you are traveling alone. I ask that you stay with her. You can strap in near the door. Our escape may get bumpy," he instructed.

Bailey nodded. She looked from him to Lina to the bench next to the door. Edge quickly exited the medical bay and turned right. He took the steps up to the bridge three at a time. He strode down the short corridor, and stepped onto the bridge. It was configured for six personnel in the small cockpit.

He slid into the pilot's seat and pressed the control on the arm of the chair. The straps engaged, crossing his chest and lap. His fingers flew across the console. A grim, determined smile lifted the corner of his mouth when the engine powered on.

He checked the ceiling of the landing bay. Dirt and debris drifted down on the spaceship as the heavy doors parted. From this angle, he could see the Waxian home planet. He could also see the hundreds of ships fleeing the Spaceport.

Disengaging the docking clamps, he gripped the controls and easily guided the ship which began to rise. With any luck, they would get lost among the masses of panicked, fleeing residents.

More explosions shook the Spaceport. Edge tilted the ship to the side when a large boulder rolled over the edge of the bay door into the opening where he planned to exit. It didn't fall inside the landing bay since the artificial gravity had been disengaged but floated in the air as if suspended on a string.

Edge timed their departure with that of a large evacuation ship beginning to emerge just above them. Rising through the outer bay doors, he hugged the underside of the vessel. Hordes of other ships moving at varying speeds passed by them. Once they were well clear of the Spaceport, he began maneuvering his way through fleeing ships. When he estimated that they were approximately half the distance to the planet below, he veered away along with nearly two dozen other ships.

"Compute trajectory for jump," he ordered the computer.

"Destination," the computer requested.

"Rathon," Edge instructed.

"Calculations complete," the computer confirmed.

"Initiate," he ordered.

Edge watched the stars turn to streaks of light. He methodically began to check each system on board the ship. He paused on the medical unit. He noted that the repairs to Lina's body were proceeding well.

His hands were trembling. He curled his fingers into a fist, breathed deeply, and returned his gaze to the stars. He could appreciate their beauty now in a way he hadn't been able to since his first trip into space.

A strange sense of disconnection washed through him when he realized that he was truly free of the Waxians. As long as he and the women were in or near the Waxian boundaries, they wouldn't be completely out of danger, but they were moving in the right direction.

Reaching down, he opened the internal communication system. "We have left the orbit of the Waxian planet. You may move around the ship," he announced.

The smile on his face turned into a chuckle, which turned to a deep laugh when he heard the cheers rising up from the level below. Several minutes later, he heard footsteps on the stairs leading up to the bridge. Glancing over his shoulder, he saw Andy, followed by Gail, walking onto the bridge. They sat down beside and behind him.

"Where are we going? Earth?" Andy excitedly asked.

Edge shook his head. "Rathon," he replied, continuing to check the systems.

"Why Rathon? We want to go home," Gail said with a frown.

From the corner of his eye, he caught the swift look of suspicion that Andy shot at Gail. He paused what he was doing. He understood their distrust, but was also a touch exasperated by it.

"The journey to Earth is almost three times as distant. From this location, we would need to travel through several different star systems, many of which are hostile or still not within the boundary of Alliance control. Our best hope for survival is to get to Alliance-friendly territory and notify them of our position," Edge explained.

"But...," Andy began, pausing and looking at Gail again.

Edge turned to face both women.

"We'll still get to go home, right?" Andy asked.

His expression softened at the worried look in her eyes. "If that is what you wish," he quietly replied.

Tears glittered in both women's eyes and they nodded. Edge returned his attention to the console in front of him. While he had told them the truth, he also hadn't been completely honest, either. The rest of the women would be allowed to return to their world, but if he had his way, one of them would remain behind on Rathon with him.

He turned his gaze back to the medical bay monitor. He heard Andy and Gail quietly leave. There was still a lot he needed to check before he felt confident enough to leave the bridge. Until then, he would have to monitor Lina's progress from here.

CHAPTER TWENTY

*E*ighteen hours later, Edge left Andy and Gail on the bridge while he made his way down to the upper-level area near the bridge. Walking along the corridor, he searched each room until he found what he was looking for—the Captain's quarters. It was the only room designed for sleeping on this level.

He stepped inside, and searched it. Whoever had owned the ship before had made sure to leave behind as few identifying articles as possible. He discovered fresh linens in one of the storage compartments. The adjoining cleansing room, again, gave no clues as to who had once piloted the ship.

He retraced his steps before continuing down to the mid-level where the medical bay was located. Bailey was lying on the infirmary bed. She sat up and rubbed her eyes.

"How did she do through the night?" he asked, walking over to the surgery unit.

Bailey slid off the bed and stretched. "Okay. That thing is pretty incredible. I thought having the tooth cleaning stuff in your water so you never had to worry about brushing your teeth was pretty cool, but this thing totally blows the rest of our medical technology right out of the water," she replied with a yawn.

He looked at Lina's stats on the monitor attached to the unit. All of her bio-stats were within normal ranges. Opening the unit, he gently pulled up her shirt, so he could check her wound. Now, only a thin, pale scar existed, about the length of his palm. The skin around it looked pink and healthy.

"Wow!" Bailey said, coming to stand next to him.

His lips twitched at the awe in her voice. "She will sleep for several more hours. The monitor attached to her neck will continue to give her small doses of anesthesia. This is being done to give her body time to heal," he said, bending over and sliding his arms under Lina's relaxed body.

Bailey frowned when he raised up Lina's shoulders and knees to hold her against his chest. He could see the confusion on her face. He ignored it, moving to step around her, but Bailey cut him off.

"Where are you taking her?" Bailey asked with a raised eyebrow.

"To our cabin," he replied, stepping to the side.

Bailey followed him. This time, it was his turn to raise an eyebrow. He was tired. He wanted to refresh both Lina and himself before getting some sleep.

"Wait a minute! What do you mean by *our* cabin? Is Lina aware of this?" Bailey demanded, placing her hands on her hips.

He frowned at the curvy brunette. Bailey might be small compared to him, but if there was one thing he had learned over the past several weeks, it was that these women more than made up for what they lacked in size with their indomitable determination. At the moment though, his only concern was his need to hold Lina. Over the last several hours that need had grown until he couldn't focus on anything else.

"She has slept in my arms for the past three weeks. Do you think she would not wish to do so now?" he asked in a blunt tone.

Bailey's eyes widened at his statement. Yes, he might have exaggerated about the length of time Lina and he had slept together, but not by much. It was closer to the past week, but none of the other women needed to know that. He impatiently waited for Bailey to move out of his way.

"Well, okay. I mean, as long as it is okay with Lina," she said, looking at Lina's relaxed face.

"Bailey." He waited for Bailey to look up at him. "I would never harm her. I swear on my life as a Trivator warrior."

He saw the expression in Bailey's eyes soften before she nodded and finally stepped to the side. She briefly touched his arm as he started to pass her. He turned his head to look into her warm hazel eyes.

"If you need anything, just call. I'm going to go get a bite to eat. I can bring something to your room if you'd like," she offered.

He shook his head. "Maybe later," he said before continuing out of the room.

Walking down the corridor, he passed by the galley. Mirela and Mechelle stopped talking as he walked by but quickly began again once he passed the doorway. He stepped into the Captain's cabin when the door slid open. It closed behind him, sealing the two of them in the dimly lit room.

Taking his time, he gently laid her on the bed and stripped the bloodstained clothing from her body. He rose and placed the soiled clothes in the clothing refresher before returning to the bed. He lightly brushed his fingers along the scar on her side.

He laid his hand over the mark, feeling the natural warmth of her skin. The knowledge that he had come so close to losing the woman who had captured his heart shook him. Taking a deep breath, he retrieved a bottle of cleansing foam and a cloth from the other room. He gently bathed Lina, wiping away the residual blood from her side and stomach. Once he was finished, he drew the covers over her.

She immediately sighed and rolled onto her side. As much as he wanted to slide in next to her, he forced himself to return to the cleansing room. He stripped out of his clothing and stepped into the cleanser enclosure. The curved door slid shut behind him. Laying his palm against the panel, he bowed his head.

Warm jets of foaming cleanser coated his body. He lifted his hands and ran them through his long, black hair. Running his hands down his body, he wrapped one hand around his cock. As much as he wanted to relieve some of the tension, he would not. In his heart and mind, he had given himself to Lina whether he wore the marks of her claim or she wore his.

Washing his body, he tilted his head back and closed his eyes as the foaming mist finished cleansing him and the unit began the rinse cycle. The cleanser tingled as it was rinsed away. Lifting his arms above his head, he gripped the safety bar above the unit and waited. Once the rinse was completed, jets of warm air swirled around him, quickly drying his hair and body.

The door opened when the unit's cycles were complete. Stepping out, he ran his fingers through his hair, divided it into sections, and braided it. His hand ran over his upper lip and chin. He had never worn facial hair before but decided he liked it. It wouldn't have mattered if he hadn't. He'd left the bag of items Lina had gathered for him on the bridge. He would have to remember to retrieve it later.

He gathered his dirty clothing and stepped into the other room. After placing the items in the clothing refresher with Lina's, he turned on the power. At least when they woke, they would both have clean clothes to wear.

Walking over to the bed, he pulled the covers aside and slid in beside Lina. She murmured in her sleep and rolled toward him, snuggling close to his nude body. The feel of her long body pressed against his drew an immediate reaction.

Edge released a tired sigh. He wanted her. His body didn't care that now was not the time. He knew her deep slumber was caused by a combination of the medication and her body's need to heal. The memory of her soft lips against his, their bodies joined as one, sent a shaft of need through him. Lifting her hand to his lips, he pressed a kiss to her palm.

"You hold my heart in your hands, my beautiful goddess. You have given me a gift I never thought possible," he murmured.

He closed his eyes. Using the strategy Lina had shown him, he pictured his home back on Rathon with Lina in it. They would swim together in the shallow cove or hike to the market in the nearby village. His body relaxed as he dreamed of their life together.

The dark, chaotic thoughts that always hovered along the edges of his mind since his capture slowly calmed. He tightened his arm around Lina when she moved so that her head was against his shoulder. He desperately clung to the vision of her in his mind as the swirling thoughts grew louder.

Lina must have sensed his unrest because she murmured his name in her sleep. He tightened his grip on her hand when she slid her leg along his calf and tucked her foot between his legs. A sense of peace and warmth flowed through him when her hand glided across his chest and she curled her fingers around the curve of his shoulder. He wasn't alone in the darkness. His little goddess was there with him.

~

Oculus IX Spaceport

Prymorus gazed down at the billowing smoke with rage while Deppar gripped the edge of the desk. The sound of more explosions could be heard going off far below them. From this view, Prymorus could see the panicked residents and visitors to the Spaceport frantically searching for a way off.

"The fires must have spread through the sewer and access tunnels. The blast doors and electrical systems were damaged. There is an outer perimeter breach on Level Two. What in the hell did the Drethulans do to my Spaceport?" Deppar demanded, watching in horror as one system after another began to fail.

"It was the Trivator and the human," Prymorus stated in a cold voice.

Deppar's head jerked up and he stared at his half-brother in disbelief. "Do you expect me to believe that a half-dead Trivator and a female could cause this much damage? I told you not to bring the Drethulans on Oculus IX. They are unpredictable. This is your fault. I will seek compensation for the damages. Our uncle will...," Deppar's rant suddenly ended.

Prymorus stared at his half-brother. Deppar's expression was frozen with shock and disbelief as a stream of blood slowly seeped from the hole in the center of his forehead. Prymorus lowered the pistol in his hand as his now dead half-brother slowly collapsed to the floor.

Turning back to look down at the city, he gripped the beam between the plates of glass and watched as the city below him began to cave in on itself. Furious, he knew in his gut that the Trivator and human female were not only responsible for the initial explosion, but that they had somehow managed to escape as well.

Prymorus continued to watch the hundreds of spaceships frantically trying to evacuate the Spaceport. It would be impossible to know which one had provided the Trivator and the human safe haven and escape. He turned when the door opened behind him.

"Sir, the structure is unsafe. The Drethulans have requested that you return to the ship so they can depart," his guard relayed.

Prymorus slowly crossed the room. The Trivator and human would try to escape beyond the Waxian borders and sphere of influence. It was time to visit his uncle and take over his new position as the future Prime Ruler of the Waxian empire.

CHAPTER TWENTY-ONE

*E*dge was locked in pleasure and he didn't want it to end. He moaned as an erotic heat surrounded his cock, causing him to lift his hips. He curled his fingers into the bedsheets as the intensity increased until he was panting.

"Goddess!" he hissed, when he felt a warm tongue swipe across the tip of his cock again.

He decided that he had indeed died on the Waxian Spaceport. He didn't believe anything in the stars or among the living could feel this good. Another groan escaped him when he felt a light scrape along the length of his cock before a sucking sensation lifted his hips off the bed again.

Opening his eyes, panted as wave after wave of intense pleasure shook him to his core. A slender hand joined the hot mouth that was moving up and down his cock at speeds varying from tortuously slow and deliberate, to fast and wild.

Edge could feel the tingling along his spine and knew that he would not last long. He had heard of such things during his time on Earth, but had shuddered at the thought of a female wrapping her lips around his shaft. A Trivator female had sharp teeth.

"You like this," Lina whispered against his cock

"Goddess, woman. You are lethal," he hissed, lifting his head to watch her.

He rocked his hips back and forth, sliding between her lips. If he didn't stop her, he would come down her throat before he ever had a chance to give her pleasure. A choked curse slipped from his lips when he partially sat up to stop her. His eyes locked on the vision of her sucking on him.

Edge narrowed his eyes when she reached the tip of his cock. She looked up at him and rolled her tongue around the thick, bulbous head. Tilting her head to the side, she teased his cock.

"What do you want, big guy? Do you like watching me eat you?" she asked, her hot breath caressing him.

He snarled and wrapped his hands under her arms, sliding her along his body. Leaning forward, he caught her right nipple between his lips. She cried out, and the scent of her arousal filled his lungs. Opening his mouth, he gently nipped the rosy nipple.

"Damn, but that feels good," she groaned, spreading her legs so that she was straddling him.

"I want to taste you," he demanded against her nipple.

Lina tangled her hand in his hair and looked down at him with a mischievous smile. "Have you ever heard of sixty-nine?" she asked with a raised eyebrow.

"I know how to count. What does that have to do with my wish to taste you like you tasted me?" he demanded.

"Slide down a little bit and lay flat, and I'll show you how magical that number can be," she said, leaning down to capture his lips.

Curiosity warred with his desire to claim her. He frowned when she released his lips and slid to the side. She motioned for him to lie down.

Gazing at her, he moved down. He widened his eyes when she swung around and climbed over him. She looked down at where he lay between her legs. Spreading her thighs, she lowered her soft mound toward his lips.

"Show me what you can do, big guy," she invited.

He slid his arm up her leg and between them, spreading her soft folds until she was exposed to his teeth and tongue. If she wanted to see what he could do, he would be happy to show her. Nipping at the pink nub, he buried his fingers deeply inside her before he began an assault with his tongue that would leave her wet and begging for release.

~

Lina's breasts felt swollen and her nipples excruciatingly sensitive. The need to come almost became an addiction. She had awakened with the sensation of Edge's hard cock pulsing against her. The pain in her body had transformed into a different kind—one of sexual need.

She had planned to just enjoy the feel of her hand stroking him. Before she knew it, one thing had led to another and the temptation to brush a kiss across his cock turned into giving in to her desire to slide him into her mouth. His immediate reaction had emboldened her to continue her seduction.

Memories of the last time they made love filled her mind. The heat of passion had been building over the past few weeks, and the fact that they had both been forced to keep the sounds of their pleasure from waking the others may have helped with the intensity. Something told Lina that no matter where they were, the passion between them would always be powerful. There was something primitive about it. She had heard of people having a chemical as well as a physical reaction to each other. She had experienced that before, but this was different. Whatever was causing the allure, she felt like she had been given a mega-dose where Edge was concerned.

She could feel her body pulsing with her desire for him. The restless feeling was about to drive her crazy, at least until Edge began his assault on her body. She didn't bother trying to control the loud cry that escaped her.

"Yes!" she breathed around his cock when he began teasing her clit.

An intense wave of pleasure struck her hard. Her hands tightened around his cock and she moaned. She would have pulled away if not for his arm around her thigh. Closing her eyes, she pictured what they looked like together. The image of them locked together, combined with his lips and fingers, was too much for her overly-sensitive body and she came with a shuddering sob, her hand and mouth tightly wrapped around him.

The touch of his tongue over her swollen clit made her release him. Her back bowed upward as her hips rotated. She took swift, gasping breaths as her body pulsed with pleasure so powerful that it bordered on pain.

She softly sobbed when he released her. She swung her leg over him. Her body started to melt down to the covers as she tried to regain control of her shaking limbs.

Edge didn't give her a chance. Sitting up, he pulled her around and under him until she was lying on her stomach. He gripped her hips, pulling her up onto her knees. She felt his hand run over her buttocks before he slowly impaled her with his cock.

He didn't take her hard and fast. Instead, he took her with tender, excruciating slowness. Her lips parted in a gasp as he slid into her. Closing her eyes, she gripped both sides of the pillow.

"You're killing me," she groaned when he began to rock his hips back and forth. "Damn it, Edge. Faster!"

He chuckled and bent forward until he was pressing deeper inside her. His warm breath caressed the skin between her shoulder blades. He slid one hand along her side and up, cupping her breast.

"You fit me like a glove. I feel every inch of you surrounding me. You are so slick and I can feel you pulsing around me, pulling me deeper," he murmured.

The vivid image of his cock sliding in and out of her, their bodies connected, and his description left her wanting more. His fingers pinched her nipple hard enough to make her hips jerk. She lifted her head when he released her breast and moved his hand back to her hip.

"Accept me as yours, my *fi'ta*. I am your *Amate*," he declared, his hands holding her as he began to rock his hips in hard, fast strokes.

"Yes!" she groaned, mindless of everything but the feel of him moving inside her.

He was hitting a spot that was causing the nerves inside her moist depths to go crazy. The combination of his rocking hips, his cock moving along her nerve endings, and how he was hitting her swollen clit caused her body to spiral out of control.

"Yes! Oh, damn. Oh, damn. Oh, damn," she cried as her orgasm swept through her and her body clamped down around him.

"Sweet Goddess!" Edge groaned, his hips pressed against her sweet ass as he emptied his seed deep into her womb.

Lina felt him shudder before he wrapped his arms around her waist and leaned over her. He continued to press against her, his cock continuing to pulse with the intensity of his release. After several minutes, they slowly sank to the bed where he spooned her protectively against his well-satisfied and now relaxed body.

She lay pressed against him, and tilted her head when he bent to kiss her bare shoulder. A soft, quavering sigh slipped from her lips at his quietly murmured words.

My Amate. You will be my wife.

A tear slipped from the corner of her eye and fell to the pillow, unseen by Edge, and she grasped the hand covering her breast. She would hold on to this moment for as long as she could before she let it go—forever.

An hour later, the sound of her growling stomach drew a chuckle from Edge. Lina lay stretched out on top of him, and he held her soft body tightly against his chest. He slid his hands up and down her bare back while he rubbed his chin against her hair. He knew she was awake from the way her fingers were drawing a pattern against his skin. They had been content to lie silently in each other's arms.

"When we arrive on Rathon...," he began.

He stopped when she lifted her hand and gently laid her fingers against his lips. She lifted her head and gazed at him with dark, troubled eyes before they cleared. In the depths, he could still see lingering remnants of sadness.

"Let's not talk about the future. I need to get cleaned up," she quietly replied, sliding off of him.

"Lina...," Edge said, sitting up and reaching for her hand when she stood up. "You cannot ignore what has happened between us."

She lifted her chin. "We still have a long way to go before we reach Rathon. Let's just take it one day at a time for the moment," she suggested.

He wanted to argue, but the stiffness of her shoulders showed that she was already rebuilding the wall between them. She reminded him of a wounded animal that was unsure of whether she could trust those trying to care for her or not. Rising from the bed, he bent over and brushed a brief kiss across her lips.

"One day can lead to many more. I will give you until we reach Rathon to accept that you belong by my side, my beautiful goddess," he murmured.

He released her and walked into the cleansing room. Behind him, he could hear her searching the room for her clothing. A chuckle shook his body when he heard a string of muttered, colorful words under her breath.

"You could always join me in the bathing tube where I can hear all the wonderful things you wish to call me," he teased.

"You are not playing fair," she growled before she stepped into the room and ran an appreciative look over his body. "Still, it might be fun to give you another bath."

Edge's eyes darkened. "Goddess, woman. And you accuse me of being unfair?" he replied.

~

Twenty minutes later, Lina emerged from the cleansing room. She leaned against the doorframe and watched him for several minutes. Every time she was anywhere near him, he was drawn to her like a moth to a flame.

"I never did thank you for carrying me, getting us away from the Spaceport, and healing me. I wish we had known about the medical device when you were so sick. I'm sorry you had to suffer," she quietly said.

He looked up from where he was strapping on his boot. His expression softened. Silhouetted by the light, she looked small and fragile against the wide door frame.

"I had you with me. That is all that matters now. Besides, I vaguely remember you carrying me to safety. Though, if you wish, you could always thank me another way," he teased, his gaze smoldering.

She wiggled her nose at him and shook her head. "You're incorrigible. I swear you really have been around us women too long," she retorted with a chuckle.

"I have actually found Bailey and Mechelle most informative in matters relating to relationships between couples on your world," he said with a thoughtful look.

"Really?" Lina replied with a raised eyebrow.

He grinned at her before he held out his hand. "Yes. Come, you need food," he said.

She looked at him with a strange expression before reaching out and grasping his hand. An uneven smile lit up her face. He pulled her close and slid his hand along her cheek.

"You have to share with me some of the things they have been telling you," she said before she frowned when another thought came to her. "By the way, who is flying the ship?"

$\sim$

Waxian Home World:

Prymorus sat in the chair at the head of the room. Out of the two dozen Generals belonging to his uncle's inner group, only six remained. Most of these men concealed their thoughts behind an inscrutable mask. Flanking these six Generals were a large number of Drethulan warriors, lined up against the interior walls of the room.

He glanced around the room. For centuries the Waxians had been considered nothing more than mercenaries for hire. No longer would they just work for others in return for a few credits. With the help of the Drethulans, he would oversee the creation of the mightiest military force the galaxies had ever seen.

In his hand, a tiny crystal fragment rolled across his palm. This was the key to his ambitions. This miniscule gem contained a tremendous amount of power. The red crystal, combined with the metal mined from Dises V would make his army virtually invincible and unstoppable.

The flaws in the Drethulan design and their refusal to follow his orders had led to their failed attempt to destroy the main Trivator bases on Earth and prevented his capture of Destin Parks. He had planned to use the brother of Razor's mate as a weapon against the Trivators. The failure of the Drethulans would not happen again. Prymorus had capitalized on the Drethulan's military fiasco to convince the Drethulan ruling caste that he alone held the key to their future—literally.

The Drethulans had at one time ruled the star systems, but an unknown species had risen up and defeated them. The Drethulan's blood had soaked into the soil of long-forgotten distant worlds. Those few who had survived were forced to retreat to their home world. By the time they arrived, only a small number of their warships had remained. The Drethulan military had been decimated by the war and their population had nearly become extinct.

During his dealings with the Drethulans, he had learned of an interesting fact from the Drethulan retelling of their defeat that intrigued him: the reference to the red crystal ships which had appeared out of nowhere – ships that were not only unbelievably fast and powerful, but were commanded by living machines.

Prymorus hadn't believed the Drethulan's legend until a recent encounter was recorded and transmitted by a Waxian fighter before it exploded. During a brief conversation with his half-brother, he had been reminded of the legend.

Deppar used to have business dealings with another Waxian named Cordus Kelman. Kelman had been in possession of another

Trivator warrior who he had forced to compete in the fight rings. The Trivator named Dagger had escaped. While in pursuit, one of Kelman's personal fighters recorded an encounter with a red crystal ship.

Curious, Prymorus had researched Dagger's history and discovered a connection between Kelman's prize fighter and the warrior, Edge, that Deppar had located for him. It was possible that if one knew about the existence of the red crystal ship, then the other would also know.

He should never have trusted his brother with anything so important. Deppar's only real concern had been ruling over the Spaceport. Prymorus clenched his hand in frustration. He was so close to having the resources he needed to bring down the Alliance.

If Deppar hadn't been so inept, he would already have acquired the information he needed. Now he was forced to waste precious time and resources in order to find the Trivator again. He wanted the red crystal ship and whatever creature was controlling it.

"Prime Ruler Prymorus, I offer you my loyalty. What is your command?" one of the generals asked.

The man stepped forward, keeping his eyes locked onto the new Prime Ruler instead of the body of Prymorus's now dead uncle, who had been the Waxian Prime Ruler. Prymorus stared back at the general for a moment. Rising from his seat, he deliberately scanned around the room, making sure to make eye contact with all who stood there. If they lived, each of the remaining men had the potential to be an integral part in the future of the Waxian Rule.

"A Trivator and a human female escaped from Oculus IX. I want them found—alive," Prymorus ordered.

"I will personally see to it, Prime Ruler," the general vowed with a stiff bow.

Prymorus watched as the man backed away before turning and leaving the room. The other men looked back and forth between Prymorus, the general, the dead former Prime Ruler, and exchanged telling looks between themselves. Irritation swept through him.

Perhaps only one of these men will be a part of the new Waxian Rule, he thought.

"What are you waiting for? Find the Trivator and the human!" he snapped before pointing to another general. "You, get this room cleaned."

"Yes, sir," the man replied.

Prymorus slowly sank down in the chair behind him. Opening his hand, he moodily stared at the crystal. He reached into his pocket and pulled out a small cylinder made from the metal ore mined on Dises V.

He placed the crystal into the modified power housing for the small laser pointer. A powerful, thin beam of red energy spanned the length of the room. With a slash of his wrist, the stone table in the center of the room, large enough for fifty men to sit around, split in two.

A grim, ruthless smile curved his lips when the Waxian Generals in the room jumped. Something so small, yet so powerful. If he controlled a whole crystal it was possible that he could destroy a planet with its power. With that type of power, he would be invincible. No one, not the Alliance, not even the Trivators, would dare to stand in his way.

A new thought coursed through him. His focus again moved to the Drethulans. He had a new project for them to add to their list. Once he had the crystal ship within his grasp, he would use the energy to destroy not one, but two planets—Rathon and Earth. Then, the Alliance would submit to his rule.

Rising to his feet again, he strode out of the room. It was time to redefine the role of the Waxian forces in their universe and unite them with a common cause. Any who defied him would suffer the same fate as his uncle and the dead generals.

CHAPTER TWENTY-TWO

"So, what is this?" Andy asked, leaning forward and pointing to another button on the console.

"The port and starboard weapon turrets. If you push this one, there are slides on each side that will extend. Each contains an XE450 laser cannon. Whoever owned this ship before made sure that it was upgraded with the best equipment. The XE450 came out fifteen years ago. I would say the ship was in the landing bay for at least three years based on the records I was able to retrieve," Edge explained.

He looked up when Lina stepped onto the bridge. They had been traveling for three days and had just left the inner boundaries of the Waxian star system. Andy and Mirela were very enthusiastic about learning how to operate the ship and its weaponry.

"How long will it take until we arrive on Rathon?" Lina asked, sliding into one of the vacant seats.

"A month, possibly longer. We will be traveling through some hostile regions and must proceed cautiously," he explained.

Andy turned in her seat to grin at Lina. "We couldn't have found a more kickass spaceship. This thing is fully loaded! It has shields and blasters and supercharged engines," she crowed with a beaming grin. "Gail and I are going to go check out the upper and lower gun turrets."

Lina chuckled. "You sound just like Bailey, only she was raving about the medical unit," she replied.

Gail snorted. "You should have heard Mechelle talking about the galley and the washing machines. She also found out where the captain was stashing her personal items," she said.

"Her?" Lina replied in surprise.

Gail nodded. "We are assuming it is a she. It would appear the former captain liked to wear fine clothing on occasion along with lots of black leather," she said.

"I wonder what happened to her?" Lina speculated.

Andy shrugged. "Her loss is our gain. We'll see you later," she said, rising from the co-pilot seat.

Lina nodded. Edge didn't comment, his gaze was focused on Lina. He waited until Andy and Gail left before he reached over, cupped Lina's hand, and brought it to his lips.

"Bailey told me that you've been by the medical unit," she murmured, searching his face.

Edge felt his gut tighten in response. He slowly released her hand and turned back in his seat. Staring out into space, he didn't reply at first.

"It is nothing," he finally responded.

He turned his head when Lina touched his arm. Tightening his lips, he shook his head and focused on the scanners.

"I thought the residual effects from the drugs had almost stopped," she continued.

"I told you, it is nothing," he said.

She released a loud sigh. "What are you doing?" she asked, changing the subject.

"The shield systems are emitting an unusual signal. It doesn't happen often, but I don't want to meet up with any Waxian or Drethulan forces and suddenly discover the shields are not at one hundred percent," he said, checking the system again and continuing to explain about the other systems on-board.

In the back of his mind, he deduced that Bailey must have suggested to Lina that she should stay close to him. The thought of his weakness gnawed at him. The episodes of uncontrollable shivers and the visions of insects crawling out of the walls and over his body were less frequent, but they still left him weak and his mind filled with chaos. The unbidden, mind-shattering swirling of random thoughts and flashes of memories worried him the most.

Even now, he fought against the trembling and visions. His fingers itched to crush the insects climbing out of the console in front of him. He had to keep telling himself that none of them were real.

The surgery bed scanner was still analyzing the compound that Deppar had used on him. Bailey had sympathetically explained that it would probably take some time and that he might need to accept that there would always be moments in his life when he might suffer from flashbacks. There had been no need for him to ask Bailey what she meant.

"Is there anything I can do to help you?" Lina asked when his voice faded.

He understood the double meaning in her words. Turning to look at her, he could see the troubled expression in her eyes. He decided right then and there that he would thank the Goddess every day for sending him such a beautiful warrior to be his *Amate*.

"Stay close to me," he admitted.

She stood up, wrapped her arms around his broad shoulders, and pressed a kiss to his forehead. The simple, intimate act had the power to still the trembling in his hands and calm the doubts in his mind. He was about to pull her onto his lap when the sound of an alarm resonated from the console. They both turned to look down at the screen.

"What is it?" she asked with a frown.

His lips tightened. "We have company. Warn the others," he instructed.

Lina nodded and turned. He heard her shouting to the others as he scanned the visuals appearing on the screen in front of him. A Waxian Class One Starcruiser. It was one of the oldest and smallest of the Waxian warships, but it was still deadly.

Data that he had forgotten suddenly filled his mind. The Class One could hold a crew of one hundred, along with fifteen fighter ships. Twin C-10 laser cannons on the upper sections were protected by smaller automated turrets. There were four small C-5 laser cannons located at the bow and stern of the Starcruiser. Both sets of cannons had a limited range of fire.

His attention snapped to the communications controls when the console lit up, indicating an incoming message. He was surprised when a Waxian hologram suddenly appeared on the screen. This must have been the previous captain of the ship.

"This is the Dauntless Explorer, freighter license XZ528, state your business," the automated voice stated.

"This is Captain Adkindas of the Waxian forces. Under the orders of the Prime Ruler, you are to be boarded for inspection," the Waxian captain replied.

The image next to him flickered, before repeating itself. There was a moment of silence on the other end. Edge used the time to program a new trajectory.

"I repeat. This is Captain Adkindas. Prepare to be boarded or we will disable your vessel," Adkindas ordered.

"This is the Dauntless Explorer...." the computer-generated image began to repeat before Edge cut it off.

He opened internal communications. It went against every atom in his body to put the women at risk and ask them to fight back. The ship was small enough and fast enough to outrun the Starcruiser but not the fighters onboard. If they jumped now, it would burn crucial energy and leave them vulnerable because the fighters would simply follow them. They needed to disable the Starcruiser first.

He activated the shields and powered up the gun turrets. Whether he liked it or not, if they were to survive this journey, he would have to depend on the women.

"I've activated the gun turrets. Be prepared for a fight," he calmly stated over the central communications system.

A startled chuckle escaped him when he heard the loud responses. The hoots and hollers followed by 'hot damn', 'yippie-ki-yay', and 'let's kick some ass' were far different from the familiar responses of his peers. He looked over in surprise when Lina reappeared next to him.

"I'm your co-pilot. I don't know shit about flying a spaceship, but if you have weapons controls here and can tell me which buttons to push, I'm pretty damn good at that," she said with a grim smile. "Gail has the top turret. Mirela and Mechelle have the two sides while Andy has the bottom one. They are all kick-ass shooters. Bailey will monitor them, and she has the sick bay ready in case we need it."

Edge cast a quick glance at her before he focused on the first target. "If I didn't know any better, I'd think you had practice at this," he teased.

She was quiet for a brief second before she replied. "We did—against the Trivators," she said.

Before he could reply, a group of fighters began pouring out of the back of the Starcruiser. They had the element of surprise in the well-armed ship they had appropriated, and the women were well versed in using it. The first four fighters were destroyed the moment they were visible. Lina was right, the women were kick-ass shooters.

"Shields are up. Lina, aim for the top turrets. We have to take out the largest cannons," he ordered, guiding their smaller spacecraft toward the Starcruiser.

∼

Nebula One:

Jag looked over the reports coming in. He glanced up when the door opened and Thunder and Vice walked in. He nodded to the two men before returning his focus to the most current reports from Jordan Sampson.

"Torch has installed the cloaking system, and it is online and working. Those Kassisan bastards have some very interesting technology. I'm glad they are on our side," Thunder commented, turning around the chair across from Jag so he could sit down.

Vice did the same with the other chair. "I'd feel a lot better if we knew what else they had," he added.

Jag frowned at the two warriors. The conditions on the *Nebula One* were more relaxed than normal, but he was still their commanding officer. He could tell by the way they glanced at each other that they were baiting him.

Lifting his hand, he rotated the holographic screen so that each man could see it. He sat back and waited as they scanned the material. Their eyebrows rose in surprise and Vice softly whistled.

"Oculus IX destroyed? Prymorus has taken over as Prime Ruler, and the might of the Waxian military forces are searching for an escaped Trivator and his human accomplice," Vice murmured.

"Human?! How in the hell did a human get that far into Waxian territory?" Thunder demanded with a frown.

"You don't think this could be one of the missing women, do you?" Jag asked, leaning forward and resting his elbows on the table.

Vice ran a hand over his smooth head. He was one of the few Trivator warriors who shaved his head. Elaborate tattoos, bearing the symbols of the desert regions, his home, decorated his arms and chest.

"It's possible, but from what we found on the ship carrying the other women, it was an Armatrux ship which took them. The Armatrux deal with the Waxians on occasion, but they have always had a strained partnership. Both sides would sooner cut the middle man out of a deal for a few extra credits," Vice replied.

"The last information we had on the Armatrux ship that took them was from over two years ago. All records indicate it was destroyed in a battle with a Jawtaw freight tanker," Thunder said, glancing at Vice who nodded.

"There is a possibility the Jawtaws took the women before the ship was destroyed. We have an informant working with the Jawtaws to find additional records on what happened. It appears the captain of the freighter didn't always record new acquisitions correctly," Thunder dryly replied.

"Not to mention the Jawtaws outlawed slave trafficking decades ago. They have a very stiff penalty for those who violate that specific decree," Vice added.

"Well, our mission has just become even more complicated now that Prymorus has taken over the position of Prime Ruler," Jag interjected.

"I thought he was killed in the battle on Earth," Thunder said, leaning forward.

Jag shook his head. "He was wounded, but managed to escape. With a small contingent of Drethulan Battle Cruisers, he has returned to the Waxian home world. Reports indicate that when Prymorus took over the position of Prime Ruler from his uncle, there was a major change in the power structure of the Waxian ruling class. An unknown number of his uncle's trusted generals were replaced," he added dryly.

"I'm assuming the replacement was cordial," Vice commented with a wry grin. "At least if Prymorus is killing off his own government and military, it will help eliminate a few of the bastards."

"Not enough. It looks like Prymorus is expanding what he began on Dises V. Jordan intercepted communication transmissions between Prymorus and the Drethulans. She is working on deciphering the encrypted messages. What we know about the current situation so far is from communications between the warships and activity surrounding Oculus IX. It seems that several days ago, there was a massive underground explosion on the Spaceport. The environmental and life support systems were severely compromised. Failure of the systems led to a mass evacuation of the Spaceport. It is believed that during the evacuation their Trivator prisoner and a human accomplice escaped," Jag relayed.

Jag watched as both Thunder and Vice studied a hologram of the evacuation and the probable trajectories of the fleeing ships. Most headed for the main planet below, but there were at least two dozen which headed for open space on various trajectories. Out of the two dozen, there were only six of them heading in the direction of safe space for anyone trying to escape the Waxian's reach.

"Our new mission is to intercept each of those six ships before the

Waxian military does. Any engagement between our military and the Waxian or Drethulan forces will be without any assistance from the Alliance," Jag warned.

Thunder and Vice nodded at him. He would make this same announcement to the rest of the crew. They each had known when they signed onto this mission that it could be a one-way ticket. The mission had now changed from a search and rescue to something far more difficult. Jag's gaze moved back to the screen. At the speed they were traveling, they would intercept the first vessel in forty-eight hours. Unless Jordan could find additional information, they would be potentially revealing themselves multiple times. Each time the *Nebula One* reappeared would increase their risk of discovery.

"I will let you know when we have more information. Be ready for a quick boarding, and see if Torch can replicate that damn cloaking device. I want that technology on each of the fighters," Jag ordered, rising from his seat.

Thunder and Vice nodded and stood up. "We've already got him working on it. The Kassisan must have realized that we might try it. He sent additional units. We can help Torch install them on the fighters," Thunder replied.

"Make it happen. Dismissed," Jag said.

Vice smothered a gruff chuckle as the door opened. "I told you he'd try to go all Captain on us before we left. You owe me a glass of whiskey," he said with a slap on Thunder's shoulder.

"I don't know why I ever bet with you," Thunder growled as the door closed behind them.

Jag shook his head in amusement. Sinking back down in his seat, he rotated the screen back toward himself again. He scanned the information before moving to the projected flight patterns of the fleeing ships. There were three heading in a direct line toward Alliance territory. He would focus on those three first. The other three were spread out further. He leaned forward and studied the ship along the outer rim.

He looked at the report. Jordan had noted that it might not be a ship because it faded in and out of the long distance scanning software, so it could be a glitch. She would monitor it to see if there was a pattern. If there was, that would prove there was something real there.

Rising out of his seat again, he walked across the room to stare out of the window. Faint streaks of light were a testament to the speed the *Nebula One* was traveling. He wondered if Torch might be able to get a little more out of the engines. Something told him that Edge and his human were going to need their help sooner rather than later.

CHAPTER TWENTY-THREE

"*W*ay to go, Gail!" Lina cried, watching another fighter explode.

She bit her lip when she saw another heading toward them. The shields lit up with a wave of color when the blasts from the fighter's laser cannons struck them. She turned her head away when one blast nearly blinded her.

Using the toggle in front of her, she aimed the front cannons at the fighter and fired. A brief flash showed she'd hit the fighter, but it veered off before she had a chance to fire on it again. The Battle Cruiser was continuing to fire at them with one large cannon and three of the smaller ones. They had been able to take out all of the others. From the last count, the Battle Cruiser was down to eight fighters out of the fifteen Edge believed were on the warship.

"Whoever this ship belonged to must have had inside knowledge on the Waxian military," Edge commented as he maneuvered the sleek ship along the underbelly of the warship. "The weapons system automatically locks onto the targets and sends out a pulse that jams their systems. That is the only explanation for the way we have been able to do as much damage as we have."

Lina snorted. "I don't give a rat's ass what it is as long as it works in our favor," she said before emitting a growl. "You sorry-ass-son-of-a-bitch! That one has learned to hit and run. Asswipe! Yes!! Mechelle, you toasted his ass."

"Right up the butthole," Mechelle laughed over the com.

"Mirela, look out, there is one coming up from behind us," Gail warned.

In the background, Lina could hear Gail firing. From the viewscreen, she saw the fighter that Gail was talking about. It looked like the one that she had hit just a short time ago. The pilot had circled around them and come up from the rear. It looked like he was going to kamikaze ram them.

"Get him, Gail!" Lina ordered.

She could hear Gail's loud, frustrated curses. "I can't, he is using the back of the ship to shield himself. Andy, do you have a shot?"

"Negative," Andy replied.

"Mirela, what about you?" Lina asked.

"Negative, I've got two on this side. Gail, can you or Andy take any of them out?" Mirela finally replied.

"I'm trying," Andy responded.

Lina watched in horror as laser fire from above streaked by the side window. She concentrated on the fighters coming straight at them. Edge was lining up for another pass by the Starcruiser. They needed to take out the small cannons housed along the belly of the ship.

"I have a line on the cannons. Firing!" Lina said.

"That asshole is still coming at us," Gail replied, swiveling around to fire on him. Lina heard Gail's joyful cry before it changed to a gasp of horror.

"What's happening?" Lina demanded.

"Mirela, look out!" Gail cried.

"Holy shit!" Mirela's horrified gasp filled the comlink before the sound of a loud explosion shook the ship.

"Mirela!" Mechelle's pain-filled cry could be heard by them all.

"Bailey, get to Mirela," Edge ordered. "There is an outer breach. I've deployed a chemical sealer. It will only last a few minutes."

"I'm almost there," Bailey replied in a calm voice.

Lina shut off her fear for Mirela. She had to stay focused on the fight. They might have been up against a more powerful warship, but their ship was holding its own thanks to everyone on board and Edge's skill at the controls.

Andy took out two more fighters while Lina, Gail, and Mechelle took out the last of the smaller cannons. The only one left was a large cannon located near the bridge of the warship. Lina looked at Edge in surprise when he suddenly veered off and away from the warship. Gail and Andy continued to fire on the remaining fighters.

"Prepare for a jump," Edge ordered.

Lina frowned at him. "I thought you said the fighters could follow us if we jumped," she said.

A muscle in Edge's jaw throbbed. "Bailey, do you have Mirela out of the turret?" he asked, not answering her.

"Almost," Bailey replied.

"You have one minute," he said, unstrapping the harness to his seat.

Lina looked up at him in surprise when he stood. "Where are you going? Edge, the fighters...," she said, looking out of the screen at the Battle Cruiser in the distance.

He leaned over her and pointed at the console. "When I tell you to, I want you to hit this button, then this one," he explained in a soft voice.

"Edge...?" she murmured.

"There are more ships coming, Lina. If we don't leave now, we won't make it," he said.

Dread filled Lina and she nodded. "I'll wait for your command," she said.

Edge nodded and disappeared through the doorway. She could hear him running down the corridor. In the background, she heard the faint sound of Edge and Bailey's voices, and Mirela's strained curses.

Touching a corner of the viewscreen, Lina watched as Edge and Bailey worked frantically to free Mirela. Edge sliced through the harness holding her friend to the seat. Unfortunately, one of the shards of metal had gone through the strap. The only way to free Mirela was to cut the strap on either side of the shard or removed the metal embedded in Mirela's shoulder. With limited time, Edge gripped the shard and pulled it free while Bailey applied a patch to stem the blood. Lina's hands tightened into fists when she heard Mirela's scream of pain followed by silence.

She ripped her attention back to the controls when a red light flared. Looking up, she stared out the front viewscreen in dismay when two more Battle Cruisers suddenly appeared. Her fingers trembled when she saw the number of fighters streaming out of them. These Cruisers were almost three times larger than the first one.

"Now, Lina," Edge's voice rang through her earpiece.

Her hand automatically moved to touch the buttons in the sequence that he'd told her. The ship violently shook for a moment. Her lips parted in dismay and shock when she saw a large section of the gun turret from the starboard side of their ship floating away before the background changed as the ship lurched into the space jump.

"Edge…," Lina called out in panic.

"Bring the starboard turret in like I showed you, Lina. I'm heading to medical with Mirela," Edge instructed.

"She's losing a lot of blood. We'll lose her if I don't stop it now…." Bailey's voice came through in the background.

The sound of Mechelle's smothered cry was heard over the com before she was cut off. Behind her, she could hear the sound of the other women's boots against the metal floor. She moved her hand to the control that would retract the turret.

Her gaze moved blindly over the controls before she stared out at the empty space in front of them. Her heart hurt, not only for herself, but for Mechelle. Memories flooded her. Memories of losing someone who she loved and being helpless to prevent it. As hard as she tried to push the memories away, they washed over her with such a crushing force that it still took her breath away. Pain, guilt, and another emotion she couldn't identify held her in its greedy grasp.

~

Ten years before: Earth

"Come on, Lina," Leon whispered, motioning for her to follow him.

Lina rolled her eyes at her best friend and soon-to-be husband. She grinned when he gave her that damn crooked smile and looked at her with a hint of challenge. She knew Tim and Destin would be furious if they knew what they were doing, but Leon loved to explore the city after dark.

Tim was still mad at her for telling him that she was going to get married. At seventeen, she knew she was young, but she also knew that Leon was her true love. They had grown up together. They had played, explored, dreamed, and watched each other's back since they were in kindergarten. When the aliens arrived, they had hidden together. At first, they were terrified. Gradually, that terror changed to fascination for Leon.

"You know Destin and Tim are going to ground us again," she murmured when they climbed up on the edge of the old parking garage to watch the alien ships take off and land at the base situated along the river.

"We're adults, they can't ground us," Leon teased.

Lina turned and leaned against the wall. She stared up at the night sky. She could see hundreds of moving lights. She had never seen the night sky before the aliens had arrived. She had lived her entire life in the city and the light pollution had blocked all but the brightest stars.

After the aliens arrived, their city, like many others, had become a war zone. The electricity was one of the first things to go. That was when Leon and she, along with the others had realized just how many aliens there were in orbit around Earth.

She raised her hand and held her palm over one of the moving objects. Some of the alien ships were big enough to see from the surface. They arrived and left at all hours of the day and night. So far, Leon and she had only seen what they looked like from a distance.

"Look at that one, Lina," Leon murmured, holding out a pair of binoculars to her.

"I don't want to," she replied, dropping her hand to her lap with a sigh. "What do you think the future will be like?"

He looked at her with a tender smile and twisted around so he could sit down next to her. She scooted closer to him when he lifted his arm. Her head rested against his shoulder, and she giggled when he cupped her breast.

"Wonderful, because I've got you," he teased, looking at her before he gazed up at the night sky with a somber expression. "I always knew we weren't alone."

"I know, I know," she murmured. "But, what do you think will happen?"

"You heard what the government said. The Trivators said they aren't here to conquer us. Hell, you've seen the damage. They weren't the ones who did it, our people did. We are so fucked up it is amazing that we've made it as long as we have," he said, still looking up at the stars. "I think we are going to see a new world. You've heard Tim and Destin talk. We'll be able to travel out there and explore in ways that we've only dreamed about. Hell, maybe even a kid like me from the streets can go."

Lina tilted her head and frowned at him." I know you've always dreamed of going, but… what about me…? What about us?" she asked.

"We'll go together," Leon promised, leaning forward to press a kiss to her lips.

~

Lina looked up when she saw Edge reappear in the doorway. She blinked the memories away. Her eyes widened in concern when she saw the blood on his clothing.

"Mirela?" she asked in a hoarse voice.

He looked back at her with a grim expression. "Her injuries are severe. Between the surgery bed and Bailey, I can only hope that she survives," he replied, sliding into the pilot's seat.

"I...," she started to say, glancing at the door, then the console, before looking back at him.

He nodded. "Go. I can manage here," he replied.

Lina unstrapped the seat harness and stood up. She paused as she started to step between the chairs. Looking down at him, she bit her lip.

"Thank you," she murmured before exiting the bridge.

She strode down the corridor to the medical bay. Andy stood at the door, staring at the floor with a tight expression on her face. The other woman looked up when she drew close. Through the doorway, Lina could hear the soft sounds of Mechelle's sobs and Gail's voice trying to soothe her.

"Is she....?" Lina asked, bracing herself for bad news.

Andy shook her head. "No... At least...." Andy looked through the door and shook her head again. "I need a drink."

Lina watched Andy straighten and turn on her heel. She drew in a deep breath and stiffened her shoulders. Over the past ten years she had heard the same sounds so many times. Just when she thought she was immune to the pain, it all came rushing back. She stepped through the door and paused when she saw the gaping wound in Mirela's chest.

"What... How bad is it?" Lina asked, stepping up to where Bailey was attaching a series of wires.

Bailey didn't turn. Instead, she finished what she was doing and pressed the panel on the wall. The glass lid slid closed over Mirela. The tube immediately filled with a mist that obscured Mirela for several seconds before it disappeared.

"She was impaled by flying debris," Bailey explained.

Lina frowned. "Impaled... How?" she demanded.

She turned when Gail released a soft curse. Confused, she watched Gail walk out of the medical bay. Her gaze turned to Mechelle who was sitting in a chair near the end of the surgery bed.

"She...," Mechelle began to say before her voice faded, and she shook her head.

Bailey watched the panel. "From what I could piece together, Gail hit the fighter that was coming up from behind. It collided with the underbelly of the Waxian Starcruiser and broke apart. Parts of the fighter pierced the outer section of the turret. Thankfully, there was a foam sealant that prevented it from shattering. I couldn't get Mirela out. The rest of the clear glass was starting to crack from the pressure. The blast door alarm sounded. It would have closed on both of us if Edge hadn't shown up when he did," Bailey explained.

Lina realized that that the button he'd had her push first had stopped the door from closing. They had needed to seal the damaged area before they could jump. Otherwise, they all would have died.

"Can the surgery bed repair the damage?" Lina asked.

Lina saw Bailey glance over at Mechelle. Dark eyes the color of onyx stared up at Bailey with pleading in their dark depths. Bailey looked back at the panel on the wall. She was silent for several seconds before she nodded.

"Yes, I think it can. Her vitals are beginning to stabilize. I won't know for sure until the unit is finished, but I saw what it did for you," Bailey said, turning to look at her before she focused on Mechelle. "How about you take Mechelle to get a drink. I'll let you both know if there is any change."

Mechelle stood up and started to shake her head. "But...," she argued, angrily wiping a hand across her ebony cheek.

Bailey walked over and wrapped her arms around Mechelle. They held each other for several minutes before Bailey pulled back and gently brushed a tear from Mechelle's cheek. A small, reassuring smile curved Bailey's lips.

"I swear. It's a small ship. You'll hear me," she insisted.

Lina stepped forward and hooked her arm through Mechelle's. She sent a swift, grateful smile to Bailey before she gently pulled Mechelle with her. They needed to talk about what they would do once they came out of the space jump. Though, at the moment, Lina had to agree with Andy—she needed a stiff drink.

CHAPTER TWENTY-FOUR

*W*axian home planet: Prison cell A11 Solitary Confinement

Prymorus motioned for the prison guard to open the cell door. The guard looked as if he wanted to say something, but he refrained when the guard behind Prymorus shook his head in warning. The prison guard stepped forward and inserted the specially made key into the panel before unlocking a dozen additional locks on the door.

Prisoner A11 didn't turn around when the door opened. Prymorus narrowed his eyes on the prisoner. Tall, slender, and muscular despite the poor nutrition given to Waxian prisoners.

"What do you know about a modified transport that was on Oculus IX?" Prymorus demanded.

A soft chuckle sounded in the room. He watched the prisoner slowly raise slender arms that were as white as his own to grasp the bars of the window. From here Prymorus could see the view of an endless sea of cells below. The sense of wariness grew inside him when the prisoner turned and gave him a sardonic smile.

"Well, well, well... The new Prime Ruler has dirtied himself already. Don't you know that you should send your lackeys to do your dirty work? Oh, wait… You tried that already," Prisoner A11 chuckled. Prymorus raised his eyebrow at the blatant lack of subtlety. He didn't miss the curious light that came into the eyes staring back at him—or the recognition. The recognition turned to a cynical expression of distaste. "Go away, Prymorus. Find someone else to answer your questions… or better yet, have the guard lock the door with you in here and we'll see how long I let you live."

Prymorus ran his gaze appreciatively over the figure in front of him. "I see you haven't changed, Katma. You are still as bloodthirsty as ever," he replied.

Katma Achler looked at the male across from her, her smooth bald head gleaming in the dim light. "You have no idea how bloodthirsty I can be, Prymorus," she replied, stepping closer to him before stopping and looking down at the chain attached to her ankle. "I've rotted for three years in this hellhole with no visit from you and now you want to know about my ship?" she hissed.

Prymorus's body tightened at the smoldering look in his mate's eyes.

"I've been busy," he replied with a shrug. "I need you now. Guard, release her," he ordered.

Prymorus watched as Katma placed her hands on her hips and glared at him. The guard who had opened the door moments before warily stepped into the cell. He gingerly knelt and pressed in the code to release the shackle around Katma's ankle. The moment she was free, she grabbed the guard's head in her hands and violently twisted it. The sound of bones cracking and the thud of the guard's body on the floor filled the room a moment before Katma released a satisfied sigh.

"Are you finished?" Prymorus asked in a dry tone.

"Hardly. What has happened to my ship?" Katma demanded, stepping over the dead body of the guard.

The other guards quickly moved to the side when Katma exited the cell. Prymorus made sure to keep his hot-tempered mate slightly ahead of him. He slipped the blade he had hidden back into the sheath in his sleeve.

"Can you find it?" he demanded.

Katma suddenly turned and faced him. Her eyes glittered with fury. She stepped up to him and grabbed the front of his shirt in her hand. The knife that he had returned to the sheath just seconds before once again slipped into his hand.

She looked at him with an expression that was fierce and filled with passion, skimmed her fingers down his arm, then gripped his hand, keeping it and the knife firmly pressed against his side. Prymorus closed the distance between them, pressing his lips against hers in a savage kiss.

"Who took my ship?" she repeated in a breathy voice against his lips.

"A Trivator and a human," he answered. "I want them alive."

"I want a warship under my command," she requested.

"You will have it," Prymorus agreed.

Katma smiled. "I pick my crew," she added. Prymorus nodded. "And the weapons I want added."

"You can have whatever you want, Katma. I want them alive. I don't care what you do to them as long as you bring them back to me breathing and able to talk," Prymorus stated.

"Anything...." Katma's fingers walked down Prymorus's chest to his groin. "I've been in solitary confinement for three years. I'll be wanting a little compensation for having to take care of my own needs," she replied, cupping him and squeezing. "You can begin payment while my warship is prepared."

A large vein throbbed at Prymorus's temple. Katma was a liability, but she was also an asset. He would use her talents to retrieve the Trivator, then he would either lock her up again or dispose of her once and for all. She would kill him if she learned he was the one responsible for her incarceration.

Katma had killed the son of one of the Drethulan warlords over a minor credit dispute. Prymorus had been in negotiations with the

Drethulans long before the incident, and he had known that he could lose their army if his volatile mate was involved in the process.

Prymorus was struck with a brief flash of regret that he had killed his half-brother. While he was the one who had ordered Katma's imprisonment, it had been Deppar who had carried out the act in his absence. The regret faded as quickly as it appeared when Katma released him.

"How is Deppar?" Katma asked with a coy smile.

"Dead," he replied.

The smile faded, and an expression of disappointment crossed her face. "A pity. I was looking forward to killing him myself," she casually replied before turning and walking down the corridor.

"I'm sure you were," Prymorus stated under his breath.

CHAPTER TWENTY-FIVE

"$\mathcal{D}$o you need any help?" Lina asked.

Edge pulled off the welder's mask and set it down on the floor. He gazed at her tired face. She was carrying a tray holding a large plate of food and a container of water.

"I wanted to make sure there was no chance that the door would rupture. Sit with me," he said, taking the tray from her and nodding to the floor. "I fear I have no chair or table."

Lina chuckled. She lowered herself to the floor and leaned against the wall. He saw her take note of the items scattered across the floor.

"I recognize some of this stuff," she commented, nodding to the rectangular device.

"The storage bay is full of items," he commented, sitting down next to her. "I assume you and the others brought most of it aboard."

Lina nodded her head before leaning back against the wall. She closed her eyes. A small smile played around the corners of her lips.

"Yes. Two years is a long time to spend doing nothing but hiding. After the first month, we decided we'd better do something, so we started collecting things. By the time we found the underground hiding place, we'd pack-ratted enough to know what was useful and what wasn't. The area underground was like having our own private treasure cave. Once Mirela and Andy found the ship, we decided we'd need to be ready to go the moment we found someone who could fly it," she explained, opening her eyes and sitting forward.

"Did you do this on your world? This pack-rat thing?" Edge asked.

Lina nodded. "Yeah. Finding and hoarding items of use became not just an art, but a necessity for survival. Before the Trivators arrived, we were ordinary women with ordinary dreams," she quietly said, looking down at her hands. "It turned out we all had a talent that when combined, worked out for us. Bailey was a Physician's Assistant. She had just landed her first job at Chicago General. Andy was a mechanic at a service distribution center. There wasn't much that she couldn't fix when it came to engines. Mirela and Mechelle are as different in personalities as they are alike in their looks." Lina chuckled and shook her head. "Mirela is in-your-face tough as nails while Mechelle is the complete opposite."

"I have noticed that. I find it fascinating," he commented, taking a bite of the stew. "What did they do before our arrival?"

Lina looked at him. "Mirela worked at a local hotel during the day and competed in regular Kickboxing matches at night. I wouldn't make her mad if I were you. She is pretty fierce. She taught us all a lot of new moves which have come in handy. Mechelle was focusing on her education. She was a programmer for a local video game company during the day and an aspiring actress at night. She was the one who gave us the ability to move around without being discovered. Her talent for making costumes is brilliant," Lina said.

"What about Gail? She is older than the rest of you," he observed.

"Not by much. I'm twenty-seven, the twins are twenty-six, Andy is thirty, and Bailey is thirty-one. Gail is forty-three. Her second husband was killed during the first wave of resistance. Both of them were veteran police officers with the Chicago Police Department," she explained. "Gail took me under her wing a year after the Trivators arrived."

Edge placed the tray aside. He didn't miss the fact that she avoided talking about herself. He could sense the wall around her again, the one that she erected when she wanted to protect herself.

"And you…. What is the story of Lina Daniels?" he quietly asked.

Lina stared across at the opposite wall in silence. She finally shook her head and rose to her feet. Bending over, she picked up the tray.

"Lina," Edge said, rising to his feet.

He reached out his hand and touched her arm. He was surprised when she looked up at him with tears in her eyes. This was not a part of her that he had seen before.

"I'm just a kid from the streets," she quietly replied, before she turned and walked away.

Edge watched her retreat. He started to follow her, but paused when he heard someone softly call his name. He didn't turn until Lina disappeared around the corner.

"She isn't just a kid from the streets," Gail quietly said, coming to stand next to him.

"What is her story, then?" he asked, turning to gaze at the older woman.

Gail shook her head. "If she wants you to know, she'll have to be the one to tell you," she replied.

"Do you blame us for your mate's death?" he asked.

Gail's lips tightened and her face became shuttered. "Yes and no," she finally replied, lowering her eyes to look around the corridor. "I could play the what-if game. God knows I've done that enough in my head, but it still comes out with the same results. Guy is dead, and I'm on an alien ship in a world that exists no matter how many times I pinch myself and try to wake up. I can't change what happened, Edge. I can only change what I do about what is to come. Lina still has to figure out that part."

He wanted to ask Gail more, but the older woman shook her head and walked away. He was left with more questions than answers.

Sighing deeply, he turned and began picking up the equipment he'd used to make sure the door was sealed. He paused when he saw his hands tremble. He looked at the welder and grimaced when he saw it was covered with insects.

～

An hour later, he stepped into the medical unit. Andy was on the bridge with Gail. They would be coming out of jump speed in another twenty minutes. The scanners were showing that there were two fighters following them.

"How is she?" he asked Bailey as he stepped into the room and nodded toward the surgical table.

Bailey glanced up from studying Mirela's chart. "Stable," she replied. "A fragment clipped her aorta. Her clavicle and shoulder blade were shattered, and she had fragments of metal in her left arm, side, and leg. All in all, she's lucky to be alive. This machine has dissolved the bone fragments and is recreating bones from a synthetic material as well as mending the surrounding damaged tissue. It is un-fucking-believable! I wish we had this in the ER at Chicago General."

"There could be one there now," he replied. "Advanced medical technology and training are part of the protocol for all new planets joining the Alliance."

Bailey gave him a wry grin. "Yeah, well, they have to put Chicago back together first. I don't know if you've ever been there, but there's this huge-ass wall down the center of it with a lot of fighting on each side," she said.

Edge frowned and nodded. "I was there. I have seen the wall. It would not last long. Razor, the Trivator Chancellor for the Alliance, would either settle the conflict or order the leveling of the city," he replied.

"Oh sure, just level the city," Bailey muttered resentfully, setting down the chart. "Did you have another episode?" she asked.

"Yes," he replied in a curt voice.

Bailey motioned for him to sit down on the chair. She stepped closer and pulled a thin penlight out of her pocket. She turned it on and tilted back his head.

"How bad?" she asked.

"Bad enough," he replied.

Bailey shook her head at him in exasperation. "That tells me a lot," she muttered.

"Do you have the results of the scan?" he asked, straightening when she pulled back.

A delicate flush rose to her cheeks. "I honestly forgot to check," she admitted.

He nodded and glanced at Mirela's peaceful face behind the glass enclosure. Between the escape, the fight, and Mirela's grievous injuries, he understood. He watched as she quickly tapped in a command on the tablet in her hand. She frowned as she studied the reports.

"What is it?" he asked, rising to his feet to look over her shoulder.

"I'm still learning your language, and medical terminology is always a bitch. I look mostly at the charts and diagrams to help interpret what the words might mean. I just don't understand this or the chemical structure of the drug," she said.

He reached over and took the tablet from her, the frown on his brow growing deeper and darker. His knuckles turned white as he read through the report.

"It is a synthetic drug using nanotechnology. The drug continues to replicate itself, supplying me with a continuous source of the chemical in my bloodstream. Deppar frequently increased the dosage until my body could no longer kill or dilute it, thus prolonging the pain while he tried to get whatever information he could out of me. He would have needed to administer small amounts of the antidote to slow the process enough to prevent my death," he said, his stomach clenching as the meaning sank in. "It will always be inside me unless we can find a way to stop it."

"But... Your symptoms have lessened," Bailey said, pulling the chart out of his hand and looking at it.

"Yes, for the moment. My body has adapted to the amount that was given to me and my immune system is fighting it. We need to run another scan. If it is what I think it is, then the number will increase until...." his voice faded.

Understanding dawned in Bailey's eyes. "Until you die of an overdose," she whispered, her eyes wide with horror.

"Yes," he responded.

"Edge...." Bailey laid her hand on his arm.

He took a deep breath. "I would like to keep this private. I will do everything I can to get you and the others to Rathon. The chemical has slowly been replicating over the last few weeks, but as the amount increases, it will accelerate replication. I don't...." he paused and swallowed.

"Patient confidentiality is part of a medical professional's job. I'll continue to research the compound and see if there is any way to reverse it. There has to be a way to synthesize that antidote," she stated with confidence.

"Thank you," he replied, turning away.

"Lina would still love you, Edge. It helps if you have someone you can talk to. I'll be here, but Lina has a right to know," Bailey murmured.

He bowed his head before lifting it with determination. "Thank you, Bailey. I will take your words into consideration," he said before he exited the medical bay.

CHAPTER TWENTY-SIX

*N*ebula One:

Jag strode onto the bridge. His piercing glance scanned the room. Thunder and Vice were standing near the communications officer, quietly talking. They both looked up when he entered the room.

"Two down, the last is along the outer rim. Was Jordan able to determine if it was a ship?" Vice asked.

"Yes. How long until we reach it?" Jag asked, wanting to verify the time he already estimated.

"We will reach the vessel in five hours, thirty-two minutes, six seconds," the navigator replied.

"Thunder, Vice, my office," Jag ordered, turning on his heel.

Thunder glanced at Vice with a raised eyebrow before he shrugged and followed Jag into the Captain's room off the bridge. Vice followed behind him. When they paused at the door, Jag motioned for both men to have a seat at a small conference table in the middle of the room. He walked over and poured three drinks. Turning, he walked back to the table and placed a drink in front of both men before sitting down across from them.

"What is it?" they both asked at the same time.

Jag stared at the dark green liquid in his glass before he lifted it to his lips and drank it in one swig. He placed the glass on the table and leaned forward. With a flick of his wrist, he activated the computer screen. The soft green glow from the image of a small ship floated above the table, this time in full three-dimensional form. Data ran along the side of the image.

"Nice! I didn't know the Waxians made ships like that," Vice commented.

"They don't. This one was reported stolen from a Kassisan development center ten years ago. The outer section has been modified, but the guts of the ship are anything but Waxian," Jag replied.

Thunder frowned. "How do you know that it is a Kassisan ship?" he asked.

Jag looked toward the shadows behind them. They both turned and started when they saw the figure of a man standing near the window looking out into space. The man turned when he felt the eyes of the other men on him.

"This is Dakar," Jag briefly introduced.

Thunder raised an eyebrow. "When did a Kassisan become part of the crew?" he asked.

"It was in the fine print that came with the cloaking devices we sent," Dakar replied in a light tone.

"Why the hiding?" Vice asked with a raised eyebrow.

Dakar chuckled and stepped out of the shadows. Jag watched the other man warily as he walked across to the bar and refilled the glass in his hand. He tightened his jaw when the Kassisan studied the screen before he looked at them.

"Kassisans don't typically hide. We prefer to observe from the shadows until we have a clear understanding of the situation—most of the time," he added, lifting his glass to Vice.

"Riiiight," Thunder said dubiously. "So, why is he here?" he asked.

Jag looked at Thunder in warning. "The fine print," he replied with a hard edge to his voice.

Jag watched as Dakar glanced down at his drink and sighed before he swung one of the chairs around and sat down. He pointed to the screen. Jag returned his attention to the images floating above the table.

"Unbeknownst to us at the time, we had a traitor working with another alien species to overthrow the leadership of our world. The fallout and repercussions of Tai Tek's treachery is still being felt. He was working with a group of rogue Tearnats, a species who was once our enemy, but has since become our ally. During that time, Tai Tek and Commander Trolis of the renegade Tearnats stole a prototype ship from us and sold it to an unknown species," Dakar shared.

"The Waxians," Thunder and Vice said at the same time.

"Actually, no.... But, it was recently brought to our attention that a Waxian stole the ship after killing the previous owner. We were able to trace the ship to Oculus IX, but it disappeared three years ago. Since then, the Kassisan star system has joined the Alliance, and we discovered a few other areas of concern that related to the Waxians and the Drethulans," Dakar explained.

"Concerns?" Thunder asked with a raised eyebrow.

"The incident on Dises V has caused us all great concern. The ore they are mining can be made into an unusually strong, yet lightweight alloy. If combined with a unique energy source and the right technology, weapons and ships could be made that would have a devastating effect in the hands of the wrong people," Dakar said.

"What unique energy source?" Vice asked, sitting forward.

Dakar glanced at Jag before he shrugged. "I'm not at liberty to say," he replied.

"Do you trust him?" Vice asked, turning to look at Jag.

Jag's mouth tightened. "Let's just say I'm monitoring the situation," he replied.

Dakar was the first one to start chuckling. Soon, Thunder and Vice joined in. Jag finally allowed a hint of a smile to show on his lips before he leaned forward in his chair.

"Now that we have the introductions out of the way, here is the latest update we have on the situation," Jag said.

Aboard the Dauntless Explorer:

"We'll be coming out of the jump soon. Hang on tight," Edge warned, moving to take the seat that Andy had vacated. He brought up the scanners.

"Are the fighters still behind us?" Lina asked.

Edge nodded. "Yes, and there are now three additional warships approaching," he said in a grim voice.

Gail rose from the co-pilot seat. "We'll gear up and be ready for the bastards," she said.

"I'll take the port turret," Lina said, stepping back so that Gail and Andy could pass her.

Edge looked over his shoulder when he felt her gaze on him. She was looking at him with a conflicted expression. He watched as she unconsciously worried her bottom lip.

"We will make it," he softly vowed. Lina's gaze moved to his hand. He turned his head and saw that his hand was trembling again. Curling his fingers into a fist, he looked up at her. "Be ready. The fighters will come in fast behind us. We will emerge near the remains of a large moon. I will use it to conceal us," he said, turning back to focus on the controls.

He heard Lina murmur a soft acknowledgement before she turned and left. Uncurling his fingers, he stared down at his hand. A soft hiss escaped him when he saw several insects rising out from beneath his skin. Swallowing down the bile that rose in his throat, he refocused his attention on the controls, and carefully programmed in the safest, fastest route to the Alliance territory. He also set up an emergency message that would broadcast on a secure channel monitored by

Alliance forces. They were still several weeks away from the closest Alliance controlled border.

He frowned when an unusual signal was emitted from the shield system again. It lasted only a brief second, but it was enough to trigger his internal warning system. An alert from the computer drew his attention to the fighters closing in on them.

The moon was made of pyroxene, a glass-like silicon type mineral, brilliant green in color. He was confident they would be able to find hundreds of caverns large enough to hide inside. The mineral's unique composition would deflect any signals from the warship's scanners. In essence, they would simply vanish.

It was a risky maneuver, but necessary. He would deploy decoy flares in different directions to divert the warships. Once the warships jumped, he would divert all power to the main engines and pass through the outer rim of Jawtaw space. While the Jawtaw were members of the Alliance, they were also neighbors to the Waxians. So, even if they wouldn't attack a vessel emitting an emergency message on an Alliance channel, they might also look the other way if the Waxian warships attacked them.

"Brace yourselves. I will bring the ship around once we exit the jump. Lina, I will angle toward the port side so we are not vulnerable," Edge warned through the com link.

"We're ready," Lina calmly replied.

Edge gritted his teeth and disengaged the jump propulsion system. The harness around his chest and shoulders tightened at the sudden decrease in speed. Tilting the retro rockets and releasing timed bursts, he swung the ship around. He reached for the forward weapons system controls even as his glance narrowed on the scanner showing the approaching fighters.

"Steady," he murmured. "Now!"

The two fighters appeared almost simultaneously from the black void. He released a series of bursts from the front cannons at the same time as Lina, Gail, and Andy did. The first fighter exploded and broke apart almost immediately. The second one verged to the left, but it was no match for the unexpected firepower of the Dauntless. In seconds, the second fighter joined the first in oblivion.

"Lina, I'm bringing in the port turret. Andy, Gail, be prepared for entry," Edge advised.

"Entry? Into what?" Andy asked before her voice faded. "You have got to be fucking kidding me! A green glass house?"

Edge chuckled. "I do not remember Earth women having such colorful language," he replied.

"You just didn't hang out with the right ones," Andy retorted.

"Obviously," he responded.

He fired three long range decoys. The missile shaped cones floated away from the Dauntless. He waited until they were a ship's length away before he fired the rocket systems at several second intervals. Each veered off in a different direction, before disappearing from sight.

With the decoys deployed, he focused on maneuvering the ship toward the moon while keeping an eye on the approaching warships. The ion trails would be easy to recognize. Not willing to use the main engines, he used the impulse jets to guide the ship toward the moon.

"I really hope you know how to fly this thing in very tight spaces," Gail muttered.

"Can you?" Lina asked.

Edge huffed as he gently rotated the ship, aligning it with the entrance to a dark cavernous hole in the moon. The lights of the ship reflected off the mirrored green surface.

"Yes, I can," he finally replied when they cleared an exceptionally narrow section.

"I think I'm going to need a clean pair of panties," Andy muttered over the comlink.

Gail's choked laugh was heard on the bridge. "You and me both, sister," she retorted.

Edge leaned forward and cut off the power to all but the most essential systems. The soft red glow from the emergency lights lit the bridge. Rising from his seat, he turned Lina's chair until she faced him. Drinking in the sight of her, he couldn't help but think she was the most beautiful, strongest woman he had ever met.

"What?" she asked with a puzzled expression.

Edge lifted his hand and ran his fingers along her jaw. He never wanted to forget the feel of her skin against his fingers or the taste of her lips against his. Bending over, he drew her up until she was standing in front of him.

"What is it?" she asked again.

He threaded his fingers in her hair. "I want you to know that I have come to care very deeply for you," he said.

"I…. Edge, I don't… I can't…," she murmured, fear, sadness, and confusion warring in her eyes.

He gently laid his thumb against her lips. "I want you to know you have given me a gift that I never thought I would ever receive. I… love you, Lina. I love you," he repeated softly before he bent and captured her lips.

CHAPTER TWENTY-SEVEN

*L*ina sat in the top turret, staring up at the green crystals. She pulled her legs up onto the seat and wrapped her arms around them before resting her chin on her knees. She had sought a place where she could be alone for a little while.

"What am I going to do?" she whispered to herself.

The incident over an hour ago had shaken her. There was no doubt in her mind that he had spoken to her from the heart. He loved her. The big Trivator warrior loved her. But... what did she feel for him?

Tears burned her eyes when she tried to come to terms with everything that had happened. She knew she was physically attracted to him. Their lovemaking was hot enough to scorch the inside of the ship. She enjoyed being around him. He had a good sense of humor, something that had definitely taken her by surprise, but he was also considerate to others, caring, and unselfish. It was a side of him she hadn't wanted to see.

"Why? Why is this happening to me?" she pleaded.

She rubbed her eyes. Bowing her head, she blindly stared at the weapon controls. She had given up on love. She had built a wall of ice around her heart. How could this wounded Trivator—one tied to the very heartache she had dealt with for so long—touch her the way he did? She should hate him.

"Out of every person in the universe, why did it have to be him?" she muttered, wiping at a tear that escaped down her cheek.

She closed her eyes and let the memories come. Memories that she had sealed behind the same wall of ice that she'd thought encased her heart. No matter how hard she braced herself for what came with the memories, it still hit her like shards of metal piercing her body and sucking the life from her.

"Leon, help me understand," she begged.

Earth—ten years before:

Lina looked up at Leon. In the faint glow from the moon, he still took her breath away. His light brown, shaggy hair drooped down over his forehead. She needed to give him a haircut. His hair grew so fast and stuck out everywhere, no matter how hard he tried to comb it. It was probably because he was always running his hands through it.

He loved the freedom of running the streets at night. He was always trying to get closer to the Trivators. Personally, she didn't understand why. The aliens scared her. They were big and looked mean.

There was one she had been watching lately down near the river. He was different from most of the others. Usually, he wore his hair long and unbound. He was also broader in the chest than most of the others and had muscles on top of muscles. Unlike the other warriors who wore a vest to protect themselves against the chilled winds coming off of Lake Michigan, he only wore a leather harness for his weapons, and his pants were low-slung.

Several of the other girls had talked about him. Hell, Mirela and Mechelle had dragged her out to go check him out three times so far. Tim had given her hell when he caught them returning from the waterfront. Colbert was causing issues, and he wanted her to stay close to the main base.

She did, except when she was with Leon. The nights were theirs. They would find spots to spy on the Trivators before finding a place where they could lay out under the stars, dream, and hold each other close. Leon's favorite place of all was the Adler Observatory along the banks of Lake Michigan.

That was where they had been heading again tonight, until they saw several Trivators, including the one with the long black hair, patrolling the area. Now they were hiding in the parking garage a few blocks away from the observatory, waiting for Trivators to pass. She slid down along the short wall of the parking garage and looked at Leon.

"I know you've always dreamed of going, but... what about me...? What about us?" she asked.

The thought of what it would be like to leave Earth and possibly never see it, her brother, or her friends again scared her. She looked up when Leon turned and grabbed her hand. He pulled her close, bending to press a kiss to her lips.

"We'll go together," he promised, his eyes glittering with excitement.

"You're crazy," she whispered with a rueful grin. "And how do you plan on doing this marvelous thing? You know Tim will probably have us both locked up if he even knew you were thinking of leaving the planet, especially with me."

"Tim, Destin, Colbert, blah, blah, blah. They have no sense of adventure. Think of what it would be like, Lina." He turned and waved his hand up at the sky. "To see the stars up close. To go where no one has ever gone before...."

"Except the aliens and all the other aliens," she couldn't help but interject.

"Except for everyone else," he chuckled. "We could see the universe, Lina! Not Paris or Rome or Key West, but the universe!"

Her heart melted when he turned to look at her. His whole face was lit up with excitement. Leaning forward, she tangled her hands in his hair and kissed him with a passion that shook both of them.

"I want to be your wife, Leon. Tonight," she murmured against his lips. "I do want to go with you to the stars. As long as we are together, we'll make our own world."

Leon started to reply when the sound of someone kicking a tin can drew their attention. They scrambled to their feet when three men and a woman appeared out of the shadows between two cars. Leon pushed Lina behind him.

"Well, well, well, what do we have here? Some lovebirds," the woman mocked.

Lina's gaze narrowed in anger. The girl wasn't much older than she was but she looked rough. She had grown up on the streets as well, but there were still parts that Tim and Destin protected her from and this was one of them.

"We were just leaving," Leon said, sliding to the side.

"I don't know what your hurry is. It looks like a fine night for a little fun," one of the men said, spitting on the ground.

"Destin and Tim will be expecting us," Lina said, hoping that dropping Destin and her brother's name would be a deterrent.

The four looked at each other and chuckled. "I guess you'll just have to be fashionably late," the woman replied, eyeing Leon with a wicked smile. "I'm feeling like having a little fun with nerd boy here."

Lina gripped Leon's arm and pulled him several steps away from the group. They had two advantages in their favor. They were fast and they knew the area. If they could get away far enough from this group, they could disappear in the rubble of the city.

The man standing next to the woman must have realized they might try to run because he lifted his hand, showing the gun he held. The menacing laughter grew when they heard Leon and her take in a swift breath. Lina's mind raced as she tried to think of a way out.

"Help! We need help!!" Leon shouted, his voice echoing through the otherwise quiet night.

She was surprised when Leon suddenly yelled at the top of his voice. She could tell that his shout for help was not what the other four were expecting either. The man with the gun lowered his arm and looked at his friends.

Twisting around, Leon grabbed her arm and pulled her after him. They ran like the hounds of hell were on their heels. She heard the woman curse and the sound of pounding feet behind them.

Leon jumped over the low wall and reached for her. She grabbed his extended hand, and they took off down the deserted street lined with broken down, abandoned cars and the crumbled remains of buildings. Darting behind a large truck, they turned down a narrow alley.

"Turn left," she said.

They turned left at the end of the alley and dashed across the street. Behind them, she could hear the heavy sound of breathing. They had made it two blocks when she tripped on a loose piece of concrete. Her hand slipped from his and she fell, twisting at an odd angle. Sharp pain lanced through her ankle, and she bit her lip hard enough to make it bleed in an effort to keep the cry of pain from escaping.

"Come on," Leon quietly encouraged her.

She tried to stand, but the pain in her ankle was too much and she fell again, bruising her knees. Shaking her head, she motioned for him to keep going. Her ankle was throbbing, and she wasn't sure if it was just sprained or broken.

"Go, I'll hide," she whispered, fighting back the tears of pain.

Leon looked around before he peered back down at her. "I'll lead them away. Be safe and don't make a sound," he instructed, straightening and turning away.

Lina watched Leon disappear down the street. He waited until he was near the intersection before he yelled for help again. She slid under a delivery truck, half lying on the ground behind the front driver's tire.

She sucked on her tender lip when she saw three sets of feet run by her. Panic filled her when she didn't see the fourth person. The sound of dry laughter pulled her attention to the end of the street in the direction Leon had taken. The fourth person emerged from around the corner of the intersection. The guy must have run down the other street in an effort to cut them off.

"I was the fastest running back in my high school. I guess I still have it," the man chuckled.

"Where's the girl?" the woman demanded.

"What do you want with us? We haven't done anything to you! Hell, isn't the world bad enough without making it worse?" Leon demanded in a loud voice.

"Why's he talking so loud?" one of the guys who hadn't said anything before asked.

The woman turned to Leon and struck him across the face. "Shut up. Where's the girl?" she demanded.

Leon rubbed his jaw. Lina bit her lip when he didn't say anything. She scooted forward when the man behind him struck Leon hard enough to send him to his knees.

"She asked you where the girl was!" the man said.

Leon looked over his shoulder and scowled. "She also told me to shut up. Which is it? Shut up or answer her?" he snapped.

"Trivator forces. Show your hands," a deep, accented voice ordered from the shadows.

Lina's breath caught in her throat and her eyes widened with hope. That was why Leon had been yelling. He'd known the Trivators were scouting the area. He knew they would stop the four from harming them.

"Fuck that! Aliens!" the man said, turning and aiming his weapon toward the Trivator emerging out of the shadows.

"Kill them," the woman yelled, lifting her own weapon.

Lina watched in horror as the group opened fire on the warriors. Leon rose up off the ground and grabbed the woman's wrist. They fought, the gun in her hand going off several times while the Trivators returned fire.

Everything happened so quickly. Leon swung the woman's arm around and to the side. Two of the alien warriors stepped out, firing at them. The woman's body jerked several times and she started to fall. Lina saw Leon stumble back when one of the bolts from the laser fire hit him in the shoulder. The continued sound of gunfire rang out for several more seconds. Leon's body jerked again, this time a dark patch opening up in the center of his chest.

His shocked gaze locked with hers as he sank to his knees. His hand lifted toward her, as if he was trying to touch her one last time. Lina uttered a gasping sob and scooted forward, trying to get out from under the truck.

A silent scream of denial reverberated through her as Leon slowly fell face first in the street. Out of the shadows of one of the buildings a tall, muscular alien with long flowing black hair stepped over to where Leon lay motionless. He bent and turned Leon over. His hand pressed to Leon's throat before he rose to his feet.

"He's dead," he told the other warriors.

Lina remained motionless under the truck. Tim and Mason found her there the next morning. She was lying under the truck, her eyes glued to the spot where Leon had been earlier. The aliens had sent a human crew to remove the bodies.

She had remained silent, in shock and devastated. It had taken her three months before she realized that she wasn't going to die from a broken heart. She decided she couldn't die from one if she no longer had a heart to break. Instead, she filled it with a cold purpose— become a soldier, stand beside Tim and Destin and, if possible, kill the alien with the long dark hair.

CHAPTER TWENTY-EIGHT

"*L*ina," Gail softly called.

Lina blinked and raised her head. She moaned when she felt the stiffness in her neck and legs. She lifted a hand to her cheek, it felt stiff from her dried tears. She must have fallen asleep.

"What? What is it? Are we...?" She looked up and saw that they were still in the green crystal cave. Brushing a hand over her face, she groaned and straightened her legs. "Is it time to leave?"

Gail shook her head. Dread filled Lina when she saw the expression of sympathy in the other woman's eyes. Pushing her hair back from her face, she frowned and looked down at Gail where she stood on the steps leading up to the turret.

"Bailey asked me to come get you," Gail said.

Lina felt her eyes widen in concern. "Mirela...," she asked, rising to her feet and motioning for Gail to move so she could climb down the ladder.

"No, Mirela's actually awake," Gail replied, climbing down and stepping to the side.

Lina jumped the last few rungs of the ladder and looked at Gail. "What...? Edge?" she asked, her stomach tightening in fear.

Gail nodded. "He doesn't look too good," she cautioned.

Lina swallowed. Pushing past Gail, Lina took off at a run along the dimly lit corridor. Turning, she jumped down the set of short steps leading to the corridor and the medical bay.

She reached out and grabbed the doorframe leading into the medical bay. Her frantic eyes swept the room, pausing on Mirela who was lying on one of the medical beds, quietly listening to Mechelle. Stepping inside, her turned to Bailey and the surgical bed.

Horror gripped her when she saw Edge on the bed. His body was bowed upward, and his hands were gripping the sides. Sweat glistened on his face, and his eyes looked wild. Bailey was tightening an extra set of straps around his legs even as his body jerked uncontrollably as if he were in the throes of a massive seizure.

"What happened?" Lina demanded, hurrying forward when Edge lifted his arm, straining to break free.

"They are eating me," he muttered, his head twisting from side to side.

"I need to give him a sedative," Bailey said, making sure the strap was secure before she hurried over to a tray near the bed.

Lina flashed Bailey a furious glare. "What the hell is the matter with him, Bailey?" she demanded through gritted teeth.

Bailey turned and stepped up near his head. She pressed the tip of the injector to his neck and pushed the button. Within seconds, his body began to relax.

"This won't last long," Bailey quietly said, placing the injector on the tray.

"Bailey," Lina gritted out.

Bailey's back was to her. She could see the other woman take a deep, shuddering breath before she turned to look at her. Bailey had the same look in her eyes that Gail had—sadness and sympathy.

"He's dying," Bailey quietly answered.

Lina could feel her head shaking in denial. The fear she had felt for Leon welled up in her throat again, threatening to choke her. Her hands trembled as she reached for Edge's hand. Swallowing, she had to try several times before any words would come out.

"Dying? How? What? I.... He can't. He can't die. He can't," Lina said in a broken voice.

She turned away from Bailey to look down at Edge. He looked so pale. Even with the sleep medication, his eyelids flickered, and she could tell he was in pain.

"It's the drugs that were pumped into him. They are some kind of weird nanotechnology. We thought that he was going into remission, but they continued replicating. They've multiplied," Bailey explained.

Lina looked at the surgical bed. "The bed.... Surely, it would help him. Can't it stop the things from replicating?" she asked in a barely audible voice.

Bailey shook her head. "No, at least not yet. The compound is unknown. It adapts whenever we introduce a new drug to counteract it. I just don't have the knowledge to fight it, Lina. I'm sorry," Bailey whispered, her voice thick with tears.

Lina stood beside the bed, watching Edge. His breathing was erratic. She lifted her free hand and brushed it across his temple. His skin was hot to her touch. Pain exploded through her until she felt like she couldn't breathe. This pain was worse than it had been even with Leon.

"What...?" She bowed her head and took deep breaths in an effort to gather her courage. "Can you slow the nano-whatever down?"

"Yes, I think so, but I'm not sure what good that will do except draw out his misery. If the fever inside him doesn't kill him, the attack on his other organs will. Unless we can get him to a Trivator doctor, I'm thinking it would be more humane to keep him sedated until...," Bailey said, looking at Edge again. "I can program the surgical bed to slow his respiratory system and lower his body temperature. That may give him some extra time."

Lina nodded. "Do it," she ordered, bending over to press a kiss to his lips.

"Uh, gals, I hate to be the bearer of bad news, but those warships aren't going after the decoys. In fact, another big-ass warship just appeared on the scanner, and it looks like it knows where we are," Andy said from the doorway.

Lina looked up at Andy. Her mouth tightened in determination. She looked at Gail, then at Mirela and Mechelle. A frown creased her brow.

"A signal…. Holy alien hell. There is a tracking device on the ship," Lina muttered, her eyes widening.

"A tracking device? Where?" Andy asked.

Lina looked down at where she held Edge's hand. Her mind ran through their conversation. He had mentioned a strange signal.

"The shield. Edge said there was a strange signal going off every once in a while in the shields," she murmured. She looked over at Mechelle again. "I need you to find it. We can't use the shields until you do. They will only follow us. Edge shut down just about everything, including the shields. Mechelle, you have to figure it out."

Mechelle looked uncertain. She glanced at Lina before turned to look at her sister. Mirela gave her a tired smile.

"I can try. I was a gaming programmer, not an alien computer expert," she said, rising to her feet.

"You did a hell of a job on the Spaceport," Gail reminded her.

The look of uncertainty turned into one of pride. "I did, didn't I?" she replied with a smile. "Okay, I'll take a look. I'll need to power on the computer system. If I can see the program, I might be able to see if there is an anomaly in the script. Binary code is the same everywhere. It is either on or off."

"Well, we need you to make sure it is off," Lina said, reluctantly releasing Edge's hand so that Bailey could attend to him. "Take care of him, Bailey."

"I will," Bailey vowed.

Lina looked at Andy. "Can you fly this thing?" she asked.

"If it has an engine, I can operate it," Andy promised.

"Ok, this is the plan…" Lina said with determination.

CHAPTER TWENTY-NINE

ebula One: Waxian Territory Outer Rim

Jag stood with his hands clasped behind his back. He was staring intently at the three large Waxian warships slowly moving over the remnants of a moon. They had arrived only moments before the warships did.

Thunder and Vice stood to his left side while the Kassisan, Dakar, stood to his right. They watched in silence as the first of the large ships searched over the pockmarked remains of the crystal moon. In the background, they listened to the communications between the ships.

"Scanners reveal the debris belongs to at least two fighters. Sir, there is another warship approaching," the Trivator to the left informed them.

"Thunder, I want you and Vice to take one of the modified fighters and search the moon. I want you to find the ship before they do," Jag grimly replied.

Thunder nodded, then Vice and he strode off the bridge. Jag could feel Dakar's unease. He looked at the Kassisan.

"What is it?" he asked, crossing his arms and raising an eyebrow.

Dakar nodded. "Four warships, at least a hundred fighters, against one. Not the best odds," he observed.

Jag shrugged. "I've been in worse. We have the element of surprise and concealment thanks to Ajaska," he said.

"And...," Dakar prompted.

"We Trivators are not without our own technology and resources," Jag replied with a smug smile.

"Sir, we are receiving a message on a secure emergency frequency," the man at the communications console said.

Jag frowned. "Play the message," he ordered.

The communications specialist nodded and activated the com for the bridge. There was a brief moment of silence before a deep voice spoke. Jag lowered his arms and his jaw tightened.

"This is Edge, Trivator warrior identification E585, requesting emergency rescue assistance. We are aboard the Dauntless Explorer in Waxian territory. I don't have much time. I've programmed the ship to jump to Jawtaw territory once we are able. There are seven aboard. Again, this is Edge, Trivator warrior identification E585, requesting emergency rescue assistance."

Jag turned to the communications specialist. "Can you lock onto the signal?" he demanded.

"Yes, sir, but it is faint. It is coming from the moon. I would need a ship to get closer and act as a booster to pinpoint the exact location. The pyroxene is distorting the signal," he replied.

Dakar turned to look at Jag. "It would help if you had another fighter out there. If Thunder and Vice discover the ship and Edge is unable to pilot it, you'll need one of us to do it while the others help provide cover," he pointed out.

Jag nodded. "Take the other fighter," he ordered before turning to the communications specialist. "Notify Thunder and Vice of the situation. I want that ship found. Elevate the ship's status to Level 5, and prepare for battle."

"Yes, sir," the communications specialist responded.

Jag narrowed his glare on the three Waxian warships. They were focused on the moon. Their scanners had detected the decoy flares, but they had ignored them.

Jag knew enough to be familiar with that tactic, and it didn't appear to be working. Edge didn't have much time.

"Sir, the fourth warship is coming out of space jump. It is a Waxian Battle Tank," the navigator informed him.

Jag took a deep breath as the massive ship came into view. The Waxian Battle Tank held five hundred fighters, had reinforced armament, and a crew of eight hundred. The three smaller ships, which could easily fit inside it, were overshadowed by this Battle Tank.

"Thunder...," Jag warned.

"We see it. Fortunately, it can't see us," Thunder replied. "We are going in."

"Dakar will assist you. I would prefer not to engage the four Waxian warships if possible," Jag dryly replied.

Jag watched as one fighter appeared on the viewscreen followed by another. He hoped to the Goddess that the Kassisan cloaking device was as good as Ajaska and Razor insisted. If it wasn't, this was going to be a brutal battle with the odds heavily stacked against them. He walked over to the captain's chair and sat down. Now, it was a matter of 'wait and see.'

~

On-board the Waxian Battle Tank:

Katma Achler sat in the commander's chair. She impatiently tapped the armrest with her fingers. Her focus was directed at the three smaller warships.

"I want the entire moon scanned," she ordered.

"Yes, Commander," the captain of one of the warships acknowledged.

"Have you found it yet?" she demanded, looking at the communications officer.

The man shook his head. "Not yet, Commander," he replied.

"Keep scanning," she said, rising to her feet. "They are in there."

Katma clenched her right fist. Her first thought had been to blow the remains of the moon to dust. The two problems with that plan were that she wanted her ship back and she had promised Prymorus that she would capture the Trivator and the human alive. She had been denied the chance to kill Deppar, perhaps Prymorus would give her the pleasure of killing the human female in exchange.

The woman was the root of the issue. She had taken the Trivator out from under Deppar's nose, and Katma suspected that this woman was also the one who had found the ship she had appropriated several years before. No one stole from her and lived. It was a matter of principle.

Patience had never been her strongest trait. Revenge, on the other hand, was, and she reveled in it. She paced back and forth while the communications officer continued to listen for the tracking code Katma had programmed into the Dauntless' computer. Then she stopped and looked out the viewscreen at the warships scanning the moon.

"I know you are there," she murmured. She tapped her foot. "Dispatch a squadron of fighters to start searching the caverns."

"Yes, Commander," the First Officer said, before he pressed the com button. "Dispatch a squadron of fighters to initiate a search of the moon."

"Now, for a little game of hide and seek," Katma murmured with a sly grin. "I do love a good hunt. It will make killing you all the sweeter."

Katma did not miss the uneasy glances between the other crew members on the bridge. She didn't care. Her focus was on standing beside Prymorus when he brought the Alliance to their knees.

Then I will do the same for my darling husband. Queen Katma... No, Empress Katma, she thought with a menacing smile.

CHAPTER THIRTY

"**N**othing," Dakar said, searching around the dark green crystal cavern.

"We are entering the next chamber," Thunder murmured into the comlink.

Small crystals floated around the fighter. The sound of them bouncing against the ship's hull reminded them that they were in a structure made of glass. Behind him, Thunder heard Vice hiss.

"This would have been better in a shuttle transport than in a fighter," he muttered.

"Did you see a shuttle with a cloaking device on it? You know, you could always take over and pilot this thing," Thunder commented.

"No, if we are going to die, I want you to be the one who gets blamed for it," Vice replied with a grin.

"Sometimes I wonder…," Thunder started to say before he whistled. "Found them."

Vice leaned forward behind Thunder and looked over his shoulder. "How the hell did he get that thing in here?" Vice hissed in surprise.

"It was definitely a tight fit," Thunder agreed. "Dakar, we have a visual. We are moving to intercept."

"Confirmed. I have no signal with the *Nebula One*. I will fall back until I get one," Dakar stated.

"Confirmed," Thunder said. "Vice, do you have a visual on an entry hatch?"

"We will have to enter from the belly of the ship. The top is practically touching the ceiling of the cavern. Can you get us under there?" Vice asked.

"I'll get us under. You get us sealed onto the hatch," Thunder stated in a grim tone.

Thunder delicately maneuvered the fighter toward the spaceship. He was almost to the hatch near the stern of the transport when he saw the turret turn, and they were suddenly facing the wrong end of a laser cannon. Sweat beaded on his brow as he stared into a pair of dark gray eyes filled with determination.

He was too close to the ship to lift his hands from the controls. Holding the fighter steady, he realized that the person couldn't see them. Making a split second decision, he shut down the cloaking device. The woman's eyes widened when she saw the fighter suddenly appear. Behind him, he heard Vice's smothered curses.

"I hope she doesn't push the button on that damn thing," Vice said.

The woman's hands slowly moved away from the controls. Thunder saw her twist in her seat and disappear. Deciding that was a good thing, he continued aligning the fighter with the underbelly of the ship and the hatch.

"Connection complete, airlock sealed. Opening hatch," Vice said, checking all of the readouts before pressing the release on the top of the fighter. "Let's see what kind of welcome we get."

Thunder released his harness and then reached up to press the release on the hatch. The first, then the secondary hatch slid open. He froze when he found himself staring down the business end of, not one, but three, laser rifles.

"I'm glad you decided to go first," Vice remarked.

"I think we found some of the missing women," Thunder said before he raised an eyebrow. "We've been searching for you."

"Yeah, you and half the galaxy. What the fuck do you want?" one woman with dark gray eyes demanded.

"He looks like a Trivator," a woman behind her said.

"Yeah, but does he smell like one?" another feminine voice retorted.

"Smell? What are we supposed to smell like?" Thunder asked in confusion.

"They do know that it only takes a single burst from one of the rifles at this range to kill, don't they?" Vice commented.

Thunder was about to make a similar comment when the rifles disappeared and another dark-haired woman replaced the older female. This one held a laser pistol in her right hand and knelt on one knee to look down at him. He could see hope with an edge of desperation in her gaze. He waited for her to speak.

"Edge is dying. Can you help him?" she asked in a soft voice.

"Take me to him," Thunder ordered, climbing out of the cockpit of the fighter and up through the hatch.

Lina bit her lip and stood near the wall. Bailey was explaining what had happened to Edge, the drug that the Waxian had used, and what she was doing to slow the damage. The two men listened intently before they looked over the chart. She straightened when the bald guy shook his head.

"Is there anything else that can be done to help him?" she asked, stepping forward.

The man named Thunder turned to look at her. Her stomach dropped when he shook his head as well. Lina looked at Edge where he lay cocooned in the surgical cylinder.

"We don't have the medical skills to do more than what you are already doing," he explained.

"He needs advanced care. The healer aboard the *Nebula One* would know what to do," Vice added.

"Then we get him to the *Nebula One*," Lina replied.

Thunder and Vice looked at each other. Shifting her focus back and forth between the two men, she lifted her chin.

"What is it?" she demanded.

"There are four Waxian warships searching the moon for you as we speak," Thunder said.

"They followed a tracking signal placed on this ship. I've disabled it," Mechelle said.

Vice turned and looked at Mechelle in surprise. "A tracking signal?" he repeated.

Mechelle nodded. "Edge told Lina before he collapsed that there was a strange signal coming from the shields. I found a script running in the background. It wasn't hard to disable it once I knew what I was looking for," she replied.

"Hey, guys! I hate to break up the welcome party, but we have company," Andy yelled from the bridge. "Shit a gold brick! I think I see some bald-headed milk duds. We've got douche bags at seven o'clock. I don't think they've seen us yet."

Lina twisted and took off at a run. Behind her, she could hear the others heading to different parts of the ship. Gail was taking the top turret, she would take the bottom, and Mechelle would take the port side once it could be extended. She was surprised when she saw Vice behind her and not Thunder.

"He will pilot the ship. I'll provide cover," Vice said, swinging down the ladder and closing the hatch.

She drew in a deep breath and hurried to the ladder leading down to the turret. They were so close to freedom and yet still so far away. She slid into the seat and swung the turret around until she was facing the two fighters that she could see through the green crystal. In another few seconds, all hell was about to break loose. The only difference was this time, she wouldn't have Edge sitting beside her.

～

A shiver ran through Lina as she waited. Until now, she'd never really thought about the saying that your life flashed before your eyes when you were about to die. She'd faced many life or death situations over the past ten years. She wouldn't say that she'd never cared what happened to her before, because she had. It wasn't like she'd had a death wish, but there had always been a part of her that just accepted that she would die young.

She had experienced plenty of things in her life that kept her fighting to live—her brother, her friends, hell, even just to prove she could do it! Yet, she realized now that she had only been existing more than participating in life. For the first time in ten years, she wanted more and a future.

Memories of Edge's face rose in her mind—the expression of awe, hope, and fierce determination in his eyes when she had stepped into his cell; the teasing looks and curiosity as he had struggled to regain his strength; the passion that burned like fire in his eyes when he looked at her; and finally the love that made them shine like the brightest star.

I love you.... The memory of his softly spoken words tore a choked sob from her. Throughout everything he had been through, he had never given up. He had grasped life and wanted a future while she had just become aimless, existing without thinking of anything more than making it to the next day.

For years she had harbored a hatred for the aliens who had come to Earth. Then she had transferred it to Colbert and the aliens who had taken her from her home. Her fingers trembled on the grips of the weapon in her hand. She wanted more. She wanted a future... and she wanted it with Edge.

She bit her lip as she remembered Tim's quiet words two days after Leon's death. *Lina, we were able to retrieve Leon's body. According to Doc, he was killed by a gunshot wound to the chest.*

The words had meant little to her at first. It hadn't mattered whether the alien standing over him had killed the man she loved or the humans had; nothing would bring Leon back. She had wrapped herself in her grief and turned her anger toward the man who had been standing in the street, simply because he represented everything that she had lost. The same man whose life would cross paths with hers again light-years from Earth.

"Powering on all systems. Be prepared for a rough exit," Thunder's voice echoed in the turret.

"What are you going to do?" Lina asked.

"Get us out of here," Thunder grimly replied. "The *Nebula One*, Vice, and Dakar will provide cover."

"We're all going to die," Andy added. "I hope you have clean underwear on."

"We are not going to die and why would it matter if your underwear is clean or not if we do?" Thunder growled before the comlink closed.

A soft chuckle escaped Lina. The exasperation in Thunder's voice reminded her of Edge. A new sense of purpose filled her. No, they were not going to die today. She had too much to live for.

"Lock and load, ladies. It is time to kick some ass," Lina said, flipping the switch and watching her console light up. Her eyes brightened when she caught a glimpse of open space below the ship. Only a thin layer of crystals blocked their exit. "Thunder, how about if I open up a new door out of here?"

"I see it. Gail, can you take out the two fighters?" Thunder asked.

"Done," Gail replied.

Lina pressed the fire button on her laser cannon at the same time as Gail opened fired on the two Waxian fighters. The ship trembled from the twin explosions. Crystal fragments floated around them, and Lina could see other large sections breaking apart.

Thunder expertly rotated the ship and angled it toward the opening. Lina's breath caught in her throat, and she was pressed back against her seat when the ship suddenly accelerated. They shot through the floating fragments and out into space.

Out of the corner of her eye, Lina caught sight of four warships orbiting above as they exited the moon. Two of the smaller ones were suddenly lit up with explosions. Fighters swarmed the area, firing randomly into space before suddenly breaking apart in a flash of light.

Out of the darkness of space, powerful bursts of laser fire lit up the shields of a giant warship.

She watched in horrified fascination as the last smaller warship tumbled end over end directly into the path of the larger ship. Several fighters turned toward them. She automatically swiveled the turret around and began firing on them. She could see streaks of added fire from Gail and Mechelle.

"Prepare to jump," Thunder ordered.

Lina braced her feet against the footpads and gripped the handles on the cannon. She felt the familiar drop in her stomach before everything sped up. In a flash of light, the last thing she saw was the huge Waxian warship firing on its smaller counterpart.

CHAPTER THIRTY-ONE

*E*dge woke several times before being swept away again on a current of darkness. There were times when the fire licking at his veins and clawing at his insides made him want to scream in agony. He was being eaten alive. When he felt like he would go insane from the pain, a tender hand would cool the flames and a soothing voice spoke of their future together.

"How much longer?" the voice of his goddess asked.

"The new medication is counteracting the synthetic drug in his system and destroying the nanobots," a voice replied.

The hand stroking his face paused. "That still doesn't tell me how long it will take or if he is going to be alright when he wakes up," his goddess retorted with a drawl of sarcasm in her voice.

Edge wanted to smile. He recognized that bossy tone. He wished he could warn the other male that it was futile because his goddess would have what she wanted.

"We should know in a couple of days. I want to keep him sedated until the Waxian drugs are eradicated and are completely flushed out of his system," the man finally replied.

He felt her soft fingers resume their tracing across his cheek and jaw. Then she stopped touching him. A moan escaped him, and he turned his head toward her. Her fingers immediately returned, and he sighed.

Time seemed to weave in and out of his consciousness. The one thing that was constant was the touch of his goddess. She was always there. At times, he could hear her arguing with someone. Her colorful language, determined tone, and grip on his hand reassured him that she would be there the next time he woke.

"How's he doing?" a voice asked.

Edge frowned, searching his memories... Bailey. This was Bailey. She sounded like she was worried.

"Better. I see small changes and improvements almost hourly now," his goddess replied.

"That's good," Bailey said before she released a loud sigh.

Edge flinched when he heard the loud sound of someone dragging a chair across the floor. The hand holding his tightened and her thumb caressed his skin. His mind slowly became clearer. He knew that they had been found. He heard familiar names and the sound of voices that he recognized but couldn't quite attach the names to their faces. The sound of the ship and the medical bay felt different as well.

"What's wrong?" his goddess asked.

"Nothing—everything," Bailey replied with another sigh. "The other gals are worried."

"What are they worried about?" his goddess asked, a wary note in her voice.

"You, the ship... well, not the ship but some of the guys on it, getting home, and some of the other stuff. The ship's captain, Jag, and Gail are butting heads with each other. She wants him to take us directly back to Earth since we are in a super-ship, and he says his orders are to take us to Rathon. I decided to come visit you when he started threatening to lock us all in our cabins. Gail said she'd like to see him try," Bailey laughed.

His goddess chuckled. The warm sound pushed him to open his eyes. He wanted so badly to see her face. A frowned creased his brow when he saw the dark circles under her eyes.

"You... are not... taking... care of... yourself," he forced out, surprised by how difficult it was to speak.

She started in her chair and turned to look at him. A soft, uneven smile curved the corner of her mouth, and she lifted his hand to her lips. His searching eyes remained locked on hers. Next to them, Bailey rose from her seat.

"I'll let the doc know he is awake," Bailey quietly murmured.

Lina nodded, but didn't say anything. Edge could see the tears glistening in her eyes. He wrapped his fingers around hers when she held his hand to her lips.

"It's about damn time you woke up. I swear I think you were just seeing if you could drive me crazy with your silence," she softly informed him.

A dry chuckle shook his large frame. "Did it work?" he asked, rubbing his thumb against her lips.

"More than you'll ever know," she replied as a tear escaped and slid down her cheek.

She bowed her head when the doc came in behind her. Edge growled and shot the healer a heated look. The healer stopped and looked at him with a stern expression.

"Bailey informed me that you regained consciousness. After all the work I did to keep you alive, you could show a little more appreciation," Stitch dryly pronounced.

"I will do that later. Right now, I want to be alone with my *Amate*," Edge retorted.

Stitch looked at Lina and shook his head. "If he has a relapse, call me. Otherwise, I will be in my office—monitoring his vitals," he replied, adding the last statement as he retraced his steps.

Edge struggled to sit up, surprised by how weak he felt. Lina immediately stood up and slid her arm around his shoulders. He took a deep breath while he waited for the weakness and dizziness to abate.

"What happened?" he asked in a gruff voice, slowly lifting his head to look at her.

Lina sat down on the edge of the medical bed. He reached out and cupped her hand in his when he saw her swallow and release a shuddering breath. Reaching up with her free hand, she tucked a strand of her dark hair behind her ear.

"A lot," she said with a wry grin.

He released a humph. "Define 'a lot'," he ordered.

She laughed and tilted her head to the side. "You aren't getting bossy on me, are you?" she teased before the smile died. "Remind me to kick your ass when you are feeling better."

He blinked, trying to understand what kicking his ass had to do with 'a lot'. His breath caught when he saw the sheen of tears in her eyes again—and the anguish. He lifted his hand to brush it across her cheek. He froze, his hand in midair, and stared at it in wonder. Turning it over, he flexed his fingers.

"The shaking is gone," he murmured, truly appreciating the control he had over his physical abilities again.

Lina nodded. "Hopefully for good. Stitch said your last three scans came back clean. It was touch and go there for a while. The drug the Waxian pumped into you began to mutate when it was attacked by other medications. With the help of some of the doctors back on Rathon, Stitch was able to make adjustments to fight the mutation and create an antidote to counteract it," she explained.

She wrapped her fingers around his hand, and drew it to her cheek. He opened his hand and splayed it across her smooth skin, then slid his hand down her arm, pushing her long blue sleeve back to expose her wrist.

Shock held him immobilized. Wrapped around her wrist was an intricate tattoo. He read the symbols, and their meaning hit him hard, leaving him shaken. Her gaze followed his.

"I am Lina, *Amate* to Edge. I love him. He is mine for the rest of my life," she murmured with a crooked smile. "I was never big on a lot of words and figured the fewer there were, the larger I could make them."

He reached over and pulled up his own sleeve. A frown creased his brow when he saw that his wrists were bare of her claiming mark. He looked at her with a confused expression.

"Why do I not have the markings?" he demanded.

Lina rolled her eyes. "You were out of it, in case you don't remember. Stitch wanted to do it, but I wouldn't let him. He was going to copy what I had him mark on me. I told him that you needed to make that decision when you woke up. You've said I was your *Amate*, but saying it and following through are two different things. You are going home and you've been through a lot. I wanted you to make the decision when you had your head clear," she explained.

"Stitch!" he loudly called, pushing back so he could twist until he was sitting on the side of the bed. "Stitch!"

Stitch came out of the office. It was obvious that the healer had expected his shout because he held the device to mark him in his hands. Edge grabbed the hem of his shirt and pulled it over his head. He tossed it to the side. Rolling his shoulders, he held out his arms.

"I wondered how long it would take you to notice. Vice owes me a case of Trusset liquor and Thunder owes me a case of Port from Earth," Stitch said with satisfaction, placing the cuffs around Edge's wrists.

"You were betting on how long it would take me to discover my *Amate's* claim?" he asked in disbelief.

"Yes, though Jag bet me that you wouldn't even make it. He owes me a month's leave," Stitch chuckled.

Edge shook his head in disgust. "You were betting on whether I lived or died as well?" he demanded with a growl.

"Don't worry. Gail overheard Jag and has been giving him hell about it," Lina chuckled.

"She isn't the only one. Now, what do you want this to say?" Stitch asked in a dry voice.

"Get out," Edge ordered, pulling his hands away from Stitch. "We will do this—without you."

"Fine," Stitch snapped. "Say your vow, press your thumb to the imprint, and it will automatically open when it is complete. I hope you know this is only the second time it has been used. I never could understand why it was a requirement to have one of these on board every ship. Now I know."

Edge watched Stitch pivot on his heel. The healer strode out of the medical bay, leaving Edge and Lina blissfully alone. Focusing on Lina, Edge slowly rose from the bed before kneeling on one knee in front of Lina. Edge tenderly cupped her hands in his and searched her eyes.

"I, Edge, claim Lina as my *Amate*. I vow to love and protect her. I give my life into her hands, knowing that she will do the same for me," he said in a deep, clear voice.

He released her hand and placed his thumb on the device. It glowed red before turning to a soft green. In less than a minute, the locking mechanism popped open. Rising to his feet, he removed the marking bands and placed them on the bed.

"I love you, Lina, with all my heart," he murmured, tenderly cupping her cheek and bending to brush a kiss across her lips.

The sound of muffled giggling near the door stopped him. Tilting his head, he glared at the five women peeking through the opening. They each had huge grins on their faces.

"I swear this wedding has to be right up there with the drive thru one in Vegas," Gail observed with a grin.

"How would you know?" Andy asked.

Gail chuckled. "What happens in Vegas, stays in Vegas. Thank you, Elvis," she added with a wink.

"Welcome back to the world of the living, Edge," Mirela replied.

Edge nodded, realizing the women were not planning on leaving any time soon. He looked down at Lina when she laughed and wrapped her arm around his waist. He stifled a groan when she deliberately ran her fingers along the bare flesh of his back and down to his hip.

"It is good to see you alive as well, Mirela," he replied before he frowned. "I still have not been told what happened," he said. "Where are we and how did we escape the Waxian forces?"

"It was so cool!" Mechelle replied with a suddenly animated expression. "I totally bet that Waxian captain is catching hell for destroying one of their own warships, not that it would have mattered because the *Nebula One* was doing a pretty good job without any help from some dopey captain that blasts a hole right through the middle of their own warship. I still think the coolest thing was the invisibility cloak."

"Invisibility cloak? Warship?" he repeated with a skeptical expression.

"You might want to sit down for this," Lina said with a laugh.

Edge listened as Lina and the other women shared how Thunder and Vice had suddenly appeared, how they had all escaped from the moon, and how the *Nebula One* had kicked the Waxian's ass. He looked up over their heads at one point to see Jag, Thunder, Vice, and a man he did not recognize standing in the doorway listening to the fantastic tale with bemused expressions.

Jag gave him a pointed look. Edge bowed his head in acknowledgement. He knew that Jag would want to debrief him on his captivity and what—if anything—he might have discovered during that time. The commanding officer would have to wait.

For now, he would listen to the women tell their exciting tale and count the seconds until he could carry Lina away to the cabin that would have been assigned to them. A smile curved his lips and he rested his chin against Lina's soft hair when she leaned against him. He held Lina in his arms and rubbed his thumb across the marks around her wrists.

"Would you like to go to our cabin and get cleaned up and eat?" she murmured, tilting her head against his shoulder.

"I thought you would never ask," he replied against her ear.

Lina's body shook with laughter. Rising to their feet, the other women quickly realized that the rest of the story would have to wait. He patiently waited as each one congratulated them on their 'marriage'. They paused by the door where Jag and the other men were standing.

"Thank you," Edge quietly said, wrapping his arm around Lina's waist.

Jag shook his head. "Our only regret was not locating you sooner. Get cleaned up and eat some food. You've been assigned a cabin. It is three doors down on the left. I want you in my office off the bridge in two...," he paused and looked at the raised eyebrow and mutinous expression on Lina's face before he continued, "three hours for debriefing."

Edge bowed his head in agreement. "I will be there," he replied as he guided Lina through the door and followed the directions Jag had given them to their cabin.

"Is he always such a hard-ass?" Lina murmured.

Edge chuckled. "Yes," he replied, knowing that Jag could hear her soft comment.

CHAPTER THIRTY-TWO

*T*he warmth of the fine mist from the shower felt good across his shoulders. He chuckled when he thought of Lina's insistence that he go ahead first. He could hear her talking to Gail in the other room.

The older woman had delivered a tray of food, complete with the 'miracle water' as Lina liked to call it. The combination of food and the nutrient enriched water had gone a long way to restoring his strength. Now that his body was free of the drugs, he could feel his energy returning.

He turned around in the shower when he heard Lina thank Gail and the door to their cabin open and close. A moment later, she stood in the doorway to the cleansing room. He brushed his wet hair back from his face. Her sparkling eyes followed the movement before sliding down over his body.

"Join me," he encouraged.

A hint of a smile curved her lips. "Good things will happen if I do," she warned with a smile before her expression changed to one of concern. "How are you feeling?"

His gaze moved over her. "Why don't you come find out?" he suggested.

Her laughter filled the room. "You really have been around us gals too long," she retorted.

He watched as she reached down and pulled her black shirt over her head. Heat filled him when he saw the lacy, black bra. She didn't remove it immediately, instead her hands slid down her stomach to the waist of her pants. She unfastened them and pushed them down. She had removed her boots earlier, so there was nothing stopping her from kicking off the pants.

Clad only in black panties and bra, she took her time removing these last two items. He feasted his gaze on the pale twin mounds of her breasts, but his mouth watered for what lay hidden by the dark brown curls between her legs. His body, rested and rejuvenated, throbbed with desire.

The dark bands of his Amate mark around her wrists filled him with pride. He slid the door open when she walked forward. She stepped into the enclosure and the door slid shut behind her.

"I love you, Lina. You are truly my goddess," he murmured, burying his hands in her hair and kissing her.

Pleasure coursed through him when her lips parted under his. Her hands caressed his body, moving from his hips, up to his chest, over his shoulders, and back down his sides as if she was memorizing him. His buttocks tightened when her hands cupped them. Her tongue tangled with his even as his cock throbbed between them.

He broke off the kiss and looked at her with burning desire. He wanted to feel her lips wrapped around his cock before he buried himself inside her. Wrapping his hands in her hair, he shuddered when she grasped his cock with both hands.

"We don't have much time before you're supposed to meet with Jag. I guess we'll have to make this hard and fast," she said, tilting her head to the side.

He rocked his hips back and forth as she caressed him. The combination of tight squeezes and fast stroking mixed with a slower, even rhythm made his cock swell in her hand. He agreed that it should be hard, but maybe not quite so fast. He reached down and wrapped his fingers around her wrists.

"This time, it is my turn to take care of you," he said in a deep voice filled with emotion.

Pulling her hands away from his body, he gently turned her. Lifting her hands, he placed them against the opposite wall. He swiped his hand over the cleansing foam option. The mist changed to a light blue.

Starting at her shoulders, he followed the light blue trail of foam bubbles running down her back. He gently massaged her skin, noting the scars on her back for the first time. He'd seen the small round one before and knew what it was from—she had been shot with a human weapon.

"How did this happen?" he demanded, brushing his thumb over the scar.

Lina bent her head. "I was on a patrol and we took some fire. Never did find out who it was. Kali Parks, Destin's sister, saw them before I did. If she hadn't grabbed me when she did, I'd have been dead. She stopped the bleeding, called in for help, and Doc patched me up. Luckily, it didn't do much more than hurt like a son-of-a-bitch," she said.

"And this one," he asked, running his finger over a long thin scar that ran along her right shoulder blade.

"Rebar. I didn't duck low enough trying to hide from a group of Trivators," she said. "That one took twenty-two stitches and almost got us caught. You guys have a great sense of smell. Thankfully for us, some other bozo decided to use the Trivators for target practice and they changed course."

"You should never have been placed in such danger," he said before he continued washing her.

Lina uttered a short, tense laugh and shook her head. "My life wasn't all that dangerous until your people came to our world," she murmured.

Edge could hear the change in her voice. He slid his hands around her and gently turned her in his arms. He glanced down at her, but she avoided looking in his eyes.

"Tell me," he quietly ordered.

She shook her head. Lifting his hand, he changed the cleansing foam to a rinse. Cupping her chin, he tilted her head back and looked deeply into her eyes.

"Tell me... please," he requested.

Her lips parted. He could see the emotion welling up in her eyes. Caressing her cheek with his thumb, he waited.

"I saw you before... back on Earth," she said, shocking him.

"When? Where? I would have remembered if we had met," he swore, trying to understand how he could have met her and not remembered it.

"We never met," she said with a shake of her head. "I would like to get out of the shower."

He watched in confusion as she opened the door and stepped out. She ignored the body dryer, and instead grabbed a towel from the shelf and quickly dried off. He turned off the shower and stepped out onto the drying vent. With haunted eyes, she finger combed her hair and stared at him through the mirror before she wrapped the towel around her body and disappeared into the other room.

He impatiently waited until he was dry before he strode into the other room. Lina was sitting on the bed, staring out of the window into space. Walking over to the bed, he sat down beside her and waited for her to speak.

"You were on Earth not long after the first wave of Trivators came," she began.

"Yes, I did three tours on your world. The first one ten years ago," he admitted, still puzzled.

She took a deep, shuddering breath. He saw her fingers nervously twisting the material of the bath towel. Reaching out, he covered her hand with his.

"Mirela and Mechelle didn't recognize you, but I did. Some call it a gift, others a curse, but I never forget a face," she said with a bitter snort.

He could see that this was difficult but very important to her. "I... don't remember much except for a few of the patrols and some of the people I met," he confessed. He'd been to many places and had done a lot of things over the years. He had vague memories, but nothing that he could connect with Lina.

Lina's fingers stilled and she breathed deeply. He could practically feel her tension. She released her nervous grip on the towel and wrapped her arms around her waist as if to protect herself.

"Do you remember a shootout in Chicago? It was dark and there were... there were four men and a woman," she whispered.

Edge frowned. He'd been on patrol with Blade and Sniper. The biggest reason he remembered the incident was because a woman was killed. It had bothered all three of them, and he had talked to one of the Trivator counselors in order to understand his guilt for not protecting her.

"Yes. We were ambushed. A human called for help and we responded. When we reached them, they opened fire on us," he said.

Lina violently shook her head and scooted off the bed. She walked over to the window, and stood there with her fist pressed to her mouth. In the reflection of the window, he could see the tears in her eyes.

Concerned, he stood up and walked over to stand behind her. She stiffened when he placed his hands on her bare shoulders, but she didn't pull away from him. He could feel her trembling.

"Tell me, please," he begged, pulling her back against his body and wrapping his arms around her.

"They weren't... He didn't...." She uttered a choked sob and paused. "Leon loved to explore at night. His favorite... his favorite place to go was the Alder Observatory by the river. At night we could see the spaceships in orbit. He dreamed... he dreamed of going to the stars. He talked about us going together," she choked out.

Dread filled him as she spoke. They hadn't planned to kill the humans, just wound them and then take them into custody, but that didn't change the fact that they had all died.

"Which one was he?" he asked.

"We were in one of the downtown parking garages. Leon saw a group of Trivators on patrol and we were waiting for them to move on. Three men and a woman took us by surprise while we were hiding. They... they planned to...." She shook her head and looked up to stare out of the window again. "Leon knew if he yelled for help, the Trivators on patrol would probably hear it and come to see what was going on. We used the opportunity to escape. We thought we might have a better chance if we ran toward you. The worst that might happen is we would get caught and maybe sent to the base. That would be preferable to what would have happened if we hadn't done anything. We made it several blocks before I stepped on a loose piece of concrete and twisted my ankle. I couldn't walk, much less run. Leon told me to hide under a truck, and he would lead them away with the hope that the patrol would come to his aid," she explained in a voice suddenly devoid of emotion.

"We came, and they opened fire on us," Edge remembered.

"Yes," she replied.

"There was one male, he struggled with the woman," he said.

Lina nodded. "She shot Leon several times. I didn't know that at first. I heard a lot of gunfire and laser blasts. Everything happened so quickly and then it was over. I saw you... I saw you step out of the shadows. You walked over and stood over Leon for several seconds before you bent down and turned him over. I heard you say he was dead," she said, shaking her head. "I thought you had killed him."

"Lina," he murmured, turning her in his arms.

She refused to look up at him. He lifted his hands and cupped her face. Silent tears slid down her cheeks. He brushed them away and pulled her, unresisting, into his arms. Holding her tightly against his chest, he soothingly ran his hand up and down her back.

"We didn't want to harm any of them," he promised. "They were shooting at us, and we had no choice. Sniper shot your Leon in the shoulder. It was the woman who killed him."

"I know. Doc told me. I had no one to hate but you. The woman was dead. I told myself that if you... that if the Trivators hadn't come, then none of this would have happened and Leon would still be alive. I didn't want to feel anything but hatred. I needed someone to focus that hatred on—and that someone was you," she confessed, looking up at him with such despair in her eyes that it made him groan.

"Yet, you wear my mark," he said, releasing her cheek and reaching down to lift her wrist up so he could press a kiss to it. "You accepted my claim."

Tears clouded her beautiful brown eyes. "I never wanted to love anyone again, and then I met you. I swore the Fates were laughing at me when I realized which Trivator the Waxian held. I wanted to leave you, but we needed you. I wanted to hate you, but…." She tried to look away, but he refused to release her chin.

"But…," he murmured.

She tilted her chin in defiance. "But then I started to get to know you. You were so damn stubborn and wouldn't give up," she said.

He shook his head. "I told you to leave me," he reminded her.

A rueful grin curved her lips. "Yes, you did, but only to protect us. Then, you closed your eyes and gave me your trust. I honestly don't know of another single person in the entire universe who would have done that on a narrow plank five stories high," she confessed.

"You threatened to knock me out," he teased.

"It wouldn't have been that hard to do it," she said with a strained laugh. "You make me laugh."

"You sang to me," he said.

She bit her lip and leaned forward to rest her head against his bare chest. "I love you, Edge. I was terrified when Bailey said you were dying. You make me want more out of life," she quietly said, her voice catching on a sob. "You make me believe that love can be worth the risk."

"Ah, my little goddess, you are the one who makes me believe. I love you, Lina. I have since you ordered me not to fucking die on you," he murmured, rubbing his chin against her hair.

"Really?" she sniffed.

"Really," he promised with a deep chuckle.

She leaned her head back and looked up at him. "How much time do we have before you have to meet Jag?" she asked, sliding her hands up his chest.

"As long as we want," he vowed, bending over and picking her up in his arms.

He turned around and walked back to their bed. Laying Lina gently on the soft covers, he opened the towel covering her. Placing one knee on the bed, he leaned forward and captured her right nipple in his mouth. Her loud gasp filled the air as he sucked on the hard pebble.

He made a path down her stomach, brushing soft kisses along her ribs before reaching her hips. He slid between her legs when she opened them for him. Spreading her soft folds, he exposed the tiny nub that brought her so much pleasure. At the first swipe of his tongue, he knew a flame was ignited inside Lina.

"My *Amate*, today I will show you how much I love you," he murmured.

～

Lina's breath caught in her throat. A rush of feelings swept through her. Every time he touched her, she felt like she was on fire. Spreading her legs farther apart, she lifted her hands to her breasts and played with them while he tortured her clit.

"Yes. Oh, Edge, yes!" she hissed, wanting more.

Liquid heat pooled inside her and prepared the way for his fingers. She cried out when he added a third finger, stroking her while at the same time torturing her clit with his tongue and teeth until she was panting. She stiffened when the first wave of her climax hit her.

She groaned when he released her. She started to open her arms, expecting him to move up her body so he could enter her. Instead, he sat up and rolled her over until she was on her belly.

"On your knees," he ordered, a slightly desperate note in his voice.

Still throbbing from her climax, Lina rose to her knees. He leaned forward and gripped her hip with one hand. Looking over her shoulder, she saw his hand holding his cock ready to enter her. Her eyes moved up to lock with his heated gaze.

"I want to take you hard," he warned through gritted teeth.

"I love it hard," she replied with a raised eyebrow. "Let me feel you, Edge."

She got her wish. His thick, bulbous head pressed against her swollen labia. He was so aroused that she wasn't sure he would fit at first. A guttural moan escaped her when he pushed forward, impaling her on his thick shaft. He gave her body a moment to adjust to him before he began moving.

Lina swore she could feel each stroke as if it were magnified. His cock, completely wet from her orgasm and his precum, slid along the sensitive walls of her channel. Shaking her head, she fought against another orgasm, unsure she could handle it.

Edge felt her stiffen. He released her hips in favor of her breasts and leaned over her body. The position pushed him even deeper inside her. Lina was ready to scream as he began driving into her with a force that took her breath away. She decided he must have been holding back before or the drugs must have had some impact on him because she didn't remember him being quite so large.

The sound of their flesh smacking together drove her wild. Hot liquid coated his cock with her arousal, and she went over the precipice, locking down on him as she came again, this time harder than the first time. Her arms began to tremble, and she collapsed on the bed. She bowed her head with her ass still in the air.

Edge released her breasts to grip her hips again. She knew he was watching his cock as it slid in and out of her. It was growing larger as the blood flowed into it. The feel of his cock as he pulled it out to the tip and pushed it back inside sent her spiraling out of control.

"Edge!" she harshly cried out, gripping the covers in her hands.

"Yes, yes, yes!!!" he groaned, jerking twice before he stiffened and held her hips in a fierce, bruising grip while his cock pulsed inside her. "Oh, my goddess."

Pulsing wave after pulsing wave locked them together. Tears burned her eyes when he leaned forward again and wrapped one strong arm around her waist. She could feel his lips against her shoulder.

"I love you, Edge," she said in a soft, rough voice.

"Not as much as I love you, my beautiful *Amate*," he murmured, easing them down onto the bed.

CHAPTER THIRTY-THREE

"*Y*ou're late," Jag said with a raised eyebrow.

"You would be too if you had someone like Lina in your arms and had also been through hell the past two years," Edge retorted before he grimaced and ran his hands through his hair. "My apologies. It was hard to leave her side."

"I wouldn't be apologizing," Thunder muttered under his breath.

Vice grinned. "I wouldn't either," he replied, lifting up a bottle sitting on the bar near the window. "Drink?"

"Yes," Edge nodded with a grin.

Jag motioned for him to sit down at the oval table. He paused when he saw the fourth man sitting quietly at the far end. He studied the man, trying to guess what species he was.

"Edge, this is Dakar. He is a Kassisan. His people were kind enough to assist with your rescue," Jag introduced.

"The invisibility cloak," he murmured, nodding to Dakar. "Thank you for your assistance."

"I will pass on your regards to Ambassador Ajaska," Dakar replied in a dry tone.

"What can you tell us about what happened to you?" Jag asked.

Edge glanced around the table before picking up the glass that

Vice had placed in front of him. For a moment, he was lost in thought. Taking a deep swig of the fiery liquor, he allowed it to warm his blood before he began.

"Dagger and I were on a mission when we were shot down. I was knocked unconscious. I don't know what happened between the crash and when I woke up on an Armatrux slave ship. I assume Dagger dragged me out. For the next year and a half, I worked in various mines until a Waxian named Deppar purchased me...," he said, relating everything he could remember, including names, places, and what was mined.

The next several hours passed quickly as Jag related what had happened to Dagger and the fact that Dagger and he had both been presumed killed in action. It was the tenacious determination of a woman named Jordan Sampson, who refused to believe Dagger was dead, that had given them hope that perhaps he had survived as well.

"Deppar wanted to know about our military operations, locations, equipment, movements of men, anything and everything. He also wanted to know where Razor, Hunter, and other leading members of the Trivator forces lived and worked," he shared.

"What did you tell him?" Dakar asked.

Edge looked at the Kassisan. He had been silent throughout the debriefing. Now, he sat back in his chair, sliding one finger around the rim of his half-empty glass.

"To go fuck himself," Edge replied with a hard tone.

≈

Waxian Battle Tank Warship:

"Commander Achler," the first officer said in a stiff tone.

Katma sat in the chair, staring out at space. Her left leg hung over the arm of the chair while she tapped the toe of her right boot against the floor. In her right hand, she held a bottle of dark green liquor that was half empty.

"What is it?" she finally replied.

"The warship should be minimally operational in less than an hour. The decks with hull breaches were sealed. Once we are operational, we have orders to return to base," he said.

Katma tilted her head. She was watching her first officer's expressions change in the reflection on the bottle in her hand. She didn't miss the two security guards who had quietly entered the room either.

"By whose order?" she asked in a deceptively calm voice.

"The Prime Ruler, Commander," he answered.

"The Prime Ruler.... You do know that I am the mate of the Prime Ruler, do you not, First Officer Waxman?" she asked, slowly standing up and turning to face him.

Waxman's face hardened and he nodded. "Yes, Commander. If you would please follow me, I have orders to escort you to your... quarters," he said.

Katma raised an eyebrow. "Well, if you were ordered by the Prime Ruler, then I must obey like a good officer," she quipped.

Waxman eyed the bottle in her hand. She could tell he was noting that it was more than half empty. Stepping around the chair, she wobbled a little before straightening. A soft giggle slipped from her lips.

"Please leave the decanter, Commander Achler. I believe you have had enough to drink," Waxman stated.

She gave him a pouty look, sticking out her lower lip. Swinging the bottle between her fingers, she shook her head and sighed. There was no way she was going to give up a fine Raftian liquor without good cause.

"As long as there is still a drop left in this bottle, I can assure you I have not had enough. Do you know that this is the first truly fine liquor that I've had in over three years? Three years, Waxman. For three years, I was left to rot in a cell on our dear home planet," she murmured, stepping closer to him.

"Commander, I must insist that you place the decanter on the floor now," Waxman said, pulling his laser pistol from his hip and aiming it at her.

She narrowed her gaze on his face and pursed her lips. With a shrug, she bent to place the heavy glass decanter on the floor. As she expected the pistol in Waxman's hand dipped along with her movements.

Rotating on her foot, she kicked his hand and swung around with the glass decanter. The heavy glass container struck him in the head, shattering his cheekbone and jaw while the pistol flew upward. Katma pushed her first officer into the two security guards standing behind him. She reached up and grabbed the pistol as it fell. With cold precision, she immediately fired three shots, killing Waxman and the two security guards.

Lifting the decanter to her lips, she drained it before dropping it on Waxman's stomach. Wiping a hand across her mouth, she stepped over the three bodies and looked up and down the corridor. She had less than an hour to gather her belongings and commandeer a transport. It would take her only a fraction of that time since she had been prepared for Prymorus's betrayal from the start.

"It is a shame that Deppar was so lousy at keeping secrets, my darling mate," she murmured to herself as she walked down to the flight bay.

"Now, to find my other ship along with the red crystal ship which my beloved finds so interesting," she replied, her eyes hardening.

EPILOGUE

 athon: Two months later

"Hey, stranger," Lina said, gazing at the viewscreen.

"Holy Mother... Lina?!" Tim's shocked voice sounded strange to her after not hearing it for so long.

"Actually, it is Goddess Lina now," she chuckled, leaning forward and staring at the image behind him. "Where in the hell are you?" she asked.

"What? Oh, Chicago. You honestly wouldn't recognize it. The city looks like something out of a sci-fi movie. Where are you? Are you on Earth? Where in the hell have you been? What happened? Hell, are you alright?" he demanded, running both hands through his already disheveled hair. "I can't believe you're alive."

Lina laughed again. "Yeah, well, neither can I nor the other gals," she admitted with a sigh. "I'm on Rathon, the Trivator's home world. Or, at least, I'm in orbit around it. We are heading down in a little bit. How did you get Colbert to agree to the rebuilding? You know that bastard is the one who sold me along with the other women to the blue dipstick," she growled.

Tim grimaced. "Colbert and Badrick are both dead. They've been dead for a while. Destin and Sula have taken over the rebuilding, though Destin has been spending more time meeting with alien dignitaries lately. The day-to-day operations have pretty much fallen into my hands," he admitted.

"Who is Sula?" she asked.

Tim chuckled and shook his head. "A lot has changed since you were taken, sis. Destin is married to Sula, an Usoleum Princess and Ambassador of the Alliance," he said before his expression grew somber. "When are you coming home?" he asked.

Lina bit her lip and looked down at her wrists. She took a deep breath and looked back at the viewscreen. With a rueful grin, she lifted her arms.

"A lot has happened since I was taken," she said with a grin. "Destin isn't the only one who is married."

"Holy shit! Lina... I swear, if some bastard has...," Tim's voice faded.

Lina knew exactly why it did when she felt Edge's hands on her shoulders. He slid them down her arms as he stood behind her and gazed at her brother with a fierce expression. She tilted her head back and scowled up at him.

"I was just telling him," she said with a slight pout.

"I know," he replied, bending to brush a kiss across her lips before he straightened and looked at her brother. "If it helps, she claimed me first."

Tim's mouth opened and closed several times before he grunted. "Why does that not surprise me?" he dryly replied.

"Everything is good, Tim. I promise," Lina softly assured him before she shared everything that had happened – with a few minor omissions like her getting shot.

They talked for over an hour about the different things that had happened. It felt good to talk with Tim again, but it also felt different. They had both grown and changed over the last two years

"Will you be coming back to Earth?" he finally asked.

Lina reached up and gripped Edge's hand when she felt his hand tighten on her shoulder. She drew comfort from his touch when he gently squeezed it. She leaned against him and smiled at her brother.

"We may come for a visit, but we will be living here. I'd like to try it. There are other humans here so I won't be alone, and Edge was given time off to rebuild his strength. We are going to go to his home for a while. It will give us some time to rest without running for our lives," she explained.

Tim was quiet for a few seconds. He turned when someone called his name. With a grimace, he turned back to her and gave her a look of resignation.

"I'm needed. These are the times when I really miss Destin," he commented with an apologetic expression.

Lina shook her head. "We are about to depart as well. We can still chat. You go rebuild Chicago. I'm... I'm going to go enjoy life for a little while," she said.

Tim's expression softened. "If anyone deserves to enjoy life, it is you, Lina. I love you, sis. Never forget that," he said.

Tears burned Lina's eyes. "I love you too, big brother," she murmured. "Talk to you soon."

"Soon... I know.... I'm coming," Tim shouted over his shoulder. "Love you, bye!"

Lina chuckled when the screen suddenly went dark, then quickly swiveled in her seat, wrapped her arms around Edge's waist and burst into tears. He gently guided her to stand up and wrapped his arms around her. She shook her head, crying and laughing at the same time.

"I'm such a wuss when it comes to emotions now. It seems like every time I turn around, I'm crying," she complained, wiping at her cheeks.

"Perhaps you should see Stitch before we leave," he suggested, brushing her hair back from her face.

She looked at him with a surprised expression. "Why? I don't feel sick," she replied with a frown.

This time it was Edge who chuckled. He looked at her with a

raised eyebrow and a mischievous grin. Bending over, he whispered in her ear. Her eyes grew huge when what he said sunk in.

"No way," she breathed, shaking her head.

"Oh, it is very possibly a way," he teased.

Her lips parted at the thought. Pregnant? Edge thought she could be pregnant?! She frowned, trying to think when she last had her period. The days blurred, and she honestly couldn't remember.

"Well, fuck me!" she whispered.

"With pleasure," Edge agreed with a grin, bending over and scooping her up in his arms. "We have time."

~

Three weeks later, Edge stood on the beach. A gentle breeze blew in from the ocean and the last rays of the sun were streaked across the sky. He turned around and was about to head back to the house when he saw Lina hurrying out of the door. She was tossing her shoes back into the house behind her.

With an apologetic smile, she ran across the soft, black sand toward him. He lifted his hand and grasped hers, then brushed a kiss across her lips. They both looked out at the setting sun.

"You almost missed it," he said.

She grimaced. "Your mom called. She wanted to know if I'd like to go to the market with her tomorrow," she said, wrapping her arm around his waist.

"Both my mother and father have fallen in love with you," he observed with a pleased smile. "I knew they would."

Lina snorted. "She wanted to go shopping for baby clothes. I told her I thought it was still a little early," she replied with a dry tone.

"It is never too early," he stated.

She shook her head. "Now you sound like your father!" she warned.

"Goddess forbid," he replied with a fake shudder.

"Oh, look!" Lina whispered in awe.

The last rays of the sun shone over the horizon while the twin moons rose. The effect, combined with the water from the ocean, made the sunset look magical. Once again, he was glad he had followed his instincts to build his home on the island of his clan. This island oasis rose up a hundred miles off the mainland.

"The stars will be magnificent once the moons set. Would you like to get up and see them?" he asked, turning her in his arms.

She lifted her arms and wrapped them around his neck. "Does that mean we need to go to bed now?" she asked with a coy smile.

"I think that is an excellent idea. I'm glad you thought of it," he said, bending to sweep her up into his arms.

Lina leaned her head against his shoulder. "You've been talking to the girls again, haven't you?" she murmured with a sigh.

"At least once a week," he chuckled. "If for no other reason than to keep them from killing their *Amates*."

Lina lifted her head and stared at him with her mouth hanging open. "They have *Amates*? Who? When? Why haven't they told me?"

Edge brushed a kiss across her lips. "Yes, they do, but they haven't accepted it yet," he said. "Now, enough of them. I think I want to explore that number you told me about again."

"Sixty-nine?"

"That's the one," he said, climbing the steps that led to the open doors of their bedroom.

"Damn, but I love your gorgeous alien ass."

Edge chuckled at Lina's heated declaration. The sounds of their lovemaking carried on the breeze. In the quiet aftermath, he lay with Lina in his arms, his hand over her stomach, and thanked the Goddess for sending her to find him and bring him home.

To Be Continued… Jag's Target

Read on for a sneak peak into the magic, new worlds, and epic love within the many series of S.E. Smith!

RIVER'S RUN

River Knight was looking forward to a peaceful vacation in the mountains with her two best friends, Jo and Star, sisters of the heart. When she travels up into the mountains of North Carolina to the cabin Star has rented for them, she is shocked when she finds the two sisters being abducted. Following them, she discovers their abductors are anything but human.

Sneaking aboard the shuttle in an attempt to rescue them, she finds herself on an unplanned vacation to the stars...

Chapter 1

"I'll be there. It might be late by the time I get there, but I'll be there, I promise," River said, sitting on the bed in the hotel she had just arrived at in California.

"Do you swear, River?" Star asked anxiously.

Star was twirling her shoulder-length blond hair around her finger and looking at her older sister, Jo. She had been trying to get through to River Knight for the past two days. It had been far too long since she had seen her best friend and surrogate sister.

"I swear, Star," River laughed. "And tell Jo she still owes me for the last time we got together."

Star grinned at Jo, giving her the thumbs-up sign. They had been trying to get the three of them together for the past year. Now, everything was set. They would finally see each other again.

∾

"She's coming!" Star said excitedly, wrapping her arms around Jo's neck and dancing around.

River let out a tired sigh, rolling her shoulders around to ease the tension. She had a lot to do in the next couple of days if she was going to meet up with her two best friends. She grinned.

They were really more like sisters to her. They were her only family now. She had grown up traveling with the circus and had met them when their parents had joined when she was five.

The Strauss Family Flyers were known for their high-wire acts. When Star and Jo's parents retired several years ago, it became the Strauss Flying Sisters. River's parents did just about everything from tightrope walking to the high wire to River's specialty, knife throwing. River had been born into the life of a circus performer just as Jo and Star had been.

They grew up moving from town to town, country to country, nomads in a modern world. The life had actually been very fulfilling. They were very well loved and protected. Their schooling consisted of learning a wide variety of languages as well as learning how to do all types of incredible tricks. They had more parents, grandparents, aunts, and uncles than any girls could ever imagine having. It had hurt when River's parents were killed in a hotel fire during one of their stops when she was seventeen, but her circus family had gathered around her and supported her.

Two years ago, Jo and Star decided they were tired of all the traveling and accepted jobs with Circus of the Stars in Florida. They bought a condo and loved the stability of living in one place. River continued traveling with the circus.

At almost twenty-two, she was the youngest of the three. The circus had just finished a tour in Asia, and she was glad to be home. The girls promised each other they would get together at least once a year.

Last year, Jo convinced River to meet them at their condo where Jo produced at least a dozen different guys for River to meet. River knew what they were up to. They thought if they could get her interested in someone, she would settle down. River still enjoyed traveling too much to put down roots. All the guys left her feeling awkward and clumsy, which was ridiculous when one considered she could hit moving targets with a series of knives while gliding through the air upside down held only by her ankles.

River just wasn't comfortable around the opposite sex. She always felt a little different. It might be her appearance. She looked more like an elf.

Oh, not one of Santa's—more like one from the Hobbit. She wasn't really tall at five foot six, but she was very willowy. She had thick dark brown hair that hung to her waist, pale skin, and huge dark-blue eyes outlined by thick dark lashes.

Most people thought she wore colored contacts when they first met her. She usually wore dark sunglasses when she was out because her eyes were so different. She didn't mind when she was performing —it helped with the mystique about her—but out in public she would often be stopped and stared at. Her parents used to tease her, saying she had been a gift from the stars, which she might have believed if her mom hadn't had the same unusual eyes.

River was glad they had decided to meet somewhere else this year. Star had picked out a cabin in the middle of nowhere. They were supposed to meet up in the mountains of North Carolina in two days. River was still in California so she had to make arrangements for a flight.

She called Ricki, who made all the travel plans for the circus, and within an hour she had all her flight arrangements done including her e-ticket and leased car. The joy about Ricki making the arrangements was River didn't have to worry about the usual restrictions for car rentals. Everything went through the company.

Pulling a big, black bag that resembled a duffel bag onto the bed, River opened it to look at her collection of knives carefully packed. She was very, very picky about her knives. They were her life, literally. She had been tossing, juggling, and throwing them since she could walk. Some of the acts her dad taught her had never been performed by anyone else in the world.

She was known as the best of the best when it came to anything involving a blade. While she made sure that everything had survived the shipping from Asia, River couldn't help but laugh at the memory of the reaction of customs officials on both sides of the ocean. Ricki had been there to take care of everything, thank God.

Now, River had the next three months off as the circus broke for a much needed rest. She would spend most of it at the cabin Star had rented, practicing new acts. Closing the bag, she finished packing her other belongings before getting ready for bed. She was so looking forward to the peace and quiet of the mountains.

Everything worked out well. She made the flight and for once she didn't have to produce documentation about her duffel bag. She had gone ahead and checked all her baggage so she wouldn't have to deal with it in the cabin of the plane for the long flight. After she plugged in her iPhone and placed her sunglasses firmly on her head, she was left blissfully alone for almost seven hours.

Picking up her two bags at the airport, she placed them in the trunk of the rented black SUV and began the three-hour drive up into the mountains. She wouldn't get there until after midnight. It was a warm evening, but she couldn't resist driving with the windows down. She loved the freedom of the wind blowing through the window.

She stopped for gas and a quick bite to eat an hour out as she didn't want Jo or Star to feel like they needed to cook for her so late. She couldn't suppress the thrill of seeing them.

She did miss them so much. No one could separate the three of them during their teenage years. River was two years younger than Star, who was a year younger than Jo. She had always been the one everyone protected the most.

There was a full moon, and the gravel road was lit up as River pulled up toward the cabin. The road for the past ten miles had been winding around and around the mountain. Star told her to park in the garage, which was located below the cabin. She would have to tote her stuff up a narrow path to the cabin.

River found the garage with no problems and pulled in next to Jo's SUV with Florida tags. River grinned when she read the bumper sticker saying "Flyers Do It Better." Grabbing her black duffel bag in one arm and her smaller carrier in her other, she quietly pushed the button to close the trunk. She bent down and pulled one of her smaller knives out of the bag to slide in her boot.

She didn't know what types of animals lived in the mountains, but if she was walking through the woods at night, she wanted at least one knife with her for protection. Moving out under the bright moon, she was glad she had worn her black jeans and put on her black sweater to ward off the cool mountain air. She would have glowed in any of her other jackets with their rhinestones.

Walking along the moonlit path up to the cabin, River was enjoying the peace and quiet until a scream ripped through the air, followed by a second one. River froze for a moment before she dropped her bags and took off at a run toward the cabin. She skidded to a halt behind a tree when she heard what appeared to be a growl. Reaching down to her boot, she pulled a knife from the sleeve hidden inside it.

Moving up toward the front porch, she jerked back when the door suddenly opened, and a huge figure moved out onto it. She crouched down so she wouldn't be seen. Peeking around the corner, her breath caught in her throat when she realized more than one huge creature was coming out of the cabin. She counted three of them; two of them appeared to be carrying something wrapped in blankets.

River shook with fear as she watched the huge creature turn at the bottom of the stairs. Its face, if you could call it that, was elongated and had what looked like scaly green skin. It turned and hissed at the other two. As they moved down the steps, River almost fainted when she saw Star's arm hanging limply down its back. The creatures started moving down another path on the far side of the cabin.

River slid the knife back in her boot and took off toward the path she had just come from. If she was going to try to save them, she needed more than the one knife in her boot. Sliding on the leaves, she grabbed her black duffel bag and took off running after the creatures. She didn't have any idea what she would do when she caught up with them.

River rounded the cabin cautiously before moving down the path on the other side of the cabin. She could hear them moving up ahead of her. She moved silently, keeping as close as she could to the trees so the shadows would help hide her. They moved at a lumbering pace, their long legs taking steps twice the length of hers.

She froze suddenly when one of them stopped and turned around. Keeping her head down so her face wouldn't be as visible, she held her breath. After what seemed like hours, the creature hissed at the one leading them and turned to move down the path again.

River followed them for almost two miles before they came to a clearing. She stood frozen behind a tree as she watched them move into what appeared to be some type of spaceship. It was almost as long as a football field. The two creatures carrying her friends moved up a platform that was opened in the back. River could see lights shining dimly in the interior. The one leading hissed at the other two as they moved up the ramp, but it remained outside the spaceship. A few minutes later, the two creatures returned. A loud noise off to the left side of the ship suddenly caught their attention. All three hissed and took off running toward the woods.

River shook with fear as she moved toward the spaceship, keeping an eye on the woods where the creatures had disappeared. She didn't know if there were any more in the spaceship or not, but she knew she needed to get to her friends and get them out. Pulling her duffel bag straps over her shoulders, she slowly climbed up the ramp, casting quick glances all around her.

Moving up the ramp, she saw a narrow corridor leading to a larger opening. Moving swiftly through the corridor she glanced around the interior of the spaceship. In front of her was another corridor that looked like it led to the front of the spaceship. On each side of her, there were a series of seats with what appeared to be storage compartments above and below them.

Chained to two of the seats were Jo and Star; both of them were unconscious. River moved toward them with a silent cry. She put her hands on their cheeks and gave a sigh of relief when she felt their warm breath against her palms.

"Jo, Star, wake up. Please, wake up," River called out softly.

She looked at their wrists and noticed they were both chained to a metal bar between the seats. She gripped their wrists to look for where the key went in to see if she could pick it. All three of them were good at picking locks. Marcus the Magnificent, the most famous magician in the world, had shown all three girls how to pick locks before they had learned how to ride a bike. She twisted the cuff on Jo's wrist around and around but didn't see where a key would fit into it. Jo gave a slight groan as River moved the cuff.

"Jo, wake up. It's me, River. Please wake up," River softly said again.

"River?" Jo whispered. Jo's eyes suddenly flew open in horror. "River, you have to run. Run, River. Don't let them get you." Her eyes flew back and forth as she struggled to free herself.

"I can't leave you and Star. We have to get out of here," River whispered back.

"There isn't time," Jo said as her eyes filled with tears. She looked at Star, who was still unconscious. "Oh, Star."

"Come on. You have to help me figure out how to get these off you before they come back," River whispered frantically. She pulled the knife from her boot and tried to pry at the metal.

"Where are we?" Jo asked weakly.

"It looks like some kind of spaceship," River replied softly. "The creatures that had you and Star carried you here. I don't know what they are. What happened?" River asked.

She was trying to keep Jo occupied while she worked on the cuff. There had to be some way to get it off them. If she had more time, she knew she could figure it out. There was always a way.

"I don't know. We were waiting up for you. I heard a noise and thought you might need some help, but when I opened the door to the cabin, it was to those creatures. I screamed and tried to close the door, but it just ripped it right off the hinges. Star ran for the bedroom, but one of them caught her and she fainted. I don't remember much after that. They put something across my mouth and everything went dark," Jo whispered hoarsely. She began shivering uncontrollably.

"They're coming back! I can hear them. Run, River. Run!" Jo began crying softly now.

"Never. I won't leave you," River said, sliding her knife back into her boot.

Looking around, she dropped down to pull open one of the compartments under the seats. It was filled with boxes of some type. Moving down the row, she hurriedly opened and closed them until she found one in the corner that was empty. Removing her duffel bag, she slid down feet first into the compartment, pulling her duffel bag in front of her, then reached over and closed the compartment.

Jo stared at River before nodding. River would not abandon them, ever. Closing her eyes, Jo let the darkness of unconsciousness take her away from the fearful creatures boarding the spaceship.

Chapter 2

River looked out the front of the spaceship she had stowed away on for what seemed like the millionth time. It turned out the spaceship the creatures used on Earth was just a shuttle to a much, much larger ship. Once they docked with the larger ship, the creatures carried Jo and Star out. River remained in hiding until she felt sure all the creatures had left the shuttle. Now, she moved about the empty shuttle, trying to get familiar with what she had gotten herself into and waiting for the shuttle area to clear out a little.

Peeking out the front view panel, River watched as about ten of the creatures moved containers about. She watched as the one creature who she suspected was the leader of the shuttle crew who had taken Jo and Star argued with another one who was almost twice as big as it was.

The bigger creature hissed loudly and pointed at Jo's and Star's unconscious bodies wrapped tightly in the blankets. The smaller creature hissed something back, then flinched when the other one roared. The other two creatures took a step back and looked like they would have preferred to have been anywhere but there. Finally the huge creature hissed something at the two holding River's friends, and they followed him. The other creature just hissed and left the shuttle bay by another exit.

River knew she needed to find a way around the ship without being seen. These creatures were huge compared to her, Star, and Jo. Looking up, she noticed a series of platforms leading to the ventilation system. If she could get to it unseen, she could move through the vents. The creatures were too large to fit in them. Besides, wasn't that what they did in the movies? If she could stay with them, she could find her friends and they could hide out until they figured out a way to get off the ship.

Satisfied with her plan, she just needed to wait until things calmed down a little. In the meantime, she explored the shuttle for any type of food or drinks and a restroom. Finding a box with what appeared to be emergency rations, she stuffed as much as she felt she could safely carry into her duffel bag. She needed to get ready in case she needed to defend herself.

Opening her duffel bag, she pulled out some of the harnesses she used to carry her knives during her performances. She pulled her sweater off, placing it in the duffel bag. She might need it later but not while she was climbing.

Pulling on a tight, long-sleeved, form fitting black spandex shirt, she strapped on two of her leather wrist holders which contained seven small knives in each holder. Next, she grabbed her back and chest holder. It crisscrossed her front and back and allowed her to put all types of knives and throwing stars in it, including two small swords which fit in an X-formation on her back. Pulling on her belt, she put additional small throwing stars in it. She used this belt when she was riding bareback and throwing them at candles lit around the ring. She had maybe twenty-five very sharp throwing stars in it.

Lastly, she pulled out several of her favorite throwing knives and placed them in the inserts she had in her leather boots. Closing the duffel bag, she pulled the straps tight so she could run faster if she needed to.

River waited almost two hours before the shuttle area had become deathly quiet. She watched as the last creature left the area, and the lights dimmed. Moving toward the opened ramp which had been left down after their arrival, River stayed as low as possible, moving slowly so she could listen for any noises.

Grabbing the side of the ramp, she flipped under it so she was covered. Peering out, she moved swiftly when she felt confident she was safe toward the nearest stack of cargo boxes, slipping between two of them. She followed the tight corridor between the crates until she was in the shadows under the catwalks leading up to the ventilation system.

River turned and grabbed the piping and began climbing. She hoped there was no video surveillance of the area. If so, she should have had company already.

Rolling over the catwalk, she took the stairs up to the highest level before grabbing hold of the piping and climbing it up to the vent. It was small, but she wouldn't have any problems sliding through it. They didn't even have a grill over it. Holding on to the pipe with both hands, she stretched her legs out until she could slide them in, then pushed off, letting the rest of her body follow. She moved back about ten feet into the vent before she leaned back and took a deep breath to calm her shaking body. She had never been so scared in all her life. The only thing keeping her going was the knowledge Jo and Star had to be even more scared than she was.

River crawled until she reached an intersection in the vent. Here it was high enough, she could actually stand up straight. She guessed whoever built it was a lot smaller than the creatures on it now.

They would have a hard time crawling as each one of them had to be over eight and a half feet tall and almost as wide. Moving to the left, which she hoped was the direction the creatures had headed when they took Jo and Star, she followed the ventilation system for hours, marking sections as she came to them with a permanent marker. Luckily she had always been good with directions, probably because she had traveled so much her whole life. It almost reminded her of the passageways under Paris, she, Star, and Jo had explored one summer.

River almost cried out with relief when she saw a schematic of the ship attached to one intersection. Pulling out one of her knives, she pried it off the wall. Sinking down, she looked over the map. It looked like there was some type of holding cells two levels up.

If she followed the ventilation system another hundred feet to the left, there should be a vent leading up to the next level. She needed to do this again at the next level to get to the one she wanted. Sliding the stiff map into her shirt, she moved off to the left.

Sure enough, she came to a vent that went straight up. It was narrow, but it had what looked like foot holds. Grabbing hold of the first rung, River began climbing.

River spent the better part of the next three hours moving through the ventilation system. She had made it to the level with the holding cells. It had taken her longer to climb up to them than she expected. They were much further apart than she expected. Once she had made it to the level she wanted, she had paused to rest and get something to drink.

At first she was leery of what was in the bottle, but on smelling it and then finally taking a sip, she was relieved to find it was water. She drank half the bottle before realizing she needed to conserve what she had. Closing her eyes, River felt the fatigue take over her body.

She needed to rest before she moved any further. She had been up for over seventy-two hours between arriving back in the States and her long flight and drive. Then there had been the wait in the shuttle until everyone had left.

Leaning her head back against the cold metal, River felt a shiver run through her body. She had no idea how they were ever going to get home. No one would even begin looking for them for at least three months when they didn't return from the mountain. By then, who knew where they would be.

Shaking off the depressing thoughts, River focused on finding her friends first. She had to make sure they were safe. Her last thought as her body shut down was that she would worry about the rest later.

River woke disoriented. She hadn't meant to fall asleep. Taking a drink, she rubbed her eyes, trying to get them to focus. She wasn't far from the first row of cells. She figured she would leave her duffel bag here and check out each cell through the vent until she hopefully found Jo and Star. Shrugging the bag off her back, she checked to make sure all her knives were securely fastened so she didn't make any noise.

Standing up, she moved to the first cell. Peering through, she saw it was empty. Moving to the next one, she found the same. On her third cell she saw a familiar pink-and-white comforter lying across what looked like some type of bed. Peeking around the room, River waited a good five minutes, listening.

"Jo, I'm scared," Star whispered. "Do you think they are going to hurt us?"

"I don't know, baby," Jo replied softly. "I hope not."

"Psst. Jo, Star," River called out softly.

"River?" Star whispered excitedly.

River pulled the vent grill up. Man, whoever designed these cells must have been thinking whatever was going to be in them would be too big to fit through the opening. It was a perfect fit for River's, Jo's, and Star's petite figures.

"You alone?" River asked quietly.

"Yes. They only come by once a day. They bring us something to eat and drink, then don't come back again until the same time the next day," Jo replied.

River was surprised. She didn't realize they had already been in here that long. She had fallen asleep earlier in the ventilation system, but hadn't thought so much time had passed. She felt guilty at having slept so long.

"When will they be back?" River asked huskily.

"Not for another eight hours by my calculations," Jo said.

River laughed softly. Jo was always the level-headed one of the three of them. River slowly lowered herself through the vent opening and dropped lightly to her feet. Star rushed off the bed and wrapped her arms around River tightly.

"Oh River, you shouldn't be here," Star cried softly.

"Oh? And where else do you think I should be?" River teased softly, pushing Star's hair back. "Whatever adventure we go on, we go together," River said softly, repeating a mantra they had said since they had become friends.

Jo smiled through her tears. "Yeah, but even we aren't stupid enough to have invited you on this one."

"Well, I wouldn't want to be anywhere else without you," River said. "Now, we need to think about how we are going to get out of here and back home."

"What do you suggest? If we are on a spaceship, and I have to believe we are, God only knows where we are. Even if we were able to get off, where would we go? It's not like any of us know how to fly one of these things," Jo said sadly, sinking down onto the bed.

"Can you understand anything the creatures are saying?" River asked, trying to think of ways to get the girls in a fighting-back mood. Usually it was Jo who was the one shaking everyone up out of the doldrums. This was a new experience for River.

"Yes. They gave us some type of translator to wear," Star said, pulling her hair back to reveal a device that looked almost like a small hearing aid.

"I need one. I've been scouting the ship. If worse comes to worst, we can disappear into the ventilation system until we can figure out a way to get off this boat," River said, holding out her hand.

Star handed her translator to River. "What should I tell them when they discover it missing?"

"Tell them it fell in the toilet," River grinned. "I bet they've dropped stuff down it before."

Jo laughed. "You are so bad." Sighing, she couldn't help but admit, "I'm glad you're here, River."

River smiled softly. "Me, too. If I am going to be hanging out here some, I need to use your bathroom. I left my duffel bag up in the vents a few cells down. I figured I could spend part of the day with you and the other part doing reconnaissance. I need you two to stay here just in case someone decides to put in a surprise visit. I'll leave you some of my knives just in case you need them. Whatever happens, don't be afraid to use them," River added seriously.

Jo and Star nodded as they took the knives River handed them from her boots. They knew this was for real, and they wouldn't get a second chance if they hesitated. River used the bathroom to freshen up and refilled her water bottle.

The three of them talked for the next few hours planning different strategies. River had Jo copy the map she had of the ship, and they made plans on where to meet if they had to disappear into the ventilation system. They had three places they set where they would meet if they should get separated from each other.

Jo insisted River get a couple hours sleep, and she would wake her an hour before their next scheduled visit from their captors, so she could hide. River was going to stay close to make sure the translator worked before she would explore more.

Over the next two weeks, they did the same routine. River began having Jo and Star explore the vents to get familiar with the ship while she stayed with one or the other. They figured she could cover up with the bedspread and act like she was sleeping if the creatures came back early.

So far, they had been left alone. It wasn't until the beginning of their third week of captivity that they knew something major was happening. The ship jerked and shuddered, tossing them to the floor as the lights in the cell dimmed.

"What's happening?" Star asked, frightened. She gripped the edge of the bed trying to keep from falling again.

"I don't know. I'm going to go check it out," River said. "Give me a boost."

Jo and Star stood and cupped their hands, giving River a boost through the vent. River closed the vent grill before whispering, "I'll be back shortly."

The sisters nodded as they staggered under another shudder. The ship moaned, then everything seemed to become deathly quiet. Moving over, they sat on the edge of the bed, holding on to each other as they waited for River to return.

Chapter 3

River moved swiftly through the vents. She was a pro at navigating her way through them now. She had even pack-ratted items she thought might come in handy. She had food and water stored throughout the ship. She had found a storeroom filled with weapons.

She had taken as much as she thought she could get away with and hidden them in strategic places as well. Her biggest find had been what looked like explosives. She figured they could always find a good use for those. Moving down, she followed a group of creatures running toward the shuttle bay. They seemed to be very excited about something.

Running, she made the quick climb down the vents until she came to the vent she had originally slipped into almost three weeks before. Staying to the shadows, she moved quietly out onto the catwalk using the pipes to move around. There was a large square duct hanging down she could hide behind, but be close enough to hear what was going on as she would be almost directly above them. Crossing the thick metal beam, she made her way across and hid behind it just as the huge creature that obviously was in charge stormed into the shuttle bay with almost twenty armed men following him.

Another ten men stood surrounding a shuttle with their weapons drawn. A small explosion caused the platform at the back of the shuttle to open. The men rushed in.

A few minutes later they came out, followed by a group of almost a dozen men. River caught her breath at her first look at the men. They were much different than the creatures that had captured Jo and Star. They were tall, about six and a half feet, but had long, black hair pulled back at their necks.

They were all dressed in leather pants and had on different colored shirts except for the one in the front who was older and wore some type of formal cloak. They were so handsome, River would have to call them almost beautiful.

They appeared almost human in form. She couldn't tell what it was about them from this distance, but she knew there was something different about them. Maybe it was their builds, which were very muscular, or the way they carried themselves, but something was different.

River watched as the huge creature named Trolis walked up to the man in the long cloak and hissed at him.

"So, *Krail* Taurus, we meet again. This time there will be no peace negotiations," the huge creature hissed.

"Trolis, you have broken the treaty signed by your people by attacking an Alliance vessel on a diplomatic mission," *Krail* Taurus replied calmly. "This will be seen as an act of war."

Trolis grinned nastily before replying, "No, *this* will be seen as an act of war."

Before anyone knew what Trolis planned, he swung a double-edge sword and sliced the older man across his neck, severing his head clean off his shoulders. The other men roared with rage and moved to attack. Suddenly, the ten men surrounding them opened fire and all the men dropped to the floor.

River shoved her fist into her mouth to keep from crying out. Silent tears coursed down her cheeks as she watched all the men drop. She almost fell from her hiding place when she heard Trolis tell the men to drag the men to the holding cells.

They aren't dead, just unconscious! She thought with relief.

She waited to hear what else Trolis had to say. She needed to know what he planned on doing to the other men. If he planned on killing them, she was going to have to tell Jo and Star they were moving up their attack on the creatures.

"Commander Trolis, what do you want us to do with the others?" one of the creatures hissed out.

Trolis swung his large head back and forth. "Two of the men are part of the royal family. I think a demonstration of who is in charge is necessary. Strap them to walls. Take the younger one with the red shirt and secure him to the center of cell block eight. I want the others to watch as he is gutted. I have plans for his older brother to suffer."

"Yes, commander," hissed the creature.

Trolis called out to two other creatures, "Clean up this mess."

River watched as Trolis walked out of the shuttle bay. She moved back along the metal beam, climbed back into the vent, and took off at a run. She had to let Jo and Star know about what happened and get to cell block eight before they had a chance to kill anyone else. She didn't know why, but she knew those men were their only hope of finding their way off this ship and back home. They had to free them.

River's Run

DUST

Dust wakes to discover the world as he knew it is gone after fragments of a comet hit the Earth. It isn't the only thing that has changed, though, so has Dust. He now possesses powers that continue to grow, but also come with a price. A deadly encounter after he leaves his home leads to a new discovery – other survivors.

Dust soon learns that another creature has risen from the ashes, one that is determined to possess the powers that he has. On a journey filled with danger, it will take the skills of not just Dust, but those of his friends, if they are to survive.

This time the race is not for the swiftest, but the deadliest in a world where a changed human boy and an odd assortment of friends must face their worst nightmares, and accept that life on Earth will never be the same again.

Join Dust and his friends as they fight to overcome an evil force determined to create a new species unlike anything the world has ever known.

Chapter 1
Before and After

Dust woke from his sleep, blinking up at the dark gray skies. He could see the swirl of acidic clouds through the hole in the ceiling. It took a moment for his body to catch up with his mind.

He often forgot to focus on it. Since the morning he woke up alone in a collapsed building that had once been his home, he realized that things would never be the same. Before, he was just a fourteen year old boy who loved playing video games and hated going to school. A year had passed since the day the comet hit the Earth. A year since the strange cloud had washed through the small town where he had lived *Before*. That is what he called his life... Before. Now, he was in the After.

His body wrenched as it came back to its solid form. He was used to the feeling now and thought no more about his unusual ability to dissolve into the shadows. Rising up off the floor, he stretched and twisted. Glancing around, he walked over to the bent metal cabinet where he had hidden his knapsack. It contained one pair of jeans, one shirt, a clean pair of underwear and socks, and a bottle of water.

With a wave of his hand, the debris in front of the cabinet rose up into the air and moved. He opened the door and pulled out the dark green knapsack he had found in one of his many excursions over the past year. Slinging the strap over his shoulder, he turned and quietly left the building.

Dust paused on the sidewalk outside the small convenience store where he had taken refuge. His disheveled brown hair stuck out in all directions. Glancing around, his dark brown eyes paused on a moving shadow between two abandoned cars halfway down the street. The sense of danger rose in his gut. His gaze narrowed on the three shadowy forms that slowly stepped out from between them.

Devil dogs.

He didn't know if that was what they were really called, but that was the name he had given them. They were like him... different.

Turning, he slipped the straps over his shoulders so he could run faster. It was time to move on. Where there were three of the creatures, there could be more. Dust felt the adrenaline surge through him as he took off at a steady pace, glancing back and forth as he ran through the center of the small town he had arrived in late the night before. He had hoped to find food. The changes to his body demanded that he eat more often.

Food wasn't always the easiest thing to find. The lack of it was what had finally forced him to leave the small town where he had lived with his family during the time Before. As the sole survivor, he had foraged for every piece of food he could find during the past year until he could find no more.

Dust didn't bother turning to see where the creatures were. He knew they would follow him. They were hungry. He knew, because he felt the same hunger. There would be a fight, of that he had no doubt. Up ahead was the shell of a two-story building. With a wave of his hand, the door was ripped off its hinges and it flew out behind him. He heard a snarl and a thud. They were closer than he'd realized.

Sprinting across the sidewalk, he disappeared into the shadows and allowed his body to dissolve. It would be difficult to keep his shadow form for long. He desperately needed food if he was going to continue using the amount of energy that he needed to maintain this form. Scooping up a metal pipe as he flew by, he turned just as the first shape came through the door behind him. The end of the pipe caught the creature in the chest, impaling it and driving him back against the wall. His body solidified at the force and the wind was knocked from him as he slammed into the wall.

The creature's glowing red eyes flashed and its jaws snapped, but he could already see the light fading. He immediately recognized that the creatures must be starving to attack him so boldly. Not only that, they couldn't hold their shadow form any longer than he could. He pressed the metal rod down to the floor and forced the metal tip further through the beast and twisted it. The creature's loud snarls turned to a scream before silence engulfed the room. Dust didn't wait. There were at least two left, possibly more.

Ripping the pipe out of the creature, he turned toward the open stairwell. The faint sound of glass crunching under heavy feet pulled his gaze to the ceiling. He could hear one of them. It must have gone through an upper level window. Dust's jaw tightened. He would have to kill all of them or the creatures would follow him and he would never find food or rest. His fingers wrapped around the cool metal and he started up the steps, taking them in a slow, steady climb. He was almost to the top when the huge black creature appeared at the top of the stairs.

Dust glanced over his shoulder when he heard a second snarl behind him. He was stuck between the two beasts. Glancing back and forth, he realized that they had set up a trap for him. A shiver ran through him. He started when the one above him suddenly jumped. Focusing, he used more of his precious energy. The creature flashed through his body, sending a wave of nausea through him. His body once more solidified and he thrust upward, pushing the rod through its soft underbelly while it was still in the air. He allowed the weight of the creature to twist him around. The force of the movement and his gradually weakening strength tore the metal pipe from his hands as it crashed into the beast moving up the stairs at the same time.

Stumbling back against the wall, he watched as the dying creature struck its companion. He gripped the stairwell and pulled himself up. He needed to find another weapon before the last beast regained its footing. His legs shook as he half crawled, half climbed the stairs. He barely had time to roll to the side before the third creature came up through the narrow opening and turned. Dust rolled to his stomach, his gaze froze on the heaving chest and foaming jaws. His arms trembled and he knew he didn't have the strength to dissolve.

He pushed upward in a slow, steady movement, never taking his eyes off the beast. He was almost to his feet when it sprang. Jumping, he twisted to the side and rolled. Almost immediately he was back on his feet and twisting around. The beast had slid into a large wooden desk. The force of its body hitting the desk shattered one of the legs and the heavy piece of furniture collapsed on top of it. He took advantage of the reprieve, darting down the staircase. He jumped over the dead creature at the bottom, tearing out the metal pipe protruding from its chest. Running, he burst back outside.

A loud crash resounded behind him. Dust didn't pause. Spying an abandoned SUV with its door partially open across the street, he pushed every ounce of energy he had left inside him to his quivering legs. He reached out and grabbed the door handle, pulling it open far enough to squeeze through. He barely had time to pull it closed before the beast hit the door with enough force to knock the SUV onto two wheels. The force of the blow knocked Dust across the console and into the passenger seat. He quickly pulled his legs up when the glass on the driver's door shattered.

Dust fumbled for the handle behind him as the beast thrust its long black head inside, its jaws snapping viciously at his legs. Blood dripped on the fine leather interior from where the ragged glass cut into the beast's neck. That didn't stop it. If anything, the creature became more enraged, clawing at the glass and pulling it away so it could try to wiggle into the vehicle. Dust kicked out, striking the canine-like snout. It jerked its head back, giving him just enough room to grab the door handle. He fell out the other side, landing heavily on his back. Kicking his foot out again, he slammed the door just as the creature jumped into the driver's seat.

Rolling stiffly onto his hands and knees, he gripped the metal rod in his hand and rose to his feet. Glancing back at the snarling beast, he took off running. It was only a matter of seconds before he heard the sound of breaking glass again. Ducking under a torn awning, he darted through the open door of another building. It didn't take long for him to realize his mistake. The back section of the building was blocked by fallen debris. The only thing separating him from death was a tall refrigerated display case and the metal pipe in his hand. Turning, he backed up as the dark shadow paused in the entrance.

"Don't move until I tell you," a soft voice said behind him.

Chapter 2
Someone Else Lives

Dust froze, his eyes locked on the blazing red eyes of the devil dog even as he wanted to turn to the sound of the voice. It was the first voice other than his own that he'd heard in over a year. Afraid he was dreaming, he stood ready, holding the bloody pipe in front of him.

The beast took another step and snarled. White foam dripped from its mouth and its yellow teeth snapped as it moved through the doorway. Dust knew it was about to attack. The sound of the voice yelling for him to move echoed through the air at the same time as a thin shaft flew past his right shoulder.

He jumped to the side, sliding under a table that was bolted to the floor. His back hit the wall and he jerked his legs out of the way as the beast's thick, black body slid across the few feet of cleared space on the dirty tile. He stared in shock at the two thick shafts of wood sticking out of its throat and upper chest. The beast's red eyes were blank and its jaw hung open as it pulled in its last breath of air.

Dust slowly scooted out from under the table, keeping his eyes on the creature just in case. He was rising to his feet when a movement behind the counter caught his attention. Turning, he held the dark gray pipe out in front of him. Two figures, one slightly taller than the other rose from behind an old display. Swallowing, Dust stared at the two dirty faces looking back at him with a combination of curiosity and fear. It took a moment for him to realize that the tall person was pointing one of the long arrows at him.

Dust waited, staring at the girl. He saw her swallow, but she didn't lower the bow in her hands. The small boy next to her scooted slightly behind her when Dust glanced at him. His gaze returned to the girl's face. He curled his fingers into a tight fist as a wave of dizziness washed through him. The hunger was beginning to become unbearable. He needed something to eat.

"Who are you?" Dust asked in a rusty voice, his eyes locked on the face of the young girl who seemed to be close to his own age.

Dust swayed as he waited for the girl to respond. He saw her swallow again and nervously bite her bottom lip. She still didn't lower the bow in her hands, even though he had dropped the pipe to his side. The small boy next to her stared back at Dust with a wide-eyed, curious expression. Dust kept his gaze fixed on the girl's face.

"Who are you?" The girl suddenly demanded, staring at him through narrow eyes.

Dust flexed the fingers of his right hand, trying to stay focused. "Dust," he said in a low, hoarse voice.

"Sammy, he don't look so good," the boy whispered, tugging on her shirt.

"What's wrong with you?" Sammy asked in a tight voice.

"Food," Dust whispered, uncurling the fingers of his left hand and letting the pipe drop to the floor with a loud thump. He felt his legs begin to shake so much that he couldn't hold himself up. "I need food."

The girl lowered the bow when his knees gave out on him and he sank to the floor. His head fell forward and he drew in a deep breath before gagging when the stench of the dead devil dog poured through his nose. Shaking his head, he closed his eyes and shakily lifted his arm to cover his nose.

"We need to get out of here," the girl said in a soft voice, stepping around the edge of the display case. "Todd, get me one of the bars."

"But, Sammy," Todd protested. "We don't have but three left."

Sammy frowned at the small boy that appeared to be around seven years old. "Now we have two," she stated, holding out her hand. "Get me one of them."

Dust didn't bother opening his eyes. He was afraid if he did that the two of them would disappear. Instead, he rested his cheek against his bent arm.

"Here," Sammy said. "Eat this, but do it slow so you don't get sick."

Dust lifted his head and opened his eyes. Sammy was holding out a small fruit bar. His mouth watered and he reached shakily for it. Their fingers touched for a brief moment and he almost jerked back. He could tell she was just as surprised as he was at the contact. Taking the small bar of food from her hand, he nodded his thanks before lifting it to his mouth and taking a bite.

All too soon, it was gone. His eyes closed again for a moment as he felt a surge of energy. It wouldn't last long, but it was enough to keep him going. His eyes popped open when he felt the tentative touch on his arm again.

"We really need to get going," Sammy said, rising to her feet and holding her hand out. "I don't know how many more of those creatures there are. I counted four earlier."

Dust nodded, reaching up and gripping her hand. He rose clumsily to his feet before bending down and picking up the bloody metal pipe. Testing it, he glanced at Sammy and Todd.

"I killed two of them. That makes three," he muttered, staring out the doorway. "I need more food."

"There's a small grocery store at the end of the street," Sammy said, uneasily. "That's where we were headed when we saw those things and hid in here. It's just a few doors down."

Dust lifted his arm, stopping Sammy when she started to walk around him. His gaze flickered from her to Todd and back again. If there was still another one of those creatures out there, he would go first.

"I'll go first, you follow," he said in a rough voice. "Keep the kid between us."

"I know how to take care of us," Sammy muttered, glancing at Todd. "Hand me the backpack, Todd."

"I've got it, Sammy," Todd mumbled. "You need your hands free."

Dust felt a tug of emotion when Sammy smiled tenderly down at the boy. For a moment, he felt a wave of envy. There were times in the past year that he would have given anything to have someone to talk to. He drew in a deep breath. Now wasn't the time to think of the past. He needed to find more food before the little bit of strength he had deserted him.

Grabbing a hold of the door frame, he glanced outside. His gaze carefully moved down along the street in both directions before pausing on the building across the street. If there were only four of the devil dogs, then they should be okay. He could kill the other one. He glanced over his shoulder and jerked his head to Sammy and Todd. Stepping outside, he walked slowly down the sidewalk along the buildings, pausing every once in a while to search the shadows.

A sigh of relief poured through Dust when he saw the sign for the small grocery store hanging at an odd angle. He really hoped there was still some food inside. His steps increased as they drew nearer. He was passing a small barber shop when a movement inside caught his attention. The shadowy form exploded through the plate glass window just as he turned.

The devil dog's snapping jaws barely missed his throat as it hit him in the chest. The only thing that saved him was the metal pipe he had raised and gripped between both of his hands. A grunt of pain escaped him when the creature's sharp claws sliced through his thin shirt and across his chest. Twisting, he tripped on the edge of the curb and landed heavily on his back in the road.

Dust jerked his head back when the beast lunged again for his neck. His arms strained to keep it back, but its front and back legs were cutting through his clothing. A hoarse yell escaped him when the beast suddenly yelped and rolled away from him. He turned onto his side, staring at it as it wobbled for a moment before it turned and half ran, half limped away, the shaft of one of Sammy's arrows sticking out of its front shoulder.

"You're bleeding," Sammy said, kneeling down beside him. "Did it bite you?"

Dust shook his head and grimaced as the pain from the numerous cuts flashed through him. "No, just scratches," he muttered, leaning on the pipe as Sammy slid her arm around his waist.

"I'll lead," she said, turning to Todd. "You help him."

Todd just nodded. His eyes were wide with fear. He stepped forward and stood next to Dust.

"What if there's more?" Todd whispered, glancing back at where the devil dog had disappeared between two buildings.

"Then we'll deal with them," Sammy said, fitting her last arrow into the bow. "I need to either get the arrows I shot or find more."

"I need food first," Dust muttered, beginning to droop again. "Food, then we'll look."

"Hopefully there are some medical supplies there as well," Sammy said with a worried glance at the blood coating the front of Dust's shredded shirt. "Let's go."

Dust just nodded. Once he had food in his system, it wouldn't take long for his skin to heal. It was one of the things he had learned after he had awoken from the change. Gritting his teeth against the pain, he leaned against Todd so he wouldn't fall flat on his face again. They stepped back up onto the sidewalk and continued the few feet to the entrance of the store.

The large front window and the glass in the front doors were shattered. Sammy lowered her bow and peered through the opening before reaching over and tugging the door open. The loud screeching sound of metal hitting the glass as it pushed against the concrete drew a wince from all of them. Sammy glanced back at Todd and Dust before squaring her shoulders and stepping through into the dark interior.

Chapter 3
The Search For Food

She and Todd hadn't known what was going on that day almost a year ago. Her dad had been at work and her mom had driven into town for a doctor's appointment. She had been watching Todd when the weather alert went off. At first, she thought it was a mistake because the skies had been a crystal clear blue, but the alert said that it wasn't and that emergency precautions needed to be made. She had dragged Todd down into the storm cellar buried out behind the house.

They were almost there when they saw the huge, dark cloud rolling toward them. Sammy had never seen anything like it. Frightened, she had ordered Todd to get down behind the boxes in the back as she slammed the door shut and locked it. Seconds later, the light on the inside had gone out and the entire shelter had shaken so hard that Sammy had been thrown to the floor.

The aftershocks continued for days and the sound of dirt and rocks hitting the door had lasted even longer. For a while, Sammy had actually feared that they might get buried under the onslaught. When it finally stopped, they had waited... and waited... and waited for either their mom or dad to come tell them that it was safe to come out. Sammy had used the flashlights stored in the shelter sparingly. Fortunately, the growing season had just ended and the huge collection of canned goods she and her mom had processed and stored for selling remained protected from the fallout.

A week had gone by before Sammy finally worked at forcing the door to the shelter open. The land around the house was barren, stripped clear by the blast. Only the shell of their house and the barn remained. She and Todd had searched the area, but they seemed to be the only ones left alive. Remembering her father's warning that if there was ever an emergency to stay put until someone came for them, Sammy salvaged what she could from the ruins of the house and returned to the storm shelter.

They had waited for someone to come, but no one ever did. When the food started to get low, she and Todd began venturing to neighboring farms in the hope they would find someone. They discovered the occasional can of food, but never another living human soul.

The first strange creature they discovered had been small. She and Todd were on their way back to the shelter from a neighboring farm. They had stopped at a narrow bridge over a dried creek to rest. The thing had come up from under the bridge and grabbed Todd's pant leg. She used a long walking stick that she had found and beat the thing to death. They had run back to the shelter and hidden for two days.

It had taken her a while to finally understand that the thing had been some type of mutated animal. That was when she searched the barn for her dad's old bow and arrows that he used when he went hunting. She spent hour after hour each day practicing until she was confident she could protect herself and Todd if need be. Two months later, their food was dangerously low and she knew they had no choice but to leave the shelter and search for some – and more survivors.

"I see food," she said, shaking away the memories as she stepped through the doorway. "It looks like the creatures didn't get all of it, only the stuff they could reach and open."

"I... I just need something... anything... for now," Dust muttered in a voice filled with pain.

Sammy glanced at the bent shelf that was closer to her. There were cans of green beans on it. It would have to do. Gripping the bow in her right hand, she walked over to the shelf and grabbed a can. She turned and wove her way along the row of cash registers, searching for something to open the can with, when she saw a can opener hanging from the tab along with other items. Grabbing it, she quickly removed the top of the can before turning to walk over to where Dust was sinking down next to a pile of shredded candy wrappers. She held the can of green beans out to him.

"Be careful, the edge is sharp," she said. "I'll go look for some medical supplies. Todd, you start picking up as many cans of food as you can and stack them near Dust. We'll figure out what to do with them once we have an idea of how much there is."

"Okay," Todd said, sliding the backpack off his thin shoulders.

Sammy glanced one last time toward Dust where he sat frantically eating the green beans, liquid and all. Her gaze flashed over his chest. She'd have to see if there were any clothes along with the medical supplies. She reached down next to him and picked up one of the handheld shopping baskets before turning to walk away.

She glanced up at the signs above each aisle. Number ten held cosmetics and bandages. She carefully walked down the center aisle, pausing to glance down each row as she went. It looked like most of the items had been either knocked off the shelves or crushed.

Turning down aisle number ten, she quickly grabbed everything she could off the shelves. Once the basket was filled, she released a frustrated groan. She would need to get more baskets. Food and medical supplies were essential. How they would carry everything, she didn't know, but for now, she wasn't going to worry about it. Remembering the blood covering Dust, she turned and hurried back down the aisle to where she had left him.

"I found some...," Sammy's voice died when she saw the four empty cans of green beans next to Dust. That wasn't what froze the words in her throat. "What happened...? How did...? What are you?" she asked in a trembling voice, staring at his chest.

Sammy's fingers instinctively searched for the bow she always carried. A curse swept through her mind when she remembered that she had set it down to gather the medical supplies. Swallowing, she dropped the basket in her hand and took a step back as Dust rose to his feet. Her eyes remained glued to his chest. There was dried blood on his skin where the devil dog had clawed him. The front of his shredded T-shirt was proof that she hadn't imagined the attack a short while ago. Only now, instead of ripped flesh there was smooth, unmarred skin.

"I don't know," Dust replied, staring back at her with an intense expression on his face. "But, I know that I won't hurt you or Todd."

Sammy shook her head, her eyes flashing from his face to his chest. She bit her lip, trying to decide if she should scream for Todd to run or stand her ground. Her gaze flickered to the front door. If they ran, how far could they get? That thing was still out there and they needed food. She was also out of arrows. In here... There was food, medicine, and... Dust. Swallowing, she locked gazes with Dust again. Could she trust him? That was the real question.

Chapter 4
What Is He?

Dust stared at the two figures walking ahead of him. He glanced down and kicked at a stone in the road when Sammy looked over her shoulder at him again. A small smile tugged at the corner of his mouth. She had been glaring at him for the past two hours. At first, she had backed away from him. When it became obvious that he wasn't going to attack her and Todd, she had tried ignoring him. They had worked quietly, gathering as much food as they could and placing it in stacks.

He found some more shirts on one of the aisles and quickly changed out of his torn and bloody one. He had also snacked on anything he could find and felt better than he had in ages. He paused when she stopped to stare inside one of the small cars left in the middle of the road. Curious, she opened the door and slid into the driver's seat. He jumped when he heard the clicking of the engine. His expression softened when Sammy leaned her forehead against the steering wheel.

"Pop the hood," he called out.

Sammy slowly lifted her head and stared at him in silence before she bent down and pulled the lever. Dust stepped forward and felt under the hood until he found the latch. Pulling it, he lifted the hood and pulled the thin bar down to hold it up. He glanced around the engine, looking for anything obvious.

"Can you fix it?" Todd asked, coming up to stand next to Dust.

"Maybe," Dust replied, touching some of the wires and hoses, before checking the battery. "Does it have any gas?"

Sammy stepped up to look up under the hood. "I don't know," she said with a shrug. "The battery is dead."

Dust grinned. "I might be able to help with that," he commented, looking around. "Wait here."

～

"Where else are we going to go?" Sammy muttered under her breath as she turned to watch him jog across the street. "Shit!"

"Sammy!" Todd exclaimed, watching Dust with wide eyes.

"Sorry," she muttered, staring at the spot where Dust had just disappeared – literally. "He just went through that door without opening it!"

"I know," Todd whispered in awe. "I wish I could do that!"

Sammy didn't say anything. Instead, she watched as the door opened this time and Dust walked out. He had disappeared inside what looked like a discount auto store. He had several things in a dark red basket. He stopped in front of the car and set the basket down before rubbing his hands nervously down the front of his pants.

"I used to help my dad in his shop," Dust admitted. "It may take a little while, but all we've got is time, right?" he joked, looking at Sammy with a slightly pleading look.

"Why are you doing this?" Sammy asked, swallowing over the lump in her throat. "What happened to you?"

Dust bent his head and shook it. "I don't want you to go without me," he said softly. Clearing his throat, he bent and picked up the tools he had picked out and set them on the edge of the radiator. "You two are the first humans I've seen in over a year. The only other thing I've seen are a few animals and...."

"And?" Sammy asked, motioning for Todd to take the pack in her hands. "Can you put this in the car?"

"Okay. Can I help you, Dust?" Todd asked with a hopeful smile.

Dust nodded. "Sure," he said. "Can you make sure everything is cleaned out as much as possible so we can load the car up when we get it going?"

Todd's face fell, but he nodded his head and kicked at a loose rock. "Yeah, I guess," he mumbled.

"If I need more help, I'll call you," Dust promised. "This is important, though. We've got to have supplies."

"That's okay," Todd replied with a hesitant smile. "Can you teach me how to go through doors like you did?"

Dust's smile faded and he bowed his head again. Sammy shook her head at Todd, who released a loud sigh and turned away. Sammy's gaze followed her little brother with a look of worry.

"I won't hurt him... or you," Dust muttered. "You asked me what happened to me. I don't know," he said, bending forward and beginning to pull the spark plugs. Both the plugs and wires were scorched. He quickly removed them and tossed them to the side. "I don't remember much after the initial blast. I was in the house alone. My mom and dad were in the barn, trying to bring the cows inside."

"What... What happened to them?" Sammy asked, watching as Dust worked.

Dust glanced at her before bending to pick up some new spark plugs he had taken from the auto store. Sammy wished she could take back the question, but it was too late. Dust turned away from her and worked in silence for several minutes before he spoke again.

"They were gone and so was the barn. There wasn't much left of the house," he said in a low voice. "I woke up buried in the cellar. I could see through the roof. I remember a strange light in the sky, bolts of lightning striking all around me and a strange dust. It all mixed together and everything began to glow. The next time I woke, I was...."

"You were...," Sammy prompted, placing her hand lightly on his arm before jerking it away.

Dust's head slowly turned and he looked at her with piercing brown eyes. "I was there, but I wasn't."

Sammy stared at him for a long time before she nodded, as if she had made up her mind about something. Biting her lip, she looked at where Todd was playing. Her heart hurt for both Todd and Dust. Life shouldn't be like this. Blinking back the tears, she looked back at Dust and blushed a little when she saw he was watching her.

"Todd can stay here and help you," she said suddenly. "I'll start bringing stuff from the store and packing it into the car. This way we can get out of here as soon as you get it started."

"Okay," Dust replied, glancing back down the street with a frown. "Be careful. We don't know what happened to that one devil dog and we don't know if there are more."

"I will be," Sammy said, stepping back. "Just... Promise me that you'll keep Todd safe."

Dust straightened. "I promise," he replied. "I'll keep you both safe – or die trying."

"Let's hope that won't be necessary," Sammy retorted with an unsteady laugh, pushing her hair back behind her ear.

"Take your bow," Dust advised.

Sammy shook her head. "I only have one arrow left. I'll borrow your pipe," she said, reaching for the long piece of metal leaning up against the front of the car. "Just get the car going."

Sammy didn't wait for Dust to reply. Instead, she focused on the task she had assigned herself. If Dust was successful, she wanted to get out of here. Her gut was telling her they didn't want to be here after dark tonight.

Dust: Before and After

GRACIE'S TOUCH

A time travel adventure full of hope, sacrifice, and love...

Gracie Jones was little more than a child when the Earth was invaded by an alien species.

Don't miss the story of the woman who became the Mother of Freedom!

Chapter 1

"Good morning, good afternoon, and good evening to all the citizens of the world. This is Gracie, reaching out to touch each and every one of you with love and hope. The Freedom Five, along with groups from around the world, are pushing back against the Alluthans. Forces around the world have freed thousands of captives over the past several weeks. Over two hundred Alluthan fighters have been destroyed in the past week. Our fight for freedom is heating up, and we expect a breakthrough soon, so don't give up!"

Gracie Jones leaned into the microphone attached to the bank of computers and continued sending out news, stories, and hope to the millions of listeners in fifteen different languages. She spent at least three hours a day during different times, sending the messages out. Adam worried it would open them up to attacks if the Alluthans traced the signal, but Gracie was a master at bouncing signals off the satellites the Alluthans hadn't destroyed.

She was just ending her broadcast when Chance came in. One look at his face and she knew he was furious. She also knew what the cause was, Adam or Adrian had finally told him about her plan. She winced when she looked at his face again. The confrontation about to come was not going to be a pleasant experience.

"This is Gracie's Touch signing off," Gracie said in a husky voice filled with emotion.

~

Fifteen minutes later she was ready to scream. She'd known it was going to be difficult, but she'd never expected it to be this difficult! She turned to Adam, pleading silently for his help.

"It's the only way! I'm the only one who can do it," Gracie said again, looking intently at the four men standing around her. "There is no other way."

"Like hell there isn't!" Chance said fiercely. He jerked away from Adam, who grabbed at him.

"Chance..." Gracie began.

"He's right, Gracie. There is no way in hell we are going to let you do this," Mark said.

Gracie sighed again in frustration. "Adam, you talk to them. You know I'm right."

Adam watched as Gracie rose gracefully from the chair in front of the row of computers. He shut his eyes briefly in an effort to get control of the rage burning inside him. He knew she was right, but he didn't want to be the one to admit it. Adam opened his eyes and looked at his younger brother, Adrian, who hadn't said a word throughout the whole argument. He had the same look of resignation in his eyes.

"Gracie is right. She is the only one who can do this." Adam spoke quietly but with authority. As the leader of one small group of New York rebels known as the Freedom Five, it was up to him to make the tough decisions. He wasn't sure he would be able to live with some of those decisions if they survived the fight for their freedom.

Five years before, Earth had been invaded by a group of ugly-ass aliens. There had been no warning, no promises of peace, nothing. The half-organic/half-robotic aliens had simply begun gathering up as many humans as possible and placing them in huge holding camps protected by a shield of some kind.

Millions perished from lack of food and medical care. It was later learned, thanks to the work of computer hackers—or geeks as Gracie liked to be called—that the aliens were planning on using the humans as renewable parts for their own deteriorating forms. The Alluthans were experimenting on the captive humans to test their limitations and compatibility.

Gracie lost her parents and an older sister when the aliens first attacked New York. Adam, his brother Adrian, and two other survivors, Chance and Mark, found her hiding in the old subway system six months later.

She had escaped with her laptop and some external hard drives, and had managed to tap into one of the maintenance room's access points to monitor what was happening. The governments of the world finally banded together to fight the threat, but not before a devastating number of humans had died or were lost in the large alien holding camps.

Gracie was the youngest daughter of two university professors at NYU. Her ability to understand computer languages, and languages in general, was unbelievable. By fifteen, she had mastered eight different languages fluently and another seven on a conversational level.

She also used her skills at deciphering computer-generated languages to stay one step ahead of the Alluthans. For the past two years, she'd focused on studying the language and computer applications of the Alluthans so she could find a way to defeat them.

Adrian looked at his brother with a tense frown on his face. "You know it is suicide. She'll never make it out."

"That's not true!" Gracie said, turning to frown at the four men towering over her petite five-foot-four frame. "I have an excellent chance of escaping."

"And how, pray tell, do you figure that?" Chance growled, folding his arms across his massive chest.

"Chance, I can speak, read, and write their language. I've been studying it extensively, as well as their computer applications. Team Two has one of their supply ships in the old warehouse down by the river thanks to me. All I have to do is program it to autopilot to the mother ship.

"Once on board, I'll upload the programs I've developed to bring down the shields protecting all their bases and prisoner camps around the world. Once it has downloaded, I'll reprogram the ship to bring me back to Earth," Gracie said with a plea for understanding in her voice. "I know I can do this!"

～

Chance walked over and drew her against him, holding her close. She was the closest thing to family he had left besides the other guys standing with them. He had lost his family also and had vowed to protect Gracie from the first time he saw her emerald-green eyes staring fearfully back at him in the dark tunnel five years ago.

He didn't want to admit for a long time that as she matured, his feelings for her grew beyond a brotherly love. At seventeen, Gracie was still too young. Chance was waiting as long as he could before he claimed her as his own, but he feared he would never get the chance to tell her how he felt about her.

"What if they find you? What if it doesn't work and you get trapped there?" Chance asked huskily as he held her against his hard length.

"They won't. It will work. I've double and triple-checked the programs to make sure they would work. You saw for yourself how the shield collapsed, and I was able to take control of the ship and bring it down. The alien didn't have a clue about what was happening," Gracie said as she wrapped her arms around Chance. She wanted to give him reassurance, but she also needed it herself.

"When do we do this?" Adrian asked.

"Tomorrow morning," Adam replied. "We've received confirmation from around the world that everyone will be ready."

Mark nodded. "You better come back, little britches, or I'm going to be mighty pissed at you."

Gracie smiled softly before replying. "I will, Mark. I will."

Gracie slowly walked into the bathroom and stared at her reflection. She tried to calm the trembling in her hands as she pushed her short, thick strawberry blonde hair away from her face so she could wash without getting it wet. Gracie wouldn't say she was beautiful—more like cute.

Her hair was cut in a bob that came to her chin; her eyes were too big and a deep, dark green. She had a short, button nose and lips just a little on the full side. She was very pale from having spent most of her time underground in the subway tunnels of New York. She was also very petite for her age, but that was mostly due to not having very much food for too many years.

The guys had finally set up grow lights in one tunnel, and they grew what they could. Mark had been the farmer of the group, having come from the Midwest in search of survivors. Chance knew a little, but that was mostly because of the pot plants he used to grow when he was a teenager.

Adam and Adrian were native New Yorkers used to the mean streets. They were the fighters of the group and had been instrumental in saving the lives of each of them on more than one occasion.

Gracie watched as her hair swished around her face as she leaned forward and drew in a deep breath. She tried to sound confident about what she was about to do, but in reality she was scared to death.

She wasn't sure it was going to work, and she knew if it did, there was an excellent possibility she wouldn't survive.

She figured it would be a one-way ticket, but she also knew that if the guys knew that, they would never let her go. If there was a chance they could turn the tide of this war and defeat the aliens, she was going to take it.

The only reason she was the best candidate for this mission was because if the aliens figured out what she was doing and tried to stop her, she had a chance of counteracting their programming.

So, scared or not, she was it. She washed her face and brushed her teeth before pulling on a comfortable pair of worn jeans, an oversized T-shirt with a picture of New York on the front, and slipped into her running shoes. She grabbed some personal items and shoved them into her oversize leather bag along with an extra shirt and her hoodie.

Last, she grabbed her tablet PC and chargers. Looking around for the last time at the little bed set up against the stone wall, Gracie pulled aside the blanket she used as a door and walked down to the main staging area.

Chapter 2

Adam, Adrian, Chance, and Mark were waiting for her by the time she got to the center area they used as a main living quarter. Chance helped Gracie up onto the platform, then stood back as the other six men who made up Team Two looked her over.

"Not much to you," one of the men said before he spit on the floor. "Maybe if they catch you they won't think there is enough of you to eat. You sure as hell aren't big enough for parts."

Adrian, who was standing slightly to the left of the man, turned in a blur of motion and struck the man in the jaw, sending him to the floor on his ass. "Shut your mouth!" he snarled, clenching his fists tightly. "She is risking her life to do something no one else can, you piece of shit. Give her the respect she deserves."

"And don't spit on the floor. This is our living area," Gracie said as calmly as she could.

The man's words had sent a shiver down her spine. They frequently received reports that the aliens were using humans for parts to repair the damage to their own organic bodies. Gracie didn't want to think of her family ending up that way.

Chance could sense how the words of the man upset Gracie, and it took everything in him to not just kill the bastard right then and there. He walked over and pulled Gracie close to his body, trying to give her what little protection and support he could.

~

"Gracie," Chance called out quietly a few hours later.

Gracie and the guys had gone over the plans again with Team Two before calling it a night. They looked over every aspect of what they were about to do. It was essentially Gracie's plan.

When she'd first worked out the programming to not only disarm the shields protecting the Alluthan spaceships, but also to override their system and bring it down using a simulator, she had been ecstatic. If a worldwide, systematic coordination of attacks could be organized, then it was possible to turn the tide of the war and possibly even bring it to an end.

It took over two months for Gracie to finally convince the four guys it was a possibility, and that only happened when she took over the supply ship now down in the old warehouse. The Alluthan on board had had no idea that it was not following a direct order from the mother ship.

Once Gracie proved she could override, control, and operate one of the spaceships, Adam began communicating with other rebel forces around the world through the ham radio and low-frequency signal setup.

Gracie knew she would never be able to sleep after the other team left. Crocker, from Team Two, said he would have the things she would need on the supply ship for her arrival at five the next morning. Everything was ready. Now she sat listening to the communications going on back and forth between the different bases of the Alluthans on the ground and the mother ship.

That is where their downfall will be, Gracie thought. *They put all their eggs in one basket, or in this case, one ship.*

The Alluthans believed the humans too primitive to attack them in space. Everything was run from the mother ship—all communications, orders, even power was distributed from there. If it was destroyed, then all their resources were gone.

Gracie started when she heard Chance's voice call out to her. Turning, she watched as he came into the small computer room the guys had set up for her. She couldn't help but smile as she watched him. She loved him so much. She had since the first time she saw him five years ago. His gentle touch had drawn her out of the alcove she was hiding in, and his strong arms made her feel safe.

She knew he loved her too. She'd tried to act upon their love six months ago, but Chance had said it was not the time. He had made a promise to Adam to wait until she was eighteen before he claimed her as his. She had argued, but Chance remained firm. Adam was the father figure to them all, and they respected him.

Adam wanted to make sure she was old enough to understand her decision. Gracie did understand. She also understood life could be short. With considerable reluctance, both she and Chance agreed they would wait until she was eighteen to act upon their physical desires.

Now, it looked like their love would become another tragedy in history—for she knew deep down she was never coming back. In a way, she was glad they had never made the final commitment to each other. Perhaps it would be easier for Chance to move on.

Gracie knew she would always regret not forcing the issue for her own selfish reasons, as she would have loved to have that memory to take with her when she died.

Gracie forced a smile on her face and rubbed the tears away as she looked at Chance's worried face. "Hey, Chance," she said in a husky voice filled with emotion.

Chance heard the tears she was fighting so hard to push back.

Rushing forward, he wrapped his strong arms around her tightly. He pulled her close, holding her like he would never let her go.

"Let me go with you," he whispered against her forehead. "Let me go with you, and we can both come back. I'll tell Adam that you need me."

Gracie squeezed Chance close to her and closed her eyes. "You can't. I'm good, but not that good. The Alluthans scan each ship for heat signatures. If they pick up two signatures in a supply ship designed for one, then they will destroy it before it ever gets near them.

"Besides, Adam needs you here to help with the attacks. You are supposed to take out the camp holding my parents and sister. You promised to see if they survived," Gracie said, looking up into Chance's eyes, pleading with him not to argue with her.

Chance slid his arms up and gently cupped Gracie's face between his large palms. He pressed a kiss to her lips, groaning when she opened to him. Tonight could very well be their last night together, forever. Chance briefly thought of his promise to Adam, then thought, *To hell with it*. Gracie was his.

"Come with me to my room. Let me love you, Gracie," Chance murmured against her lips.

Gracie was torn between wanting to push Chance away from the hurt she knew he was going to feel when she was gone, and her own selfish desire to grab what little life she had left. The feel of Chance's hand on her breast made the decision for her. She would be selfish and take what little happiness she could with her.

~

Chance squeezed Gracie's hand as he pulled her after him out of the alcove set up as a computer room. He hated that he could not give Gracie a real bed for her first time or even the promise of a full night. Instead, all he could give her was a small pallet on a cold stone floor and a few hours at best. He resolved to make it the most beautiful experience that he could for her. She deserved that and more.

They had almost reached the area he claimed as his own when Adrian came running up to them. He was breathing hard and looked pissed as hell. Chance instinctively pulled Gracie closer as his stomach knotted. Something had happened, and it wasn't going to be good.

"Fighters are headed this way," Adrian blurted out. "Word is they are going to level this part of the city, including the holding camps."

Gracie gasped. Her parents and sister, if they were still alive, were in the holding camp. If the Alluthans took out the warehouse down by the river, then their chance of bringing down the mother ship would take much longer and more lives would be lost.

"I have to leave... now," Gracie said. "When are the fighters expected?" she asked as she pulled away from Chance.

"A couple hours at most," Adrian responded grimly.

Gracie nodded and looked back at Chance one last time before turning to follow Adrian. "Gracie," Chance said hoarsely knowing his time with her was coming to an end.

"I love you, Chance," Gracie said, letting one of her hands run up and over his cheek as a single tear coursed down hers. "I always will."

~

The next hour was a blur as the teams worked together to get everything in place. All those who could be evacuated were in areas outside of the attack zone. Gracie reviewed the instrument panel of the supply ship and hooked up her laptop to the control panel. The software program she developed quickly uploaded. She designed a type of dump upload, so the program uploaded immediately, then unpackaged. This made it easier to get all the files on the system as fast as possible.

Gracie nodded to the men from Team Two as they began filing out of the supply ship. Crocker looked at Gracie for a long moment before saying anything. Gracie waited patiently for him to say what he had to say.

"You know, if you succeed you'll be a hero. If your program does what it is supposed to do, you'll have saved the Earth and millions of lives," Crocker said gruffly.

Gracie smiled at the big man with the gruff voice. "I don't want to be known as a hero. Just as another human who refused to give up or give in. I couldn't have done this alone. It took everyone..." Gracie's voice faltered as her throat thickened with tears at the thought of all the senseless deaths, "... everyone who has lived and died over the past five years to get to this point. I just hope it works. I'm tired of being afraid," Gracie ended softly.

Crocker leaned down and brushed a kiss across Gracie's forehead. "It is Gracie's Touch that has given all of us the hope of seeing that day. Take care, little girl, and come back home."

Gracie nodded as she watched the big, gruff man walked off the ship. She turned all the way around and watched as the four guys who she considered her closest family walked onto the ship. Adam was first, followed by Adrian and Mark, with Chance coming up in the rear.

"You stick with the plan. If you have any problems, if you get even the weirdest feeling, you abort and get your ass back planet side, do you understand?" Adam said sternly.

Gracie smiled as she watched his Adam's apple move up and down. It was the only way to tell when Adam was upset about anything. "I understand. I will, I promise."

Adam hugged Gracie tightly to him and kissed the top of her head. The thought of never seeing her again and being the one to give the order for her to complete this mission was killing him inside. His arms tightened for just a moment before he released her and walked out without a backward glance.

Adrian cleared his throat. He was the quietest one of the group and held his emotions close to his heart, never letting on he felt anything. He stared down at her for a moment before saying anything.

"Come back," he ground out before brushing a kiss across her cheek and turning to follow his brother.

Mark looked down into Gracie's eyes and smiled. "Come home to us, little britches," Mark said gently as he pulled Gracie into his arms and rocked her gently back and forth for a moment before kissing her on the lips. "Come home for Chance."

Gracie's eyes filled with tears as she felt Chance's arms come around her and pull her away from Mark. She turned and buried her face in his strong chest. She wanted to remember what he felt like, what he smelled like, everything about him. She wanted... needed... this memory to give her the strength to turn away from him and leave. Gracie bit back a sob that threatened to escape. It wasn't fair! She should be looking forward to having a future with Chance, not leaving him. She loved him so much.

"Gracie..." Chance choked out. "I... Don't do this. Stay. We can find another way to defeat them." Gracie was about to respond when the ground shook from an explosion several miles away. The attack had begun. She forced herself to pull away from Chance and looked up into his eyes one last time.

"I have to do this. Go on, go, while I still can. Go, Chance, please," Gracie begged.

"Chance..." Adam called out from the platform. "Let her go. We need to move now."

Chance growled out his frustration as he crushed his lips to Gracie's in a brief, hard, passionate kiss filled with love, anger, and pain. "Come back to me, Gracie. You fucking come back to me," Chance bit out harshly before he turned and walked down the platform.

Gracie pushed the control to close the platform door, watching as Chance slowly disappeared from her sight. She blew one last kiss to all the guys and smiled before the door closed, sealing her fate forever.

Chapter 3

Gracie moved into the pilot's seat and strapped herself in. She could feel the vibrations from explosions, but ignored them as she set the supply ship's course for the mother ship. She opened the front view screen panel so she could watch what was happening as she left the

Earth's atmosphere. The supply ship lifted off smoothly and moved rapidly upward following Gracie's pre-programmed coordinates.

Gracie looked in dismay at all the destruction to New York. She could see the fighters in the northwest highlighted against the fires burning from their attack. She prayed everyone was able to evacuate in time. In moments, she was thrust back against the seat as the supply ship went through the Earth's atmosphere.

As the blackness of space engulfed the small ship, Gracie got her first look at the mother ship. She stared at it in a combination of awe and despair as she saw how enormous it was. It had to cover at least the size of Manhattan alone!

Gracie knew if larger ships were coming, the Earth would never stand a chance. She needed to destroy this one. If she could take down the mother ship, it would not send for additional ones.

From what she was able to learn from the files she had accessed, these ships traveled great distances alone, one mother ship and its "offspring"—meaning the fighters, supply ships, and ground forces. If a planet was found to contain an abundant amount of resources, then the mother ship would send for more. If not, it would use what it needed before destroying the planet and moving on to the next one. Gracie needed to destroy it before it decided on either option.

She listened as the supply ship gave the needed code for admittance to the mother ship for refueling. As soon as the large panel doors opened on the outer edge of the ship, Gracie patched into the computer system through a backdoor she'd discovered a couple of months ago. The Alluthans were getting better at closing the doors, but they were still arrogant enough to think the humans too primitive to learn their language, much less their computer codes.

Gracie left a digital copy of her notes on deciphering both for Adam. She wanted to make sure all her work over the last five years was not wasted. That was one nice thing about having parents who were researchers, they believed in taking notes and showed their children how to do it also.

Gracie smiled as the virus she uploaded finished. It was a simple one that grew every time it was uploaded to another system, changing its signature to make it more difficult to detect. It would wipe their system clean once finished. The Alluthans would lose control of everything.

Gracie watched as the supply ship connected to a docking port, and an arm extended, recharging the fuel cells. She monitored the activity, frowning when she heard a disembodied voice on one channel, giving directions for the attack on specific sites around the world. They were pinpointing some of the major areas where the rebels were.

Patching into the channel, she watched as the programmed instructions flooded her screen. She frowned again as she focused on the rush of data scrolling down it. Her breath caught as she picked out keywords.

Typing quickly, she began redirecting the fighters to other areas away from the original commands. Most of the areas were over open water and shouldn't pose a threat to humans.

A warning flashed at the bottom showing a probe flash as the intrusion was detected. Gracie glanced at her other screen. The program to disarm the Alluthans defense systems was almost complete. It was spreading, but not as quickly as she wished. Gracie quickly typed in a few commands and watched as the warning faded.

She continued uploading one code after another, determined that if the Alluthans found and stopped one virus, they would not be able to stop them all. She uploaded the last one and looked at the power-cell indicator. Refueling was done, and it was time to leave before they opened the platform to begin loading and found her.

Gracie punched in the release code and waited anxiously until she heard the sound of the fuel arm disengaging. She hit the program that would take her home with a sigh of relief.

Maybe, just maybe, I will get to be with Chance, she thought as a wave of hope swept through her.

She felt the thrusters kick in as she started to return the same way she had come, and was almost to the open panel doors leading out into space when a voice came on over her audio com. She listened as it gave a command for her ship to return to the docking port.

Gracie punched in a command to override the auto-command when the operator tried to take over her controls. She listened as the voice came over again.

"Supply ship 100982 return to docking port 2-225."

Gracie smiled as she saw her programs kick in. She had an ace up her sleeve if she needed it, but she needed to be far enough away when she dealt it not to get caught in it.

Gracie flipped the audio and gave her announcement to the millions of resistance fighters on the Earth far below. Gracie's eyes gleamed with tears as she gave the command that would hopefully bring this war to an end.

"Good morning, good afternoon, and good evening. This is Gracie reaching out to touch you with love and hope. Today the people of Earth are ending the siege of the Alluthans. Rise up and fight, for freedom is ours. This is Gracie's Touch saying, *Freedom for all!*" Gracie's husky voice called out to all the millions on the beautiful blue-and-white ball below her.

She watched as lights flared all over the globe as the united governments and rebel forces joined together and made a decisive assault against the aliens who thought them too weak to win.

Gracie was about to hit the button that would speed her way home when the supply ship shuddered violently, throwing her to the side. Gracie's eyes frantically flew to find the cause. She punched in the command to silence the alarms as she fought for control.

No fighters followed her as they were unresponsive due to the command to shut everything down. Gracie could see multiple failures occurring on the mother ship, but it would take longer for each system to completely shut down. The mother ship was turning to follow her. It sent out several bursts from its pulse cannons.

Her shields immediately came online, but the bursts took a toll on them, and they read eighty-five percent. Gracie felt dread seep through her. If the mother ship followed her and the self-destruct program activated, Earth would be in peril from the fallout. The only way to ensure the mother ship did not endanger the Earth was to lead them away.

Gracie quickly programmed a new route into the navigation system. Tears blurred her vision as she sent the command and felt the supply ship turning. She increased her speed, knowing it would not be long before the mother ship lost all power and the self-destruct initiated.

She braced her palms against the front console as another jarring jolt hit the supply ship. She was moving as fast as the supply ship could go without sending it into hyperdrive. The navigation panel said they were nearing Mars.

She didn't know if the signal she sent would make it to Earth or not, but she had to try to send one last message. She had to tell them she was sorry and say good-bye. Gracie opened the communications program and typed in the password for one of the satellites she used to send her transmissions.

"This... this is Gracie," Gracie waited a moment. She trembled as she continued. "Chance, this is Gracie saying I'm so sorry. I won't be coming home after all." Gracie drew in a shaky breath and forced herself to continue.

"I hope you get this message. I wanted to tell you I love you. I want... need... to thank all of you for saving me so long ago. Chance, you and Adam, Adrian, and Mark will always be with me. Please keep up the fight for freedom, knowing I'll always be with you every time you think of me. Th-this is Gracie, saying goodnight and good-bye, my love," Gracie ended the transmission as tears choked her and her vision blurred so badly she couldn't see anything.

Impatiently, she brushed the tears away. If she was going to die, she was going to take those pissant aliens with her. Gracie programmed the supply ship to enter hyperdrive and set the mother ship's navigation system to follow. She also set the self-destruct to half the time. Both ships would explode during the light jump making sure nothing else was damaged.

Gracie watched out of the front view as the stars seemed to blur together. Within seconds, she was pushed back against her seat. She closed her eyes and waited for the end. Everything seemed to slow as she felt the push from the mother ship as it exploded. The shockwave threw the ship forward with such force, the shoulder strap on the harness broke, throwing her forward. As darkness descended, Gracie drew a picture in her mind of Chance holding her in his arms and smiled.

~

Grand Admiral Kordon Jefe strode into the conference room in a dark mood, but his grim thoughts didn't show on his face. He'd just finished reading the report sent in on the latest attack by a new alien species on one of their remote mining planets. Everyone was dead and the planet stripped of most of its resources.

The last message received from the mining colony was sent two weeks before. Some imbecile captain on the remote station of Atphlon didn't think it important enough to investigate the emergency signals being sent out until two days ago. That captain was now washing floors on Atphlon as a private. Kordon didn't tolerate idiots under his command.

He didn't bother to nod to the other officers standing around the table waiting for him to sit first. He moved to the chair at the head of the conference table and sat, pulling the data grid closer to review the information the frigate sent to the site looking for survivors. He already knew every detail in the report; now he wanted answers.

"What have you to report?" Kordon looked at his head of security.

Chief Bran Markus cleared his throat before answering calmly. "Two hundred and fifty-eight colonists dead or missing, any resource worth having gone, the colony destroyed. The source appears to be the same as before. We were able to get a brief glimpse of some of the attackers and one of their vehicles before communications were terminated." Bran nodded to a center screen displaying the mining foreman as he sent the distress signal.

"We are under attack by an unknown force. They... they have captured most of the men as they came out of the mines. All women and children have been killed." The man wiped his face as sweat dripped down it. "Those bastards have some type of shield we can't get through. We need immediate assistance." A loud explosion could be heard in the background. "Th-they've breached the complex head-quarters. Th—" The transmission ended as screams filled the air.

Captain Leila Toolas, his chief medical officer, responded. "From the details I've been able to retrieve from the bodies left, whoever was there killed any female not able to reproduce and the young children immediately. From the list there were fifteen females within a breeding range unaccounted for. The men..." Captain Toolas paled as she continued. "The remains of the men show body parts missing. Limbs and internal organs were removed with surgical precision."

Kordon kept his expression blank as he took each report. He finally came to his communications officer, a Ta'nee. The Ta'nee were known for their language and communication skills. The rich red hair down the center of Lieutenant Mohan's head flared with different colors as she spoke.

"I have never encountered the language or signals recorded by the mining foreman. It was very perceptive of him to record the commu-nications being transmitted. It will take time to decipher it as there is no known database to compare it to," Mohan said. The fur along her cheeks changing to a slightly darker color as all eyes turned toward her.

Kordon nodded, ignoring the changes. He knew the Ta'nee were very shy and did not like being the center of attention. He looked at each officer intently so they would understand what he was about to say. He had worked with all of them for the past twenty years with the exception of Mohan, whom he brought on board almost a year ago.

"I want answers. Find out if there are any signature marks from their ship. I want to know every ripple in space that has occurred in that region within the past month. Mohan, monitor all frequencies. Let me know if you hear anything out the ordinary.

"Toolas, get me a detailed report on the bodies. I want to know exactly what you know and what you think in the report. Bran, get me a report on the types of weapons that could have been used to cause that amount of destruction. I also want information on what types of shields they could have used. Report back in four hours."

Everyone stood immediately as Kordon stood and strode back out of the conference room. He walked over to the commander's chair on the bridge and gave the order to the helmsmen to proceed to the mining colony. He wanted to look at the destruction first hand.

~

Three years after crash landing

Gracie moved quietly, stalking her prey. It was a small creature not much bigger than a squirrel. She didn't know the names of any of the creatures on the moon she had crashed on—in truth, she didn't care... at least, not at first.

Gracie had woken up three years ago to the alarms sounding and a terrible headache. She finally managed to shut off the alarms resounding through the supply ship. She was amazed she was still alive.

When the computer indicated the supply ship had crashed on the surface of an unknown moon it took Gracie a minute to realize that something strange—besides not being dead—had occurred. It didn't matter how hard she tried, the response from the computer system came up the same—unknown. Gracie shut everything down except life support, even though the system verified the atmosphere was suitable for her life form.

A week after she landed she was finally so sick of being confined to the small supply ship she would have fought a bear to get out of it. Her first step onto an alien world should have been filled with trepidation, but Gracie was beyond that.

She was alone. She no longer feared death, but welcomed the

possibility. A part of her knew she was grieving the loss of Chance. It took almost six months for her to finally talk herself into moving forward, and to begin stretching out of her comfort zone.

The first six months she stayed close to the supply ship. She focused on finding enough food to supplement the MREs Crocker had stowed aboard the ship. It was strange, but it was almost like he'd expected her to need them. Gracie didn't need much. She had gotten used to living on very little during the years they'd lived in the subway system.

As the months turned to years, she'd learned to hunt, gather, and forage for most of her food supplies. She often wondered if this was what early humans must have done and felt when they fought for survival. The moon had a few predators, but Gracie learned to avoid them. For the most part, they were primarily just small mammal-type creatures like the one she was hunting now. She made sure to only seek them out a couple of times a month so she would not reduce the population, although they seemed to be plentiful.

Gracie aimed the bow she'd made and let the arrow fly. It had taken her over a year to get any good with one. Gracie grimaced as she approached the dead creature. She still got queasy when it came time to kill and clean them though. It was only because she had no other choice that she did it. It was that or starve to death, which she'd come very close to doing.

She swung the bow over her shoulder and walked over to pick up the dead 'squirrel'. She would have protein tonight. Working her way back to the supply ship, she marveled at how fast the plants on the moon grew.

In the three years she had been on it, there'd never really been a winter. The coldest it seemed to get was in the thirties, if she had to guess. *Not near as cold as a New York winter,* Gracie thought before she could stop herself. She fought against the wave of sadness that flooded her. *This is why you shouldn't think about it,* she scolded herself.

Quickly, she pulled away some of the vines that threatened to cover the platform door before she walked down to a nearby stream. The water was good as long as she boiled it for at least five minutes first. She neatly and efficiently cleaned her supper and set it in a large container she used as a pot, to cook over the open coals of the fire she kept burning. Laser guns were good for starting fires, she'd discovered after several failed attempts to do it the Girl Scout way and in a fit of temper.

Several hours and one full stomach later, Gracie turned the supply ship's power on. She did a systems check at least twice a month to make sure the fuel cells were not leaking and to check for any communications in the area.

She felt comfortable that the moon was uninhabited except for her and the few creatures she saw. In three years, not a single space ship nor communication had been seen or heard. She figured she must have traveled at least a fifty-mile radius from the ship, and there was also no sign of additional life.

Turning on the power, Gracie set a random pattern for the computer to scan for any type of signal. She leaned back and carefully pulled the last picture of her with the guys out of the protective sleeve she kept it in. Gracie smiled and gently touched the tip of her finger to Chance's cheek. She wondered if they were all okay. She liked to dream Chance had found her parents and sister and moved on.

Perhaps the Earth was now free, and Chance had married someone else. He could have a child by now … one that looked like him. She imagined sitting with the guys, her and Chance's son or daughter on her lap, while the other guys cooked barbeque and drank beer. She remembered her parents having friends over and she and her sister playing with the other kids. Gracie was so focused on her daydream it took a moment for the sounds coming through the communication systems to register.

Gracie sat up straight in shock as the voices came over the system again. She didn't understand them, but she might be able to figure it out eventually. It sounded just like the chatter she used to listen to between the ham-radio operators. Her fingers trembled as she set the computer to record.

Gracie listened to the traffic for almost an hour before she made a decision. She could hear the different cadences and even laughter.

Laughter was good, she kept telling herself. Looking around the small supply ship, she figured she had two choices—die alone on this small moon or try to find a way off it and back home. Either way, she would eventually end up dead.

Pushing the transmission button before she could talk herself out of it, Gracie leaned forward and began talking softly, hesitantly at first. "This is Gracie's Touch reaching out to anyone who can hear this. I am currently stranded on an unknown planet or moon. If you can understand this, please respond. I repeat... this is Gracie reaching out to touch any friendly ship who could offer assistance. If you receive this message and can respond, I need assistance."

Gracie repeated the message over and over before she felt she needed to power down for a while. The solar cells could power the supply ship's systems for a short period, and she wanted to conserve the power as much as possible. She would listen and try again tomorrow once the sun was up.

"This is Gracie's Touch saying goodnight," Gracie said before she shut down the system.

Her heart was pounding as she realized she had either done the smartest thing she would ever do or the dumbest. Only time would tell. Looking out through the front view screen at the dark forests slowly devouring her little home, she knew there was no going back.

Gracie's Touch

CAPTURE OF THE DEFIANCE

Makayla Summerlin is excited to join her grandfather, Henry, in Hong Kong during a college break. She plans to help him sail the next leg of his journey around the world on the *Defiance*, but events take a frightening turn when her grandfather is kidnapped and the *Defiance* disappears! Unsure of what to do, Makayla reaches out to an old friend for help.

Brian Jacobs' work at the Consulate General in Hong Kong is just a stepping-stone for his political career. His life for the foreseeable future is carefully optimized for success, but everything is turned upside down when he receives a frantic call for help from a friend. Their meeting quickly turns into a race for survival when Makayla is almost kidnapped in front of him. Seeing Makayla again awakens old feelings inside Brian and he knows he will do everything he can to help her, no matter the cost.

When the situation turns deadly, both Brian and Makayla find unexpected help from another old friend and a Hong Kong detective. Together, the four race to find Henry and protect Makayla. Their efforts to unravel the mystery of why a wealthy crime lord would target Henry and Makayla; and to find the *Defiance* will take them further than they ever expected to go, but will they be able to discover the truth before time runs out for Henry?

Chapter 1

Hong Kong

The figure of a man pushed through the crowds gathered along the Graham Street Market, uncaring of the curses he was drawing. Sweat beaded on his brow despite the cool breeze and temperate weather. His gaze swept the collage of faces. Almost immediately, his eyes locked with the intense, dark gaze of a man searching the crowd – for him.

Gabriel Harrington swallowed and backed away. He stumbled when he ran into an older woman who turned and began admonishing him. Pushing past her, he ignored her tirade when she continued to yell after him. His frantic flight that had started earlier that morning was now one that meant life or death.

Turning sharply, he cut between two of the merchants' booths, pushing the colorful material hanging down on display out of his field of vision as he rushed through. He had already passed the irritated merchants before the men could say anything. He made another sharp turn along the sidewalk toward the busy intersection, urgently glancing behind him. If he could just get across it, he could lose himself in the crowd of pedestrians.

The skin on the back of his neck tingled and he could feel the sweat sliding down between his shoulder blades under his shirt. He slipped his hand into his pocket for the small box. It was still there.

He breathed a sigh of relief and glanced over his shoulder again. Slowing to a fast walk, he relaxed a little. He didn't see the man who had been following him. Reaching into his pocket, he pulled out his cell phone and quickly dialed the number he had memorized.

"Do you have it?" The voice on the other end asked in a terse tone.

"Yes, but I'm being followed," Gabriel muttered, glancing both ways before entering the intersection.

"Where are you?" The voice on the other end demanded in a brisk tone. "I'll send backup."

"I'm leaving the market near Shelter Cove. I'll... Shit!" Gabriel hissed, pausing about three-quarters of the way across the intersection.

"What is it?"

"There are two of them," Gabriel said hoarsely. "I'll try to get the package to you."

"I have a team en route," the man said.

"It's too late," Gabriel replied with resignation, turning and seeing the other man he thought he'd lost standing not more than fifty feet from him. "I'll hide the package and notify you of the location as soon as I can."

"Negative," the man hissed, but Gabriel was already turning to cross the intersection at a diagonal angle.

He had only taken a few steps when he saw a third man appear on the corner in the direction he had been about to go. Twisting, he bumped into an older man carrying several canvas shopping bags. Gabriel muttered an automatic apology under his breath, even as his hand slipped the package from his pocket and into one of the bags. His gaze swept over the old man's face, trying to memorize it before he backed away.

He darted across the intersection. He was almost to the curb when a van, trying to beat the red light, turned the corner. Gabriel registered the impending impact just seconds before his body hit the windshield. He rolled several feet before coming to a stop. In the distance, he could barely make out the old man turning to see what had happened before everything went black.

∾

Makayla looked around the Customs area of the airport from her place in line. There was a sea of people arriving from all over the world. Her lips curved upward when she saw a harried mother trying to grab a wayward toddler in front of her. The smile turned to a sympathetic grimace when the little boy started crying when his mother picked him up. Several people standing behind her gave the woman an annoyed glance.

Makayla started to turn away when she noticed that the woman had dropped her passport on the ground when she had bent to pick up the little boy. With a murmur, she motioned for the two people behind her to go ahead. With a tired sigh, she waited until they had passed her before she stooped to retrieve the fallen documents.

"You dropped this," she murmured, glancing at the woman's name on the open passport. "Would you like some help, Hsu?"

"Oh, yes, please," the woman stuttered, startled, before she breathed out a tired sigh. "It has been a long trip."

"Where are you traveling from?" Makayla asked politely, adjusting the diaper bag that had fallen off the handle of the stroller before she pushed the baby carriage forward along with her own carry-on.

"Seattle," Hsu replied with a grateful smile. "Thank you so much for your help."

"You're welcome," Makayla replied with a sympathetic grin. "My name is Makayla, by the way."

"That is a beautiful name," Hsu responded, moving forward with the line. She gave a relieved groan when she saw they were next and awkwardly adjusted the little boy who had finally fallen asleep on her shoulder. "I think I can put him in the stroller now."

"Oh, yes," Makayla said, quickly moving the diaper bag so that Hsu could carefully place the sleeping boy in the stroller.

"Where are you from, Makayla?" Hsu asked politely, straightening and placing a hand on her lower back before she took the diaper bag Makayla was holding. "He is getting heavy."

"I'm from Florida," Makayla said, adjusting her backpack on her right shoulder. "He looks it. How old is he?"

"He will be three next month," Hsu replied before she turned to the Customs agent. "Thank you again for your help, Makayla. I hope you have a pleasant visit in Hong Kong."

"You too, and good luck!" Makayla replied, watching as Hsu pushed the stroller up to the window.

A moment later, it was Makayla's turn. She walked up and presented her passport. The agent behind the window briefly glanced up at her and then down at her passport.

"What is the purpose of your visit?" The agent asked in a cool, disinterested voice.

"Vacation," Makayla replied with a polite smile.

"Are you traveling alone?" The man asked, suddenly more focused on her when he looked up from her photo to her face.

"No, I'm joining my grandfather who is already here," she replied, keeping the smile on her face, even though the man's sudden assessing gaze was making her uncomfortable.

"How long will you be staying?" The agent asked with a smile.

"A week," Makayla answered.

She quietly answered several more questions before she breathed a sigh of relief when he stamped her passport and handed it back to her. She quickly passed through the gate and into the main section of the airport. She was relieved to get out of the crush of people. Fortunately, she was able to bypass the wait for baggage claim. Twenty minutes later, she was in a taxi heading for the marina where her grandfather was docked at the Royal Hong Kong Yacht Club in Shelter Bay.

Sinking back into the seat, she stared at the tall buildings and crowded streets. She didn't even want to think about how the taxi driver was able to navigate through the streets without hitting either a pedestrian or another car. All the sights, sounds, and colorful assortment of people were overwhelming for her exhausted brain.

"Is this your first visit to Hong Kong?" The driver asked, glancing up in the mirror before returning his gaze to the road in front of him.

"Yes," Makayla answered, staring out the window.

"You have friends here? I can tell you the best places to go for young people," he said, laying his hand on the horn when a car cut in front of him. "There are lots of young people here."

Makayla shook her head. She knew he would think she was

strange if she told him she preferred to be in places where there weren't that many people, or buildings. That was one reason she had gone into the field of study that she had chosen in college. As a marine biologist, she could escape from the mad rush of urban life and spend most of her time either in a lab or on a research ship.

"No, thank you," Makayla finally replied when she realized that the driver was waiting for her response. "I'm meeting up with someone."

"Okay," the driver replied.

He finally took the hint that she wasn't a very talkative passenger and refocused his attention on the traffic instead of her. She knew she was attractive and was used to drawing men's attention. It wasn't that she was a beauty. She wasn't delusional enough about her looks to think that. It wasn't until she had overheard a couple of guys talking about her in one of her classes that she finally realized what it was about her that drew attention.

It wasn't her looks, but her attitude and appearance of aloofness that was like a red flag to guys. They liked the challenge of trying to get her to open up for them. She had never been very social and really didn't care to be around a lot of people. It had taken a while to finally figure out it was a defense mechanism – a wall between her and the world. Deep down, she knew it was probably because of the way she had been raised. Oh, she didn't blame her mom. Her mom had enough baggage without Makayla adding to the load. Makayla had learned at an early age that life could suck, and she didn't want to fall into the same dark hole that her mom had.

Her gaze softened when she thought of her mother. Her mom had been doing so much better since she married Arnie Hanover three years ago. Makayla liked Arnie. He had been there for her mom, supporting her, encouraging her, and calmly waiting until her mom was ready to take control of her own life. It was something that Makayla had secretly wished for through the years, but had doubted would ever happen.

Pushing the memories back into the box that she kept them in, she refocused on the landscape. It took her a moment to realize they were already traveling outside of the city. It would take almost an hour to get to the yacht club. Henry, her grandfather, had offered to pick her up, but Makayla had told him it didn't make sense for both of them to spend the money to take a taxi to and from the airport. It would give her time to unwind as well.

Makayla leaned her head back and closed her eyes. At twenty-two, she was fortunate enough to be in a better position than most girls her age. Her father had died before she was born, but he had left a trust fund that she had inherited when she turned twenty-one. The fund had grown over the last twenty plus years, and while she wasn't wealthy by most standards, she had a nice nest egg that had allowed her to focus on her education without having to worry about how she would pay for it. Between the trust fund income and the summer internships that she had worked, she had never had to touch the principal to live on. It also helped that she didn't need much. When living in a small dorm room or on a research ship, there wasn't a lot of room for material things.

Makayla opened her eyes when she felt the taxi slow down and turn. She blinked her eyes to clear the gritty tiredness from them. She sat forward when she realized that they were turning into the yacht club.

She quickly fumbled for the information her grandfather had sent her and her passport to show identification to the security guard at the gate. She pressed the button on the window when the guard leaned down to talk to the cab driver.

"I'm here to see Henry Summerlin," she stated, holding out the documents showing Henry's membership card and her ID. "He should have notified you that I was coming."

"Good afternoon, Ms. Summerlin. Welcome to the Royal Hong Kong Yacht Club," the security guard greeted in a polite professional tone. He glanced at the documents before returning them to her. "Mr. Summerlin is located in E40. Please go down to the turning circle. It will be located on the third turn. Have a nice day."

"Thank you," Makayla murmured, impressed with the efficiency of the guard.

Her gaze swept over the man's immaculate uniform of dark

bluish-gray pressed slacks and white short-sleeved shirt with the emblem of the yacht club on the shoulders. The man's black hair was cut close to his head, and his dark brown eyes were as warm as his greeting. A small, relaxed smile curved Makayla's lips. The journey from the airport had been less stressful than she had feared.

Within minutes, the red and white taxi drew to a stop at the beginning of a long dock. She could see the numbers depicting the dock slips in several different languages. She quickly leaned forward and paid the driver before grabbing her carry-on and backpack. She drew in a deep breath, relieved to have finally arrived from Florida, pushed open the door, and stiffly slid out of the taxi.

Chapter 2

Makayla rolled onto her toes and stretched the soreness out of her muscles as the taxi pulled away. She glanced around and lifted her face to the fading sunlight. It felt good to be out of the cramped confines of the airplane and taxi, and to be out in the wide open spaces again.

She shielded her eyes and gazed around her. In the distance, she could see low mountains behind the tall high rises of the city overlooking the sapphire blue waters of the bay. Excitement filled her when she stared out at the variety of sailboats, powerboats, and multimillion dollar yachts either berthed or anchored in the surrounding waters. She couldn't help but shake her head at the thought of how out of place Henry's small sailboat must look there among the larger vessels.

Adjusting her backpack strap on her shoulder, Makayla bent and pulled up the handle of her carry-on and headed down the long dock. She gazed across the long line of boats to the coastline, enjoying the gentle, cool breeze against her face. The temperature was a nice seventy degrees Fahrenheit, but she knew it was expected to drop after sunset.

Her steps slowed as she came closer to the slip where she could see the *Defiance* moored. A slight movement and a tuft of gray hair peeking out near the back of the sailboat told her that Henry was there and probably working on one of a probably endless list of repairs. A rueful smile curved Makayla's lips. She had once heard that the acronym for the word 'boat' was 'bring on another thousand'. She imagined that was true, especially if you owned a sailboat and were sailing it around the world.

"You know, old man, I heard tell that the two happiest days in a man's life are the day he buys a boat and the day he sells it," Makayla called out in greeting.

Henry turned in a quick circle, surprisingly fast for a man in his late sixties and grinned up at her. He wiped his hand across his cheek, leaving a dark smear of grease above the silver whiskers that coated the lower half of his face. The smile on her lips grew when he realized what he had done. He muttered a soft curse and pulled the rag out of the back of his pocket and scrubbed at his cheek while staring up at her.

"Well, seeing that I'm not of a mind to do either one at the moment, I guess you'll have to wait to find out," he replied with a huge grin. "You made it."

Makayla nodded and looked over the deck of the sailboat. "Yeah, I made it. It's good to see you, Henry," she said, pushing the handle of her carry-on down and handing it to him when he reached up for it.

"You, too, girl," Henry murmured, setting her bag down and reaching up to help her onto the sailboat. "I'm glad you're here," he added, pulling her into a tight bear-hug the moment she was on board.

～

Makayla finished stowing her clothes in the cabinet that Henry had emptied for her. It didn't take long. She glanced up through the companionway and saw that the sun was about to set. Quickly pulling out some lunch meat, cheeses, and condiments, she prepared two turkey and cheese sandwiches on whole wheat with a side of potato chips. She grabbed two bottles of water out of the small refrigerator, carefully balanced them with the stacked plates, and slowly climbed the steps.

"Perfect timing," Henry said with a grin. "I just finished cleaning up. Let me go wash my hands. Mm, that looks delicious. I haven't eaten since this morning. I wanted to have the blasted engine maintenance done before you got here, but had to wait on a part."

"No problem," Makayla replied, placing the plates and bottled waters down on a teak table that Henry had cleared and uncovered. "Take your time. I'm going to enjoy this beautiful sunset."

Henry chuckled and looked over at the mountains. "It is a beauty, isn't it? I'll be right back. I might take a quick shower as well," he muttered with a wrinkle of his nose. "I stink."

"I wasn't going to say anything about that, old man, but since you brought it up, you smell like a diesel engine," Makayla laughed, relaxing against the seat and laying her arm along the back of it.

She affectionately watched Henry head down the steps muttering about ungrateful passengers. She chuckled and tilted her head back to look up at the sky when he disappeared from sight. She took in a deep breath, and held it for a few seconds before releasing it. She gazed upward, staring at the faint dots of light beginning to appear. Against the darker backdrop, she could just make out the first few stars that were beginning to shine through the twilight hues.

Her mind drifted in a kaleidoscope of thoughts and images. She turned and tiredly rested her chin on her arm. The last six years of her life had been a blur of activity. It was hard to believe so much had happened in such a short span of time. Most of it had been good, but some of it had been sad as well, she thought.

"Why the sad face? You aren't having second thoughts, are you?" Henry asked, emerging from the galley.

Makayla turned and smiled. It was a good thing Henry was practically bald on top, otherwise his hair would be sticking up everywhere from the way he was rubbing it dry. As it was, it looked like he could use a haircut for the sides. She'd have to see if he had any electric clippers on board.

"I'm sorry about Breaker," she murmured, twisting back around. "He was a good dog."

Henry grunted and hung the towel over the side of the opening to dry. He grabbed two beers out of the refrigerator while Makayla watched him in silence. He twisted the tops off and held one out for her.

"I think we can celebrate your arrival and Breaker's long life with a beer instead of water," he said, picking up one of the plates and sitting down. "He was a damn good dog. It'd be hard to find one like him again, so I didn't bother trying."

"Kind of like Grandma?" Makayla asked with a raised eyebrow.

Henry's hand paused as he raised the bottle of beer to his lips and he shook his head. He took a long swig of it before he set it down on the table. Makayla could see the amused twitch to his lips and in his eyes.

"Anyone ever tell you that you are a lot like your Grandpa?" Henry asked, picking up his sandwich and taking a bite.

"Only everyone who knows you," she retorted, picking up her own sandwich and biting into it. "So, tell me about your trip so far. How was the trip from Australia?"

They spent the next three hours eating, drinking, and talking. Makayla slowly felt her body relax from a combination of exhaustion and contentment. It felt good after the exhausting flight. Being back on the water aboard the *Defiance* soothed her soul. She raised her hand to smother a yawn. She should have stuck to the bottled water, she thought, lowering her second bottle of beer.

"So, are you seeing anyone?" Henry suddenly asked.

Makayla blinked and dropped her hand to her lap. Her lips pressed together and she rolled her eyes, a habit that she thought she had given up when she was sixteen. Leave it to Henry to bring up her love life on the first night.

"That is none of your business," she replied, lifting the bottle of beer and finishing it. "You know most grandfathers wouldn't give their grandkids a beer, don't you?"

Henry shrugged and grinned. "You're over twenty-one and won't be driving. Plus, I hoped between the jet lag, exhaustion, and the slight buzz that you might let me know if you've found someone," he said.

"Well, you've got those three things right, but I'm not talking," Makayla retorted, pushing up off the seat and lifting a hand to her head. "I'm done for the day."

"You get some sleep. You can have the front bunk and I'll take the one in the galley. Don't worry about this stuff, I'll clean up," Henry instructed, rising to his feet.

"Thanks. I'll be more coherent tomorrow," she replied, holding onto the side of the companionway to keep from stumbling.

"Makayla...," Henry called quietly.

Makayla glanced over her shoulder, her foot on the first step leading down into the galley. She could see the love and concern in his eyes. A part of her wanted to look away, while another part wanted to reassure him that everything was fine. In the end, it was the need to reassure him that won.

"I'm okay, Henry. You don't have to worry about me. I'm not broken. I've just been a little busy with school. I haven't exactly been out of touch with the world, either," she murmured. "I'll see you in the morning."

"Have a good night, sweetheart," Henry said after searching her face to make sure she was telling him the truth. He seemed satisfied with what he saw there. "I'll see you in the morning."

Makayla nodded and made her way down the steps. She passed through the galley, grabbed her small toiletry bag from off the shelf, and made her way to the head. It didn't take her long to brush her teeth, hair, and wash her face. She didn't bother with a shower. She was too exhausted and would probably fall asleep in it. Instead, she changed into a pair of pajama pants and an oversized T-shirt.

She barely made it to the bed before she collapsed. Rolling, she pulled the covers over her and wrapped her arms around the pillow. For a fleeting second, the image of a face from her past flashed through her mind before it was gone. Makayla didn't even bother trying to hold onto it. The memory was gone before she knew it, lost in the fog of her exhaustion. She was too tired to think about anything but sleep at the moment.

Chapter 3

Two days later, Makayla sat back and gazed out over the water. She could already feel the itch to leave. She refocused on where she was polishing the safety railing. Henry had made some modifications to the *Defiance* over the last few years to make it more of an ocean-going vessel. She was still amazed that he had made it over halfway around the world already. This would be her fifth time joining him en route and the longest distance since he had started.

"What do you think?" Henry asked, standing near the mast.

Makayla glanced over her shoulder and raised an eyebrow. "I try not to," she joked, watching an expression of exasperation cross his face at her snarky response. She laughed and turned to face him. "I was just thinking how impressed I am that you have made it this far. It is an incredible feat. You know, Mom still thinks that you've totally lost your mind."

Henry bent and sat down next to her. She could see the thoughtful expression on his face while he gazed out across the harbor. His fingers played with the wire he was holding, rolling it back and forth between them.

"I've been smart about it," he commented, turning back to face her. "I watch the weather and stay in the major shipping lanes. I've made some of the longer legs along with other boats. I've been planning this trip my whole life and I have to admit – I don't have a single regret. I've seen places and met people that otherwise would have been impossible."

"You've also had a few close calls," Makayla reminded him. "The Philippines...."

Henry waved his hand. "I know, but that's life. There are never any guarantees. One thing your grandmother made sure I never forgot was that there are never any guarantees in life. Her death was a huge blow not only to your mom, but to me, Makayla. When Mary Rose was dying, she made me promise that I wouldn't let fear stop me from living my dreams. She reminded me every day to grasp life with both hands and live it, because as she pointed out, you never knew when your last day might be. I raised your mom and uncle as best I could. I wasn't perfect, but I can say I did my best. Having you back in my life made me realize just how fortunate I am."

Makayla sat in silence for a brief moment before she shook her head. "I think that's the longest thing I've ever heard you speak," she reflected with a grin before it faded and she grew serious. "You did good, Henry. Mom doesn't blame you for what happened in her life. And as for me – well, I'll be the first to admit you changed mine," she said in a quiet tone, glancing away to look at the water again.

"You already had a good head on your shoulders, girl. You just needed to know what you had inside you," Henry replied in a gruff tone. With a grunt, he stood up. "I'd better get the wiring completed if we are going to leave the day after tomorrow. We'll be following a couple of cargo ships down to Guam, then over to Honolulu."

Makayla nodded. "I saw the charts. It's good to know we won't be alone. The Pacific Ocean is a mighty big place to get lost in," she said, picking up the polish and pouring more onto the rag she was using.

"There's a market about a mile or so from here. I've got a couple of bikes and thought we could stock up on some supplies later," Henry commented. "I went there the day before you arrived. They have a nice selection of items."

"That sounds like fun," Makayla said. "I could use some exercise."

Henry nodded. "Looks like a good day to go, tomorrow it's supposed to rain," he reflected. "I'd better get the new wire run for the lights if we want to be able to see where we are going."

Makayla turned back to her task. Henry turned on some music and all around them other boat owners talking could be heard. She glanced up when she saw a helicopter flying over the marina. Shielding her eyes, she saw it land on a yacht anchored offshore.

"That must be nice," she muttered under her breath before a familiar song caught her attention and she became lost in it while she worked.

~

Makayla brushed her hair out and twisted it up into a messy bun. Several strands of dark brown hair fell and she impatiently tucked them up into the mass of twisted hair. Her gaze flashed to the clock on the microwave.

"Henry, if we are going to go shopping, we need to do it before it gets much later," Makayla said, grabbing a pile of canvas shopping bags from off the table. She frowned when she heard Henry's muffled reply. "What?"

"I've got at least another hour or two of work," Henry said, glancing up at the sky. "I need to get this done now, especially since the front is expected to move through starting tonight instead of tomorrow."

Makayla could see the frustration and regret on his face. She could also see the dirt and grease. Shaking her head, she glanced up at the sky before looking at him again.

"I can go," she said. "It isn't far. I saw it the other day when the taxi brought me here. I'll go get what we need and be back before the weather turns bad. If you need my help here, we can wait and go tomorrow."

Henry gave her an appreciative smile and shook his head. "If you can go today, it would be better. I'm not that wild about shopping, if you remember. At least if you go, I know we'll have something worth eating," he said.

Makayla nodded her head in agreement. They had been living on turkey and cheese sandwiches for the past two days. She had quickly discovered that was all Henry had in his refrigerator. At least he had also purchased some bread.

"If you're sure you've got this, I'll handle the food," Makayla promised, stepping up onto the back of the sailboat before jumping down onto the dock.

"Coffee!" Henry called out behind her. "Don't forget the coffee."

"I won't," Makayla responded, placing the canvas bags in one of the baskets attached to the bike Henry had placed on the dock. "Anything else?"

"Just whatever you want," Henry said, already focusing back on the wiring. "Don't talk to strangers."

Makayla didn't even reply to Henry's last comment. Instead, she adjusted the small purse she had draped across her chest and slid the straps of her empty backpack on. Grabbing the handlebars of the bike, she turned it and pushed it up the dock. Once at the end, she slid her leg over and kicked off.

She enjoyed the exercise of riding the bike. She followed the road around to the front entrance. Raising her hand in greeting to the security guard, she rode down the short drive before turning right onto the bicycle path.

~

"What did you discover?" The man standing in the elegant office overlooking the bay asked.

Sun Yung-Wing poured himself a cup of tea from the small, antique silver teapot. The steam rose from the delicate white china teacup. He lifted the fragrant brew to his nose and inhaled with appreciation. The tall, slender, elegantly dressed man that had entered the room politely waited until his employer turned before he answered.

"Mr. Harrington is still in a coma," the man stated.

Yung turned to look at the new man in charge of his security. The last one was now at the bottom of the ocean. He carefully studied Ren Lu. The man's slender frame, perfectly cut black hair, and calm face were very deceptive. There was an air of something dark and barely controlled under his polished exterior. Ren Lu had dispatched with his previous boss without hesitation when Yung gave the order after the man screwed up with dealing with Harrington.

"He is still alive?" Yung asked with mild surprise.

"Yes, Mr. Sun. Until we can locate the information that was stolen, I thought it best not to kill him. There is no guarantee that he will survive. If he wakes, I have personnel in position to extract the information before eliminating Mr. Harrington," Ren Lu explained in a quiet tone.

"And what are you doing about locating the information that was stolen from me?" Yung asked in a deceptively pleasant voice before he took a sip of his tea.

Ren Lu stared back at his employer with a cool confidence. "I have accessed the security cameras situated around the marketplace. I was able to narrow in on an encounter Mr. Harrington had with another individual shortly before he was struck by the van. The video was inconclusive, but I believe Mr. Harrington may have given the information to the man. There is a section of the video where it looks like he pulled something out of his pocket. It is unclear if the American was a contact of his or not."

Yung walked silently over to his desk and placed the teacup down on it before he pulled out the chair behind the desk and sat down. Sitting back, he once again studied the man in front of him. The recent discovery of Harrington's double cross had stung. He had prided himself on his ability to recognize someone who was being deceptive.

"Have you located this individual?" Yung asked.

"Yes, sir. The American has a vessel berthed at the Royal Hong Kong Yacht club," Ren Lu replied.

"Bring him to me," Yung ordered. "I have business offshore. I want no mistakes this time. I want the information that was stolen returned to me and anyone involved eliminated."

"Yes, sir," Ren Lu replied with a slight bow.

"Mr. Lu," Yung said, stopping Ren Lu when he started to turn.

"Yes, sir?" Ren Lu responded.

"Remember what happens to those who fail," Yung stated in a cold voice.

"Yes, Mr. Sun," Ren Lu replied, bowing his head once again.

Yung watched his new security chief exit his office. He sat in silence for several long minutes before he reached for his cell phone. Pushing his chair back, he rose and walked over to the floor-to-ceiling, tinted glass windows and stared across the bay. In the distance, he could see the marina in question.

"Send for the helicopter," he ordered his assistant on the other end.

With a press of the button, he disconnected the call. This was one situation where he would need to be personally involved. There was too much at risk. If his clients were to discover that their identities and locations had been compromised because of him, the United States and British governments would be the least of his concerns.

Capture of the Defiance

ADDITIONAL BOOKS AND INFORMATION

If you loved this story by me (S.E. Smith) please leave a review! You can also take a look at additional books and sign up for my newsletter to hear about my latest releases at:

http://sesmithfl.com
http://sesmithya.com

or keep in touch using the following links:

http://sesmithfl.com/?s=newsletter
https://www.facebook.com/se.smith.5
https://twitter.com/sesmithfl
http://www.pinterest.com/sesmithfl/
http://sesmithfl.com/blog/
http://www.sesmithromance.com/forum/

The Full Booklist

Science Fiction / Romance

Cosmos' Gateway Series
Tilly Gets Her Man (Prequel)
Tink's Neverland (Book 1)
Hannah's Warrior (Book 2)
Tansy's Titan (Book 3)
Cosmos' Promise (Book 4)
Merrick's Maiden (Book 5)
Core's Attack (Book 6)
Saving Runt (Book 7)

Curizan Warrior Series
Ha'ven's Song (Book 1)

Dragon Lords of Valdier Series
Abducting Abby (Book 1)
Capturing Cara (Book 2)
Tracking Trisha (Book 3)
Dragon Lords of Valdier Boxset Books 1-3
Ambushing Ariel (Book 4)
For the Love of Tia Novella (Book 4.1)
Cornering Carmen (Book 5)
Paul's Pursuit (Book 6)
Twin Dragons (Book 7)
Jaguin's Love (Book 8)
The Old Dragon of the Mountain's Christmas (Book 9)
Pearl's Dragon Novella (Book 10)
Twin Dragons' Destiny (Book 11)

Marastin Dow Warriors Series
A Warrior's Heart Novella

Dragonlings of Valdier Novellas
A Dragonling's Easter
A Dragonling's Haunted Halloween
A Dragonling's Magical Christmas

Night of the Demented Symbiots (Halloween 2)
The Dragonlings' Very Special Valentine

Lords of Kassis Series
River's Run (Book 1)
Star's Storm (Book 2)
Jo's Journey (Book 3)
Rescuing Mattie Novella (Book 3.1)
Ristéard's Unwilling Empress (Book 4)

Sarafin Warriors Series
Choosing Riley (Book 1)
Viper's Defiant Mate (Book 2)

The Alliance Series
Hunter's Claim (Book 1)
Razor's Traitorous Heart (Book 2)
Dagger's Hope (Book 3)
The Alliance Boxset Books 1-3
Challenging Saber (Book 4)
Destin's Hold (Book 5)
Edge of Insanity (Book 6)

Zion Warriors Series
Gracie's Touch (Book 1)
Krac's Firebrand (Book 2)

Magic, New Mexico Series
Touch of Frost (Book 1)

Paranormal / Fantasy / Romance

Magic, New Mexico Series
Taking on Tory (Book 2)
Alexandru's Kiss (Book 3)

Spirit Pass Series
Indiana Wild (Book 1)
Spirit Warrior (Book 2)

Second Chance Series
Lily's Cowboys (Book 1)
Touching Rune (Book 2)

More Than Human Series
Ella and the Beast (Book 1)

The Seven Kingdoms
The Dragon's Treasure (Book 1)
The Sea King's Lady (Book 2)
A Witch's Touch (Book 3)

The Fairy Tale Series
The Beast Prince Novella
*Free Audiobook of The Beast Prince is available:
https://soundcloud.com/sesmithfl/sets/the-beast-prince-the-fairy-tale-series

Epic Science Fiction / Action Adventure

Project Gliese 581G Series
Command Decision (Book 1)
First Awakenings (Book 2)
Survival Skills (Book 3)

New Adult

Breaking Free Series
Capture of the Defiance (Book 2)

Young Adult

Breaking Free Series
Voyage of the Defiance (Book 1)

The Dust Series
Dust: Before and After (Book 1)
Dust: A New World Order (Book 2)

Recommended Reading Order Lists:

http://sesmithfl.com/reading-list-by-events/
http://sesmithfl.com/reading-list-by-series/

ABOUT THE AUTHOR

S.E. Smith is an *Internationally Acclaimed, Award-Winning, New York Times and USA TODAY Bestselling* author of science fiction, romance, fantasy, paranormal, and contemporary works for adults, young adults, and children. She enjoys writing a wide variety of genres that pull her readers into worlds that take them away.

CPSIA information can be obtained
at www.ICGtesting.com
Printed in the USA
BVOW08s1447010418
512177BV00003B/173/P